NOT PROVEN

NOT PROVEN

The Second Book in the Punanai Series

David James Elliott

IGUANA

Copyright © 2022 David James Elliott
Published by Iguana Books
720 Bathurst Street, Suite 410
Toronto, ON M5S 2R4

Not Proven is a work of fiction. Names, places, events, occurrences and
incidents are either products of the author's imagination and/or used in a
fictitious manner. Any resemblance to actual persons, living or dead, or to
actual events is strictly coincidental.

Publisher: Meghan Behse
Editors: Paula Chiarcos and Amanda Feeney
Front cover design: Ruth Dwight, designplayground.ca

ISBN 978-1-77180-571-1 (paperback)
ISBN 978-1-77180-570-4 (epub)

This is an original print edition of *Not Proven.*

Chapter 1

Channing Hart was getting a long overdue second opinion on his legal issues from an unusual source. Prison Bob, his cellmate at the Don Jail, was a skinny guy in his late fifties with a penchant for telling stories with a lovely, soft Scottish turn of phrase. Hart was everything Bob was not: tall, well built, good looking, and in his midthirties. If they'd met at Clancy's Tavern, Hart would've ignored his mentor, thinking he was just another bum on the hustle. But this wasn't Clancy's Tavern, and PB was the only guy here willing to talk to him. Hart wanted to ask why he made everyone call him Prison Bob, but then he thought better of it. There were so many crazy rules, so many ways to blunder into fights.

The range was a comfort after the close confinement of the cell. There was no direct light in the cellblock, but the air was fresher. It smelled of disinfectant, which was an improvement over the damp smell of seldom showered men. Two fat old bastards in orange jumpsuits were gathering the linens and putting them into a canvas laundry cart. Even that much colour and movement was a treat. The unending despair of this place was rooted in the eternal present. Hart took three rapid chews on his bitter nicotine gum before he was reminded how to use it by the burn on his tongue.

PB's claim to fame was that he had once smoked a joint with the storied Stopwatch Gang. They'd never done a job together, but even so, in jail, things like that mattered. Connections gave a man a certain *gravitas*. You could see it in the way he held his head slightly cocked to the right when he spoke of it. PB was awaiting trial on bank robbery charges. He wasn't in the elite end of the stick-up business any longer, but he knew everything there was to know about trial and error.

The purchase of a Mars bar and a bottle of Coke had exhausted Hart's canteen money. But it was turning out to be the best investment he ever made. The sugar hit turned Bob the conversationalist into PB the evangelist.

"Home ice advantage, that's what we're talking about. First game of the series is always played in the other team's rink. Gives the cops the upper hand. Those buggers don't got to tell the truth when you're being interrogated. Think nothing of sitting there, making shit up, calling you a liar. Those wankers always think they're being so sly. They got the psychology. That's how they put the fear into you. Say they got evidence and witnesses, put you right up against the wall — when in fact they don't." PB frowned and shook his head. At some level, this wickedness distressed him.

"That's when they start skimming from the till. Tell you they need to know everything that happened, say they like you, they understand how this wasn't your fault, but you see, they can't put what happened in the right light for the judge if they don't know the whole story." PB looked over his shoulder to make sure no one was listening. When he was satisfied, he resumed but in a lower register.

"They don't say it out loud, but you can tell from their faces, they feel bad about having to arrest you. That's the moment when you get your cup o' coffee and pastry. You're no' like the other guys. They can see that. It's convincing because it's exactly what you want to hear. They never let up. Hell, they'll keep you up for so long you won't know your own name at the end, and that videotape keeps on grinding, waiting for you to say the wrong thing."

"That's what happened—"

"That your first time talking to 'em?"

"I've never been in trouble before."

PB grimaced as he took another slug of Coke. "It's a magical charm. Damn shame you wasted yours. Cops like to feed your name into their computer and watch it spit out every wrong thing y'ever did. That's a grand moment for 'em. They can never use it in court, but it does get their piggy little minds in gear. Doesn't take a four-star chef to follow the recipe on the back of a box of biscuit mix. If you been nailed before, and most of us have, it's that much easier to put you in the frame."

Hart was aching to make a point, but Bob silenced him by raising his palm.

A surge of anger straightened Hart's back. *This guy thinks a lot of himself.*

PB leaned forward. "If they don't, you've still a chance. Which is where you went from man to monkey."

Hart was getting annoyed with being talked over. He raised his finger to interject.

"You've got to keep your mouth shut. I repeat, as a point of emphasis, put a sock in it. Guys who been through this don't talk to the cops. It's pointless. Cops got all the advantages. They're taping you, getting your fingerprints and DNA, and talking to everyone you owe money to. Don't make it easy. Look 'em in the eye and say you want a lawyer." The little Celt smiled from ear to ear.

"They hate that more than anything else. Always come back with something slick, like 'innocent people don't need lawyers.' Hell they don't. These guys think they're social engineers, getting rid of the bad seed. What you did or didn't do has nothing to do with it once you're sitting in the barber's chair. They're shortly gonna give you a haircut you'll no' soon forget. The thing they know that you don't is that justice is what you can convince a judge is right on any given afternoon." PB pointed his right index finger directly into Hart's face.

"How many guys since you got here told you straight up they rob houses for a living, but the only house they didn't rob was the one they're serving time for?"

Hart said quietly, "The cops framed them..." But that wasn't what he was thinking. He was having trouble getting his head around what he was hearing. This was beyond being a moral inversion. He could live with the cops telling a few little lies here and there, but what he couldn't buy was the crooks being the only ones with any integrity. He wouldn't have believed a word of what PB was saying if he'd been sitting in a jury box or even standing on the other side of the bars. But he was on the wrong side of them now, and that changed everything.

The sugar was really kicking in. Bob was having a hard time keeping still. "That's what I mean by following the recipe. They look at your record, then match up what you like to do with something they got hanging around on the books. They can fit you right off the rack."

Hart was about to ask a question, but PB pre-empted him again, this time by holding his palms over his ears.

"Now the second game of the series is always played in a neutral arena. Now it's a fair fight. Your lawyer shows up and they got to charge you, let you go, or make a deal. Can't pretend, can't lie, and they've to show your guy what they got — those are the rules. S'okay to speak up to your lawyer, give him a few facts to work with, but don't ever say you did it. Got it? Your man can no' plead you innocent if you squeal on yourself. Presumption of innocence and burden of proof are beautiful things."

A pigeon was waiting out winter's wrath in the roof girders overlooking the range. He swooped down and landed on one of the tables to peck at the bread the two laundry men had smuggled out of the mess for him. All conversation stopped for a full minute as the bird tucked into this treat.

Bob got to his feet. "Now the mistake you made here, after running your mouth, was to follow the advice of your lawyer. All he does is drunk driving, and for him, one size fits all. He looked at the fee, the hours he had to put in and decided you needed some time in jail. Good for the cops, good for your lawyer, but very bad for you."

Hart felt sick. "So you're saying—"

"Don't interrupt!" PB barked at him this time. "I'm teaching you how to keep your mouth shut. Do not rise to provocation. Do not embrace the proffered hand of friendship. Still your tongue like the good book says. Now if you hadn't fouled up in stage one by talking to the cops and in stage two by trusting your smarmy lawyer, why, tomorrow you coulda played in your rink in front of your fans. That's where you want to decide this, in a court of law, wearing a nice new blue suit that makes you look ever so respectable."

A crushing sensation of loss washed over Hart.

"That is the first time you have the advantage. The cops can't beat you up, or keep y'awake, or put you in a cell beside a stenographer who's gonna write down everything you say or make shit up if you don't. Most important, when you get this far, the rules change. If there's a tie, you win. If they're no' sure it's a tie, they gotta give you the benefit of the doubt."

The pigeon took to the air with a big piece of bread in his beak. Bob pointed to him as he flew. "That is what should have happened for you."

"I don't want to go to court…"

Bob took out his comb and went to work on his hair and beard. "Oh, court is a beautiful place. They know you did it. But can they prove it? That's what it comes down to. Putting an innocent man in jail — that's the end of the world for 'em. It's millions of dollars in your pocket when you win the prison lottery. Then the real fun starts. The cops who set you up and the judge who co-signed their bullshit gotta retire. Every case they ever tried's gotta be reviewed. Imagine what that costs. So no, they don't trouble their own house. The only guy who knows for sure what happened is you. So if you don't talk, they've nothing. And the thing is this — if you never been collared before, it's double damned difficult to prove you're a crook."

The brief moment of hope Hart had felt halfway through the conversation had long since slipped away. "So what do I do tomorrow?"

Bob looked sadly into the now empty plastic bottle. "You been swindled. All you can do now is play out the hand. You can't win, but you can still do yourself some good. Read the heartwarming little speech your lawyer gave you. Try and make it sound real. Everyone in that room has permission from God on high to hate you. Don't make it easy for 'em. Don't argue the science. Keep shtum. That's all you can do."

"How does that do me some good?"

"Presumption of innocence is powerful. They know you were in a blackout. They took your blood, examined the scene, and didn't find a damn thing. If they had, you'd know about it. Let 'em fret they have this wrong. Your job is to look like the fella who was in the evil place at the unlucky hour."

Hart put his forehead on the table. "I still don't see how that helps."

PB rapped his knuckles hard right beside Hart's ear. "Were you no' listening? This is your first time. Judges know what policemen and lawyers get up to. Mostly they don't care and why should they. I'm up on a bank robbery charge. With my record, there's no doubt I did it. Even if I didn't, the judge is going to figure, what the hell, send him off to jail for the one he got away with. But your case is different. It requires careful scrutiny. The judge knows if you'd called a real lawyer the first night, we wouldn't be having this conversation. Tomorrow tell 'em you feel awful about what happened to that poor family. Cry if you can. But don't tell 'em anything else. You need to look badly taken advantage of."

"That might turn out to be the truth."

"Judges have a wonderful way of calling bullshit. That is your one remaining hope. They don't care about what happens to you any more than they do about that lady. This is all about appearances, nothing more." PB looked up and saw two men approaching. "We need to go. These two are trouble."

Hart stared at the men coming toward them. *Why is PB afraid of them?* His misgivings found words. "I thought that killing somebody gave you the run of this place."

PB lowered his voice. A look of fear crossed his face. "Stick a crowbar in a biker's eye 'cause he parted his hair on the wrong side, then yeah, you might get an extra pork chop on your lunch tray. But you killed a lady while you were drunk and that makes you the lowest of the low. Any guy who harpoons you will get a hall pass from the guards and the lads." PB turned and began walking toward their cell. "A charge like yours can get you killed — and me too 'cause I'm your pal." He glanced back to make sure Hart was following. "Did I mention how important it is to keep your mouth shut?"

Chapter 2

The New Life Institute was once housed in a fine old fieldstone mansion on Admiral Road, in the district of midtown Toronto known as the Annex. But the craze in cryogenics turned out to be a fad after all. After 1985 or so, the demand for their new flagship product, the Chamber of New Life, fell off dramatically, as did the need for a prestigious location.

Barstow Higgins still burned hot with passion for his craft, but he was now getting on in years and had been forced to make a humiliating peace with his much younger rival, Pritpal Virk. For over twenty years, these two industry titans had fought tooth and nail for supremacy in the field. But increasing costs and falling sales devastated their margins, and one night over drinks, the men reluctantly decided to merge their two magazines, *The Life Pod* and *The Cryogenic Newsletter*, into a new joint publication, appropriately titled *New Life*, and combine their storage vaults at a new low-cost location — the Granite Glen Nursing Home on Madison Avenue, just a short walk from Flannerman's Funeral Home. Barstow's nonagenarian mother owned it and resided there. And the Glen had a diesel generator that kicked in when the power went out. It was tested monthly. This made the Glen an ideal location for the cryotanks.

But money was still a problem. Postdated cheques and preauthorized deposits continued to flow in, but every year, one or two families would lose interest or die, and fewer new ones joined. There were seven in 2009 and fourteen in 2010, but then just four in 2011 and only one so far in 2012. Barstow felt personally responsible for seeing his clients through this difficult time, and he fully expected to catch up on his billing when they were all together and safe again in some much happier place. But in the meantime, there were hydro bills to pay and expensive maintenance to be done on the aging tanks.

Just last week, tank three, an old Lawrence Meteor that dated from the 1960s, needed service again. The chief problem was the deterioration of the seals. Warm, moist air was seeping into the tank and causing frost to form on the clients. On two occasions the buildup of ice had actually lifted the lid off the cryotank. The situation had become so desperate that Barstow had to chip ice off several clients using an ice pick that had lain unused in his kitchen drawer since the 1950s.

Barstow was philosophical about all of this. He had known his calling as the new Noah was never going to be easy. He stopped drawing a salary and supported himself with part-time work at the supermarket. But he was sick at heart when he contemplated the changes that would inevitably come after he died and the unprincipled Pritpal took over. The man had no real feeling for the work. On more than one occasion, Barstow had dreamed of Pritpal tossing the frozen head of a delinquent account holder into a dumpster.

Yet Barstow felt he had no choice. It was more than business arguments that compelled him to take Pritpal on as a partner. The final straw had been the horrifying realization that, after he was gone, only Pritpal would have the skills to fit him up for his state-of-the-art Chamber of New Life. That insight broke his heart. Having to trust someone with his death made him feel unwell.

Chapter 3

It was Kaiser's first week as the phone guy. Matt Brown, who was supposed to be doing the shift, found a way to weasel out of it. Serious trouble with his mother's health. He wept when he said it. Kaiser knew crap when he heard it and had to fight the urge to phone the old girl and ask her if she wanted to go play bingo.

There were lots of bright-eyed young kiddies who could've done this shift. Wasting the talents of the top man on this nonsense was petty. But no recent outrage came to mind when he contemplated the wherefores and the whys.

He took out his comb to give his curly blond hair a touch-up; unnecessary for a man doing phone work, to be sure, but it made him feel better. He looked as good as he felt.

Kaiser picked up the phone on the third ring. "This is Punanai and I'm Kaiser. How can I help you?"

The male voice at the other end of the line was surprised. "I didn't expect a real person to pick up."

"It's annoying when all you get is voicemail."

"You can say that again!"

This guy sounded far too sensible to be a client. There was no flim-flam in his voice. His process was calm, linear, and respectful.

"Benny Fergus suggested I give you a call."

"The chaplain at the Don Jail?"

"Yes. My ... my son is there."

"Oh, that's a rough spot for a kid to be in."

"That's why I'm calling — but he's not really a kid anymore. He's twenty now. Daniel has been in and out of trouble with the law..."

"And your name, sir?"

"Oh, sorry — I'm Grant Philips."

"I'm making a few notes here while we speak, Mr. Philips. Is your son a drinker?"

"I don't know. I haven't been able to get a straight answer out of him since he was twelve years old. But, well yes, he drinks, but that's not all that's going on with him. We find stuff hidden in his room ... even the wife doesn't know what it is sometimes and she's a nurse."

"Okay, so it sounds like he's what we call a poly abuser."

"A poly..."

"It's very rare these days to find a client who only uses one substance. People mix and match. One substance to get them going, usually alcohol or pot, then something else to take them where they want to go, like cocaine or opiates, and then, finally, something to bring them back down, and that could be anything — alcohol, benzos, or pot."

There was a moment of silence. Grant Philips seemed to be digesting this information. "That would be Daniel. Always something going on, but you never see him exactly the same way twice. For years, I thought he was crazy."

Kaiser started to tap his pen on the note pad. "So how can we help you?"

"Our lawyer says we can get him out of the Don if we send him for treatment."

"We need to talk about the risks of doing that. This is what we call the get-out-of-jail-free card."

"Free? Benny says you guys charge big money."

"If your son isn't paying, it's free to him. We don't like our intakes to come straight from jail."

"But—"

"Mr. Philips, experience has taught us that it's better for everyone to go into this with their eyes wide open. We want to help your son, but what you have in mind may not be the best way to do it."

Grant started to shift in his chair. He really wanted to do this in one sitting. "Jail isn't helping him."

"Pain and fear might be doing him a world of good."

"The place is a cage for wild animals. Susan and I are afraid he's going to get hurt."

"What's he in for?"

"He breached his probation order — again."

Kaiser heard the anguish that can only be carried on that word. "How did he do that?"

"He's not supposed to drink or be out after eleven p.m. He's not allowed to leave the house without Susan or I. They put a bracelet around his ankle."

"So on Saturday night he went for a walk?"

"It was Thursday, but yes. He slipped out the basement window. Two policemen came by asking for him. Then they sat outside our house for almost half an hour with their lights on to make sure all the neighbours knew something was up. Next morning there was a call from the station. They'd arrested him in a crack house."

There was a pause. Grant was feeling it all again. Kaiser gave him the time he needed by doodling on the pad.

"We wondered where he got the money. He was beyond broke. That was the only way we could keep him sober. A week later I went in to have a look at my coin collection." Kaiser heard Grant catch his breath before he continued. "Those coins were for him. They were a legacy. Daniel knows how I feel about them. When he was a boy, he'd sit on my lap and we'd look at them together and wonder where they'd mined the ore and who'd minted them, and we'd try to imagine who'd spent them and on what. They're perfect little sculptures, beautiful, eternal…" Grant may have been crying; Kaiser wasn't sure. "But now it's all gone. Even if I got them back, I couldn't look at them now, not the same way. They would always remind me of what he did." He stopped again. "The betrayal of the thing hurts worse than anything else."

Kaiser gave him a moment.

"You still there, Kaiser?"

"Yes. I was about to give you a long speech about what we call *powerlessness*, but you beat me to the punch. What Daniel did defines the problem. He knew you loved those coins. He knew taking them would break your heart. He knew he could only get ten cents on the dollar for them, and if he left the house, he'd get caught and end up in jail. But the point is — he did it anyway. All that *knowing* didn't stop him. That's what addiction is."

The poor man looked over his shoulder to make sure his wife was out of earshot. "Susan says sometimes she … she thinks Daniel is evil, that he likes to destroy things and make us cry. She worries he gets a sick kick out of it."

Kaiser started to doodle a jail cell window on the pad. The hacksaw gave him trouble. "There are people like that. Like I said, I don't know your son, and he could be mentally ill. But I see another possibility. People who are addicted always get into trouble like this. The thing that separates addicts from everyone else is what we call *craving*. It's one of those things you have to experience before you can really understand it. Have you ever been a smoker, Grant?"

"Years ago. I gave it up after I had a bypass."

"You remember what that felt like?"

"Lying there in a hospital bed, aching to smoke a cigarette … going back and forth in my head, hating the very thing I wanted. I knew I'd be letting everyone down, and most of all myself—"

"But that's exactly what you wanted to do."

"I couldn't think about anything else! Like I was going to die if I didn't. Thank heavens I was hooked up to a whole wall full of monitors."

Kaiser smiled as he imagined himself in that situation, disentangling himself from the apparatus. "Well, give yourself some credit then; people do unhook the wires and head for the exits." The doodle now boasted a rope being lowered to the ground and Daniel rejoining his happy stick-figure parents. "Grant, I want you to remember what it felt like — lying there, wanting a smoke — while I explain why we don't like to get our clients this way. A guy in jail is under enormous pressure all the time. It's relentless. The guards are a threat, the other prisoners are a threat, and you can't relax or shut your eyes for even a second to get away from it all. People in the Don become hypervigilant and it makes them crazy. When guys get out of jail, they vibrate for weeks. They have a kind of post-traumatic shock."

The doodle was taking too much of his attention. Kaiser knew he had to concentrate. He pushed it away. He could hear the swivel chair that Grant was sitting in begin to rock back and forth.

"Now look at the problem from Daniel's point of view. He's scared to death. He's exhausted, full of guilt and shame — and then the court offers him a way out. All he has to do is come here. He'll agree to anything. And when he signs the papers, he probably wants to come. But then when they let him out, all that stress starts working on his mind. He gets what we call *triggered*. Suddenly he wants to use so badly, he'll do anything to get some cocaine — even if it means going back to jail."

The light of day burst into Grant's consciousness. "Like leaving the house and stealing the coins?"

"You have it, my friend. We've had families set this up, pay the whole shot, only to have the client jump out of the car at the first red light. Or they show up drunk or with a vial full of pills. Sometimes they check in and have dinner, then wander off into the night."

A dark shadow crossed Grant's face. "Don't you lock them up?"

"We're not that kind of place. The only people we want here are people who can, at least grudgingly, admit they have a problem. We can't help anyone who's still in the middle of the madness. If we bring Daniel in and if he decides to stay — two very big ifs — he may be so rattled from his experience in jail that he won't be able to hear what we have to say."

"So you're saying you don't want him?"

"For your sake, no, not this week, not in the state he's in." Kaiser started to play with his tie as he spoke. "Try and deal yourself a couple cards. Set this thing up so it has a better chance to work. Get the courts to put him back under house arrest. We'll get him set up in a day program somewhere, say at a detox, and make him attend twelve-step meetings every night."

Grant had a sour look on his face. "What good will that do?"

Kaiser sat up in his chair and then got to his feet. "Bodies and minds heal, but it takes time. He may be able to calm down enough at home to make use of what we're going to teach him here."

Grant's mounting frustration turned to anger. "But what if he runs off?"

Kaiser arched his back and stretched his powerful shoulder muscles. "Well, he might. And if he does, you're right back where you started, but you have one big advantage."

"What's that?"

"You won't already have paid a non-refundable fee to us."

Grant didn't like the sound of that. "Why is there no refund?"

"When you have a refund policy or if you charge people for treatment on a per diem basis, it becomes a deal-breaker in the first week of treatment. A child who has bankrupted his parents using drugs will draw the line at them having to foot the bill for his recovery. It's one more rock to hide behind. We want the whole family on the same page. We don't want to take your money if we can't help you."

"But that's crazy — how do you stay in business?"

"By getting this thing set up the right way." Kaiser reached for the doodle once again. It needed a police car. "The kind of intervention we do will change everything in your family. We'll stop you and Susan from enabling Daniel, and we're going to ask him once and for all how he's going to live his life. No more pretending and no more going back to the way things used to be. The end of pretending is strong medicine."

Grant frowned. He needed this settled and he didn't know how to do it. All the previous advice had come to nothing. In desperation he gave the truth a gentle tug. "The Crown prosecutor says this is a take-it-or-leave-it deal. He wants Daniel in treatment right now."

Kaiser started to colour in the police car but stopped long enough to scrawl the word *fibber* over the family reunion. "That's discouraging."

Grant had made his choice and powered through to the end. "They'll let him go tomorrow if I show up with a contract from you today."

Kaiser sighed. "Well, come on by this afternoon then, and we can do the paperwork." Kaiser switched the receiver to his other ear. "How does your wife feel about it?"

"It's odd, but she says she likes it when he's in jail."

"I know why."

"Astonish me."

"The only time she can get a good night's sleep is when he's in jail or in hospital."

"That's right. How did you know?"

"My mom used to say the same thing."

Chapter 4

There were six men in the van that took Hart from the Don Jail to the courthouse at Yonge and College Street. They were shackled together like links of sausage in a butcher's window and anchored to a common fastening point. There were no amenities and no gas stations on the itinerary, so if you had to go, it had to be in your jumpsuit. Even the pressure washer couldn't get rid of that kind of evidence. Before they loaded the prisoners inside, their hosts sprayed the interior of the van with a wax vapour intended to deaden the sense of smell, but the best it could do was plead the charge of criminally rotten down to misdemeanour awful.

Hart shut his eyes and, with an effort of will, envisaged the clubhouse sandwich from Clancy's Tavern. The old bastard made it to perfection with a side of chips that were hot and steamy on the inside while remaining brown and crispy on the outside. All he needed was a miracle and some bail money, and then maybe he could get himself one. He tried to rest his back against the padded side of the van, but the chain was too tight.

They always find something special to do for you.

The van stopped at Metro West to pick up the final two passengers. Hart was delighted to be reunited with two of his doper friends. They'd been growing some herbs in a quiet little spot in cottage country. As it turns out, it hadn't been quiet enough.

Zipper, the older of the two, was glad to see Hart. "Hey, knucklehead, I didn't know you owned a suit."

The younger one, Doss, was a wise guy. He addressed the other prisoners as the van door closed. "He's renting the suit by the hour, so don't talk too long. Just plead guilty. That way we can get the suit back before five p.m."

The guys all smiled. One of them said, "I don't know why — he looks good in orange."

Hart liked the two herbsmen. They had played three-handed bridge for hours on the range at the Don when they'd all been there together. PB had shown obvious displeasure at his choice of friends. Hart gave them a playful jab in return: "I better say goodbye to you guys now. You get twenty years for the kind of weight you were hefting."

They both laughed.

Zipper nodded his head and smiled broadly. "Not going to happen."

Doss cracked wise. "We thought it was a new kind of kale. It's all leafy green shit. We're not rabbits. How we supposed to know? We pick anything you pay us to pick."

Hart forgot his own troubles for a second. "You think that's going to fly?"

Zipper rubbed his beard. "Her Worship owes us forty bucks from the last batch."

Hart chipped in, "You want me to be a defence witness?"

Clean-shaven Doss took up the thought. "You could say you were sitting in the office and heard that pig-faced sergeant bragging to his corporal about framing us."

A voice from the back of the van added, "Tell them it bothered you. You couldn't sleep. Felt you had to come forward."

Doss approved of the suggestion. "Sergeant's got such shifty eyes. Jury can't help but notice once it's pointed out."

Zipper gave his beard another tug. "You could tell the judge he's very polite when he takes the bribe. Doesn't even count the money."

A sudden lurch told them they were moving again.

Zipper tried to settle into his seat, glad to be moving after their long wait on the loading dock. "One thing is for sure. You can't say the judge isn't impartial."

Doss delivered the punch line. "She doesn't care if the cops lie or make shit up. It's all the same to her."

With a laugh, the voice from the back of the van added, "So long as you put your hand on the book, it all comes out the way it should."

Another pull of the beard. "Great thing that book. Why is it the cops don't have to touch it?"

"Man, don't you know? It catches fire when they do."

———

The College Park Courthouse in the old Eaton's building on Yonge Street was where a guy ended up when he couldn't manage his own affairs. It wasn't hard to sort out who was who, because the room was a study in vivid contrasts. The officers of the court were barbered, shaved, well dressed, and unfailingly polite and attentive to the public. The prisoners looked uniformly ridiculous in their bright-orange prison jumpsuits. They were manacled and kept behind a glass partition. Any presumption of innocence or credibility was damaged by their sleepless looks, their bumps and bruises, their ragged beards. No one looking at any of these men could — even for an instant — imagine them innocent.

Hart was wearing the suit that his lawyer, Chaim Levy, had picked out for him, but it did him no good; he still had to sit in the prisoner's box until his case was called. He was one of the condemned.

A few of the prisoners felt compelled to shout or whisper their testimony to the spectators in the court. The hardened criminals tried to look calm and let their lawyers do the talking. This display of indifference elevated them above the riff-raff and entitled them to sit with the other hard men at dinner. The drug addicts looked tired and paranoid.

The families and supporters of the prisoners all looked vaguely like people who'd missed their bus to work and were worried about being fired. They wondered what was going to be worse: watching them go away or taking them home. They could've used a smoke to settle their nerves.

You never know when your case will be up. The court has an order that only insiders understand, and it goes about its business in a linear manner and at its own pace. Some cases are over in a minute and others drag on for an hour. You dare not step outside for fear of missing what you came to see.

At half past ten, a disciplined crowd entered the court, marching silently like soldiers on close-order drill behind a beatific-looking clergyman wearing a Roman collar. These people had never been to court before. They looked angry and a little bit sad. They were here to support Alice Gibson, the pretty young girl with the crutch who'd been a media focal point for a month now — ever since she had been released from hospital.

Hart felt a tap on his shoulder. He stood and allowed the guard to remove his shackles. He walked over to the defendant's table. *They could have taken those off outside. They wanted everyone to see. Everyone to know.*

Her Honour, Judge Anne Sullivan, was fifty years old. On her own time, she was a lively, vivacious spirit, much given to French cooking and the breeding of corgis. Attired in a wig and gown, she looked like an eighteenth-century gentleman, severe and mistrustful. The case before her concerned a Mr. Channing Hart. Chaim Levy had pled him guilty to a reduced charge of vehicular manslaughter.

Channing Hart, who had no previous legal history and no street smarts, had, on the advice of counsel, been waiting for months in the Don Jail for his case to be heard. Judge Sullivan wasn't happy with that election. She would have granted bail if an application had been made. Levy was playing the long game: A client lingering in jail is at no risk to reoffend, give damaging interviews to the press, or otherwise frustrate a well-thought-out legal defence. Furthermore, because of the appalling conditions at the Don Jail, remission of sentence was granted at the rate of three days to one for every day spent in custody. Levy had told Hart to think about it as overtime.

Hart's fervent hope this morning was that he might be granted bail prior to sentencing. He hadn't been home since this nightmare started. He hadn't had a good day, a good meal, or a good night's sleep in so long that he was finding it hard to focus. Sometimes he gave way to trembling.

The court had just heard the last of three tearful victim impact statements. Hart tried not to cry when the little girl, Alice, spoke about her own injuries and the loss of her mother, but to no avail. He didn't really hear her words; it was the tone of her voice and her horror-stricken face that broke his heart. He felt ashamed of the tears rolling down his cheeks. He was afraid of what the other prisoners would make of this. They had so many crazy rules about how to behave.

The judge's voice called him back to the present. "Mr. Hart, do you have anything to say to the court?"

Hart rose to his feet and looked warily at Levy for support. Levy gave him an encouraging nod that seemed to say, *go ahead and tell them what I told you to say*. While he didn't like the script, Hart knew he couldn't spend another day in the Don Jail. He was willing to throw the dice. Any decision that didn't send him back to that godforsaken hellhole was a victory.

Looking around the courtroom, he noticed with some bitterness that not one of his friends had showed up. He had no flesh-and-blood family in Toronto. His whole world revolved around work and the big table at Clancy's Tavern. The local tabloids had taken pains to paint him as a monster. Hart felt an awful fullness in his core. He simultaneously wanted to cry and vomit. Something alien inside him needed to crawl out and die.

The looks of indifference on the faces of the other prisoners intimidated and confused him. What he didn't know yet — because he was new at this — was that it was a point of honour among the prisoners not to react to another man's charges. A vacant look in an overcrowded, highly charged atmosphere was often the best they could do to protect another man's privacy — to pretend to be somewhere else. To do otherwise invited retribution once back at the range.

Hart faced the judge as instructed. The absence of any emotion on her face was unnerving. He expected her to be sympathetic because she was a woman. Surely, she would understand. This was his first chance to speak since the whole nightmare began, and now he couldn't find his voice or remember his lines. He panicked.

Hart's first attempt produced only a choking sound. There was a terrible silence before he was able to find the first word of the phrase he had tried to memorize. "Hearing the victim impact statement read by the Gibson family…" That was a far as he got before his voice failed and his knees began to tremble. The ensuing silence damned him. In desperation he blurted out the first thing that came to mind. "Sometimes it's hard for me to get a breath."

There was another long silence. Hart had a stunned look on his face. The more experienced onlookers were waiting for the lie of desperation.

Levy looked mildly concerned. Hart was off message. He willed him to speak the lines he had been given but to no avail. His client was coming to a lovely simmer in his own juices.

"I don't know if I was driving that night. I want to believe with all my heart that I wasn't." Hart's voice deserted him again. You could hear the spectators in the court breathing disapproval. He was so glad he couldn't see their faces.

His voice exploded in grief. "A mother has been taken away from her child, and a wife from her husband. They blame me. I hate myself. I hate where I am. I hate what this makes me look like. But more than anything else, I hate not knowing."

Nobody yelled, *It ain't so, brother!* In the silence his thoughts took a different direction and he heard a nascent truth. *Nothing is going to be right in my life ever again.*

Judge Sullivan made a note. There was only the sound of a pen scoring a legal pad as she wrote. Without looking up, she said, "Thank you, Mr. Hart." She glanced at the defence counsel and the Crown prosecutor. "Mr. Levy, Mr. Summers, would you approach please." Both old dogs had been long schooled in the art of the courtroom. Their movements were slow, sure, and dignified. She spoke to them in a voice that could be heard in the front rows of the court. "I would like to see both of you in my office when we're finished." Levy and Summers nodded. A deal was in the offing.

Judge Sullivan addressed the gallery with an expression and a tone she had not used for the prisoners or the barristers. It was like she was talking to friends and family. It was the look that Hart had so badly wanted to see. "I'm going to adjourn these proceedings for today and set a date for sentencing. This has been a long and painful ordeal for the Gibson family. I would like to thank them for being here today and for their patience with this court. We're adjourned."

The Gibsons didn't know what to do next. The family gathered around Alice, who was still clinging to her now useless script. The formality of the proceedings had been a blessing in that it offered some insight into how one should behave. The memory of Alice's mother, Margaret, demanded that they put on a brave face and show their quality to the world. But the show was over and it was time to go home.

But go home to what? A house that ached for a mother's presence, with a little girl who now walked with a crutch. Physiotherapy, painkillers, and prodding by strangers had replaced bedtime stories and long, satisfying hugs. The world had turned on an unseen axis, snatching away a hoped-for future and replacing it with a vile counterfeit.

———

Anne Sullivan's office was well lit and airy, and she'd moved a lot of her own furniture in. There was even a small kitchen and a fridge. It was a place to feel safe and sane when, really, circumstances didn't warrant it. She'd found a hundred ways to stay above the fray and keep her eye on what mattered.

She prided herself on her gourmet coffee. When Levy and Summers entered her office, she gave them each a cup and pointed them toward the conference table. She leaned back in her chair and enjoyed her first sip, taking in the full fragrance of the beans. Outside, the custodial staff were hard at work clearing last night's snowfall. The sound of metal scraping pavement spoke of peace and good government.

"Mr. Levy, I'm inclined toward giving your client a break. But I have considerable difficulty in doing so."

She turned toward the prosecutor and nodded in a way that told him not to be alarmed. "Mr. Hart will be getting a considerable custodial sentence. What he did was inexcusable. But what I find encouraging in this case is that he agrees with that estimation. It's rare to hear despair and a longing for wholeness coming from the prisoner's box."

Summers looked at the dregs in his cup. *Oh God, here she goes again.* He snuck a look at Levy who, perhaps wisely, scarcely seemed to be in the room at all.

She paused and gathered her thoughts. "Mr. Levy, I want your client to attend a treatment program. He's well off, is he not?"

Levy smiled as if he had known all along that they'd end up here drinking coffee and casting dice. "He is, at least until the civil suit."

Summers nodded at the witticism. Anne didn't like Levy's smile. He always looked like a policeman lying under oath, sure of his ground and well schooled in suborning perjury. She had to fight the urge to smack him. She used her judicial tone. "Very well then, if there are no objections, I'm going to order Mr. Hart to attend an alcohol treatment program of my choosing prior to sentencing."

She smiled at the two counsels, who both had the good sense to look like they agreed with her decision. *These two think I'm soft in the head. Fine. Let them grumble. This is the right thing to do.* "I'll make some calls and have my assistant get back to you. Thank you, gentlemen, and good day."

Levy and Summers put down their cups and left. They kept the friendly banter for the courtroom and the jury. They were both far too competitive and overloaded to really be friends.

Chapter 5

Barry leaned up against a pillar, eyeing his followers as they straggled in. The crooked old ghost had unilaterally decided to make the display window at Holt Renfrew the permanent meeting site for the Canadian Council of the Undead after the lucky occurrence of having Sharon and Helen spot the group while they were window shopping the Mink Mile. This had swelled their ranks to ten. The faithful were in a happy mood. A high-end popcorn maker was being demonstrated just inside the entrance, and shoppers were given a small cone of the product as they arrived. The ghosts were enjoying the aromatherapy.

In life, Barry had been thin and stooped with spondylitis. The condition had been painful, and his once-handsome face was deeply lined with the marks of frowns and grimaces. His niece, who may or may not have been high at the time, had insisted that his black hair be slicked back with Vaseline by the funeral director. As she was his only living relative, what she said went. The dark suit completed the vampire look. He was horrified when he saw himself in the box but powerless to make a change.

The problem facing him today was Peter's insufferable friend, John. Barry didn't want the annoying ghost at the meetings. He couldn't abide his nonsense. He'd considered asking Peter to tell John that he was no longer welcome. The man was disturbed. But Barry hadn't yet worked out a way to drive a wedge between them. Splitting with John would be a real test of Peter's commitment to the group. Barry was shrewd enough to know that telling John he wasn't welcome was the one surefire way to make sure he never missed a meeting again, and if Peter was too soft hearted to do the right thing, he might lose them both.

The Christmas display in the window had given way to a new theme: a leisurely sun-drenched southern vacation. A whole series of small barrels were tied together with rather coarse-looking hemp ropes, suggesting some kind of fishing apparatus was being stored on the stern of a sleek, powerful motor launch. The scene was populated by eyeless young women wearing the latest in sun wear, and blanched young men in white trousers and blue blazers that gave them a nautical air. The finished product looked like the front cover of a romance novel.

Making believe and pretending, thought Barry as he looked around at the store display. How terribly apropos for this group. If this is a task force, then I'm a Dutchman. He looked at the ghosts and frowned. There were the Bailey brothers, Fergal and Declan. Identical idiots, incapable of anything other than bickering. He looked past them. And dear, sweet Maddy. It's a shame she can't fetch coffee because that's about all she's capable of doing. *And Rosa. How the hell did we end up getting saddled with that old bore? As our oldest member, she should be our link to the distant past, which is another way of saying we're trapped in the present. I can't stand the sight of her. And then there was Jack — quirky and murky. Why is he so suspicious? And he plays with matches too.* Barry shuddered. *He turned to the two young women who showed up last week and frowned again.* Who knows about them, *he thought.* Which leaves me no choice but to consider Peter my strong right arm. But he's such a pompous pain in the ass.

How hard is this? We're supposed to be investigating the light. That's why we meet as a group. Last week we all agreed to go after the light full force. But none of them did what they promised to!

He set his face like a flint and made his way into the centre of the stern deck. "You guys really let me down on Sunday. Not one of you showed up."

All eyes drifted to the floor. They looked like a Scout troop whose tents had blown over in the wind. They were disgraced. Barry let the sting of his accusation linger in the poisoned air. He crossed his arms and stuck out his chin. "You all say that you want to get to the bottom of this, but then you don't do anything. We had a plan."

There was more introspection. All of it painful. Barry was enjoying himself. This was fun. He turned his head toward Bloor Street and looked off into the distance. "After all I've done for you, I thought you would've supported me in this work. I can't believe you wouldn't do the thing you all swore you would do — with your very lives hanging in the balance."

Helen, the taller of the two new young women, raised her hand. Barry looked at her blankly. He wasn't finished berating the group. He waved the back of his hand at her.

Helen either didn't notice or didn't care. She got to her feet. "Hello, you up there, I've forgotten your name. You'll have to forgive me, I'm still new at this." *She pointed to her companion.* "So is Sharon. And we were wondering what the hell you're talking about."

Barry shook his head. He looked around the room to gauge the mood of the group. This was impertinence writ large. This was an attack on his leadership. How dare she! He looked at her and tried to take her measure. Could she even have started high school? What note should he strike in his response? Should he play an angry parent or the nurturing father? Which would get him back to where he needed to be?

He cleared his throat. "Helen, I know you've never been to one of these meetings before, but the way we do things here is one of us runs the meeting so everyone gets to have their say."

"But I don't know what you're talking about," *Helen said.* "And that's rude."

Sharon piped up. "Yes, rude. And while we're talking about it, who put you in charge, Mr. Guilt Trip? Who the hell do you think you're talking to?"

Barry was taken aback. He was also a little angry. First the dead wood doesn't pull its weight and now insubordination from the adolescents. *Barry looked at the others again — still trying to gauge their mood, still searching for the tack he needed to take this group off the rocky shore and back into the deep, navigable waters.*

The Baileys let loose a hail of covering fire for the pretenders.

"Out with the shameless villain," called Declan.

"Put him to flight girls — let's see the heels of his boots," Fergal hooted.

"Five bucks says the arse is out of his pants."

The room roared with laughter and the bluster deflated Barry. Peter took it in with a glance, rose to his full height and gave the room a smouldering look.

Rosa, too, got to her feet and started to jump up and down. "Hello," she said. "Hello, this has happened before, it has all happened before, back when we used to meet in the playhouse on Gardiner Road. Oh, it was a lovely spot. Lisa and Spencer used to invite us there in the good weather, and everyone came until the light showed up and scared us all half to death."

Peter bellowed, "Mr. Chairman, a point of order, if you please!"

Helen was very angry now. "I ask a simple question and the whole place is falling down around our ears. What's wrong with you people?"

Barry held out his hands trying to restore order. He tried not to look put upon. But the dagger had plunged deep and tasted a vital organ.

The Baileys couldn't have stopped themselves even if they'd wanted to.

"Look! He has his hands up. He's giving up. No backbone."

"Out with the charlatan, out with him, I say. Let's have some new leadership."

"Helen, we need you to take a turn at the helm. Are you up to it?"

"I'll help," said Sharon. "We can do it together."

"I'll help too," said Rosa. "Oh, it'll be like the old days. Maddy, you'll join us too, won't you?"

Maddy looked at Barry and Peter and then back at Rosa. "Oh, yes, I would love to. I—"

"Oh crap!" screamed Jack. "Look! Outside the window."

They all wheeled as one. A very young girl in a pink dress was standing on the other side of the glass with what looked like a cell phone in her hand. But while she looked as if she was about six years old, she was well over seven feet tall and standing in a pool of light. She grinned and waved to the astonished ghosts.

Peter and Barry took to their heels, followed closely by Jack. They made their way, under their own power, out of the display window and into the store, landing a two-foot jump in front of the escalator without a backward glance. The effort left them exhausted. By a happy chance, the trio was able to grab a young boy of about eight by the collar, a technique the group referred to as "button hooking." The little fellow was making motorcycle noises and running up and down the escalator in a pair of rubber boots that were two sizes too large for him while a bored security guard watched and weighed her options. Even so, the boy provided the impetus for the middle stage of their escape.

At the top of the escalator, they let go of the boy and grabbed on to an executive who towed them to the corridor that led to the subway entrance. They hung on to him until they got to the sidewalk, where Jack caught hold of a youthful jogger while Peter and Barry seized the sleeve of a matron going in the other direction. Jack caught the first train out of Bay Station. It wasn't going in the right direction, but he didn't care; he had strong survival instincts.

Peter and Barry found themselves alone on the subway platform. They sat back to back, like infantry men, watching for further signs of trouble.

"That was close," said Barry.

"Did everyone get away?"

"Who knows. It was every man for himself. What a panic."

"Now what do we do?"

Barry arched his aching back. "What can we do?"

"It's a good thing that Jack spotted her when he did. We were trapped in there. And those two troublemakers—"

"Which ones? Fergal and Declan?"

Peter turned to face Barry, looking increasingly frustrated. "Them too, but the other ones, Sharon and thingy."

Barry shook his head. "Rosa or Maddy?"

"Both of them too, but that other new one. Oh hell, I can't remember her name."

"Helen … Ah, Peter, what are we going to do?"

"Buck up, Barry. We'll get through this somehow."

"Not with this bunch of losers."

"What do you mean?"

"Peter, you and I are the only members of the council who ever had jobs."

"What?"

"Didn't you know?"

"It never came up. Why didn't they work?"

The bent ghost struggled to find a more comfortable position. "Well, Rosa did, but she cleaned houses. Declan and Fergal, well, the best they were ever able to do was go prospecting. Got lucky too. Made a fortune."

"What about Jack?" *Peter asked.*

"Don't know. I think he must have been an axe murderer or something, so secretive. It took me a year to get a name out of him, and I'm almost certain he made that up on the spot."

Peter gave Barry a look. "So they didn't work. I never worked either. I sold real estate."

"That's work."

"Not like shovelling coal or butchering hogs. What about you, Barry?"

Barry squared his shoulders as best he could. "I was in charge of labour relations at Canada Post."

"It's a shame we can't get John involved," *said Peter a little wearily.*

"That man's attitude is poison."

Peter swung his legs around and dangled them over the edge of the subway platform. "But he follows through, you have to give him that. His word is his bond."

Barry was gobsmacked. "He's crazy and he lies!"

Peter looked at Barry and shook his head. "Really, I hadn't noticed. He's always played fair with me."

Barry got to his feet. "When he's in the group, he's always talking to someone who isn't there. At first I thought he was turning poltergeist. He walks around the rest of us like we're mannequins. You see him sometimes mugging for the camera, like there's a play going on and only he knows it."

"He does seem self-absorbed…"

"I'd call it disturbed."

"Not to worry; we can bring him around. Leave it to me."

Barry looked unconvinced. "When will you see him next?"

"Tomorrow. We meet at Flannerman's."

"Peter, you have to get him on side. The light is no longer passive. It's hunting us. Who knows how many got taken today. We were lucky to get out alive. You need to get John by the scruff of the neck and drag him from where he is to where we need him to be."

"Like a speech! I could do that!"

"Put some backbone into him. Pump him up. We need a man of action, not some over-the-hill naysayer."

Chapter 6

Anne Sullivan gathered the coffee cups from her desk and took them to the sink. She pressed the play button on her Bose radio and heard the sombre notes of a half-finished symphony. It was heaven to have something this simple to do. She ran a sink full of warm water. The cleaning staff would have done this for her, but it was one of her rituals. A few minutes of warm soapy water and unguarded thoughts dissolved her game face and restored her focus.

What am I going to do with this guy? If he did it, he deserves harsher treatment than I can give him. And if he's innocent, that really would make this the perfect mess. A blackout cuts both ways. No confession and no physical evidence makes this worse. And I have to play God. Is there no way to know what really happened?

Anne closed her eyes and rubbed her palms against her temples. Difficulties both personal and professional gave her pause. There were dozens of other places she could send him to and the idea of phoning her ex-husband rankled. *What would that look like? What will a bastard like Levy make of that in the Appeals Court?*

Anne opened her eyes. *Doug and his thugs are the only ones who can make sense of a guy like this*, she thought. *I can't turn this guy loose, and I don't have the stomach to send him back to the Don. But if he's in treatment, I'll know where he is. And they might be able to get to the bottom of this.*

She picked up the phone and dialled.

Doug Moore picked up the private line in his office when he saw Anne's name on the display. His former mate's voice filled him with a sentimental glow.

She got straight to the point. "Have you heard of Channing Hart? You know, the man who's charged with killing Margaret Gibson and injuring her daughter, Alice. It was in all the papers. He's pleading guilty to a reduced charge, and I'm getting ready to send him to prison."

"Okay ... how can we help?"

"I want him to attend your program." A pause and a lowering of her voice signalled a shift from professional to personal. "Doug, he woke up in a jail cell and they told him that he killed someone. He doesn't remember anything about it. He deserves an explanation. Without some insight, he's never going to get past wondering if he did it. A man who has his head on right can live well, even in a prison. What was it your old boss used to say? The bars are all in your head."

Doug smiled and shook his head fondly. "The things you remember. Is he still in custody?" Doug caught something at his twelve o'clock. One of the clients — a tall, thin man pushing forty with angry eyes — was watching him through the window in his door. He tried, unsuccessfully, to make eye contact with Doug several times.

Any fool could see that Doug was on the phone. But for an alcoholic, everything is a matter of life or death. After a few more seconds of staring, Sean Miller opened the door. Doug scowled and waved him away. Sean looked perturbed and retreated to the other side of the door, but he continued to glare through the window. This phone call with Anne was a precious opportunity. Doug was desperate to keep the irritation that was rapidly consuming him out of his voice.

Anne, of course, was unaware of the drama at the other end of the phone. She was desperate to avoid anything that looked like a conflict of interest. Impartial had to be just that.

"No, he's out on bail, but only long enough to take your program. If he leaves, you have to call the police. The usual arrangement. I'm taking a risk here. If I'm wrong about this guy and he gets behind the wheel of a car — well, you can imagine."

Doug was still watching Sean, who was pacing now and occasionally leering through the window, obviously spoiling for a fight as he jerked his thumb in the direction of the front door. Doug swung an emphatic arm that said, *get lost!* — and the negative energy found its way into his voice. The words "Is he going to pay or is he looking for one of the charity-sponsored beds?" were set to the raucous tune of *this marriage is over.*

Anne was astonished by his manner. She stood her ground. "I want him in right away, and I expect him to pay for it." Doug's tone had brought up issues from their failed marriage. Before she could weigh them, the words were out of her mouth. "Did you think I was asking you for a favour?"

Doug calmed himself and switched back to a friendly tone. "I'm sorry, Anne. One of my guests is behaving badly and distracting me. Give me a second to restore order here, will you?" Doug left his hand off the receiver so Anne could judge for herself what was happening as he gave vent to his feelings of irritation. "Mr. Miller, can't you see I'm on the phone?"

Sean couldn't hold out for a second longer. "Somebody stole my coat — my brand-new four-hundred-dollar coat."

"I'm on the phone. Have a seat outside and I'll be with you in a minute."

Sean was hopelessly tangled up in his past and unable to control his anger and his growing sense of helplessness. He shouted, "So you don't care if someone in this house is a thief!"

Doug had murder in his eyes. "Plant it."

"Fine!" yelled Sean, loud enough for the neighbours to hear, as he slammed the door. Still spoiling for a fight, he went back to pacing back and forth and glaring at Doug through the window.

"Anne, I'm sorry. One of the guys burst through my door. Someone stole his coat."

Anne laughed. "Still a den of philosophers."

"Give Mr. Hart my direct number and I'll be happy to sort him out."

Doug's moment of peace didn't last. Mr. Miller was still on the prowl. Doug could hear him snarling through the door. Then he was in the living room, shouting his accusations to the heavens. "I left it at the front door! I was only gone a minute and some creep took it. I can't go to a meeting tonight without a coat. And a fat lot those do-nothings in the office care about it…"

Doug burst out of his office full of purpose and energy. "Relax, nobody took your coat. Did you look in your room?"

Sean was now close to hysteria. Too many people had played with him like this in the past. "The coat was hung up by the front door and now it's not there."

Doug was starting to see a familiar pattern. "No one has ever stolen a coat here. It's misplaced."

"So now I'm a liar!" Sean's body moved reflexively, as if in movement he'd at last find peace. He stormed out of the living room, through the fire doors, and onto the back patio.

Doug entered the counsellors' office and closed the door. "Is it just me or does Sean Miller seem a little off this morning?"

Reg Topping got to his feet with difficulty. His spina bifida was playing him up, and so he was using both his canes this morning. He wanted to observe Sean's behaviour through the window in the office door. "It may not look like it, but I'm dealing with this. He's so hot right now, he's going to say or do something and get himself thrown out. I see no point in pushing him when he's this angry. When I get him to settle down, he'll remember where he put his damn coat."

"How did a guy from the mission get a four-hundred-dollar coat?"

"That's why he thinks it's stolen."

"Anger really tells a story on this guy."

"It sure explains a lot. He has a good trade but can't hold a job. I think we know why now."

"What's he like when he's drinking?"

"Has to be better than when he's stark raving sober."

Doug shook his head and smiled. "Put on your game face, youngster. Here comes General Custer again."

Sean was so overamped, he was acting as if from divine revelation. He opened the office door and walked right into Doug's personal space. "Are you guys going to get up off your asses and do something about this?"

Doug saw through to the heart of the problem. There was a time when he'd have done the same dumb thing. He set about restoring order, one step at a time. He fixed the angry man with a no-nonsense stare. When he spoke, his voice was a wonder: a mix of majesty and calm. "Do not come barging through a closed door again. You knock and wait to be invited in. Are you clear on that?"

Sean was caught off-balance and he gave ground. He'd expected the conversation to be about the coat.

"But…"

Doug's voice escalated one notch. "Mr. Miller, no *buts* … everything after *but* is always bullshit."

That was the wrong thing to say. Anger gave way once again to rage. They were going to blame him so they wouldn't have to pay for the coat. "So you're not going to help me."

Reg knew his role here. These two were too much alike. They would destroy each other arguing over the loss of the coat and then deeply regret doing it. "We're trying to help, but you keep getting mad at us. Let's try again. Where was your coat?"

Sean was willing to deal with Doug because he was the head man, but he wasn't going to suffer an underling. "By the front door, you moron."

Doug was calm. "Mr. Miller, I'm going to ask you to leave if you do that again."

Reg was still trying to keep the peace among combatants. "Show me."

Sean felt he was getting somewhere now, being taken seriously for the first time. He followed Reg to the front door. "It's a black leather coat."

Reg put his hand to the rack. "There are two of them hanging here. Is one of them yours?"

Sean looked uncomprehendingly at the two coats. He looked at the label in the first one and then pushed it aside with disgust. He put his hand into the outside pocket of the remaining jacket and felt the familiar presence of his cigarette lighter. It was fascinating to watch the elation on his face turn first to disbelief, then shame as the implications of what he'd said and done became apparent.

Reg smiled. "Go have a smoke. You'll feel better."

Back in the office, Doug flung himself into a chair with a goofy look on his face. "Are you guys going to get up off your asses and do something about this?"

"Well, while we're on the subject of conversations that seem to be about one thing when they are in fact about another, check this one out." Mike Sage, the office manager, had the good sense to never interfere in what one of his counsellors was trying to achieve with a client. Sensing that the crisis had passed, he spun his computer monitor around to show them what he'd been looking at. The image of a pretty young woman appeared against the backdrop of a dating site. "My niece, Sarah — that's her picture there — was on a dating website on the weekend. She met this guy from Georgia. They seemed to click and so they exchanged a few emails. But then Sarah sensed something wasn't right. It took her a couple of emails before she got him to own up to being fifty years old. She's only twenty-five, so it wasn't a match. When she told him she was moving on and thanks for the bullshit, he came back with a line about being particularly well endowed so might she want to reconsider. She replied that she hoped that by *well endowed* he meant he had twenty acres of bottom land, five acres of pasture, and ten acres of hardwood."

Doug shook his head. "Dating is all in the details."

Reg was inspired. "If she likes bad boys, we could set her up with Miller."

Doug had to laugh. "He has an expensive new coat. Don't leave that part out when you tell her."

Chapter 7

Hart rode back to the Don Jail in the van with his bridge pals. They were in a good mood. The evidence against them had been misplaced. The Crown said it was a mix-up in the paperwork that would be corrected shortly. Zipper and Doss had exchanged a knowing smirk when Prosecutor Summers had shamefacedly made the announcement to an obviously displeased Judge Sullivan. They were in a mood to celebrate. They were seated opposite each other at the back of the van with the dejected Hart in the narrow seat between them.

Doss spoke up first. "You did good, kid."

Zipper continued. "I thought you spoke very well."

They winked at each other and gave Hart a playful jab in the shoulder. "Judge, I didn't kill anybody you could take to the club, just some old lady."

"And did I mention how very sorry I am and how I'll never kill her again?"

They both got a little hysterical. Hart was too beaten up to care.

Doss tried again. "You should have offered to take one of the cats. Would have shown you in a very favourable light."

Hart laughed in spite of himself. He didn't want to. It came out like a sneeze and left his face burning with shame. "You guys are whacked."

Doss was wiping tears from his eyes. "You're not so bad for a sauce hound."

"Well, he's not much of a driver."

"This is what happens when you drink rum. It makes you crazy. Then the next thing you know, boom! Here you are."

Zipper jumped in. "Someone needs to set you straight. With booze, you lose. With dope, there's hope. You should've come to us for some chronic. If you had, instead of being hooked up with us here like a Christmas light, you'd be back home, stoned, thinking that maybe the old lady don't look so bad this morning."

Hart shook his head. *Dopers and juicers, we don't breathe the same air.*

———

The paperwork for Hart's release was waiting for him when he got back from court. They said, "Sign here," and he did. They said, "Follow us," and he followed. A clerk behind plexiglass gave him his copy and a clear plastic bag. He didn't bother reading it. He wanted to get this over with before they yanked his freedom back.

The walk through the range was familiar to him now. It didn't and couldn't hold the horror it did the first night they brought him in here. No one ever forgets the first time they hear the cell door slam behind them or the crazy shouting the incumbent prisoners lavish on their newest colleagues.

The men catcalled him when they saw the clear plastic bag, but he did nothing to give offence as he passed. He knew he was going to be back here soon enough. When they got to his cell, the guard stood in the corridor with his back to the wall, listening and watching, as relentless as videotape.

Hart didn't want anything in the cell; he only made the trip so that he could say goodbye to his friend. He threw a few toiletries into the bag to make it look good. "Bob, do you want any of this stuff?"

Prison Bob had mastered life on the range the way some men master a trade. He had everything he was allowed to have in plain sight, and a few forbidden luxuries hidden here and there. "Nope. I read all the books and the clothes don't fit."

Hart took a last look around the cell. "I can't say I've enjoyed being here."

Bob laughed. "I'll have to have the decorators in."

Hart smiled. "But I'm glad I got you as a cellmate. You're a good guy and I'm going to miss our talks. I appreciate you wising me up. I wouldn't have lasted long around here without your help."

PB pointed to the guard outside. "So how did your little speech go?"

"I couldn't read it. The little girl made me cry."

"So what did you say?"

"I'm not sure. Everything happened at once. It felt like jumping off a cliff."

"Like I told you, it's hard to find the right words when you can feel the sweat running down your rib cage. Well, it got you bail so you must have said something right."

Hart wanted to give Bob a hug, but Bob had a reputation to worry about, and Hart didn't want to start trouble. So instead, they did the ridiculous jail handshake that looked more like two toddlers fighting over a toy than a gesture of goodwill.

The next point of call was Levy's office, located conveniently across the street from the jail. It was a storefront operation. While Hart waited in the cane chair near the front window, he had a chance to read the agreement he had signed. A lot of it didn't make any sense.

The hope that he might get out on bail was the thing that had sustained Channing Hart while he was in custody. It was all that he had to look forward to. To be safe again, to have access to a shower and a toilet of his own, to eat food that a biker in a hairnet hadn't scooped out of a grey steam-table pan with a soup bowl — these things, these simple pleasures, were what he dreamed about. That and maybe having a drink or two.

Chaim Levy didn't like Hart. He saw him as a dangerous, self-indulgent wimp who'd finally blundered his way into killing someone. Hart was the kind of guy who drifted from crisis to crisis, feeling sorry for himself and finding other people to blame for his problems. He couldn't even read four lines from a script when his life hung in the balance. Levy had made a career out of rescuing mutts like him.

"Channing, this isn't an option. The judge wants you to attend a treatment program before you're sentenced."

"I'm out on bail. These last moments of freedom are precious to me. Why can't I attend something while I'm *in* jail? I'll have a lot of free time on my hands then." Hart was shifting back and forth in his chair. "Besides, I still have to pack up my place and sell my stuff. I have a million things to do."

"Like get drunk and foul this whole thing up?" Levy was feeling underappreciated. Had he not just rescued this moron from a double-digit prison sentence? And now he had to sit here and listen to him whine. His misgivings didn't change his studied tone of voice: "Channing, I put a lot of time and effort into bringing your good points to the fore in this case." *You killed an innocent woman while you were drunk. It's not easy to put a bastard like you in a sympathetic light. But I found a way.* "My strategy swayed the judge. She's now inclined to give you a break. I had to work hard to get that for you. Don't mess this up!" He fought the urge to poke Hart in the shoulder with his finger. "You embarrass a judge at your peril. The only reason you're not sitting in a jail cell right now is because you're going to treatment tomorrow. That's the deal!"

Levy was smooth. He'd given out a lot of bad news in his time and he was good at it. He tried being fatherly. He put his hand on Hart's shoulder in a gesture that said it was going to be all right.

Hart's body language said it all. He jerked his shoulder away. Levy tried a different tack, switching to the role of insider. "Channing, we have almost stickhandled our way out of this mess. In your place I might feel the same way, but we need to use our heads here and follow through on this like it's a good idea. We have to play the game."

Hart was looking down. He was shaking his head. This was wrong.

Levy barked at him, "Try and look interested."

Hart looked up, feeling betrayed. PB had called this one.

Levy didn't like Hart's look. "Let me make myself even clearer. You need to do what I instructed you to do. Either that or find yourself another lawyer. There's only one way out and this is it. Do you understand? You're out of options. If you're not careful, the wall we've been holding up with wishful thinking and bright, shiny faces is going to come crashing down on your head."

———

Hart had lived in the same comfortable low-rise in Weston since his mother had died. Most of the people in the building were from Cape Breton. There was always someone hanging around in the lobby, waiting for their laundry to dry, that he could talk to. The local kids were friendly. They liked to hang out after school in the parking lot behind the building, the one that overlooked the ravine. There were little trails cut in the hillside that led back onto the heavily overgrown hydro right-of-way — some for walking dogs, some for a first kiss, and others for smoking a spliff. The kids chased each other and their dogs up and down the trails until it was time for dinner.

The lobby was strangely empty when Hart arrived. The mats had been rolled back, and the floor, freshly washed and waxed, was drying. The air smelled strongly of disinfectant, but it was an odour that Hart liked. It was the smell of home.

Hart opened his mailbox and discovered it was jammed with bills and flyers. They were wedged in so tightly that the first items had been crushed by the weight of what had followed. While he was busy disentangling the mess, a young woman scarcely out of her teens opened the inside door of the apartment and stepped into the lobby. There was a hollow thud as the air pressure equalized. Hart heard the familiar sound and, forgetting himself for a moment, looked up eagerly, hoping to see a friendly face. It was Mary Pearson, a long-time neighbour. Hart didn't have a little sister, and Mary had taken that spot in his psyche. He was sweet on her in a big brotherly way. He smiled and gave her a little wave.

The smile on Mary's face vanished. She put her head down and bolted through the lobby and out the front door without stopping. Hart watched her go in stunned amazement. She looked back over her shoulder several times as she trotted away. She was frightened. Afraid that he was going to come after her.

Damn it. He had watched her grow up.

A fresh wave of terror gripped him as he connected the dots, the same way it had that first day in the Don Jail, when he was trapped in that dangerous, predatory place. *Does everyone in the building feel the way she does?*

He left the mail in the open box and walked down the long empty hallway toward his apartment. Halfway down the hall he gave way to his feelings of panic and started to trot, then run until he came to his door. He fumbled for his key. His hands were shaking. He cursed both them and the locks. He couldn't close the door behind him fast enough.

He pressed his back against the door as if someone were trying to push it open from the other side. He told himself he was home, he was safe now. But the apartment was deathly quiet and felt sinister. The air was dry and overheated, and for the first time in years, it didn't smell of stale tobacco. His plants were drained and discouraged. The magic that had made this space his was gone. Only the dead-battery beep from the smoke detector was there to offer him welcome.

He dropped his plastic bag and coat on the floor. He went straight to the refrigerator and opened the door, looking for some kind of comfort. The fridge was full of beer. Bottle piled on top of bottle, the way they did it at Clancy's. He stood there admiring the geometric pattern while the light from the fridge illuminated his face.

How can a three-dollar bus ride separate this room from the jail? Is this even the same planet? He had a moment of self-forgetting. Instinctively, he reached into the fridge and grabbed one of the bottles. It felt safe and familiar in his hand. He was thirsty and drained the bottle while the fridge door was still open. He was halfway through his next beer when the horror of what he was doing became clear to him. He had to be sober for three days before he went to Punanai. It was that or jail. *Why the hell am I drinking?*

He looked at the half-empty bottle in his hand the way he would a hieroglyph on a stone. Something inside him had been struck dumb. He tried to finish the beer but he couldn't swallow. He was still shocked and running on instinct. He got down on his hands and knees and took the cold beer out of the fridge, loading it back into the case it came in, like it was evidence of a crime.

The sun was low on the horizon, and it would soon be dark. He walked quietly out the fire door into the parking lot. He left the case of beer where he knew the kids would find it. He couldn't have told you why.

There were a million things he should be doing, but none of them wanted to happen. His body was brewing with an energy that couldn't find a focus. All he could think to do was put on the kettle. He put his head down on the kitchen table and felt its cool surface on his cheek. He was exhausted. The scream of the kettle coming to a boil wasn't enough to break his inward gaze.

Chapter 8

Kaiser had been in tough spots before. Lots of them. If the truth be known, he thrived on them. Nothing filled him with dread like the prospect of a peaceful Sunday afternoon with nothing to do but nap, read the newspaper, or snuggle up with a loved one. Action was the cure for everything that wore on him.

His appointment was for three o'clock, and he'd been cooling his heels in the waiting room for forty-five minutes.

The receptionist had been warned that looking up from the papers on her desk, doing something with her hair, or smiling would result in her immediate discharge and the death of her toy poodle. She didn't want to have anything to do with the clients. What they had might be catching. Clients got one of two verdicts here: Either they were done or they should take a long European vacation while they still could. The promise of graceful repose in old age was not on the table. The eternal ledger had a tale to tell.

Kaiser had put on his best suit and gotten a haircut before coming. It felt wrong to not look his best when he heard the final verdict. This had been a long time coming. He had smelled the end, in no uncertain terms, five years ago. He'd had quite a scare. But he couldn't bring himself to deal with it, so he went wild. He decided that only money could fix this. He took all the money he could raise or borrow, and he staked it all on one high-risk venture.

He made a little bit. Not enough to solve the problem, but enough to whet his appetite for risk. His second foray into the overheated market got his head above water and set him up perfectly for the disaster that followed. Now he was here. He wasn't going to be able to hustle his way out from under this landslide. But maybe that was never in the cards.

A fat man in a pair of baggy grey pants — last ironed by his wife the day before she left him — opened his office door and called Kaiser's name. The fat man wheeled around and went back to his desk without greeting his guest. He had the endearing quirk of taking off his glasses to read fine type. He put his shaggy grey mane a few inches from the tabletop, as if he was preparing to listen for the vibrations coming from an approaching train — maybe it was the train coming to take Kaiser to hell — and peered at the documents spread out there.

The office smelled of mildew and an undisciplined, possibly hyperopic cat. As Kaiser took his seat opposite the diagnostician, he could see paw prints, dusty from the cat litter, everywhere. Clearly this was progress. He had been ignored outside by a minion, but now he was being neglected by bigger fish. The ill-kempt man grunted and sat up straight. He took a mechanical pencil from his pocket and made a fevered note in the margins of a document. Whatever he found must have been a whopper because he suddenly became aware that Kaiser was in the room.

"You're Mr. Kaiser?"

Kaiser nodded.

"I don't have any good news for you."

"I wasn't expecting any."

"Your situation is hopeless."

"How long do I have?"

"That isn't for us to know. It could happen anytime."

"What should I do?"

"Go home and put your affairs in order. It's all you can do."

"Should I get a second opinion?"

"No, there's nothing ambiguous here. This is as bad as it gets."

Chapter 9

Paul Bethune stretched his arms over his head as he made his way down the hall to check on Hart's progress. He'd spent the previous hour hunched over his phone. The clients had wrongly assumed he was texting. What held his full attention was the image he was photoshopping. He loved manipulating the moments he'd captured. Pushing and pulling and twisting the fabric until the finished garment revealed itself as a suit that fit perfectly. Endless patience and attention to detail served him well as a photographer. The same traits made him a formidable counsellor.

Paul stuck his head through the doorway with a wide smile on his broad, handsome face. "Mr. Hart, how's the paperwork coming?"

Hart had his head down. He was surrounded by his luggage. In spite of Paul's assurances it would be safe, he refused to let it out of his sight. He was trying his hand at reverse engineering, attempting to figure out what kind of place this was by analyzing the intake questions. He was being careful and taking his time. After his cheery chat with his lawyer, he was on full alert. Prison Bob's notes were still fresh in his mind too. He was treating the old con's insights as holy writ. He wasn't in a trusting mood and he had no intention of testifying against himself.

"Well, I think I'm almost done. I wasn't sure how to answer some of these questions. They seem kind of ambiguous to me…"

The word ambiguous got stuck halfway up Paul's nose. He heard the siren cry. He wanted to say something caustic but refrained. He needed to get this assessment done before lunch. Paul ran his powerful hand through his thick dark hair, momentarily revealing some grey around the temples. "Okay, do the best you can. Come see me in the office when you're done."

Paul left the interview room and spotted one of the new guys standing by himself, looking a little lost. He decided to have some fun. He walked through the living room with his back pressed hard against an imaginary wall, looking like a mime traversing the dangerous ledge of a skyscraper. The dumbfounded client looked at him in wonder.

"For God's sake, don't look down!" Paul said, trying not to laugh.

Back in the counsellors' office, he found Mike was fretting the time too. Doug was trapped in a meeting, and that left Mike in charge and free to wiggle out of both his suit coat and his tie. Had Doug been on vacation, the shoes would have been next. "How's his book coming? He's been in there for an hour. Is there any ink left in his pen?" Mike asked.

Paul flopped into the nearest chair and crossed his massive arms across his thick chest. He had a bull neck that made him seem a little coarse if you didn't look closely enough. It was his face that broke the frame of that impression. His skin was as smooth and unmarked as a child's. He had deep sensitive eyes and a compelling grin. "He strikes me as being the earnest type. He's colouring in the pie charts now."

Mike interlocked his fingers and stretched out his arms. "It's always fun to get a chance to meet the man behind the face you see in the tabloids."

"Yup, it usually shakes my faith in newsgatherers."

———

When Hart handed his intake assessment to Paul, he was told to help himself to a coffee. As he sipped it in the living room, he was greeted by every client who walked through the room. *Maybe this place is different.* He leaned back in his armchair but couldn't settle. *Best not let my guard down, not yet.*

Ten minutes later Paul collected him and they set up shop in the interview room. The two men eyed each other like rivals at an auction getting ready to bid on something they both had to have. Hart's face had strong features. His eyes and chin dominated his appearance. Handsome was out of reach but prepossessing was well within his grasp. Today, though, wasn't the day for a close-up. Three months in the Don Jail had left him shaky and pale. Pronounced dark circles under his eyes gave him a sad, almost comic aspect. His arms and shoulders spoke of strength and endurance, but jailhouse carbs had distended his stomach and swollen his jowls. His clothing was good quality stuff from the L.L.Bean catalogue. But what used to flatter him no longer fit.

Paul understood the terrible psychological strain Hart had been under. His attempts to build rapport had thus far been politely declined. He could see suspicion in the man's eyes. He gave up on trying to finish on time and decided to let Hart talk.

Hart was looking at his hands, which were cold and perspiring. "I'm afraid to close my eyes," he said. "I'm terrified I'm going to remember what happened and it's going to be worse than what I'm feeling now. People want to talk to me in my dreams. They get right in my face but then a bus passes or a plane goes overhead and I can't make out what they're saying. I saw that dead lady a couple times. She just stared at me and then walked away. That broke my heart."

Paul saw the torment Hart was describing make its way across his face. The corners of his mouth drew in and he seemed to turn inward. Away from Paul, away from the conversation. Some place safe where he didn't need to choose his words. After a moment, he spoke again.

"Last night I had this dream about a woodpecker. He was exploring the tree outside my window. He was chipping away at the wood, looking for a soft spot. The tree was old and the timber was rotten and huge chunks of bark scattered in all directions."

Paul smiled encouragingly.

"I never worried about my dreams before this happened. They didn't mean anything. Sometimes I would see someone I'd lost and that was nice. But now, holy smoke — it's like when I go to bed, I'm in a movie theatre and the show is about to begin."

Paul looked down at the notes. "Are you a smoker?"

"Had to quit when I was inside. Everyone had to go cold turkey. They gave us a patch but it didn't help. There was a fight every five minutes."

Paul got to his feet and removed his suit coat. "When you quit smoking, your dreams become much more vivid for a while. I know this is stretching the meaning of dreams, but can you tell me what you want to happen? What would put a smile on your face?"

Hart was surprised by the question. No one ever asked him what he wanted. He'd been dealing with liars and bullies and hoping for a miracle that hadn't come. Maybe a miracle that couldn't or shouldn't come. He hated hope. It made him vulnerable. People used it to hurt him. *They only give you hope so they can take it away again. That's what Bob said.* He looked at Paul but felt no connection. No better and no worse than the other guards. *They don't negotiate. They burrow their way inside you. They inject their poison, and when you're paralyzed, they lay their eggs. You feel the tearing inside. Your nostrils flare and your nose runs. You fear them and hate them until you need them because there's no one else.*

He didn't know what he wanted. But he did know what he didn't want and that was another person leaving muddy footprints inside his head. The only person who'd made any sense to him was Prison Bob, and PB was adamant that these guys could not be trusted. All the professionals were making a good living playing the game. They were doing fine. That left the hoi polloi to shift for themselves.

He watched Paul roll up his sleeves and sit down again. *Is that who you are? Another stooge on the payroll? You gonna sweep me along until the next broom picks me up? Could I tell you what I really think? Not one of you bastards knows what you're talking about. But that doesn't stop you from cashing my cheques and telling me what to do.*

"I'd like you to tell me there's nothing wrong with me," Hart said. "I want to be normal again. I'd like to pick up the paper in the morning and be bored. Do you know what it's like to see your face on the front page? Especially when *they* get to crop it. They kept me awake for three days. And then — *presto* — there I am in handcuffs, looking as guilty as a man can look, under a banner headline: Killer Gets His Day in Court." Hart looked out the window at the garden below. The shrubs in their burlap and the young saplings in their sleeves were better prepared for a winter's nap than he. "Sometimes I wanna go to sleep and never wake up again."

Paul smelled what he thought might be the faint odour of duplicity and unwisely explored that possibility. "In some jurisdictions, they'd be glad to do that for you."

The look of anger and surprise on Hart's face told Paul that he wasn't the first one to disappoint this man. Hart had a reservoir of ill will to draw on, and Paul wondered how long it was going to take to bring it all to the surface. He put his hands to the pump, hoping to find the next wrong thing to say. "Do you know that most people choose to come here? I know you were forced to, and that stinks. But here we actually help people with addiction problems."

Hart laughed and shook his head. "There's no need. Where I'm going, they don't serve drinks."

Paul's face brightened. "Oh, they serve drinks all right. They mix them up in a fire extinguisher instead of a martini shaker, but they get the job done. You think that's all there is to an addiction, simply the drinking?"

Hart suddenly felt like he was talking to the police again. His voice became tentative. He was determined to keep his own counsel until he figured out what the deal was. If only PB was here to whisper the right answers in his ear. Without meaning to, he started to minimize. "I don't drink every day. A couple times I even quit on my own. It was hard but I did it."

Paul recognized that he'd been pushing too hard too soon. He'd inadvertently dressed himself in a copper's uniform. His voice took on a more casual tone. "What prompted you to quit drinking?"

"You're kidding, right? They say I killed a lady…"

Paul wasn't put off by the remark. "No, I meant the time before when you quit. Why did you do it? Were you on a diet?"

Hart shrugged. "It was a lifestyle thing. I was dating a woman who didn't like drinking. I really wanted her and so I quit. It was tough but I was able to do it."

"How old were you then?"

"I don't know, maybe twenty-three or twenty-four."

Paul snuck a look at the file. "So now you're thirty-five."

"That's right."

Paul realized that Hart had no idea how addictions worked. No one had ever explained the facts of life to him. "What do you think an addiction is?"

Hart continued to distance himself from the problem. "Well, it's when you can't take care of yourself. You see people like that all the time. They're fat, they need a haircut, they're out on the street or couch surfing most of the time. Sometimes they're dirty, their clothes never fit right, they show up for work late and smell like stale whisky. They're always getting fired. I worked with guys like that. There were lots of them in jail. I may drink too much, but I'm not a drunk."

"What do you make of the guys here? Have you talked to any of them?"

Hart felt the ambush coming. *I see what you're trying to do.*

"They seemed okay to me. I'd have to see them in action in order to make up my mind." Hart needed a friend. But so many of his recent attempts to make one had ended badly. Could he trust Paul? "Can I talk to you about something off the record?"

Paul leaned into the space that separated them. "Off the record? When you say it like that, it sounds kind of ominous."

Hart leaned forward too. "Well, I tried to be honest filling out the paperwork, but I kept coming back to the fact that I'm going to be sentenced when I'm finished here. The judge is going to see everything that gets written down."

Paul prompted him very gently: "So you want to control the information?"

That one stung enough to break the logjam. "Have you ever been on trial? Do you know what that's like? You have no voice. People talk about you while you're right there in the room. And they get everything wrong. That prick Summers got hold of my financial records, he talked to the people I work with and scared the hell out of them. Next thing I know, people who barely even know me start giving interviews about me to the newspaper. Saying shit that isn't true. The cops took my computer and tore it to bits — who knows what they were looking for. It's a nightmare. My file's the size of the friggin' Yellow Pages. Two days before the accident, I'll bet you not twenty people in the world gave a damn about me, and now I'm a household name."

Hart suddenly became acutely aware that he'd said the wrong thing again. He put his head down and took a breath. Then he looked up at Paul, who was watching him with interest. "So here's the thing. You want me to tell you the truth. Okay, I can do that. But I live in fear now. Do you know what that feels like? To be powerless. To have people look at you like the lies are true."

"We talked about privacy before we started. Do you remember?"

"Yeah, you made a joke, said I couldn't tell anyone that I saw you here. That took me a minute to figure out."

Paul's face lit up; he enjoyed his own joke. "Our reports are deliberately vague. We report attendance and outcomes. When these things get to court, all that matters are the notes — the written record. If the notes say we had a conversation, then we had a conversation. If there are no notes, then we didn't have the conversation. You and I can talk about anything you like inside this office, and as long as I don't make a note, your privacy is protected. Besides, in this case, the damage is done, isn't it? The cops know everything there is to know about you by now. So, look, I'm putting my pencil down. What's on your mind?"

"But you'll still remember. You could be called to testify."

Paul smiled at his new friend. "You'd be surprised. This stuff goes in one ear and out the other. I usually remember the story but not who it happened to. We hear so many of these tales that they all become a blur after a while. I talked to our spiritual adviser, Father Phil, about this one time. A client had told me something in confidence that upset me, and it was eating at me. I asked Phil how he kept his head on straight with all the secrets from other people he had stored in his memory. His answer surprised me. He laughed and asked if I had heard a hundred confessions yet. I said no — this was still early days for me. He said, 'Don't worry, you remember the first hundred, but after that, they're all gone very quickly. People are often quite annoyed that you don't remember their deepest, darkest secrets.'"

That was a lot of new information. Paul gave Hart a moment to think about what he'd said. "Let me ask you a question. You said when you were twenty-four, you stopped drinking for a girl. What got you going again?"

Hart smiled. "We broke up after a few months. She said I was hard to get along with."

"Maybe you were feeling the strain of not drinking. So after that you drank on a regular basis?"

"You make it sound like I drink every day. I'm not like that. But, yeah, I drank and sometimes I drank a lot. I liked it. It was something I could always rely on to make myself feel better. I worked hard. I've done okay for myself. I'm not like the guys out there," he said, pointing out the widow to the circle of smoking men.

Paul looked down at the file while Hart was talking. "Never married, no kids, not like other people at all." Paul spoke slowly and gently. "Must have been lonely."

Hart was alarmed. That wasn't the impression he wanted to make. How had Paul seen through him so easily? He started talking very fast. "I worked. I worked hard every day and I saved my money. I didn't go on vacations or buy fancy cars and clothes. I took all the overtime I could get. I played sports with the guys at work. And we all hung out at Clancy's after work. We had a darts league and a pool league. There was always someone around to talk to and have a drink with. We would bet on football and hockey. We'd rent a bus once a year and go to a Bills game. It wasn't so bad."

Paul didn't lose his way or raise his voice. "Did you want a family?"

Hart felt an awful wave of sadness. "I think I did, but I…" His voice became a whisper when he said, "I could never connect with a woman. I would meet lots of them at Clancy's, but after two or three dates, they'd all make that face — the one that tells you this is the last date — and then they'd disappear. One minute, I'm twenty-four and a hot property, and the next thing I know, I'm thirty-five and on the front page of the newspaper. It all went by like a freight train."

"How did it feel when you sobered up and they told you that you'd killed someone?"

Hart was stunned by the question. All the blood drained from his face until he looked like a figure in a wax museum. No one had asked him about this before. "I woke up in a cell with a blinding hangover. I was thirsty, my head ached, my stomach was hot and empty. My gut was full of acid. Everything hurt. The cell was freezing. My head and neck were so stiff, when I moved I got dizzy. The whole room swam when I tried to sit up. I asked a policeman for some water and he gave me a Dixie cup. I asked for another and he told me to shut up."

Hart started to replay the conversation, taking both parts. "So I ask him, 'When do I get out? Why am I here?' I was hoping for a smart answer, but this guy looked grim. He scared me. He said, 'Don't you remember?'" The life flowed out of Hart like air out of a balloon. "I don't think there's a question I hate more than that one. 'Buddy,' he said, 'you killed a lady. The detectives want to talk to you.'"

Hart's face went blank. He was so deeply immersed in feeling that he forgot he was speaking to another person. "I started walking around the cell, pulling at the bars. Looking for a way out. I didn't know if I had murdered her or what had happened. In a way, it was a relief to find out I'd only killed her in a car crash." He caught himself there. "Listen to me — only killed her in a car crash."

He got to his feet and walked over to the window. He put his forehead on the windowpane and rocked back and forth on the balls of his feet until the world righted itself and he could breathe again. He opened the window a crack and rejoiced at the cold, cruel air rushing to his rescue. Swirling around the Arctic for months had purged it of anything like human feeling or off-gases. It was only itself.

"When we got to court and the family started to talk about her — Jesus! She was a good woman, coming home from a family party with her daughter. She reminded me of my mom. That made me feel even worse. At least if I killed someone with my bare hands, I could've comforted myself with the thought that they'd done something — anything — to piss me off." He said it, but they both knew he didn't mean it.

Paul's face radiated calm. He was where he wanted to be.

"And her daughter is all busted up. She was in court…" Hart paused as a sob came up from his gut. That little girl. There was no getting over that little girl. "I don't remember getting into the car. It belonged to Connor. He says I stole it. That's the problem with not remembering — I don't know if I did or not."

Paul changed the subject ever so slightly. "This forgetting. We call that a blackout. Is this the first time it happened?"

Hart was still overcome with remorse. "Do you think I kill someone every day?"

Paul was calm. "No, I'm exploring the forgetting part. Have you ever woken up somewhere before and not remembered how you got there?"

Hart started to give it up: "It happens from time to time. Some of the guys even say, 'If you remember what you did at the party, you didn't have a really good time.'"

"But what about you? How do you feel when it happens?"

"The first time it happened, it scared me to death. I remember waking up in my own bed, but I didn't remember how I got there. I went back to Clancy's and got Clancy to show me my tab from the night before. It was hefty, but not the biggest one I ever had. Clancy told me not to worry, said lots of people get blackouts. At least then I had a word for what happened and someone telling me not to worry. Clancy and I sat down and had a short one to celebrate." He took a minute to think about that. "That's crazy, isn't it?"

Paul was pleased to be hearing the truth. This was progress. "Unlike me, Clancy is not in the business of embarrassing drunks." Paul's face lit up. He blundered by pushing too hard. "Wait a minute! You broke confidentiality. The relationship between the barman and the drinker is sacred. Lawyer-client, doctor-patient, penitent-priest. That sort of thing."

"You're not serious?"

Paul tried again. "No, I was trying to have some fun with you. You're not ready for that yet, but maybe you will be soon. The serious point here is that only alcoholics have blackouts."

Hart wasn't having that. "Half the guys at the bar get them all the time and they're not alcoholics." Hart's head came up and his eyes opened wide. Had he heard the lie in his own words for the first time?

Paul smiled; he knew now he could work with Hart. "It would be interesting to find out where they draw the line between normal and abnormal drinking."

He pushed the envelope a little further. "I'll bet they have you down as a pathetic drunk after what happened."

Hart got the jolt that he had been fearing would come in his dreams. *Oh shit, no. They all would have been talking about me. Who was there, and who saw what, and who tried to stop me from driving. Oh shit.*

He put his head in his hands as he recreated the conversation in his mind that surely had taken place that Saturday afternoon around the big table at Clancy's. Everyone tucking into their steak and eggs with all the sporting papers spread open on the table. Hart felt sick. *That's why no one showed up in court.* The photographer in Paul was as full of anguish as Hart was. The face in front of him was a *Life* magazine cover. But even if he had brought his camera, he wouldn't have been able to use it.

Hart's eyes narrowed as he worked out what must have followed. When he began to speak again, he was only vaguely aware of Paul's presence. "That's how they would have left it. Me, a monster, and them, heroes. I've seen them do it to other guys. I never thought they'd do it to me…" He thought about those other scandals. How he had listened while reputations were destroyed. How it made him feel to sit in judgment. "They think I did it."

Paul leaned back in his chair with his head tilted slightly. "So what's the deep, dark secret you want to keep out of the record? Is it something you need to talk about today? Is it something you'd feel safe talking about with me?"

Hart liked Paul, but not that much. He couldn't quite shake the feeling that Paul disapproved of him. "I wish you were a clergyman; this would be easier."

"I could comb my hair like Spencer Tracy, if you like."

"You make very strange jokes…"

"Hart, privacy means very little in a treatment centre, and even less in a homicide investigation. So let's take a deep breath here and have a conversation about the conversation. We have a real clergyman, Father Phil, who comes in once a week. You could talk to him and that would be a protected conversation. Phil has told us on several occasions that he'd rather go to jail than break the seal of the confessional." Paul's face brightened. "That would be good. You guys could get adjoining cells and really get to know each other."

Hart had had enough. What was up with this guy? "Yeah, I want to talk to Father Phil."

Paul smiled. It's not every day that you drain a forty-foot putt on the first hole.

Doug and Mike had installed a new set of speakers on the computer in the main office. They were exploring possibilities when Paul entered the room and, rather theatrically, collapsed in the swivel chair, fanning his face with the manila file.

"What's happening with our front-page celebrity?"

"He's a funny guy, Doug. I was expecting to meet a stone-cold killer. That, he is not. He sure hates seeing his picture in the papers."

"But is our boy an alcoholic yet?" asked Mike.

"He's working on it. This is all new to him. He has some funny ideas about who is and who isn't a drunk. His big worry is that he's suddenly going to remember what happened. In his dreams, people try to tell him things — important things — but he can never hear the words. He's afraid of what they're going to say, certain that whatever it is will destroy him, but still desperate to know. I think he's waiting for someone to tell him why his life sucks and afraid that someone's going to tell him he's an alcoholic."

Mike's curled-up nose said he wasn't buying it. "That's too much freight to carry on a dream. Get him to show you his bar tab — that'll settle it. If we let this guy set the agenda with this kind of nonsense, then the whole court thing is all we're going to talk about. It's a shame we can't have him when his sentence is over."

Doug spoke up. "He's going to be damaged when he gets out. He might be unsalvageable at that point. If we don't wise this guy up, prison will destroy him."

Chapter 10

While the boys had veered left in their panic to escape the little girl outside the display window, the women had followed Maddy, going right, and had ended up at a dead end. But the onrushing Rosa had forged her way to the front of the group and ordered them to link arms as she grabbed a passing interval trainer. They followed in the runner's wake like paper chains constructed by children. They soon found themselves at the corner of Yonge and Bloor, where Rosa abandoned the runner and laid hands on a Purolator driver who was intent on taking an L-cart up the escalator that funnelled shoppers into the Hudson's Bay store. When he got off on the fourth floor, the women made their way to the furniture department on the fifth floor under their own power and quickly. The considerable effort of moving on their own took the fire out of their limbs and left them breathless. Rosa had to a stop at the top of the escalator.

"Why are you stopping?" sputtered Sharon, more than a little out of breath.

"I'm all in," wheezed Rosa.

Helen bent over in exhaustion and placed her hand on Sharon's forearm. "Is that girl still chasing us?"

Sharon was taken aback and looked at her friend. "We're not running from her, surely?"

"Who did you think we were running from?" asked Maddy.

"I didn't have time to ask," said Sharon, making a face.

Rosa asked the practical question. "What about the men?"

"They were looking out for number one. Not a glance backward to see if we were safe," said Sharon. Helen nodded in vigorous agreement.

Rosa was breathing hard but was otherwise undamaged. "I'm bushed. I'm far too dead to run like this anymore." She made her way toward a living-room setting and sat down next to Maddy on the couch. "I come here sometimes to sit and remember happier times in my life."

"Let's make this our meeting place," said Helen as she chose a comfortable-looking straight-backed chair that was upholstered in red velvet. More fun to look at than to own.

"We won't tell the boys," said Sharon, settling herself in the chair next to Helen's. "Too much testosterone spoils the picnic."

Helen was feeling better now. She felt safe again. "What was that awful Barry trying to get us to do?"

"I didn't like the way he was talking to us," said Sharon. "And the way he was looking me up and down made me want to slap him."

Maddy giggled. "The way he goes on about the light, like there's nothing else worth talking about."

Rosa opened her purse and started to look inside it for her glasses. "I died right after the war and a lot of the ghosts back then were badly beaten up. Some of them had done dreadful things and they were scared to death of going to hell. Whenever the light showed up, they'd take to their heels. A fat lot of good it did them. One by one, they became poltergeists and that was the end of them. In spite of all their plans and bluster, they went quietly in the end. When the light finally came for them, they just stared at it like it was a big balloon at a birthday party. I always think about that when the men start to get crazy with all their talk."

Maddy was fascinated. "Have you ever seen it happen?"

"Twice in all my years."

Helen was smiling broadly. "But that was the very thing they were talking about. Why didn't you say something?"

Rosa chuckled as she finally put her hand on her specs. "It was too much fun watching the men make fools of themselves. They all see themselves as Christopher Columbus out to conquer the new world."

Helen felt a certain satisfaction as she revisualized the meeting and its abrupt ending. "That is funny. You sitting there with the answer, and them too arrogant to ask you."

Maddy was curious about Rosa's past. "What have you been doing all this time?"

"I've been overlooked my whole life. Didn't have the looks, you see. In my day, what with all the men getting killed in the war, it was a buyer's market in matrimony. Then I died. I don't know why I didn't move along. I watched my sister's family grow up and that was kind of fun. It sort of made up a bit for what I missed, but watching people isn't really satisfying. I never got to take my turn. It isn't the same as loving and being loved."

Maddy dug a little deeper, trying to understand this new perspective. Rosa's experience was so different from the others that had been shared in the group. "Aren't you afraid of the light?"

The old ghost smiled. "No more than I am of anything else I don't understand."

"Then why did you run?"

"It's silly," said Rosa, "but when someone screams, Run! — well, I do. You don't think to ask why. I haven't done anything wrong. In my whole life, I never did anything that anyone ever cared about."

Sharon chimed in with a smile on her face. "Me neither, but that didn't stop me from running."

"How did you die, Rosa?" asked Helen.

"Don't know. Just woke up dead one morning." The women all nodded in sympathy. "I saw the coroner sign my death certificate. I didn't understand what *he put down as the cause of death. But no matter, dead is dead. Then I hooked up with Lisa and Spencer — oh, they don't make ghosts like them anymore." Rosa smiled to herself. "Spencer was bound and determined he was going to read every book in the Swansea Public Library before he went, and he was damned close to doing so when he died, and so he stayed at the library day after day waiting for someone to check out the books he wanted to read. Trouble was, the more he read, the more he wanted to read. Then one day he turned around and said that he'd had enough — but, you know, in a really good way. Lisa had loved him forever and refused to go anywhere without him. She waited and watched until he was ready and then, finally, away they went together. How I miss them." The old ghost looked sad and ready to curl up for a rest.*

Helen was still curious. "Why didn't you go with them?"

Rosa almost blushed. "They were meant for each other; they needed to go together. I knew they liked me, but I wasn't a part of them. Ghosts are never a family, in spite of what Barry tells you."

Sharon nodded. "You saw the way they left us to get scooped back there. So typical. In death as in life."

Helen stuck out her feet to get comfortable and was surprised when her chair lurched back a few inches. Everyone laughed. "But we don't have to be that way."

Rosa agreed. "Let's form our own group and talk about what's important to us."

"No men," added Sharon.

"Just the women," Maddy added.

Helen had a wistful look. "I wonder what that little girl is feeling right now. She looked sad when we ran."

Rosa spoke up. "She may not be a little girl. The light is whimsical. It takes on a form that kind of makes fun of you in a loving way. One of the old drunks used to see it appear as the Johnnie Walker figure on the Scotch bottle."

"No..." Maddy clapped in delight.

"Another guy, who was a big eater, used to see it as a giant hot dog."

"No religious themes?" asked Helen.

"Oh, the Sacred Virgin all the time and every saint and angel you ever heard tell of."

Sharon's face darkened. "But why?"

Rosa shook her head almost in wonder. "That has always been the debate. I was trying to tell Barry that before he told me to shut up." They nodded as they recalled the exchange.

"No one has ever been able to figure out if the light takes on a shape we love to comfort us or to lead us to harm, the way a lure catches a fish."

"There really is only one way to find out isn't there," Helen said.

"It's funny. I was so afraid of dying when I was still alive," said Maddy. "I have to say I expected things after death to be straightforward. I never imagined a muddle like this."

"And all we get is more uncertainty," said Sharon.

Rosa, as always, was practical. "It makes you wonder what it would take to finally make up your mind one way or the other. I think when you're ready, you weigh the evidence and you trust in your own judgment."

"The one thing we do know is we can't stay here forever," said Sharon.

"This really is a decision that no one can make for you," said Maddy.

They all had the same idea at about the same time, but it was Helen who spoke first. "Do you want to go down and talk with that little girl?"

Maddy was reluctant but not opposed. "Let's talk among ourselves a bit more."

"I'm tired of playing hide-and-go-seek," said Rosa.

"It would be better to know than not know," said Helen.

"What about the fellas?" asked Sharon.

Helen had lost interest in them. "Can't save them from themselves. They'll be trying to give the little girl a hotfoot if I know them."

"More like track her to her lair," said Sharon.

Maddy was laughing now. "There's only one thing we can be certain that they won't do."

"What's that?" asked Rosa, putting her hand on Maddy's arm.

"Listen to her," said Maddy with an infectious grin.

Sharon took it up one step. "They'll tell her what needs doing."

The women all laughed.

"I like this group," said Rosa.

The tripartite response was. "Me too."

Chapter 11

Sean Miller was lying on his bed, waiting for lights-out and listening to the flurry of activity that always preceded it. Showers were hissing, toilets were flushing, and the guys were all talking over each other in the hall. It was a good time to relax and get ready for sleep. Sean and Hart had been talking for about an hour, getting to know each other, when the conversation turned to Hart's unwelcome notoriety.

"Look, I know I'm only a mystery-novel fan, but, dude, you have a very bad lawyer," Sean said.

"No shit. He charged me twenty thousand dollars to plead me guilty. I could have done that myself."

Sean enjoyed puzzles — they gave him a good reason to light up a smoke. "It doesn't add up. How did you get the keys? How were you able to find the car when you were that drunk?" He got to his feet and started to look around for his shoes.

Hart was staring at the ceiling. "Everyone knew where the car was. That green Mustang was Connor's pride and joy. He was always taking girls for rides in it. Parked it at the far end of the lot so it wouldn't get scratched."

"Well, it's damn well dented now."

"Flipped right over, from what I'm told. The cops charged me with not wearing a seat belt." Hart leaned up on his elbow. "But I was. My pelvis was black and blue." He pulled the waist band of his track pants back and examined himself. "You can still see where the belt cut me. Later on, they dropped the charge and said I must have undone it and tried to crawl out."

"Couldn't they tell by the belt marks if you were driving?"

"That only works with three-point restraints."

"What about fingerprints on the wheel?"

"I was wearing gloves."

"Why didn't you lie? Tell them it was Connor."

Hart sighed. "You can't tell a lie if you don't know the truth."

"Well, what if it was him? He coulda given you a ride. Maybe he felt sorry for you standing there at the bus stop in the cold. That's why your fingerprints aren't on the steering wheel. Connor did this — not you."

Hart felt a sick feeling deep down in his gut. "Connor has an alibi — the guys at the bar all swear he was there."

"Yeah, like they'd know. Is he their dealer or something? The local tough guy?" Sean blew out a stream of air. Then he thought of something else. "Besides, the witnesses were all drunk."

"Yeah, but—"

"And how far away from the bar were you when you crashed?"

"Don't know, a couple blocks."

"He coulda walked that. You've been had." Sean was getting wound up. Why did this matter so much to him?

Hart felt his gut tighten. It was like he was right back in that jail cell hearing the news for the first time. Why did he have to open his mouth? PB was right — this kind of talk was trouble. This could push the deal off the table. He was suddenly very afraid of Sean and of what he might do. He read from the script that had been prepared for him. "Levy says it doesn't matter if Connor drinks and drives every night of the year. He wasn't at the scene. They aren't interested in before or after, only who was there that night."

Sean could feel his heart racing; this story was making his blood boil. "How can you be so calm about this?"

Hart was still behaving like this was happening to someone else, maybe someone he cared about, but definitely not him. He put up his right hand, palm out, in a gesture that said to leave it alone.

This is lame. No wonder everyone thinks he did it. Sean had put on his coat and was ready for his smoke. He pressed Hart again. "You have to fight this."

Hart ducked a second time. "Levy said the Crown will always take something instead of nothing. Justice not only needs to be done, it needs to be seen — that's why they make deals. When shit like this happens, getting charged is as good as being convicted. You saw the headlines — did you think I was guilty? Better to cut a deal, get my face out of the tabloids, and fade away into the shadows. I'd rather spend a few years in a jail for first-time offenders than do time in the federal system. The last thing I need is the press counting the days until I get out."

Sean couldn't get his head around that. "But it's wrong—"

"It's even worse to roll dice in a game you know is crooked." Hart rolled over on his side and pulled the blankets around him. He was done talking and listening. He wanted to be alone and at peace for a few hours. Some place with no bullies, no confrontation, and no fear about his future.

Sean was full of energy. He was a part of this story now. He felt connected to it in a way he couldn't articulate. Something definitely had to be done about this. He looked at his watch and ran down the stairs, hoping to have a quick smoke and a word with Paul.

Chapter 12

To the Bailey brothers, the howl of excited ghosts exiting the Holt Renfrew display window had sounded like a jet flying overhead, and it had lasted about as long. It was all over in less than ten seconds. Outside the window, the giant little girl had a sad look on her face. Inside, the two Baileys remained sitting on their barrels.

"Is there a reason, Declan, why we didn't scream like lunatics and run for our lives like everybody else?"

"Breeding. It's unseemly to run for your life when you're already dead."

"We have good genes."

"And good manners."

"What's the little girl going to do, do you suppose?"

"Well, I think she's finished growing. If she fills out, she'll be a beauty."

"If I'm reading her lips right, she's saying, 'Come outside and play.'"

"Do you suppose it's the glass keeping her out?"

"No. She could walk in through the front door like the rest of us if she really wanted to."

"This is like one of Father O'Donnell's logic questions."

"Oh, I used to love those. So what's the logic of this situation?"

"There's nothing stopping her from coming in here. So maybe she doesn't want to."

"Is she afraid of us? Two horrible-looking old ghosts."

"Not likely … she's a good chunk of a girl."

"So what should we do?"

"Three options: run, talk, or sit and wait for her to go away."

"It's been a long time since any girl wanted to talk to me. I say let's palaver."

"Speaking of which, where do you suppose our girls went?"

"You would have to ask them. My running days are over."

"And our fearless executive? Hard to believe that a fat fella like Peter could run right up the back of that coward Barry."

"I didn't hear them cry, 'Women and children first!'"

"It looked like the losing side of every battle ever fought."

"Yes, the perceived social order didn't survive the challenge of danger."

"Leaving the questions of leadership and procedure unresolved and, I hope you noticed, my dear fellow, no date fixed for the next meeting."

"Funny how it worked out. Barry giving us a supreme scolding for not going looking for the light, and then the light shows up and off they run like spooked

deer in the forest. You'd think they'd be happy to see the very thing they were searching for."

"Someone should have thought to bring a blanket to throw over her head."

"Would that have helped?"

"I don't know, but that was the direction that the group's thinking seemed to be going in."

"That's right. Capture the light and make it do our bidding."

"There's the way to get to heaven all right: Put the muscle on an angel."

"Why do you suppose it is that we try and work out our individual salvation in a group?"

"It's illogical."

"Father O'Donnell would agree. The individual conscience: That is what sets us apart."

"Oh, look, she's coming in. Look, it's a tight squeeze too."

"Is this the end, my dear fellow?"

"I don't think so. She doesn't look mad."

"No, she looks quite an agreeable sort."

"I don't know about you, but I'm feeling chuffed all of a sudden."

"Me too. It's been a while since I felt this good. It's getting warm in here."

Chapter 13

After his first full week in treatment, Eustice Czombo was feeling better about himself. He was examining his image in the mirror as he brushed his teeth. His beautiful green hair was being let down by dark roots. He needed a touch-up. Thank heavens he'd packed his dye. *I'll do that tomorrow.*

He had initially despaired of having any fun in this godforsaken hellhole. He despised the staff. He hated his dull-witted, pathetically annoying Employee Assistance Program counsellor for sending him here. But most of all, he loathed his ill-fated roommate, Arthur Wilberforce Cardel. Thanks to some good luck and quick thinking on his part, that Boy Scout was now working on his next merit badge somewhere else. *Good riddance.*

Czombo now had the room he'd shared with Arthur all to himself — the spoils of victory — and he'd started to make some improvements. He was quick to recognize and exploit opportunities. As he looked at his reflection, he wished that he had something other than peach fuzz on his chin. A beard would have been the making of him. He was thin and dressed to the dictates of a canon that no one over the age of twenty-five would even recognize as a fashion statement. There were only two clubs where what he wore was cool. But in those clubs, he was the coolest. He needed to get back.

He was only twenty, but already he understood that institutional living preserved the body at the expense of the soul. Frozen vegetables were the perfect metaphor for what happened in these places. Treatment preserved your colour and texture but rendered you flat and inedible. Czombo knew that no one was ever going to willingly help him do what he wanted to do with his life. Oh, they'd help him, just not willingly. They would need some love.

It was easy to get lost in the crowd at Punanai. The hour before lights-out was ripe with possibility. When he turned off the lights in his room and closed the door, it had the same effect as a Do Not Disturb sign on a hotel doorknob. During the day, the very anal staff required all the bedroom doors to be left open as a security measure, but in the evening, people could expect some privacy. His plan was to slip out the side door on the north side of the building, unnoticed. No one would miss him in the hubbub of getting ready for bed. Nobody ever missed him, because outside of the clubs, nobody liked him — unless it was absolutely necessary. He made very sure of that.

On one of his nocturnal prowls, Czombo had discovered that the house next door to Punanai had a garage the owners never bothered to lock, in which they stored unwanted furniture and off-season goods, such as waterslides and bicycles. He made his way there under cover of darkness. There was a lovely old La-Z-Boy recliner that Czombo had repositioned in front of the dark-green glass window. He kept his chronic and some rolling papers in the side pocket, the one originally designed to hold magazines. He hefted the baggie and smiled. More than enough for the rest of his stay. His practised fingers effortlessly produced a perfect cylinder. He switched on the ancient oscillating fan he had found on top of a heap of books and sparked up his creation. He was obsessively careful not to let the smoke touch his person.

From this vantage point, behind the green glass, he had a periscopic view of Doug's office and a large portion of the living room. He could also hear everything that was being said on the patio below, where the guys smoked. The guests were getting ready for bed.

The green glass he was peering through was a godsend. It had some very special optical properties. In the daylight, with the help of his sunglasses, he could see out with some difficulty, but no one could see in. He was very sure of that. He'd left a red baseball cap on top of the La-Z-Boy and tried to view it from every portal in the house and in all kinds of light conditions: The new Cardinals hat remained invisible. At night, when the lights were out, he could see everything from inside the garage, but it was fuzzy and out of focus in the way that cheap store-surveillance cameras always are. However, once he knew the players, it was easy to identify them by their movements and habits.

He thought about the week that had passed and the week that was to come as he felt the bud begin its slow dance through his body. Getting rid of that little shit Cardel and his cowboy pal had made this place bearable.

Those two assholes made it hard to breathe, what with all their positive recovery chat. They honest-to-God think this shit works. Well, they'll find out soon enough. Saturday night has a way of rolling around. A seed exploded in his joint and sent a shower of sparks cascading down onto his sweater. He punched out the fire. That was a dangerous tell.

Cardel had made it so easy. Heading into a boiler room for some bang-bang instead of listening to some poor old sod sing the blues at a CA meeting. The bud tweaked his love of parody. He slid effortlessly into character. *Arthur, what were you thinking? And after all the splendid progress you made, your goals and your aspirations all neatly laid out on lined paper for the counsellors to inspect. What does this say about your commitment to sobriety? Your personal failures are shaking my faith in the process. If I relapse, it's on your feckless head.*

Czombo couldn't help but smile. He'd made the call from the cell phone he wasn't supposed to have when he twigged that Arthur was up to something, and then he found a quiet spot from which to watch the fun. He expected a lot of yelling when Mike Sage showed up twenty minutes later to haul him and the girlie out of the boiler room, but he was disappointed. Everyone was so calm. The lovers even had their clothes on.

They had to be doing a porno in there. I hope he has the good manners to post it. She wasn't hard to look at.

From his perch in the garage, he'd sparked a joint and watched the aftermath: all the stone-faced elders trooping into Doug's office and sitting solemnly around the big discussion table. He'd have given anything to hear the dressing-down that little prick got. He chuckled to himself.

Joe College gave me the creeps. I sure hope they sent him to jail. The guys there will know what to do with him!

Czombo took a long final pull on the joint, ground it out on his boot, then exhaled a savage spirit into the room. He stood in front of the fan, hoping it would remove any residual smell of pot from his hair and clothing. He reflexively gathered his long green hair into a braid and smelled it. It was clear. Even so, he'd head straight for the shower when he got back. No point in taking chances.

Czombo scoped out the house before exiting the garage. He could see Paul sitting on the sofa in the living room talking to Sean. Sean Miller was the next prick on his list. An idea struck Czombo as funny, and he started to laugh. *I really shouldn't do this*, he thought and laughed some more. But he couldn't help himself. He dialled the house. Maurice, the night man, picked up. Czombo did his best British accent. "Bloody indecent. Do you know you have a man jerking his johnny out the window? That's what I said. My wife was taking a breath of air and the cheeky bugger waved at her. No, I don't know what floor he's on. Well, you're damn lucky I'm calling you and not the cops. Next time I'll snap a pic and that will be the end of it."

From his invisible perch, he watched the reaction to his call with tears running down his face. Maurice came running out of the office in a blind panic. He and Paul exchanged a few words before retreating to the office. When Paul emerged, he had a priceless look on his face. Czombo was still convulsed in laughter when the phone vibrated in his pocket. It was Maurice. All he'd get was the answering machine telling him that Mr. Hilary Versenken's mailbox was full.

———

Hart's chore for the first week of treatment was mopping the floor in the dining room and adjoining hallway. He'd get a new assignment after the Sunday Straight Up meeting. Czombo was supposed to be helping him by moving all the tables and chairs out into the hallway. But he was useless. Czombo always showed up — with an improbable excuse and a shallow apology — when the work was done.

Hart thought about complaining to the staff but decided against it. PB's insights on informers had coloured his views for life. Czombo was a waste of skin. He wasn't worth a push, let alone a shove. Big eyes were on Hart. He had to be careful.

Besides, Hart enjoyed the light exercise. It felt good to move his muscles again. The thing he had hated most about the Don Jail was the lethargy. Being that cramped and inactive reminded him of long car rides when he was a kid.

The linoleum floor at Punanai was of such an advanced age that no amount of washing would ever make it look good again. Too many chairs and tables had been dragged across its surface over the years. Hart had waited for the kitchen staff to finish their monthly meeting, during which the three chefs — Norma, Millie, and Sylvester — met to discuss schedules, meal plans, and ongoing irritations. He then asked Sylvester for some bleach to put in the water.

There was a rhythm to mopping that Hart had come to enjoy. It was regular. He loved watching the swirl of the mop as it traversed the pockmarked and dented calico surface. It was almost hypnotic. His first job as a teenager had included swinging a mop in a pizza joint. The old cook had shown him how to do both a proper job and a quick and dirty version. He had never forgotten. Up until that point in his life, floors had mysteriously washed themselves in the same way that groceries arrived in his kitchen and laundry showed up clean and folded in his drawer.

Hart had taken his mom for granted when he was young. Why not? She always seemed to be so relaxed and in control of everything — well, maybe a little sad around the eyes. She always had time for whoever was passing through the house. His dad was an enigmatic figure. He was up early and out the door before Hart got out of bed every morning. He'd often not return until long after supper was over. He dragged moods, disappointments, and the outlines of quarrels with him when he made his way home. Hart never knew what to expect when the front door opened. Sometimes he went for the hug, but more times than not, he hid, watching to see what was going to happen. *So long ago now. Forgotten really. Why am I thinking about this?*

He surveyed his masterpiece with considerable satisfaction. The floor had the same sheen as an ice rink after the Zamboni finishes its work. He could see little wisps of steam dancing over the drying surface. Here and there, a dry spot emerged from out of the warm, soapy deluge.

Wouldn't it be great if fixing my troubles was as easy as washing this floor? But my mess isn't like this. I no sooner get the damn thing mopped when in come Summers and Levy to throw a pail of slop on it. I hate lawyers. I'd love to find one of them staggering drunk at a bus stop.

Suddenly he felt heat rising to his face. *What good is sending me to jail? That lady is dead. There's nothing to be done for the dead.*

He frowned, the mop still clenched in his fist as he stared at the floor. *Life can be over for a long time before you die. My old man showed me that. In a few days, it'll be like I never existed. Like I was a kid born with multiple devastations — someone who doesn't really count. Someone who you whisk off to the margins and have a good cry about.*

He patted his shirt pocket, looking for a smoke. It took him a second to remember he didn't do that anymore. It would have helped. He rested his chin on the mop handle and watched the floor dry. *I didn't kill that lady. I would've remembered. Something someone said or did would've triggered something. But it doesn't even matter. The cops don't care and neither does her family. They have their guy and now they're all working on the to-do list. Have the funeral. Publish an incomprehensible poem. Give away her clothes. Send the monster to jail.*

That's what you can do when you don't know what else to do. That's how you pass the time when you can't get out of bed. But does it make them feel any better?

Another thought popped into his head. *What am I going to do with my place? My whole life is there. I'm going to have to put everything into storage. The bills will eat the rest of my savings and I'll come out of jail penniless and unemployable.*

Won't that be a treat? All those cool prison tats and no one to show them to.

His mind drifted to the paring knife in his kitchen drawer. The tip of the blade had broken off when his father had used it to open a beer bottle. Hart had hung on to it like a sacred relic because every time he touched it, he felt a connection. He loved to cut apples into slices with the crooked blade. It always left the same jagged pattern in the flesh of the fruit. It had been his mom's favourite once. That's what made it special for him, even if it was now broken. Every time he picked it up, he had to decide whether to throw it out, and every time, he decided to keep it. Where could he find a place for it now?

The floor needed five more minutes. He thought about going through the big double doors and having a smoke. A smoke was a great way to celebrate a small victory like this. A way to steal a little time away from an employer or a problem. He thought about the Don Jail. The guys who smoked all got locked up together while they detoxed from tobacco. He never wanted to go through that experience again, and certainly not with that crew. No. Better not to start when you know that you'll only have to stop again. He settled for a breath of winter's air and stepped out onto the patio.

Do I even want to drink again? I won't drink in jail. Don't want to go blind. But what about later? Even before I go away, my apartment's going to be gone, my records and paintings and photographs. The only thing I'll have left to come home to is the big table at Clancy's. Will they take me back? Will they even know who I am? What would happen if I went there tonight?

That didn't bear thinking about. The way they had all run for cover told the tale. Maybe they'd never been his friends. Maybe the big table wasn't the centre of the universe. The only place left on earth where you could really tell it like it was. Talk radio without the microphones.

Hart pursed his lips and exhaled. *It's all the worst kind of bullshit. You have to land right in it before you wise up. Nobody cares about me and nobody ever will. At least I know that now.*

Through the patio door, he saw a skinny shadow coming along the corridor. *Right on cue.* Czombo entered the dining room, acting like he was horrified at being late. He actually looked surprised to see all the work done.

He did that well. But I saw this production yesterday and the day before, so I know how this ends.

Czombo walked across the floor in his wet boots and joined Hart on the patio. "Sorry, man. Reg was giving me hell and he wouldn't let me go."

Hart glanced at the fresh footprints on his clean floor, then looked into Czombo's face and laughed like a mad man. He couldn't help himself.

"Are you laughing at me? Who the hell do you think you are?" Czombo demanded.

Hart handed him the mop. "You need to learn how to cover your tracks better, kid."

Chapter 14

The morning census meeting got bogged down during the discussions about what to do with Channing Hart, who Paul had taken to calling Yardy. Hart had made no progress by the end of his first week. The positive changes that the staff had hoped to see were not forthcoming. He was blocked, which wasn't surprising, but the urgency of his situation had become a concern. He wasn't going to have the luxury of time or the support of a loving AA group to mentor him where he was going.

Hart was a sturdy East Berliner trying to tunnel his way to freedom without a compass. He was working hard and moving a lot of dirt, but he was going to come to the surface still on the wrong side of the wall.

Mike had been keeping a close eye on him and taking extensive notes. "This guy is stuck between *what if* and *whatever*."

Greg Bass, the overnight counsellor who would be the eyes and ears of the team for the next twenty-four hours, was writing in the treatment record. He was wearing his grey suit this morning. The blue pinstripes made him look like a rocker on his way into court, the grey suggested a Rolling Stone top executive signing off on an article. "I like that. You should have been a writer," he said.

Reg pantomimed outrage. "Why him and not me?"

Greg frowned at him — a look he had perfected raising two rambunctious sons in a bungalow. "Well, for one thing, you ate the last Danish before I got to have one."

"How does that make me not a writer?"

Mike broke in. "Do you know why we're still talking about Hart? I may be just an incredibly good-looking guy dating a psychologist, but let me tell you what I think. He's the nearest thing we have to a celebrity. His face is in the papers, and when we sober him up, we become heroes. The problem is this guy isn't changing. This happens every time we get a rock star or a pro athlete — the whole staff goes Hollywood. Stop treating this guy like a celebrity — he's a drunk. Get down there and crowd him with it!"

Paul had spent more time with Hart than anyone else. He didn't agree with Mike's approach. "With this guy, it's two steps forward and three steps back. When you're there in the room with him, you can get him to see reality. But then twenty minutes later, it's like the conversation never happened. I think we're getting to him, but we need more time. He needs an extra week. Would the court go for that?"

Greg piped up. "He still needs to pack up his place. Don't forget about that."

Doug made a note on his pad. "I'll consult the missus." That earned a smile from the veterans. They hadn't heard that nickname since the breakup. "But is this the new answer to everything? It's a theme that I keep reading in all your reports. Someone is doing nothing, so you recommend keeping him an extra week. Is that all we're going to do? This man has ponied up big money. What have we done for him?"

That didn't sit well. The sullen silence that followed suited Doug. "This is what I hear you self-satisfied gurus saying. We know where this guy is stuck. He doesn't know if he killed that lady. He's working this out as an all-or-nothing proposition. If he killed her, well then, fine, he's an alcoholic and he has to do something about it. But if he didn't, or they can't prove it, then he can still go back to his old life. Before he can decide if he's an alcoholic, he needs to know if he's a killer. His time here is spent going back and forth between fear and anger."

The counsellors were all looking at him with blank looks on their faces. Doug knew that meant they were listening. Ever the consummate pro, Doug got to his feet and walked over to the window. He took it up a notch and flooded the room with cold, clean air. "He understands what we're saying about the disease — he's not a stupid man. But he isn't convinced that he's an alcoholic. What gets said at the meetings isn't about him, it's about other people. That's why his behaviour isn't changing. It's all going on in his head, not in his gut. Ours is one more opinion in a sea of seething bullshit. Two weeks after he leaves here, he won't remember anything."

Mike waded in. "This is a lot for him to absorb. On top of which, he's scared to death."

Doug saw the ideal end game clearly for the first time. "Our goal is to get him to see that he's an alcoholic without resolving his criminal case. That's what he needs and that's why he's here. He has the problem upside down. He needs to address the alcoholism first and then the criminal matter." He sat down on the windowsill and gave his chin a thoughtful stroke. "I'm going to turn Kaiser loose on him."

Reg shivered. "Kaiser will club him like a baby seal. Let me do it. I have some rapport with this guy."

Doug thought about it for a moment. Reg was not an obvious choice for this task. But he stalled too, and if Mike was right, he was starting to burn out. Reg's feud with Kaiser left no doubt about that. Reg deserved a chance to do the heavy lifting; maybe he had it in him. There was only one way to find out. "Okay, but make it count. Look him in the eye and tell him what you really see."

Greg moved on to the next client on the list. "That brings us to the other jailbird in our care: Mr. Daniel Philips. He's avoiding confrontation like a hemophiliac with arthritis. He hasn't killed anyone yet, but other than that, everything you said about Hart also applies to Daniel."

Reg tried to place him. "This is the kid who stole his dad's coins?"

Mike nodded. "In spite of that, he figures his mom is going to buy him some new runners on the way home from treatment."

Doug closed the window. "Okay, give him the business too. The rest of you, keep your eyes open. Find a little time to have a chat with these two after Reg stirs the pot."

———

The daily census meeting was a respite for the rule-breakers. For one blessed hour every day, the heat was off — the big eyes were glaring somewhere else and every man did what was right in his own eyes. Most guys went down to the corner. They could sit at Tim's and enjoy the morning paper, or wander over to BMV Books, or just sit in the park and listen to the birds sing for an hour. Some read novels. Others lay on their beds and ate potato chips.

Hart loved to take an after-breakfast nap. As soon as the door to Doug's office closed, he'd sneak upstairs. Privacy and quiet were sacred for him. This was one of the many reasons he'd found jail so nightmarish. Privacy was impossible there. At Punanai, it was a short ration, but it could be obtained, if only on the down-low.

Hart had been well schooled by Sean Miller in counter-surveillance techniques. He knew enough to have one of the textbooks he was supposed to be reading lying on his chest. That way, if he got caught napping, it would look like he had been doing his reading and been overcome with sleepiness — not an uncommon event for people in early recovery.

When he closed his eyes, time began to slow down. He found himself thinking about his favourite football game of all time. He'd had a lot of money riding on the underdog Steelers. As he drifted toward sleep, he saw with perfect clarity the football spiralling ever closer to Hines Ward's outstretched hands. And in that moment, the image slowed and the world blurred and became only silence, peace, and warmth.

Some time passed and Hart became aware of something going on in the distance. He imagined himself sitting in a darkened theatre while the stagehands moved the props around. He felt the pleasant sensation of expectation. The house lights came up slowly as the orchestra began to play.

Hart found himself sitting in the big booth at Clancy's. The boys were wasted and talking nonsense. Every sentence started with either "Shut up" or "Listen." Hart felt a speed wobble. He hadn't had more than usual, but he must have been tired because tonight the drinks were taking a toll. He felt the urge for home and his bed. He got to his feet and headed for the door. It was cold outside. He buttoned his coat as he walked to the bus stop. The streets were deserted. The wind was everywhere and sudden and poking at him, looking for a way in. He stamped his feet and moved his arms to keep himself warm. He heard a toot from the parking lot but ignored it. A minute later, a green Mustang pulled up in front of him, and the passenger door opened.

Chapter 15

Peter let himself get locked up for the night when the cleaning lady finished moping the floor around the Chamber of New Life. Lately there'd been a puddle under the tank most nights. He sat on the bench in the dark, looking at the steady green light emanating from the control panel. He felt connected. But more than that, he felt at peace. After the events of the last week, he needed some time away from everything that distracted him. This wasn't much of a home, but it was all he had.

"What's a person to do? How does God expect us to sort ourselves out in all this confusion?" He looked over at the cryotank where his love lay sleeping. "Terri, my lovely Terri, how I wish this bench was an armchair and that cryotank our living room couch. It would be heaven to sit here for an hour and watch you sleep. To be able to reach out and touch your hair."

A look of fear broke first around Peter's eyes and then settled all along his face. He vented into the silence because he didn't know what else to do. "You're not winding down. You're not about to run out of steam." That thought brought him no comfort. He got to his feet and put his hand on the brass plate that bore her name — allowing his fingers to trace the block letters like a pen etching a signature. It was a lover's touch.

He spoke to her softly with his head pressed against the side of the tank. "We're still connected, still inseparable. I can feel it in my heart."

It took a minute, but the anger came and hard on its heels, the sorrow. No, that's not true. I mustn't start by telling myself things that are wrong, only because I want them to be real. That damn little girl is a force to be reckoned with. I can't wish her away any more than I can wish Terri back. Barry's right, we don't need to chase the light anymore. It's caught our scent in the wind and now it's looking for us. I have to find a way to stay two steps in front of it.

He started to gently bang his head on the side of the tank. If that little girl had snuck by Jack... *He felt a stab of grief.* Terri would be lost and alone. She'd never know what I did for her, for us, how I moved heaven and earth so that we could be together.

The idea that Terri could be abandoned forever without hope and without him pushed Peter into the abstract. He couldn't bear the pain. He took a step back from reality and attacked the problem from a metaphysical angle. Are we flies in amber, caught forever in a moment of approach? Or are we two beautiful snowflakes descending from the very gates of heaven above — falling and spinning until, finally, we land together on the tongue of a joyful child who releases us from our frozen prison? *That took some of the sting out of it.*

Sometimes Peter wanted to go into the light. He was tired. And lonely. The math is all against me, *he thought.* I don't know what I'm doing. If it was only me, I'd give it up and lie down in the dirt and die. But it's not just about me. It's about Terri. She's counting on me. I won't let her down again.

He turned and punched the tank softly a dozen times with his fist. Thinking and planning had gotten him this far. I won't give up on my principles just because I'm in trouble. I need to know what the light is. I need to know how it works. But God help me. I can't see my way. I can't see a way out of this mess. I'm in quicksand ... no, not quicksand, the mud at Passchendaele. *He thought of it sucking him down into the cold filth as if it had sinister appetites of its own.* If I give up and let that happen, well, then it will have her too. I need to stay focused on what she needs. She's counting on me.

Peter pushed himself away from the cryotank and flopped back onto the bench. He lay on his back and looked up at the ceiling. Barry is right about one thing. I need John. He's the only one who follows through on things. He's resourceful. He gets things done. But he's a pain in the ass.

Peter sat up and removed his suit coat. He made a pillow out of it and lay down on the hard bench again. He wanted to bend this light to his will, to ride it to where he wanted to go. He'd lost his nerve the last couple times. He'd turned and run the first time he saw it, and then there was that horrible mess at the ZiggZagg club. Well, I won't lose my nerve in all that emotional mush this time. I have a dream. I know what to expect now. It took me by surprise last time, but now I'm ready for it. I'm going to trap an angel and shake her exactly like Jacob did in the Bible, and I'm going to slap the truth out of her. But first I have to lay a trap. I know what she wants but I don't think she knows what I want. That gives me an advantage.

The cryotank gurgled and the green light flashed to red. Peter was alarmed and got to his feet to investigate. He looked at the control panel, trying to fathom its secrets. The light turned green again, and after a moment, he made his way back to the bench. Why did I ever open this can of worms? I didn't have to do this. Nobody made me. I'll own this — I need to. I lost Terri and I'd do anything short of murder to get her back. The day after I died and found myself still around, I had a moment of real hope. Hope is a strange thing to feel after you die.

But I'd guessed right. I could exist beyond the grave. I had all the pieces of the puzzle at last. But I don't know how they fit, and I don't know what's going to happen if I try to force them.

That is my can of worms. A great, big frozen-solid can of worms. But that's not right either. Worms don't belong in a can. You can't pick them up off the supermarket shelf that way. You dig for worms, and you put them in a can because you want to go fishing. That's the politics of the thing. There's a purpose driving the events. You want to use worms to catch fish. It doesn't matter what they want. All you care about is the thrill of catching trout. But do the worms lack all ambition? Does what they want mean nothing?

A worm in a can is in an unnatural position. It's unsustainable. It's a lot like being a ghost, now that I think about it. There's nothing to eat, no way to tunnel in the soft dirt, all kinds of weird shenanigans and sensations going on that you don't understand. Is it any wonder that they want out?

A much more sinister thought occurred to him. I guess it's good they don't have to live knowing that some fresh-faced kid plans to impale them on a hook and drown them. Maybe they can't imagine the world being that cruel. Well, I sure as hell can. That little girl doesn't fool me for an instant — she's a monster and she's brought along her trout rod.

Another thought from the past intruded on the others and softened his focus. It was of a pleasant spring afternoon when he and Terri had gone to the creek. Terri loved to fish, she loved the water, but she could never bait her own hook. Peter didn't like it much either, but he did it for her. When they lost the bait, they would go looking for more. While they were gone, the worms would stretch to the top of the can and try to slither down the outside, heading for the Promised Land. Peter and Terri would scoop them up and put them back in the can.

He smiled at the memory. Then a thought struck him. That's got to be what the light is doing. It brought us here, and it's keeping us here. What would it matter to the light if Terri and I quietly slithered out of the can and vanished into the hillside? There's no shortage of worms. What's one or two more or less? Couldn't the universe look the other way this one time?

He got to his feet and leaned his forehead on the cryotank. He tapped lightly three times on the container. It was the way he said goodbye. He thought about his father and mother. He thought about Terri. He thought about God and about praying. But mostly he thought about the light. Going over it again and again in his mind. What was the point of this purposeless bit of cruelty? Why treat him like a worm? Why put him in this rusty old can of an existence? Why deny him his chance to be with Terri? Even if they could only be together like this, as ghosts, running out of steam and heading for oblivion, at least that would be something.

Chapter 16

Reg was feeling alive. Standing as he was at the crossroads of imminence and self-actualization, how could he feel otherwise? He caught a final glimpse of his neurotic, careworn companion and keeper of secrets as he adjusted his bow tie in the mirror. The certain man he would surely now become turned away from that discarded version of himself and gathered up his canes, ready for battle. This was the first time Doug had sent him on a mission to raise hell. He'd seen it done and had lent a hand — but that wasn't the same as doing it on his own. *Kaiser can answer the phone from now on.*

Reg had spent one full quarter of his forty-year lifespan here at Punanai. He'd worked long and hard on his game. This was the payoff. The birth of Reg the Torpedo. A dangerous new creation. He liked the sound and feel of it so much that he burst into a swagger.

There were two parts to the patented Punanai talking-to. The first was a direct confrontation coming from someone who had lived the ordeal and recovered. That was the key. They had to have recovered. There was no hiding from or lying to such an individual. Only they could provide the full alien abduction. The second part was the reconciliation. No one wants a friend more than a man who has just taken a beating. Kaiser, with his love of risk and confrontation, was the perfect choice for part one; and Reg, with his deep love of humanity, was the obvious choice for part two. So why switch the gunfighter up with the saddle tramp?

Both of these cowboys were riding mounts with bucked shins and quarter cracks. Ten years in addiction work was a long time. People don't like to hurt other people, although they sometimes say otherwise. Even when the pain they inflict means the difference between life and death. There are only so many bullets in that gun, and a wise person saves the last one for themselves. Casting out demons takes a toll. One that creeps up on you like the compound interest on a credit card.

That's why Doug was mixing things up. Trying to develop a new set of skills in both men that he hoped would allow them to function for a few more years. Perhaps giving them the gift of perspective and possibly even some peace at the end of the day.

Reg had two names on his list. They'd both been badly rattled by an extended stay in the Don Jail. But the pain they had suffered there hadn't changed them. They had become numb to it. They were stuck, and stuck always ended badly. They were both desperate to find someone, anyone really, to co-sign their bullshit. Daniel Philips needed a shake while Channing Hart required a shove. Their being jailhouse jangled would make them respond one of two ways: either with a blind rage, which would serve no purpose; or with an initial rage followed by a healing despair, which was needed — that moment they realized their pain had been right all along, that instant in which the weight of experience crushed their delusional hope.

The meeting room was hardly big enough for the twenty-person table that was crammed into it. The chairs were crowded around it with just enough room for one person to come and go at a time. There were three windows that allowed the afternoon sun to enter and that opened to admit fresh air. There was a glorious view of the property next door with its outbuildings, gardens, patios, and balconies, all of which called to daydreamers and escape artists. On the walls were more of the numbered prints of Group of Seven masterpieces, all of which had been donated by a grateful benefactor who chose to remain anonymous. Likely a recipient of a previous talking-to.

Last week some rather nice brown drapes, provided by the decorating committee at head office, had been put up and really elevated the tone of the room. Reg popped a red-hot peppermint into his mouth while he watched the doorway and imagined what this room communicated to its occupants the first time they saw it. He had a general's eye. Where a civilian saw a peculiar backward slope in a meadow, he saw an advantageous terrain that, working to support the artillery, would overturn the fortunes of an army — and then, a nation.

Reg had taken his seat at the head of the table, near the whiteboard, ten minutes before the group was scheduled to start. Sean occupied the lone space at the far end of the table. Hart was at Reg's four o'clock. Czombo's traditional seat at two o'clock was empty. Daniel and Larry entered together and occupied ten and eight respectively.

Reg observed the men carefully as they entered the room. You could tell who was interested by the order in which they arrived. Talking about getting sober in a group was a high-energy experience. The guys who were doing well looked forward to it and treated it like a meal. But in any group, there was always that one guy who had no intention of getting sober. The one who fanned the flames of resistance with looks and gestures that said, *this is so uncool.* In this group, that guy was Czombo. He did adolescent disdain to perfection. Never with a word, because words had consequences. But always with a look and a slow exhalation.

He was invariably the last one through the door and the first to leave. When one of the volunteers had been asked to lead the group last week, Czombo gave him the type of runaround that exasperates supply teachers. He put his feet up on the table and leaned his chair back against the wall — daring the counsellor with a hostile stare to make him sit up straight. The volunteer was afraid of offending him and let it go. But scuttlebutt picked it up. Reg wondered if Czombo had the nerve to try a stunt like that with him in the room. He hoped so.

Clients had been coming to him with complaints all week. The green-haired monster was politicking on the smoke deck and discounting everything said in the group as posturing and foolishness. Reg knew this was true because he had observed the angry faces as the men stood in a circle, smoking and talking. Czombo was always at the centre of the group, pointing an accusing finger.

The staff didn't worry about the serious guys. They'd had a talking-to and made their peace with it. They were busy working out their own salvation. They needed someone to feed them, keep this space drug-free, and supervise the linen. They could do the rest of it themselves. Czombo was perversely useful to the serious guys as a sparring partner. Arguing with him helped them sort out the narrative that was forming in their own minds.

Reg turned his attention to the guys who didn't feel safe and who hadn't made up their minds: Daniel Philips and Larry Lorne. The youthful pair might get sober. But did they really want to? That was always the issue with the young ones. They lived in the hope that they could carry on drinking and using for a while longer before they had to stop. If you hit them up with sodium pentothal, they'd look you right in the eye and tell you they could quit anytime they wanted to and that they would if they ever got as bad as the rest of these guys.

Their pained frowns announced in tandem, *my life, my rules.*

A group that was still making up its mind had very low energy — but that was a necessary part of the process and could not be rushed. A consensus took time to form. But that wasn't what was happening. This group was going nowhere, and a lifeless group said loud and clear that there's no such thing as recovery. That challenge needed to be answered.

The last time this group had really functioned well was during Arthur Cardel's tumultuous stay, when his roommate, RK, had been the acknowledged leader. While RK had ruled the roost, the conversation had sparkled. The uncertain ones were drawn to his certainty. It had been a pleasure to teach that group. But no one had stepped up to fill the leader role after RK left, and several of the other strong personalities had graduated and gone home last Monday. That leadership vacuum created this crisis, and Reg was here to administer the appropriate counterpoison.

Addicts and alcoholics experienced a firewall between their emotions and their thinking. This maladaptation changed everything. It was like viewing the world through a camera obscura. They could see only an outline and an inverted one at that. This distorted perspective allowed them to justify all their nonsense. From their promontory they saw only the thing that was right in front of them and, of course, that thing was always an object of desire.

Reg knew that the power to change had to come from the gut. These guys wouldn't recover until they let themselves experience despair. Something truly awful had to happen. Something they couldn't live with. Some event had to crush the idea that it was okay for them to use drugs. Hart had experienced a calamity that fit the bill, but he was desperate to avoid the reckoning. The cold swirling waters had covered his nose but not yet drowned him. Drowning men would cling to anything that kept them afloat. They put up with anything in the hope of drawing one more breath. Hart let other people make his choices and then hated them for it. Not much of a defence, but it kept him from draining the bitter cup of despair.

He was afraid of retribution. He despised his own weakness. He was paralyzed by the emptiness at his core. Looking at him you would think otherwise. He seemed well put together. But the fact remained, the only time he felt safe was when he was hiding. He couldn't face his demons that way. He needed to be standing at centre stage with the klieg light beating down on him for that to happen. Someone in the wings was going to have to drag him out of his dark box and push him out onto the stage.

Daniel Philips was frail, with long brown hair and an earring. He looked as if he might do well in modelling. He had that classic kind of face. He'd find out today that he was staying for another week. The Don Jail experience had badly unsettled him, even though he had spent most of it in protective custody. He felt trapped in a never-ending round of jail, house arrest, court appearances, and family squabbles. His only solace: his all-too-infrequent lapses into oblivion. He had secrets that went deeper than his drug addiction, and no one he could talk to about them. He didn't know it yet, but his situation had changed. His parents had been wised up by the family counsellors. They weren't fuzzy and confused anymore. They were prepared to watch him be thrown headfirst into the lake. They loved him enough to watch him sink in the hope that he'd learn to swim.

He'd smirked when they told him he wasn't coming home. They'd threatened and made angry faces before. This latest display of temper would blow over. His dad always got the maddest and made stupid rules, but then he'd cool down and disappear back into his hobbies. His mom was always going to be there for him. He could finesse this. He always had. One night on the street and a cut lip was all it would take. They'd come to get him in a taxi and wrap a blanket around his shoulders.

It was no accident that Larry was sitting next to Daniel. The young ones often sat together without realizing that a few hundred thousand years of hunter-gatherer tradition informed that choice. It just felt right. Larry was more what Daniel's parents had in mind when they'd conceived him. He possessed an open and honest face that communicated a born-in-the-country lifestyle. No big-city living for him. He liked fresh air and peaceful evenings on the porch. His go-along-to-get-along attitude worked for him. He occupied a space halfway between Hart's refusal to choose and Daniel's certainty that any choice he made had to end in disaster.

Reg's plan was dangerous. He had to revisit the crises that should have changed their lives but hadn't. Without that energy, no change was possible. He had to recreate that explosion without them being able to move away from the epicentre. If you had a small child who was full of anger and didn't know what to do about it, you could press them until they lost control. The point would be to help the child put a name to what they were feeling and then help them understand why they felt that way and show them what they could do about it.

Children are small and easy to control. This was a much riskier strategy to try with a grown man. It was even more dangerous to try it in a group. Anger was one thing, but when it got all jumbled up with fear and sorrow and self-loathing, the mixture became explosive. The anger management consultant who had instructed the Punanai staff on the use of this technique had warned them that he himself had been seized by the throat by an irate client on more than one occasion.

Throwing a sprig of parsley on last night's entrée and trying to pass it off as a new dish was lame. But when the deception worked, it made all the difference. It took the listener right back to that moment when they first learned how to fudge the figures. Reg ran his fingers through his hair. *They never forget hearing the lie in their own voice for the first time.* When that technique didn't work — and it frequently didn't — well, that was when people started hollering for a lawyer. Father Phil had suggested an appropriate prayer. "Oh Lord, put me in harm's way and keep me safe." That was the answer both Reg and Kaiser were seeking. A way to do this like an actor in a play and not like a high school senior menaced by street thugs.

Czombo took his seat three minutes after the hour had struck. *Game on*, thought Reg as he played his first card. "Should we be judging you guys by your intentions? What do you think?"

Czombo knew he was required to speak at least once in every group session, and so he thought he might as well get the unpleasantness out of the way. "With drugs, your choices are steal, deal, or quit. You guys" — he pointed at Reg with his thumb and jerked it three times — "you all agree that we can't quit, so where does that leave us on the subject of intention?"

Reg nodded and gave him a little frown. He had a point.

Larry was next in the inexorable counter-clockwise rotation of speakers. "A lie is not always a bad thing. I do things that would scare the life out of my family all the time. I keep them to myself because I love them." Reg again said, *next* with the movement of his eyes.

Daniel rolled his eyes in return. "Covering your tracks is the most important thing in an addiction. The best way to do that is to tell people you're trying to change." He smiled at the group. "That's when they feel bad about bugging you and give you money." That earned a laugh from everyone.

Hart shook his head. "People never believe you. They might say they do, but they don't. Where does that leave judgment and intention? It's all bullshit and everyone knows it."

Sean spoke last. "What gives people the idea that they can judge us anyway? What the hell do they know about us and what we've been through?" That hint of defiance carried the day. All the heads nodded in unison.

When they'd finished, Reg leaned back in his chair and smiled at them. "Okay, you're a complicated bunch, but let me see if I've really heard what you've been saying. You acknowledge that you've stolen on occasion to get your drugs, but you don't really feel like you're a thief. You're in a difficult situation that blurs the distinction between right and wrong."

The looks around the table resembled those at a poker game when the guy who raised twice unexpectedly checks.

Reg kept his voice calm, trying to sound like a man who was working out the right answer as he spoke. "You have to lie sometimes to get what you need or to cover your tracks, but then you feel hurt when people don't believe you when you do tell the truth. So you're misunderstood." Reg watched their curiosity and anxiety jostle with each other. "We're kind of at that place where you want to be judged by your intentions, but your family has a strong preference for judging your actions." He sat up in his chair as if a new idea had suddenly come to him. "You don't think it's fair to judge you on one incident. You'd rather be judged on the totality of who you are and what you've done." Reg slapped his palms down on the table. "This sets up a classic stalemate. Two people are looking at the same facts and figures but interpreting them in contradictory ways. Let me ask you a question. Is there a limit to what you would do? How hard would you push to get what you want?"

Reg looked around the group, and his gaze landed on Daniel. The young man had an angular face. The first thing that struck you about him was his impressive forehead and eyes. The eyes looked at you knowingly, like you were in on his secret. His dark hair was long but trimmed neatly around the ears. His bangs covered half his brow, but the whole thing looked neat and easy to manage. His thin lips covered good teeth that he seemed very reluctant to show. His expression was that of the boy caught looking at someone else's paper. There was fear in his eyes, shame etched in crimson on his cheeks, and anger evident in his clenched teeth. He had taken a singular meaning from Reg's last remark.

Reg leaned forward and looked at Daniel and asked in a seemingly innocuous tone, "Would you kill your mother to get a drink?"

There was a stunned silence in the room as the men checked in with their neighbours. Did he really just say that? A poison dart doesn't make much sound and it doesn't do any harm on impact but, oh Lord, this one found an artery. Only Czombo had his head up and a smile on his face.

Daniel's anger exploded into the centre of the room. "What kind of fucking question is that, you word-twisting asshole? That's what we should call you — twister. You take what we say and spin it and spin it and spin it and you don't care how much it hurts." Daniel found himself on his feet.

Hart was horrified. *They'll kick him out for this.* He wanted to say something, but he was afraid Reg would single him out too if he spoke up. He instinctively looked over to Sean, but Sean was busy measuring Daniel. The group had its new leader. The kind who emerges in the middle of a street fight gone horribly wrong. Not a spokesman. Not a mentor. But the guy who turns to face the danger and, in doing so, draws you deeper into the fray. Life or death now. No running away.

Reg realized how badly he'd blundered. He held out his hand, palm down, and made eye contact with Daniel in a classic stare down. His voice was full of power. "Daniel, calm yourself. Why are you getting so bent out of shape?"

Daniel wasn't fooled by the cool exterior. He'd watched the blood engorge Reg's ears. What the man with the bow tie intended was half a world away from what he'd accomplished. The hot lava started to make its spirited run toward the sleeping village below.

"You stupid, ignorant, fucking prick. You come to me all sad faced and interested. You tell me some of your own troubles. You get me talking about stuff I don't want to talk about and where do we end up? What a stupid question! I'm sick of you and sick of this place. Even jail is better than this. You think you know so much? Well, you don't. My mom isn't going to let my dad kick me out. She's the only one who knows who I really am. She loves me — the real me — and that isn't going to change. I'd never hurt her…"

He looked from face to face, going around the room, looking for support, trying to get his bearings. Most of the group looked embarrassed when his gaze landed on them and they looked away. They didn't know what to do. Only Sean Miller gave him the look he needed, the one that said, *stand your ground!*

But hot tears were aching for release and they began to cloud Daniel's eyes. "I love my mother, and I would never do anything to hurt her…" His words stopped when he recalled her face the last time she'd come into the police station. It was her eyes. That was all he could see. The lie fell away like a bedsheet dropping to reveal a sculpture. For the first time, he realized he'd done all that and more. He couldn't get a breath.

Reg saw the sea change and he knew what it meant. "Daniel what just happened for you? Your face changed. You look like you've seen a ghost."

Daniel was feeling so many contradictory things, he didn't know what to do. Reg had hurt him. That last insight was devastating. Here he was, fully exposed, in a room full of men — most of them older, all of whom intimidated him, just like in jail — and he was red-faced with anger and yelling at a counsellor. It was too much. He was terrified that he was going to cry. He didn't have the skills to back down. He shouted, "Screw you!" and lurched for the door. Sean Miller perfectly anticipated his exit and calmly held the door closed with his palm. No running away from this brawl.

Reg knew a blessing when he saw one. He'd sown the whirlwind and miraculously reaped the olive branch. If he had barred the door, Daniel might have punched him. Sean Miller was a different matter. This was the part of the job that Reg loved. He found it exhilarating being a tower of calm while the seas raged all around him. Reg had deliberately plunged this group into chaos and now he was going to give his blessing to the new group leader. His voice was calm and loving. "Mr. Philips, relax. This is treatment, things get heated. What do you think, fellas? Should he stay?"

They murmured their assent. They wanted him to stay. Daniel was sure he was nothing to them. He looked at their faces in wonder. Was it possible they were not going to taunt him?

"Sit down please, Daniel, and let me explain where I'm going with this."

He turned and looked at Sean. "Thanks, Sean. That was the right thing to do, and it took some courage to take a chance like that. I couldn't have made it over there fast enough."

Sean wasn't finished with Reg yet, but he had the good sense to take his seat. He'd have a chat with him later.

Daniel was still seething. "It's not right," he said as he took his seat. It felt good to have something solid underneath him again.

Reg was enjoying the rush of feel-good chemistry that always followed a hail of poorly aimed cartridges. He hoped the guys were in a mood to judge him by his intentions and not his marksmanship because the next thing out of his mouth was a necessary lie. "It was my fault that got out of hand, and I apologize. I phrased my thought badly. What I should have said was, do you guys ever drink and drive with your family in the car? Late at night, do you ever go down to your special chair in the den when everyone else is asleep and have a few drinks? Ever pass out with a cigarette burning in your hand? Ever bring shady characters home from the bar for a drink, only to find them passed out on the couch the next morning? Any one of these things could result in a fire, a robbery, a brawl, or an accident. I asked if you would kill your mother for a drink. I didn't mean to suggest that you would feel good about it. I was asking if you would risk the most precious things in your life to get what you want. This is what we're getting at when we ask you if your drinking is more important to you than your family."

Hart thought he was going to be sick. He could see Alice Gibson standing in the courtroom. *I didn't kill my mother. I killed hers.* He could feel his skin grow cold and clammy. His hands started to shake and all the hairs on his arm tried to take wing.

"We don't mean to…" said Daniel, struggling to find the words he needed.

Reg spoke as softly as he could and still be heard. "We do things drunk that we can't live with when we're sober." He counted to twenty and then went for broke. "Daniel, how did you feel when your mother told you that you couldn't go home?"

The young man's eyes grew wide with terror. This might as well have been the grand inquisitor's final question. The answer was that he didn't know because he never seriously considered this as a possibility.

"I can't say … not here."

Hart found his compassion but not his words. He stretched across the table and touched Daniel on the forearm.

Larry Lorne leaned forward too, his muscled arms resting on his powerful legs. It was one of the first things people noticed about him — how strong he was, how thick through the chest. His blond head was normal sized, but it looked improbably small sitting on his massive shoulders. His front tooth was chipped and he'd obviously broken his nose more than once. The olfactory organ had a gentle curve to it that ran along its length and suggested a player not afraid to venture into dangerous areas. "I'd like to hear what you have to say," Larry said. "I think it would help me understand my own situation better."

Daniel looked at Sean Miller, who gave him a nod. Czombo put his head down on the desk and covered his ears with his arms. The rats were back in his pantry. He'd have to clean house again.

———

When the session was over, the guys filed out of the room. They wanted a smoke but, more than that, they needed some privacy. They wanted to talk. They had Reg issues.

As they poured out the door, Reg motioned to Hart. Czombo was far too intent on getting a smoke to notice, but the rest of them picked up the danger sign and hung back. The look on Reg's face was ominous. He was having a hard time getting a read on what was happening with Hart. His face was a study in turmoil as he wondered if now was the right time to act. After his recent blunder with Daniel, Reg chose his words carefully. He wanted his invitation to sound harmless. "Channing, can I see you for a moment?" The words didn't give him away, but the look on his face and the edge to his voice made it obvious he was up to something.

Sean Miller got there first and said under his breath. "Power-tripping prick."

Hart tried to make light of Reg's look and tone. He'd just put in a hard hour of thinking and feeling about unintended consequences. Truth be known, he'd had all he could take. "What'd I do?"

The hangers-on were wary and ready for trouble. They stood shoulder to shoulder in the hallway, intent on protecting one of their own. But like all good predators, Reg had separated his intended victim from the herd. He stood blocking the doorway, his broad back to the rescuers, leaving Hart alone in the room, cut off from any avenue of escape.

Reg's tone was subdued and controlled. Like the red spot on a spider, it spoke of deadly poison near to hand. "I've been watching your non-performance in the group. What's going on with that?"

Hart was genuinely perplexed. That session had cut bone. "I don't know what you mean."

Reg was deliberately winding him up, picking a quarrel the way he had with Daniel. Sean could see that, and he knew what Reg was up to. But he was standing in the hall. For Hart, it was different. Reg was blocking his only exit. When you're being berated in front of a group of men, perspective vanishes. Reg's words became spear points, dancing in midair, hot to find a new home in Hart's flesh. Reg wasn't saying anything new. These were reheated leftovers, but to Hart's burning eyes, they seemed like a fresh torment. Reg was hoping against hope that this time the pain would overwhelm Hart's crumbling defences.

"You look like a guy who gives a damn, but that's all you're doing."

Hart didn't know what to say; but worse still, his thoughts wouldn't become words. When he tried to speak, nothing emerged from the boiling chaos of feeling. Just like in court.

"Is that the hustle?"

Hart's windpipe was holding his feelings of rage. He wanted to shout or run or punch Reg, but he couldn't. He stood there, flat footed, frozen in place. "I don't…" was as far as his protest got.

Reg managed a useful smile. "Yeah, that's the hustle. Do a little time and clean the slate. No one could expect anything more than that, could they? A couple years in the slammer, maybe get a college degree, and then back to the head table at Clancy's as the new resident badass."

Hart struggled in vain to howl at this outrage. A murderous feeling was welling up from his gut. It produced only a choking sound.

Reg moved a step closer. "Smile and nod like you got it. And, if you can make your eyes go all wide, so much the better. That's all you've got to do. We're beyond dumb. We'll buy your bullshit. Why, we'll even put it in a letter for the judge."

Hart took a half step to the right, looking for a way to push past Reg and out into the hallway.

Reg leaned into his personal space and pointed his finger at Hart's face. "You're pretending. You pretend a lot of things, don't you? Why are you just standing there? Why don't you call me a friggin' liar? That's what you'd like to do, isn't it? Take a poke at me. Shut me up. Prove me wrong. But that shrewd alcoholic mind of yours says, no, stay cool, stay in character, stickhandle your way around this bozo."

He paused as though he had been struck with an idea for the first time. "Oh, but you croaked that woman, didn't you? You have to remember to pretend to feel bad about that. It looks bad when you forget. Yeah, that makes a mess of everything."

There it was — the verdict — the one Hart had been dreading. Someone finally came right out and said it. Reg had put into words everything Hart had been distressed about for weeks. All those silences. The way people looked at him. The way they looked away, ashamed and afraid, when they recognized him. Or the way they avoided looking at him altogether, the tone of their voices, and that look, that dreadful look, the one that told him he was no longer human, no longer welcome around the fire.

Hart stared back at Reg like a wounded animal. What could he say? This was the least sympathetic view that could be taken. It assumed that he'd been fully aware all along of what happened and that he was lying in a cynical attempt to escape a badly needed and long overdue reckoning.

Reg's voice changed from authoritarian to familiar. "If you don't start telling us the truth, we're going to ask you to leave. Everyone else in your group is taking big chances. They're having a hard look at themselves. But not you! Did you kill that woman while you were drunk or didn't you? Are you going to kill someone else before you take responsibility for yourself? Do you even care about the bodies piling up?"

Hart pushed past Reg, almost knocking him off his canes, and then split the line of onlookers like a cornerback running for the goal line. Reg dropped his books and had considerable trouble gathering them up. No one offered to help him. They left him alone on his knees in the classroom. Reg barked at them as they departed. "As for you guys, get out of my sight or I'll show you what I think of snoops." The guys all scattered, pretending to be going somewhere. Only Sean Miller turned and stood his ground. He gave Reg a withering look as the counsellor painfully regained his feet and limped past with his shirt now untucked and hanging out below his suit coat. When the fire door slammed, the mice all came running back to see what the cat had done.

Chapter 17

John was in the front pew of Flannerman's Funeral Home, looking uncomfortable but not repentant. He knew he was in for a scolding for missing the weekly meeting. The slender grey spectre had put the time to better use by working out a few of the performance details for a character he was developing. The work had prospered. If a price now had to be paid for his truancy, well then, better an hour of Peter's anger and ongoing intrigues than a minute of Barry's insights. He had no idea what he had missed. The giant young lady would have focused his mind like a grail quest.

When Peter arrived a few minutes later, he didn't bother to remove his coat or take a seat. He wanted to give John a blast, but he was afraid that in the heat of that long overdue moment he might forget the speech he'd spent the entire night sitting in the Chamber of New Life perfecting. The business at hand was too important. He didn't want to risk a pointless quarrel. He had a lot on his mind and more still in his heart. His dream was slipping away. Yesterday could've been the end of everything. He needed to get John and Barry pulling in the same direction. But that had to remain top secret. They despised each other and would never work together. Managing his new crew would require the inveterate touch of a bomb-disposal expert.

Peter rose to his full height. "There are matters of universal importance that we need to discuss, John. I'm going to give it to you straight."

The consummate thespian responded to the clarion call. He settled into character and gave Peter a look ripe with vulnerability, hoping to provoke him. "Tell me. I'm ready."

"God doesn't play dice with the universe — he plays seven card stud!"

John couldn't believe his luck. He threw a log on the fire and sat back to enjoy the blaze. "You're being cryptic."

Peter had memorized his lines. He could repeat them without interruption, but any intrusion destroyed his focus, and the ad libs that followed left out critical steps in his reasoning and important factual points. "Don't interrupt me. It's rude. But more than that, it puts me off my train of thought."

John sat up in the pew and opened his arms wide, palms up like a preacher about to talk about God's love. "You're not at the council now; it's just the two of us here. There's no funeral until this afternoon. The flowers are beautiful and the room smells agreeably of floor wax, furniture polish, and brewing coffee. The morning sun is streaming in through the windows. If an atmosphere like this puts you off your thoughts, then you're more than halfway to becoming a poltergeist."

A storm cloud formed over Peter's majestic brow. "That's neither here nor there. We need to think about our current dilemma. We need to focus on the light.

There have been developments of which you are ignorant. I alone now know what needs to be done and why."

John looked up at Peter and smiled. He knew this might be the only entertainment on offer today. Peter's ramrod-straight posture and the gravitas in his tone promised carloads of fun. "Please," he said and held out his hand with his palm up, looking for all the world like a beggar putting forth his bowl.

Peter was satisfied that he'd created an atmosphere conducive to making his point. "I've been thinking back over my life. Thinking about what I was told as a young person, what I have observed since then, and about the lessons life has taught me. I remember when I was a boy in church, they talked to us about predestination. It was a painful carbuncle on the backside for the preacher, I can tell you that. It gave him no joy whatsoever to terrify a room full of shiny-faced children by telling them that, while a few of them were destined from birth for heaven, most of them were reprobates destined for the fires of hell."

The god of mischief poked John in the ribs. "Did he mention Flannerman's Funeral Home as a third possibility?"

"He did not! Why must you always crack wise when I am speaking of weighty matters? It's a habit badly in need of amendment." Peter closed his eyes for a moment and tried to regain his composure, but John could still hear the anger in his voice as he continued. "But here's the point: I never understood predestination until now. It always gave me a headache. The kids made fun of it after they got over the terror of hearing about it for the first time. 'Damned if you do, and damned if you don't,' they'd say."

John impulsively slid into another character in his burgeoning cast, taking on the role of confidant. He imagined himself standing by the fireplace with a glass of port in his hand, discussing with a learned companion the finer points of the careers of vampires or how to undo werewolves. "I won't pretend to understand what predestination is. You make it sound Christian. It's foreign, though, isn't it? One of those filthy Eastern ideas?"

Peter belatedly recognized that a direct assault on the citadel could not prosper, and so he resigned himself to digging in and taking the fortress of John's reason by siege. He settled himself by the window and took up his narrative. "No, it's very Christian. The idea is that while all human beings are sinful enough to deserve hell, a few of us are spared for reasons known only to the Almighty. The idea is that you have to be saved by grace and not by some good work you do. In short, you're powerless in the matter of your own salvation. Nothing that you do and nothing that you don't do makes any difference to the outcome because it was all decided long before you were born." There was a pause, as if he had allotted some space for John to say something objectionable, and so John peevishly chose not to, leaving Peter on his back foot.

"And," Peter said loudly, shouting down the anticipated but unuttered objection, a move clearly intended to add weight to his conclusion, "God has always known who would be saved and who would be damned."

He said it with such dignity and conviction that John might actually have believed it had he been listening. His attention was drawn elsewhere. There was a patch of white on Peter's forehead — John had observed it once or twice before — and he was sure that he could see a glint of moisture on the fat ghost's brow. Ghosts are as dry as gunpowder — everyone knows that. John tried to say something before the anomaly vanished, but Peter froze him with a look. Like a preacher, he was waiting for an amen.

John obliged with a prompt of his own. "At best, that's an interesting thought, but what has it to do with us?"

Peter rounded on his colleague, his face full of fury. He spat his anger like bullets. "My family lived by those precepts. I always thought in the end I would know a moment of peace and connection with another human being. We were the godly. We were the elect. But the payoff never came! Thank heavens I came to my senses at the last moment and took drastic action."

He gave John another disagree-with-me-if-you-dare look, so John shined him on with a tiny little lie. "Oh, Peter! I've never seen you this angry."

"Let me tell you how the world really works. Oh, there's predestination at work, all right — of that you can be sure — heartless, hateful, and efficient. The sins of the father are visited on both children and grandchildren without mercy. But the agency isn't sin. No, my friend, the devil here is genetics. Bad choices add up. Go ahead, be soft-hearted and soft-headed. Marry a halfwit husband and see what you get. Put up with a lunatic or a drunkard and you can look forward to more of the same."

The white patch on Peter's forehead mysteriously vanished and then returned. John waved at it and pointed in vain. But Peter's passion was too great. He trampled John's objection with a cascade of words.

"It all happens before we're even born," Peter said. "Imagine yourself as a fledgling spirit, seated at a poker table with a dozen other neophytes, all waiting for their cards, all waiting in their mother's womb to be born. The name of the game is seven card stud. But they play it a little different in heaven. They do it with genes and chromosomes."

The wonder of the thing wasn't lost on John, who gave up on the patch and smiled broadly at his teacher. Here is madness coming to fruition. Time to take notes!

Peter sat down beside John on the pew and put his broad palm on the slender ghost's shoulder. "The dealer gives you two cards face down. It's maddening to know they're there but you can't turn them over until after you're born. These cards will define you. You never have to look at them if you don't want to. You never have to show them to others. But they're your only advantage." John's visage was a blank slate, which Peter misread as rapt attention. "These two private cards allow you to value everything else that follows. They're the lens through which you will see the world. They're the only part of this game that gives you any measure of control. They represent your best chance to do something worthwhile with your life. But what are we told about them when we're young? We're told these are dangerous, selfish cards. Most people are far too afraid or ashamed to look at them, and after a while they forget they're there. That was my mistake. I did as I was told. I followed along. I never looked at them and that's why I ended up here. That's what the light is all about."

John considered asking him what these cards were, but you can't put an avalanche on pause. Peter was red hot with the passion behind his argument, and the flow of his words gathered in strength and intensity the further he went.

"The next four cards are public, brutally public, dealt for the whole world to see. The first card to hit the table is the looks card. Ah, hard luck, old son — but in and of itself, the ten of clubs isn't the end of the world. No job in the front office, but at least they won't put you in the circus. There might still be some hope for you with blind women or some employment for you as a character actor.

"Next comes the family connection card. As you can imagine, there are far more deuces then aces in the deck for this one. Even so, the four of hearts is disappointing. Still, wealth and power can be earned, they don't always have to be inherited.

"Moving on to the third card: Are you smart? That's the wild card, all right. Smart at what? There's the point. Be a mathematical genius brought up in a slum and see how far you get or be a writer of mystical talent born a slave and see what the world holds for you. You get the queen of spades here, and while it's encouraging to finally get a face card, there's no hope of a flush, only a remote chance at a straight. And with five cards now dealt, you have yet to get even a pair. You can feel your foot start to tap. For the first time you're afraid of being born.

"The fourth card is the health card. Are you robust? Do you have the kind of body that can get you where you need to go? The jack of diamonds is good for long life and good health and could conceivably combine with the queen of spades and ten of clubs to yield a favourable overall result."

His voice dropped into a lower and slower key. For here was the heart of the matter. "But that's where the trouble starts, John. That moment of perception is the genesis of human misery and failing. We see a remote possibility of being extraordinary and we invest it with all our hope and begin to treat it like it's our birthright. What we have isn't enough. Don't you see? Now that you actively want something, the hoping and the fearing and the bargaining and the manipulation start. You can't bring yourself to value what you have in front of you. No, now all your energy goes into hoping for the one magical card that will lift you out of obscurity and make you a winner."

He got to his feet and made his way to the window. With his back turned to John and with the sun on his face, he whispered to the glass in a voice choked with emotion.

"The final card is all about election. A nine or a king. That would straighten this mess on the table out. Give it some shape. Give you some reason to hope, some reason not to despair, some incentive to ante up and take your chances with the rest. But that card is dealt face down. Not to be turned over until you're well into middle age. All that potential for good, face down and forgotten, hidden from view. *All our energies looking outward for a solution instead of being focused inside on our own hidden strengths.*"

He had come to the end of his strength. He leaned on the windowsill beneath the stained-glass rendering of St. George slaying the dragon with its wonderful shades of blue and green and yellow in such sharp contrast with the red of the dragon's ruff. John was desperate not to spoil the moment. Peter was certain in his own mind that he had untangled the Gordian knot and that all men could now see what before had tormented them with its complexity.

"So you sit there at the big green table and eye up your cards for the hundredth time, and you look frantically around at the cards everyone else has showing. The laws of probability start to become an integral part of your thinking. You start to count the cards and figure the odds. But there are simply too many unknowns.

"After a while, all you see are endless possibilities. The hidden cards could combine in any number of ways to yield the winning hand. The girl across the table has exactly the cards you need for a straight. But would a straight win this hand? Is there only one winner in this game? Does God truly have only the one blessing? Is that how life is going to work? Be the best or be damned!" Peter looked at John the way a prosecutor looks at a jury after he's demanded of them the sentence of death.

John left mischief and merriment behind and landed on sadness. He was feeling Peter's energy, but he had no idea what Peter was talking about. And the horrible thought that followed fast on its heels was this: Neither did Peter. What happens in nature when a ghost takes leave of his senses? Do plants wilt? Does a car backfire?

Peter bowed his head, his voice soft now, his eyes ripe with softness. "That is what the light is." He looked up at John. "It's an angel, here to get us to turn over our cards, the hidden ones, the ones we're afraid to look at." Peter gave a weary smile. "Maybe no one in the game can move on until all the cards are played. That's why we can't leave. The light is after the cards. We need to turn them over, and we need to do it now before it's too late."

John felt like he'd been punched hard enough to break his nose and suffered an intern making a bad job of packing his nostrils with cotton. *What in the world is Peter talking about?* he wondered. *We don't have any cards. Cards would be a godsend. Oh, to play bridge again. John frowned. This filibuster is obscure, even by Peter's standards. What is happening to his mind?*

John looked up from his thoughts, but Peter was gone, leaving him with only sunshine on his face and his own dark thoughts for companionship.

Chapter 18

Hart was lying on his bed, staring at the ceiling and still clutching his workbook to his chest. The fan was putting in an effort more for show than effect. The kind of work you produce when there is nothing to do and the boss is passing. The air lay heavy on his skin. There was a mechanical hum he'd never heard before coming from the fan, perhaps harmonizing with a cricket sound coming from somewhere deep and dangerously oppressed inside his skull. When he moved, the sound moved with him. The sound was him. A CAT scan of his brain would have yielded a test pattern. No that wasn't right. Static. White fuzzy dancing snowflakes of electricity.

Consciousness was returning the way that deep sleep gives way to wakefulness. Slowly and in stages. No one had ever spoken to him like that. Parents, teachers, employers, girlfriends — all left contusions, but never a wound this deep and dirty, one certain to become septic. Even the cops had better manners. He'd paid his money in good faith, and they had counted it and weighed the goods and delivered them free on board from their warehouse: the trademarked Punanai talking-to. The one that connected your head to your heart with a rivet. The cargo was his from the moment he pulled away from the dock.

It chafed worse than watching Alice Gibson cry. All she wanted was to have her mother back. The universe wouldn't even pony up for that. Where did that leave him?

Outside his room, the hallway was filling with the sound of Sean and the posse looking for their friend. They looked grim. As if they expected to find a body. Hart had been so deeply immersed in shock that he'd walked straight past them after the meeting, like they were strangers. He was right back in that dreadful police holding cell, hearing the news for the first time.

Sean stood in the hallway, unsure. It wasn't like him to be this attached to a roommate. But something about Hart's ordeal had touched him. This was his fight now.

Sean pushed the door open. Entering their room felt like trespassing. What he saw made him angry. Hart was rolled up inside a blanket with his face to the wall.

Sean sat down on the edge of the bed. He wanted to say something meaningful, but all that came out was, "Not again."

Hart pulled the blanket over his head. "I can't take any more."

"You need to talk to Doug."

Hart recognized this for what it was. His new normal. This is how prison was going to shake out — assault, pain, cowering in the dark.

Sean was resigned. "How do they expect anyone to get sober when they treat them this way? We have to do something about that power-tripping prick. Catch your breath. I'll be right back."

———

Reg kept his game face on as he headed back to the safety of the counsellors' office. It felt good to close the door behind him. The other counsellors were eager to hear the news. They all had serious doubts about Reg's ability to administer the coup de grâce. Reg was great at what he did, but he was no Kaiser.

Doug looked at Reg's face for a clue. "How did it go?"

Reg smiled ruefully. "Mission accomplished."

Doug wasn't satisfied. There was no trace of the fanatic in Reg's eye. "How did he take it?"

As Reg thought about the confrontation and how to answer Doug's question, he felt a twinge of conscience. *I really hurt him.* He saw the look of agony on Hart's face again. But this time he also felt it. He tried a lighter tone, hoping the feeling would dissipate. "He went to his room. He's either packing, loading a pistol, or rewriting what I said in his head."

Doug took off his glasses and rubbed his forehead. "Do I still need to send Kaiser in?"

Reg put his misgivings aside. "No, I got the job done. Hart's face changed halfway through the conversation. I got around his defences. Let's give him some time to react."

Doug gave Reg a playful punch on the shoulder as he made his way out of the room. A second later, there was a sharp knock at the door. Sean barged into the office. He pointed a finger at Reg. "I need to speak with you."

"Aren't you supposed to be in class?"

"We need to talk."

The other counsellors started to exchange looks. Maybe Reg's version of events wasn't universal. Reg knew what they were thinking. He had to get Sean out of the office before someone picked a fight with him to find out what happened. They'd shortly find themselves right back at arguing about the coat. Besides, Reg knew what Sean wanted to say.

"Okay, come with me. You can watch me smoke." Reg struggled to get to his feet and then made his way painfully and slowly to the front porch. He knew this display of vulnerability would mess Sean up.

As they departed the office, Mike smelled danger. He was still a little concerned about the possibility of violence from Sean, so he put on his coat and followed them outside, taking up his station at the far end of the porch.

Reg lit his cigarette. "What's up?" he asked, as if he'd just arrived at work.

Sean was outraged by his insouciance. "Hart is upstairs in shock. You did that to him on purpose. Is this a sicko pleasure for you?"

Reg was prepared for this. He wanted to say, *He's lucky it was me and not Kaiser,* but he didn't. His tone was calm and kind. "That's none of your business."

Sean was so deeply enmeshed in the quarrel that his energy spiked. "It's going on in *my* room. Is this your idea of treatment? I heard what you said to him — we all did! It was brutal."

Mike saw the energy rising and stepped closer. "Why aren't you in class?"

Sean didn't respond but shot him a look of pure contempt.

Reg held up his hand. "This is on my head. Can you give us a minute?"

Mike wandered away, pointing theatrically at his watch. But he didn't leave.

Reg leaned into Sean's personal space. "Why are you here and why is Hart sulking in his room?"

"You can ask a question like that after what you did?"

Reg tried again. "But why are *you* here and not him? You're too angry right now to understand what I'm saying. I want you to come see me this afternoon so we can sit down and discuss this. But the short answer is don't ever take away from an alcoholic the pain they need to change their lives. If you care about Hart, leave him alone. Let him feel what he needs to feel."

Mike was still pointing at his watch and starting to look angry.

Reg looked at Sean in a way that said, *I take your point.* "Go on down to the meeting. I'll go check on Hart."

Reg took the elevator to the second floor and walked down the musty carpeted hallway. It was a long walk.

Why the hell did I do this? I know better. Even when you do everything in the right order at the right time ... God don't let him be dead. I don't want to hear about this every day for the rest of my life.

Kaiser would have pushed the door open. Reg knocked gently and waited for a count of five before he walked inside. Hart was asleep. Reg left the room, closing the door softly behind him.

When the lunch bell rang, Hart was still in his room. Sean had to run upstairs to collect his friend when he was missed at the head count. Reg had a horrible moment when he considered where Hart might be and what he might be doing. He was very relieved to see him come through the door, looking only a little dishevelled.

With all the drama swirling through the place, lunch was a distraction. It resembled one of those seminal moments in television when everyone is watching and waiting to see what happens next. The first part of the prayer had come to pass: Reg was fully in harm's way.

Chapter 19

Czombo needed to find a urine donor PDQ. The next collection date was tomorrow, and he was going to fail convincingly if he had to take the test. He'd brought some sample jars with him from home, but they weren't the right kind, so he waited until everyone was asleep, then stole out of his room and went on the prowl. He discovered a stash of urine sample jars in an unlocked desk drawer and helped himself to a few. Half the problem remained.

He'd paid very careful attention to the way the samples were gathered. He'd been in a lot of hellholes since his twelfth birthday. On average, about one every year and a half. Every facility handled things a little differently. The first sample was always used to establish a background level for the donor. In the past, when he'd been collared about a high reading, he'd sheepishly own up to smoking a lot of dope the day before he came "to use it up," and then he'd add a little shamefacedly that he'd been scared and couldn't help himself. A little contrition and an appeal for sympathy usually worked because it was what the staff expected to hear.

But for that story to stay afloat, the levels of THC in the next batch of his urine had to come down, if only a little bit, and continue to decline for the remainder of his stay. His frequent visits to the La-Z-Boy for his chronic were going to keep his THC levels impossibly high, and not smoking wasn't one of the options he was looking at.

Czombo didn't really care about getting tossed out. Why should he? His employer was paying. He'd been to so many treatment centres that he'd lost track of them. Centres for tweens. Shelters for teens. Scripture camps. There was no end to their folly. Why couldn't they let him do what he wanted? He was playing the current game to stay on benefits after his unfortunate injury. His last useful relative had called in all his markers to get him a job leaning on a broom in the building trades. The pay and the hours suited, but he hated all work because of what it did to his social life. He knew he had to stick it out here for another fourteen days if he wanted to continue to cash short-term disability cheques well into the summer. His employment counsellor had even set him up with a computer-programming course, which was an option that appealed to his larcenous nature. But that wouldn't start until the fall.

Now that he had the jars, what he needed was some clean pee, and the new guy, Larry Lorne, looked like the most likely source. Larry was about his age but lacked his sophistication. He looked like the most pressing thing in his life was playing on the softball team. Larry had shared about his dope smoking in the afternoon group and Czombo realized he'd be a perfect donor. His THC levels would have been high, but he'd been abstinent since he arrived, so his levels would be falling. Exactly what Czombo needed. But how should he approach his country cousin on this most delicate of subjects?

When faced with this dilemma in the past, Czombo had tried threats and bribes, but they seldom worked in the long term. Some of his donors even tried to extort a hefty bonus out of him for their continuing service. He wasn't going to go down that road again. What he needed was an idealist.

Larry gave off contradictory signals. He seemed pretty passive, even to the point of allowing himself to be abused, all of which was greatly in his favour as a candidate. But Czombo had seen that smiling face give way to a terrible anger in the blink of an eye when he felt betrayed or, worse still, when he felt he'd been made to look foolish. That was his kryptonite. Yesterday, one of the clients, a trucker named Vince, had pegged Larry as a wimp who could be bullied and had unwisely helped himself to one of Larry's cigarettes without asking. For a split second, Czombo had seen murder in Larry's eye.

Czombo figured Larry was like a lot of the guys he'd met in jail, the ones who were secretly terrified of their anger. Those guys thought that if they ever really lost control of their feelings, they could kill someone. It was a delusion, and anger management in jail was full of guys like that. They called them *feeling stuffers*. Larry wasn't a killer, but he didn't know that.

From what Czombo had seen, Larry's anger almost always took the form of blurting out the truth. That's how he'd handled Vince, and that trait made him a bad candidate. When Vince stood his ground, Larry got right in his face and started yelling out his accusations. Czombo stepped in and took Vince by the arm. He was more than willing to be led away. He needed time to sulk and lick his wounds before he got to work on searching for an easier target.

Sean had taken charge of Larry and got him calmed down too. You could see the gratitude on his face. Czombo suspected that Larry would do anything for a friend. Bribery and intimidation wouldn't work on him. The first time he lost his temper or felt put upon, it was highly likely he'd grab a counsellor and that would be the end of that. No, the way to play this one was to work on his sympathy.

Czombo took him to Tim Hortons and bought him a coffee and donut. Czombo had pulled his long green hair into a ponytail, hoping to look more Greenpeace than pot maven. He'd removed the bathtub plug from around his neck and actually looked quite presentable in his jean jacket and black cords. He looked across the small oval table at Larry, trying to take his measure. Larry's huge frame was hunched over his coffee as he furiously tried to stir all the sugar he had poured into the cup into solution. When he glanced up, his eyes were bright and friendly, suggesting he had the self-awareness and manners of someone who'd grown up in a loving household. The perfect set-up.

"Larry, I'm in trouble and I need your advice."

Larry was flattered. "Really, what's up?"

"I'm about to get caught in a lie." Czombo sold that one with a tortured look that would've dampened all but the most calloused eyes.

"That sounds ominous. What happened?"

Czombo clenched his teeth and pulled his lips back as far as they'd go in a grimace that landed halfway between shame and disgust. "Last night I snuck out after lights-out and went to see my girlfriend, Kelly."

"Holy cow."

He tilted his head to the left and squinted as he pressed his lips tight. "I had to. She phoned me and said she was going to kill herself."

The first canary stopped singing. "You got a phone?"

Czombo looked away like he was ashamed. "I got a lot of guilty secrets. I don't know why I do this stuff sometimes. I'm trying to change but..." There was a pause that lasted a full minute as he fidgeted.

Czombo's abdication of power emboldened Larry. "So what happened?"

"She was just fucking with me — she loves to do that." Czombo started to play with his coffee cup like the answers he needed might be hidden inside.

"When I got there, she was lighting a joint. And the next thing you know, I'm toking too. Then, for good measure, she screwed my brains out. You know how this stuff goes." He paused. "She doesn't want me to be here. She wants me to smoke dope with her. She's afraid to buy it on her own."

As the receiver of this kind of confidence, Larry began to feel increasingly worldly. "Oh crap."

"By the time I figured out what she was up to, the sun was coming up. So I came here and waited for the first guys from the house to show up, then I joined them when they went back."

"You're gonna get caught."

"Don't I know it, and I'm going to lose my benefits and my place and everything else, and for what — one stupid mistake. Why can't I say no to her?" The look of torment that crossed his face said the amen.

Larry didn't need to say he understood that point only too well. "So what are you going to do?"

Czombo shrugged. "My whole life is hanging by a thread here. You know how persuasive women can be."

Larry nodded vigorously. Czombo wondered if he really did know, seeing as how he was eating up his bullshit without asking any awkward questions.

Czombo looked both ways before he continued. "I went into the room where they keep the medical supplies and I stole six piss bottles."

Larry was alarmed. "Do they count them?"

"They were all in a huge box. Musta been five hundred of them in there. Anyway, this is what I've come up with. They always hand you the jar and write your name on the lid. They ask you to leave the door open a crack so they can listen to you piss, but they don't actually watch you do it. So I figured if two guys were standing in line together, like they were buddies, like us, no one would notice one of the guys filling up two bottles."

"But they'd be identical. We'd get caught."

"No, that's the beauty of this: They only flag a range with these tests."

Larry was frozen with fear. "This could never work."

Czombo played the innocent and tried to look distressed. This had worked beautifully every place he'd tried it.

"That's what I thought too, until I worked it all out. See, what they're looking for are guys trying to change the sample. So, if you pissed in the jar twenty minutes before the test, your piss would be cold and that would be a dead giveaway. They also see if it's been watered down — lots of guys been burned on that one. But if it comes back hot, in the right jar, with the nurse's handwriting on the lid, they're not gonna look twice at it."

"So I would do what, fill up two of them and leave one behind the door?"

"Anywhere out of sight. I'll be the next in line."

A wave of conscience swept over Larry. This was wrong. He liked the idea of putting one over on the staff, but he had to think about himself here too. If he got caught, he'd be tossed out. He also wondered if he should be shielding Czombo from the consequences of his own folly. Nobody made him smoke that joint, after all. He'd done that on his own. For the first time, he seriously considered the possibility that Czombo was lying.

Czombo was still out ahead of him. He smiled and looked away like he was embarrassed. "I can tell, just by looking at you, you don't do stuff like this." He put his head down and looked defeated.

Larry felt for him. He'd been caught a few times doing things he shouldn't have, and he knew how hard it was to ask someone for help.

Czombo sighed and asked for the sale. "I'll ask someone else." He let his voice trail off like he was utterly defeated and demoralized.

The locus of control shifted, as he knew it would. Larry, without realizing it, squared his powerful shoulders and sat up straight in his chair. "If you keep asking people, they'll find out." He looked over his shoulder, then lowered his voice. He ran his fingers through his hair and then bit his lower lip. "Maybe I can…"

Czombo looked at him like he couldn't believe his ears. "You'll do it?"

"Yeah, but this has to be our secret." Larry felt a wave of wellbeing sweep through him, one that made him feel invulnerable. He'd found a friend at last.

———

The first urine test went smoother than draft straight out of the tap. Larry was so nervous he was blushing, but that didn't matter. Lots of guys have trouble producing urine samples for women. When they were finished, it was hard to leave the room without high-fiving each other. A victory like this called for a celebration, but Czombo couldn't very well share a joint with Larry. He took him for a Tim's and a donut instead.

Larry liked being a bad boy. This was a whole new continent for him to conquer.

"That was such a rush! I'm still tingling."

"And all you had to do was piss in a bottle."

"What do guys feel like when they stick up a bank?"

"Scared sick." Czombo smiled at him in a knowing way. "Taking a chance can be kind of fun, like what we just did. But sometimes you get so scared you shit yourself. When I was in the joint—"

"You were in jail!" A second canary fell over dead.

Czombo stayed in character and pretended he was embarrassed about it. "Well, we're friends now and I'm hoping I can trust you. I was in for a year on a conspiracy charge. That's why I'm here. My probation officer made me come." He glanced at Larry. "Does it bother you that I was inside?"

Larry felt embarrassed about his reaction. "I never had a friend who was before, that's all."

"It wasn't so bad. It's not like what people say."

"What happened?"

Inspiration struck Czombo, and he remembered a story he'd heard in Metro West that could be brilliantly adapted to suit his current needs. "Remember that girl I told you about? Kelly? Well, she deals. Gets other people to do the heavy lifting and in return…" He smiled sheepishly. "She does favours, ones that you don't want to miss. She had me go to a warehouse downtown and hand a guy an envelope. He told me to go to a coffee shop and wait for a few minutes and then a completely different guy came by and sat down at my table uninvited. When he left, I had a backpack full of drugs. I finished my coffee with my heart beating through my chest. And with all the cool I could muster, I picked up the bag and tried not to run out the front door." He took the last bite out of his muffin and wiped his hands on a napkin.

"What happened next was the wildest stroke of bad luck. On my way back to her place, I got hit from behind by a bike courier. Broke my ankle. The dude musta been on something 'cause he went nuts and started to beat on this lady in a car with his tire pump, screaming it was her fault. I wanted to get the hell outta there, but I couldn't stand." He frowned. "You can guess what happened when the cops got there. Walks right past 'em, asks me if the backpack is mine. Why the hell did he care about a backpack when the courier is kicking the hell out of some old lady's Buick five feet away? I said it wasn't mine, but then I realized that was exactly the wrong thing to say, because then the cop grabbed it and looked inside.

"The courier said it wasn't his and tried to hit the cop, which I thought greatly helped my case as an innocent victim of a deranged cyclist. I was praying the whole time no one had been paying attention to me before the accident. So they took me to St. Joe's and got me fixed up, and then they seemed to lose interest in me."

He leaned in a little closer. "Now here's the thing. There never was any dope, just a transmitter in a block of fake hash. The guy who came up to me in the coffee shop was a cop and they were planning to follow me back to Kelly. I went home for a couple days to rest up after the accident and wait for my head to clear, then one night I snuck out and crutched it over to Kelly's to tell her what happened. I knew enough to stay off the phone. They were waiting for me when I got there. They already had Kelly."

Larry liked the story. He forgot all about the two dead canaries. This kind of stuff never happened in the country.

"So I got a year for conspiracy, and that shoulda been the end of it. But Kelly landed on her feet. She had a good lawyer, and they threw her beef out on some kind of technicality. Maybe the judge read something in the report about her being arrested in her schoolgirl outfit. She wrote me a Christmas card when I was inside and invited me over for dinner when I got out. Told me she felt bad, wanted to make it up to me. Boy, did she ever. It's hard to stay away from the good life."

Larry started to feel protective. "She used you."

"I guess."

"Are you going to see her again?"

"I shouldn't — but I know I will." A little-boy lost look crossed his face.

"You won't be able to stay sober."

"Well, that's what I'm struggling with. How the hell can I stay sober if it means giving up Kelly? Larry, what am I going to do?"

Larry liked being the newest counsellor. "Find a girl who doesn't smoke dope and get you in trouble."

Czombo put his head down like it was costing him something to say this. "But she won't do the fucked-up shit that Kelly does, that's for damn sure!"

Chapter 20

Doug settled himself into the deep and welcoming recliner in his den, but the air was slightly damp and cool, so he regained his feet and turned on the gas fireplace and adjusted the lights. It would take a few minutes before the room got cozy. The maid had been in, and the place was in apple-pie order, smelling agreeably of Murphy Oil Soap, leather, and hardwood. He didn't want to think about anything this evening, let alone work, but he was coming up against the clock.

While he waited for ideal conditions in the den, he went upstairs to make a cup of coffee. As the water came to a boil and the smell of freshly ground beans began to fill the room, he thought about spring and walking around without an overcoat and feeling the sun's warmth on his face as he drove home from work with the windows open. The good life was commonplace for him. What did Channing Hart have to look forward to?

Doug had read Hart's file very carefully. Paul had done a good write-up. He'd grasped that Hart was a classic underachiever. This guy had the tools and the skills to really do something with his life. He'd achieved some limited success, earning a lot of money for himself working blue-collar jobs and making shrewd investments. Never in trouble with the law. Not so much as a complaint from a neighbour. All that was missing was a picture of him delivering Meals on Wheels on his day off. What was holding him back? Doug smelled a sick parent. He collected his mug of coffee and plodded carefully in his slippers down the narrow wooden stairs, saying softly to himself, "Do not fall down the stairs. Do not fall down the stairs."

The recliner exhaled with relief as Doug took up his station. He let his mind wander over the facts and his impressions, moving them around in his head, trying to find a new order to put them in. *How did this Boy Scout end up on the front page? This guy always colours inside the lines and then puts the crayons back in the box when he's finished. Well, booze is the great undoer of order and intent — maybe this mess is a John Barleycorn masterpiece.*

He sighed. *This is the kind of crap I'd expect from Czombo. He doesn't give a rat's ass. Nothing gets to spoil his fun.* It took a full minute before it occurred to him. *That's why he can't own this. It's a double bind. He never lets himself go and he hates himself for it. He wants to but he can't, and now he's going to jail for something he knows he couldn't do drunk or sober.*

Someone, somewhere, at some time, had destroyed Hart's sense of agency. He not only let other people tell him what to do, he needed them to. *He can't work it out on his own.* Doug stopped himself. *The fact that he hasn't done it yet doesn't prove that he can't.* Doug looked back through the paperwork, looking for something to support that idea, but there was nothing. *Is that how the drinking fits in? Is it the glue that keeps the house of cards from blowing over? Hart has proven he's capable of running a big prosperous company for someone else. Why can't he start a business of his own?*

The treatment record supported that insight. He always made his bed and did his chores and usually showed up on time for meals and meetings. The externals were always in order. But all the counsellors had picked up on his dualism. Each, in their own way, had noted that Hart didn't believe in anything. He kept waiting for someone new to show up and sweep him up into their reality. The first time they let him down, he showed them the door. The man was pure disciple.

Doug had seen this mask before. A fierce temper is often hidden by a pleasant expression. But sometimes a tender soul needs a tough exterior to keep the corrosive world at bay. Hart may have had good reasons for resorting to masks. Masks may have saved him from a lot of pain in the past, but they'd landed him here. What he needed was for someone to pull off his mask. He needed a dose of truth that he could swallow and digest, not one that obliterated him. The fight with Reg had to have him looking for a friend.

He's a contradiction all right — the secretly angry and remote client that everyone likes. He appears to respond to treatment, but it only goes so deep. He's so damn frightened by the world that he plays one neurotic game after another. Does he really think someone's going to come along and put this right?

Doug looked into the reassuring flames in the fireplace as his mind wandered. In that perfect simplicity, he imagined the conversation that must have passed between the volatile Sean Miller and the passive Channing Hart after the savaging that Reg had imparted. Mike was famous for putting the damnedest people in the same room. It was his superpower. He'd outdone himself with this pairing. But no amount of imagining could fit Sean Miller for the role of John the Baptist.

Does Sean Miller know he's the umpteenth guy to try and save our Mr. Hart? This game-playing lunatic is recreating Clancy's Tavern right here in treatment. I won't have it. I'm going to need Kaiser after all.

———

The next morning Doug had a quiet word with Kaiser about the conversation he wished him to have with Channing Hart. Kaiser gave his long-suffering boss an I-told-you-so grin as Doug described the ragged road that Reg and Hart had traversed the day before. Kaiser imagined with pleasure the thwarted look that Reg always got on his face when things went sideways on an ice-covered hill.

So much for the tough-guy-in-training program.

Doug let him have his moment. Kaiser was more than happy to get away from the phones. He was beginning to feel like he was working in a call centre chasing deadbeats for overdue cable bills. He needed a fire, then a flood, and finally an earthquake to restore him to sanity.

The conversation he had in mind required a grand entrance. Kaiser chose his dark blazer and supplemented it with a dark fedora someone had left behind many years ago. He could see when he looked in the mirror that the hat sent the right message. When he was dressed, he walked slowly and calmly to where Hart and Sean were holding court on the smoking deck. He was wonderful at communicating power and authority through his body language.

As he approached the group first, one head turned his way and then they all did. The musk oxen reacting to the approaching wolf. Without saying a word, he'd become the focal point. The conversation they were all so invested in a minute ago first slowed and then stopped. Larry and Daniel actually moved a half step closer to Sean Miller — two calves taking shelter behind the bull.

Kaiser stopped when he was still ten feet short of the group. *Look at that. We got a new sheriff.*

Kaiser and Sean eyed each other in silence. Kaiser was used to this type of respect. Clients were always telling him they felt safe when he was around. A few of them had gone so far as to say that when they felt weak and overwhelmed, the very sight of him would put some fight back into them.

Sean Miller inspired the same kind of confidence but had no idea how or why. The street version of a stare down always ended in a brawl, which suited Sean fine. But being the new leader of a spiritual community required a different set of gifts — skills he had yet to master. The best he could manage was to look tough and angry.

Hart viewed Kaiser's approach with alarm. *He's here for me.* Hart had convinced himself the drama was over.

Kaiser picked up on his terror and spoke very gently and respectfully to him. "Mr. Hart, can I have a word with you?"

Hart had a jarring flashback to Reg's overture to a conversation, but Kaiser's look and voice were saying the opposite of what he expected to hear and see, and this confused him. He was wary of Kaiser but intrigued by him too. And part of him really wanted to go with him. He tried to look cool. "Sure…"

Kaiser looked up at the bright morning sunshine. "It's a beautiful day. Grab your coat; we're going for a walk."

The men all exchanged a look that said, *don't go.*

Kaiser waited outside the front door while Hart ran upstairs to get his coat. He wanted him running around: It set the tone and put his quarry on the defensive. He intentionally kept his distance from the other counsellors who were outside having a smoke after the morning census meeting. He kept his back turned to them. His severe body language and separation from the others was sinister. He wanted to look the part of a man steeled to perform a painful duty.

Larry Lorne and Daniel Philips met Hart as he came down the stairs from his room, putting on his winter coat as he went. They didn't know what to say, but they wanted to be there for him. Hart was surprised and delighted but didn't know what to say either. They did a fist bump.

Hart opened the heavy oaken door and walked out into the bright January sunshine. His feeling of connection vanished when he saw Kaiser standing alone with his back turned to the other counsellors. His sense of curiosity give way to a wave of anxiety. He tried to figure out what was coming next by looking for clues in the faces of the other counsellors as they smoked. He felt trapped. Kaiser's black leather coat and curly blond hair mashed down under the fedora made him look like a hit man.

Kaiser turned and made eye contact. He set a lively pace as they walked north on Madison Avenue. "We haven't talked before, have we?"

Hart had a hard time accommodating himself to Kaiser's long strides. "No."

Kaiser adopted his high-hat persona. "Well, that would certainly account for your lack of progress. If you want the big results, you need to consult the top man." The joke fell flat. Kaiser took it down a notch, from comic to confidential. "Okay, I can see you're still a bit wound up, but tell me, how do you feel about what Reg said to you yesterday? That couldn't have been pleasant."

Hart perceived Kaiser's attempt to build rapport as a trap. He got a shot of adrenalin. He began to speak very, very quickly, the way a young child does when they know they are about to be shushed. "How much more of this do you think I can take? You know my situation. Hell, everyone in the world knows all the details of my personal life. Rock stars don't get the kind of coverage I do. I'm alive to give other people something to disapprove of. Do you know what that feels like?"

Kaiser looked at him blankly.

A fresh urgency empowered Hart's speech. "You're not worried about being recognized. You can go anywhere and nobody notices. Not me. People see my face and I can see the wheels start to turn. *I know this guy. But from where?* If I'm lucky, I'm out of there before they put it all together. Three times since I've been out people have stopped me on the street and said, 'You're the guy in the paper.' One dirty old lady gave me the evil eye and spat on the sidewalk."

Kaiser continued his stately pace. The playful part of him wanted to speed up and slow down, to make it awkward for Hart to stay at his side and to see how he'd react to being dominated, but he wisely put that thought out of his mind. This was serious business. "Well, so far it's only you and me on this walk, no lynch mob. So tell me, who are you? Do you even know?"

Hart was desperate to avoid another confrontation. Why couldn't Kaiser just say what was on his mind? Why did these guys always make him play the guessing game? Why couldn't they say their piece and then let him decide how he felt about it? "What do you want to know?"

"You spend a lot of time telling everyone that you're being treated unfairly, that you're getting a lot of unwanted attention." Something about Kaiser's tone communicated to Hart that he had the counsellor's full attention. "Well, here's your chance. Let me be your judge. Tell me, who are you really? If none of this court stuff ever happened and I met you in a coffee shop, would I like you?"

Hart felt a moment of despair. "You wouldn't notice me. When I'm not at Clancy's or at work, I'm the invisible man. I don't stick out and I don't take chances. I always try and get along with people. I hate being the centre of attention. I like things to run smooth. That's when I feel at home. That's when I feel safe."

Kaiser knew he had winning cards to play. For the first time he had real hope for Hart. "I'm a little surprised you know that about yourself. Do you know how others see you? I'm not trying to be a prick here. I'm trying to give you some feedback. Do you know how to accept feedback?"

Hart shook his head. "I don't know. People don't confide in me — they either give me shit or take me for granted. They know I don't bite."

Kaiser's voice sounded almost loving. "Well, that's what has to change. Channing, we see you as being very much the way you describe yourself. But here's the thing: We don't want you to do what we tell you to do simply because we tell you to do it; we want you to do it because you think it's the right thing. You go along with things to keep the peace. That's got to stop. We need you to take a stand. We want you to occupy a space. Draw a line in the dirt and dare anyone to step across it. Own your life. You're a ball of mush. You're what we call a people pleaser. Do you know what that means?"

Hart didn't like the term. He'd heard this before. There'd been too many amateur shrinks in the pack of girlfriends and barstool companions over the past two decades. Everyone knew how to fix him after a few drinks. His shoulders rounded and he shoved his hands deep into his overcoat pockets. "Lots of people have said that…"

Kaiser came to an abrupt stop and turned to face Hart. "Well, let me tell you why, as an addictions guy, I have a righteous stake in this. People pleasers go with the crowd, they go with the flow. So while you're with us, you're willing to be sober. But once you're gone, the first person who insists you go for a drink will be all it takes to get you started again."

That was all so logical and clear that it took Hart by surprise. Could it be that simple?

Hart didn't like standing still but didn't feel that he could just start walking. "I need to think about that…" His foot was tapping although only Kaiser noticed it.

Kaiser gently steered him in a new direction as he resumed the walk at a much more sedate pace. "Nope, don't think about it. Thinking about your feelings is the way you justify all your nonsense. I want you to *feel* about it. Let it roll around in your gut. How does it *feel* to have a dirty old lady spit on the street when you pass?"

Hart laughed at the suggestion. He hadn't thought about it that way before. "Well, you make a good case."

"Or how does it feel to have Reg give you shit just because he felt like it."

That shell landed right on the money. Hart went quiet but it was a good quiet.

Kaiser's face radiated a calm acceptance of the situation. "See, you're still doing it. It's a hard habit to break. When we get back to the centre, I want you to find a nice, peaceful spot off all by yourself and sit down quietly and clear your head. Then I want you to decide once and for all — are you going to get real and tell people what you think and want and feel? Or are you going to keep going in the wrong direction, drinking and compromising and pretending that you have a life? Because, Hart, that really is the choice."

Kaiser stopped again and turned to look at him. "Do you get so drunk you don't know what you're doing? Drunk enough to kill a woman and not remember, and maybe not even care? Because that's what it looks like." He reached out and gently touched the lapel of Hart's coat. "Are you the kind of guy who doesn't have enough backbone to face what he's done drunk when he's sober? Will you put up with anything as long as you know, at the end of it all, you can have another drink?"

Hart couldn't believe that two human beings could talk to each other like this. He looked stunned. But deep inside he felt relieved. But he didn't know why. Kaiser did. That would come next.

"That's a bit much to remember, isn't it?" said Kaiser, handing him a lined index card. "Have a look at these three questions and then come see me at four o'clock. We can put on a pot of tea and talk some more."

Chapter 21

John kept regular office hours at Flannerman's, hoping against hope that Peter's foray into mania was a one-and-done event. He expected that, after an awkward entrance including the appropriate head shaking and muttered apologies, the crazed firebrand persona would be put to rest and replaced by his more tractable self. Three days passed with no sign of either high priest or penitent.

John amused himself by spying on the Flannerman's staff: The three were hunched over their Tupperware with the radio on. Smelling-of-formaldehyde Franklin was using the lunch hour to worm his way into stately Pamela's affections. It was hopeless. She was perfect in every detail from the crown of her head to the polished heels of her shoes. The care she lavished on the departed was the standard she insisted upon for herself. Lumpy and awkward might have been overlooked if she'd had enough wine, but Frankie chewed with his mouth open, and no amount of money or other compensating charms could ever undo the spell cast by that particular misfortune. Her love of classical beauty meant she had eyes only for the limo driver. He ate with delicate fingers and deliberate care. His job was to look dignified in a dark suit and to drive. Pamela thought he managed both tasks. The way she mooned over him left no doubt that it was back to jars of bourbon and old movies for Franklin this weekend.

Peter was visible from time to time through the window in the lobby, quickly moving up and down Madison Avenue. But he never stuck his head inside to say hello. That was unusual. John wondered if they'd crossed a line in their relationship. The line that separates a healthy ghost from a poltergeist isn't a clearly defined thing. In the long silence of the lonely afternoons, John was coming around to the idea that he was watching Peter's swan song. Sitting alone in a pew with no one to make fun of might be the new normal.

John was relieved to see Peter on the fourth day. He arrived in quite a state. His hair was mussed and his shirt untucked. He looked simultaneously angry and afraid. He tramped down the centre of the chapel and flung himself heavily into the pew with a groan.

"Peter, what's wrong? You look like death warmed over."

The stout spectre's concerned look suggested a martyr making sure the firewood was all in good order. "We're beset on all sides by difficulty."

After his last tirade, John had decided to give him as much time as he needed to compose his thoughts. If indeed such a thing was still possible. This looked like Looney Tunes part two.

Peter turned violently in the pew to face him, his body language showing defeat and imminent demise. He was murmuring.

John tried to lighten the tone. "What happened? Have you seen a ghost?"

Peter blew out a jet of angry air. "Naff, something almost that upsetting."

When no further details were offered, John poked the fat man again. "Get your income tax back?"

Peter had a story to tell and no inclination to jibber-jabber. He was in a tough spot. He was still very angry with John but had no one else to tell his troubles to. He knew this had to end badly but what other choice did he have? "If we can't be serious, what hope is there? The crisis is upon us John — we're at war."

There was a long pause. He looked at John, hoping to see the man of action he needed. Alas, only the wily naysayer looked back at him with mischief in his eyes. Peter rose to his full height and waved his fist in John's face. "These are deep and personal feelings and I'll not have them exposed to ridicule!" He fixed John with his familiar smouldering-hot look.

John acquiesced. What choice did he have? He couldn't bide his time and find out from the local gossips anymore; they were all inexplicably gone. The angry bull in front of him had an exclusive on this story.

"I'm sorry if I offended you, Peter. I sensed your torment, and I was trying to cheer you up."

"Well, if that's the case, you can be forgiven, my boy."

There was a silence. Peter was an actor waiting for his cue. John's training in the dramatic arts came to the fore; his task was to ask the leading question. The glowering ghost gave John a slight nod of the head to confirm what was required of him.

John knew Peter's sense of timing in these matters ran to the majestic. He brazenly counted to forty before the look in Peter's eyes announced that murder was on the horizon.

His tone would not have been out of place had he been awarding the Nobel prize. "Are you composed enough in your feelings, Peter, to tell me what happened?"

For a split second, John thought he'd been sussed out. He braced himself for a fiery blast. But no, Peter had been using the time to organize his soliloquy, and having been properly prompted and invited to centre stage, he made himself comfortable. He intended to stay there for a good long while.

"For the first time since our arrival here, I recognize that the human heart isn't the hearth of our deepest feelings. Since we parted the ether and left that organ behind, I have come to expect little in the way of good feeling. The things I used to love, like walking the dog on a brisk morning, a cup of coffee, or even a home-cooked meal, don't exist for us here. I feel like a cursed penitent denied meat in my broth, an outcast barely tolerated at the margins, longing for companionship and the goodwill of my brothers as I try and worm my way back into God's good graces. I'm cursed for a sin that I cannot shift."

Is that what this is? thought John as he willed his face not to register the mix of confusion and wonder he was experiencing.

The ghost of the sorrowful countenance held up his right hand and pointed his index finger toward heaven. "It's lonely being a ghost. The only emotion I still have regular access to is sadness. It's funny — my face is dry to my touch, but in spite of that, I can feel tears running down my cheeks. They're cold and bitter. In the old days, tears like these brought sweet relief from pent-up pain. Oh, John, I'm close to despair."

John gave him a thorough visual search. He couldn't see any tears, but Peter's hair had suddenly gone grey in a patch around the top of his head, giving him a kind of comic appearance very much out of step with what he was saying. But before John could interject and make him take a look at himself in a mirror, he was bulldozed.

"The business at hand took me to Bloor Street a few minutes ago. I forgot who I was and what the conditions of my existence were. I was lost in a reverie of a softer and fuller time in my life, when there was still a spring in my step and a burning desire for love and connection in my heart."

He took a deep breath and lowered his voice. "I was thinking about that one special girl I knew. She was young and full of an energy I could never get enough of. I was rethinking all the bridges to happiness that I'd experienced with her and how each in turn had failed to support my weight, as if I was in some kind of accursed state and so incapable of achieving human happiness. I'm often so when my dry tears are upon me." Peter put both hands on the back of the pew and let loose a pitiable groan. "Oh, Terri, my Terri, my beautiful Terri." For once John's need to interrupt was overtaken by curiosity.

"It was as if I'd left the cool of the forest and entered a sunlit glade. The air stopped moving and was suddenly warm on my skin and full of fragrance. The wanting over distances of time and space vanished, and there she stood. She had Terri's eyes."

John wanted to ask a question but dared not. Peter had forgotten he was here. This was his holy of holies.

Peter rose again to his full height. "It made the whole struggle and all the pain worth it, not only in the here and now, but for the next hundred years to come. This was a moment to define a lifetime of doubt and faith. I really mean it. For the first time since I died, I was happy. It had all come to pass.

"I reached out my hand to touch her hair, and then it all came unravelled. It took an age for me to realize she was not the woman I loved, but another."

John drew closer to better hear the trembling voice assailed by the loud gulps of air.

"The look on her face didn't change when I embraced her. She was fixed on something farther away. She looked right through me with that welcoming, living look. That perfect smile. I turned to see what was going on behind my back.

"I had not mistaken the look. Her eyes were full of love and promise. But she wasn't looking at me, John. It wasn't my Terri come back to me. In my place was a callow youth with the disinterested look of a street tough."

A look of deep sadness creased Peter's face, but in an instant it all turned to anger. Peter spat out the words: "One of your Gothic types. He had the paper-thin cool that all the young ones affect these days. This acned, hackneyed wraith was holding her attention while I passed slowly away from her, unnoticed and unloved. Oh, John, the pain of that moment still smoulders in my soul. It was so close. It was all so close. I was sure it was here." He sounded finished. John felt a little sick himself. "I know now that my dreams are never going to come true. The distance between wanting and having cannot be breached. I never truly felt dead until this morning."

Chapter 22

Paul was standing in his shirtsleeves while he wrote his lecture notes on the blackboard. He didn't have to turn around to know Channing Hart was stressed out. *The guy's sweating like a whore in church*, he thought. *Blackouts are just about the last thing in the world he'll want to talk about, but I bet he can't stay away from the subject either.* Paul remembered his own first foray into that horrible headspace. That first experience of a blackout. Waking up, often in a strange place, with no memory of how you passed the previous evening. Sometimes days went missing. Paul loved teaching this segment. The phrase that came to mind was *the knife edge of panic*. Nothing else captured the feeling quite so well of wanting and not wanting to know.

Paul turned to face the room. All the participants — with the exception of Czombo — had the anxious look of note-takers who are fearful that the teacher will erase the board before they're ready. Dark questions were forming in the lines around their eyes. They didn't like where these bullet points were heading.

When they were ready, he began in a slow calm voice. "Blackouts only ever happen to alcoholics. They never happen to social drinkers. That's why they're called the smoking gun for alcoholism. If you've had one, then you belong here. Now, for the purposes of this discussion, I'm going to dumb this down quite a bit. Blackouts come in three flavours. Do you know what they are?"

Sean piped up first, which was no surprise. He was, after all, the new shop steward and expected to behave like her majesty's loyal opposition. "Mild, medium, and suicide?"

Paul laughed, delighted that the group now had a leader. "Close enough. When we talk about them informally, we call them greyouts, brownouts, and blackouts. You've probably experienced all three of them without really knowing how to sort them out and then been too ashamed to talk about them afterward."

He looked around at them all. "First is a greyout. You go to a party and the next day you remember almost everything. You remember speaking with someone, but you can't remember what you talked about." He scanned the room. They understood. Lots of those on the curricula vitae.

"A brownout is more severe. Again, you remember everything about the party — until about ten p.m., then it all gets foggy for an hour or so. But after that, you have a clear memory of going home in a taxi."

Paul watched the heads nodding as they made a note. This, too, was familiar territory. They were comfortable talking about the first two. But were they ready to move on to the third? He looked at Hart. The man's lips had disappeared and, in their place, a horrible parody of a grin was taking shape. It looked as if a madman had used a razor to put a smile on his face. This was costing him something. But he sat still, staring straight ahead with his pen at the ready.

Paul took a breath and then plunged in. "A blackout is when you wake up somewhere and have no idea how you got there. It's the same process as a brownout and a greyout, but at a higher level of intoxication."

He looked around at them all. "There are lots of little rituals that go with blackouts. People turn off their phones when they start to drink, or they hide them in a drawer because they're afraid they'll start calling people in the middle of the night when they're drunk and lonely. I used to spring out of bed in the morning and go looking for my wallet. If I still had my wallet and if there was some cash left in it, then I probably didn't do too much damage. Did you ever do a walk-by on your car the next morning, looking for dents and blood?"

Paul noticed some of the guys looking away a little sheepishly. "Surely someone has a blackout story?"

Unexpectedly, Vince lifted his hand. Paul smiled. The trucker had been pretty quiet for the past few days, after an angry exchange with Larry on the smoking deck. He was out of step with the rest of the group. His focus was on everything but treatment. Not unexpectedly, his only ally was Czombo. Paul didn't fully understand the emerging dynamic between the two men. He would have taken action if he had. Czombo had yet to figure out what he could get Vince to do for him, but that was okay. The first task was always to isolate your new minion from the herd.

Vince slouched down a bit and mumbled, "Oh yeah. I'd wake up in the morning beside the old lady and she'd be pissed. I'd say good morning and she'd give me the look. I'd lie back down and try and remember what I did or said. I'd remember a bit here and there, sometimes nothing at all. Would usually take till four in the afternoon to get her to talk about what happened. First I'd chase her to find out what I did, then when she told me, I really didn't wanna know. Was that a blackout?"

Paul nodded. "That's what we're looking for. I see another hand."

Czombo smiled ruefully and glanced at Vince beside him. He didn't like his right-hand man talking to the opposition, but he didn't see how he could do anything about it just this minute. From his position at the far end of the table, the place that the counsellors referred to as the denial chair, he checked out the rest of the room. Paul stood near the head of the table. To his left sat the boy band: Daniel, Larry, and a new arrival who looked too young to drink let alone be addicted to something. Across from them were Hart and Sean. It was hard to watch Hart, who looked as though his oral surgeon had just exclaimed in wonder that he'd never seen a larger or more infected wisdom tooth.

A voice broke the silence. It was the guy who had arrived yesterday. Paul was embarrassed because he couldn't recall his name. "Sometimes I would pass out and be gone for hours. Was that it?"

Paul shook his head and answered gently. "No, that's a coma. It comes a few drinks after the blackout. You eventually arrive at a place where they could do surgery on you and you wouldn't feel a thing. The difference is this. In a blackout you're still walking around and getting into trouble, but your memory isn't working. That's why they're so frightening. We do things when we're drunk that we would never do if we were sober."

Paul saw another hand. "Yes, Tom?"

Tom Anderson was taking a big risk. He hated talking in groups. He sat with his chin on his chest while his powerful fingers locked in a fearful embrace. A little wisp of sweat was forming on his balding pate. "I have trouble sometimes remembering what the hell I'm talking about." The group roared with laughter. "Oh yeah, laugh at me," he said defeated and unable to continue.

Paul stepped in. "The laugh means they do it too, Tom. Finish your thought."

Tom treated the limelight like quicksand. He lowered his gaze and focused on a point five feet in front of him. "I get into the middle of a sentence and I can't remember what the hell I was trying to say. It's like I get sidetracked. I feel like an idiot."

When nobody laughed at him, he looked up and seemed to find his voice. His face brightened. "I keep talking, hoping that whatever thought got away from me will eventually find its way home. Sometimes it does."

Paul turned his head to the side and looked slyly at the ceiling like an accomplished vaudevillian. "But not always?"

Tom looked defeated. "People call me on it too. They roll their eyes. They talk over top of me, like what I had to say wasn't important."

Paul was low key yet still confrontational. "But you can sort of see their point. If you're talking nonsense because you drink too much and can't remember what you just said, why should they have to listen to it?"

Tom retreated behind a grimace. Paul thought about taking a minute to comfort him but then thought better of it. *Let that sit for a minute. I'll talk to him later in the office.*

Sean Miller was out ahead of the group. "What's wet brain?"

Paul abandoned the chalkboard and took his seat at the head of the table. He refreshed himself with a sip of water. "Wet brain is the final stop on the tour. It happens when the blackout becomes permanent."

Several voices landed simultaneously on an amalgam of "Is that possible?"

Paul couldn't resist telling a story. "Don't you guys know about Popeye the Sailor Man?"

"We know Popeye."

"Popeye had wet brain. The cartoonist who drew him was making fun of all the late-stage-three drunks in the nineteen twenties and thirties. Think about it.

Popeye had all the symptoms of wet brain. He muttered and chuckled to himself, he walked in a comical way because he couldn't keep his balance, and he was inappropriately violent when people crossed him. If you substitute rum for spinach, you can see where they were coming from. The thing that got Popeye cooking was booze."

"But he loved Olive Oyl."

"There's a babe for every bandit."

Chapter 23

Hart found a good spot in the sitting room. The afternoon sun was streaming through the window and illuminating the colourful tub chairs. This room was a treasure. It was great for reading or sunbathing or simply getting away from the noise. When Sean stuck his head through the door, he found his friend staring at the index card that Kaiser had given him. The frown on Hart's face extended to his eyes, down through his sloped shoulders, and into his twisted, tapping extremities. He looked up when he saw Sean enter the room and handed him the card. "What do you make of this?"

Sean took the offering and read it: three very straightforward questions. "Where did you get these?" he asked as he handed the card back to Hart.

Hart got to his feet and arched his aching back. "Kaiser gave them to me on our walk." Hart's weariness made it clear that this offering was a Rubik's cube, infinite in complexity and frustration. "I was expecting him to give me supreme shit. That's what he's famous for. I would've known what to do with that. But he didn't. We walked and talked like we were friends. He told me I needed to come back here and clear my mind and decide what I'm going to do with myself. It seemed to make perfect sense until I had a look at these."

He read them aloud: "If I'm not for myself, who will be for me? But if I'm only for myself, what am I? And if I can't change this behaviour now, when will I?" He looked up at Sean and grimaced. "I'm going to jail for something I didn't do. So the answers to these questions are *no one, alone,* and *when I finally get a break.* When I get out of jail, the answers are going to be even worse: *parole officers, outcast,* and *never.*"

He made a face and put the card down. "It became clear to me while I was sitting here — they're never gonna let me go. I've been thinking I'd be gone for a couple years and then get everything back. That was as much awful as I could take in. There is no coming back. Some fat prick in a baggy suit's gonna follow me around like bad news till I fall over dead."

Sean didn't say a word.

"I'm going to spend the rest of my life answering questions like these. There's no answer for me. I pretend to listen, and they pretend to care."

Sean picked up the index card. Something about the questions drew him in — something that someone had said. "Let me write these down." He took out his pack of cigarettes and made a note on the lining.

Hart turned his attention back to his friend. "What have you got on for this afternoon?"

Sean returned the index card to Hart and slid his smokes back into his shirt pocket. "If you're right about things, Reg and I are going to take a turn at making believe."

———

When Sean arrived, Reg was sitting in the living room talking to Vince. Reg made eye contact with Sean but allowed the trucker to finish his story. Then Reg struggled to get out of the deep armchair and to his feet. He nodded toward Sean. "I need to have a talk with this character. I'll see ya later, Vince."

Sean and Reg strolled down the hall until they found an empty counselling room and made themselves comfortable. Sean handed Reg the three questions he'd jotted down on the flap of his now empty cigarette pack. "Have you ever seen these before?"

Reg glanced at the words and smiled. "*Pirkei Avot* by Rabbi Hillel — it means 'the ethics of our fathers' — one of my favourites. Where in the world did you get this?"

"Kaiser gave them to Hart. What do they mean?"

"It means Kaiser is stealing my best stuff. Hillel was a contemporary of Jesus." Reg handed the cigarette pack to Sean. "So what do you make of them?"

"Are you Jewish?"

Reg didn't like the question. "No. Would it bother you if I were, you anti-Semitic prick?"

Sean had a thick hide and ignored him; he was intrigued by the brevity and clarity of these three gems. "They're brilliant. Should be in the workbook!"

Reg thought about that. "No, that wouldn't work. This insight is very special. It's like chemotherapy. It's not for everyone. Strong medicine."

"Why did Kaiser give them to Hart?"

Reg tried to look modest. "I can't comment on another client's treatment. But you can. Why do you think he did it?"

Sean lacked only a professional vocabulary. "Hart's a bit of a wimp."

Reg liked where this was going. "Is that why you feel the need to protect him? Ask yourself the three questions."

He picked up the repurposed cigarette liner for dramatic effect and held it six inches from his eyes. He didn't need to read it. He fixed his eyes on Sean as he paraphrased the familiar words.

"If you're not looking after Sean Miller, who is? What about that?" He didn't give him a chance to answer. "If you waste all your time and energy trying to save someone who can't be saved, where does that leave you?" Sean had an answer for that but never got to give it, as Reg powered right over him a second time. "And if you can't change this behaviour today, when will you?"

He flipped the cigarette pack like a playing card back toward Sean. Sean ignored the gesture and kept his thoughts to himself. He didn't like being talked over.

Reg framed his face by leaning his chin on the hook of his cane. "Do you remember me telling you to mind your own business? This is what I meant. Hart is always looking for someone to fight his battles. You're not the first guy to do this and it hurts both of you. By meddling, you take the heat off him. You're keeping him from feeling the pain he needs to feel. He can't get well until he owns it. And where does that leave you? You're so busy helping him put out the fire in his garage, you don't notice that the flames have now set your roof on fire. Stop being helpful. Be useful. This game you're playing is going to screw both of you. This is how whole families get sick and sometimes stay sick for generations. If you work on you and let him do what he needs to do, then you'll both get well. Do it the other way, and all you have is mush."

Sean hadn't heard what he said. He was stuck on the second question. Reg had given him too much information too soon. He hadn't gotten that far yet and he was desperately afraid he'd lose his place if he looked up from what he was feeling to consider any new possibility. "I'm going to have to think about that."

"That's okay. Nobody gets this stuff in one sitting."

———

Sean wanted a smoke beyond badly. Kaiser's three questions kept running through his head. Worse than any advertising jingle. They made it hard to think about anything. They were as infuriating as those stupid blue dots that move in a circle when your computer takes over and changes things that you don't want it touching while you sit there fuming and cursing.

The guys on the smoking deck were standing in a tight circle when he arrived. Something was up. Vince had the floor. The big trucker had been put down by Kaiser in front of the group earlier in the week, and he'd been largely silent since then. He was still smarting and looking to even the score. He was older than most of the guys by about two decades. He was going bald on top and a little grey around the sides — deficiencies he camouflaged with his cowboy hat and thick trucker wallet, both of which suggested a power and purpose that had once been his. Sean noticed the group around him was fidgeting — all except for Czombo, who had a smile on his face. He forgot about the questions and got close enough to listen.

Vince had belatedly figured out what he should have said to Kaiser. The perfect version of events that explained why he'd been right all along and Kaiser not only wrong, but undeniably mean-spirited for trying to make him look the fool. Three days too late, but today was a good day to expose a nest of hypocrites.

Clients who didn't like the Punanai talking-to frequently responded by first finding fault with the counsellor who confronted them. There had to be something wrong with the counsellor, who was obviously a bitter, small-minded man. The alternative opening, or the second port of call, was to suggest that the counsellor's beliefs were the culprit and that any fair-minded examination of his philosophy would easily explain and discredit his criticism. The two rejoinders were used in tandem so often that the staff referred to them as the left hook–right cross combination.

There was always a supposition at work in these philosophical autopsies that turned the burden of proof on its ear. There was what met the eye and what was really going on. Vince had worked it out and he knew he could take down Kaiser or any of the others anytime he wanted to. He'd seen through to the bottom of this charade. But before he took a step that drastic, he wanted to try out his new superweapon in front of a live audience. "This stuff is goofy."

Tom Anderson didn't like Vince. He'd called him stupid last week as he struggled to find his words. "So why are you here?"

Vince put his hands on his hips and looked Tom straight in the eye. "Good question. You want me to answer that for you straight up? I will, you know."

Tom smelled bullshit. "That'd be good. Getting a straight answer out of you."

"I'm gettin' blamed for something my boss should be taking the fall for. It's like the poem: I don't own the Choo Choo and I don't ring the bell, but watch this thing come off the track and see who catches hell."

Tom wiped a meaty hand across his bald head. "That's your point?"

Vince trotted out the pained expression he used for idiots. "I been trucking for twenty years now and never had a crash. Always make sure my load is tied down good before I take off. But five years ago, we got bought out by an outfit from Hamilton. First they fire us all and hire us back as independent contractors. Then on our next paycheque, all our benefits, gone. They can't afford to give us a raise, but they can give us more hours. They don't do maintenance, they don't follow rules, and they tell you plain and simple, if you don't phony up your logbook, you don't work for us."

The group was all ears. This was an almost universal experience for a working man.

Vince lowered his voice. "Then there's the other side of the business. We carry all kinds of stuff we ain't supposed to, and we get paid big money — and sometimes drugs. Oh yeah, we pop pills all the time too. That's how we stay awake."

Larry Lorne waded in. "That happened to my dad a couple years ago. He had a bad crash and the guys at head office threw him to the wolves. They told the papers he was unstable. My old man wasn't like that, and they knew it. But they were warned by their insurers, if they had one more funny crash with bald tires on their rigs, that'd be the end."

Vince nodded. "At our place, drivers were turning themselves in at the weigh stations. Had to beg the guy to call the inspectors. It was the only way to get these pricks to fix the damn trucks. Some of 'em had no brakes for chrissake."

Larry tossed his cigarette butt in the smouldering coffee can. "My old man said if you're not doing your maintenance, sooner or later there's gonna be a crash, and that's negligence. But if you can make it look like some dumb driver did something stupid, they can't raise your rates — that's an act of God."

Sean saw the parallel that Vince was trying to float. "So you're saying that being here doesn't work. That this is more of the same bullshit. Is that your point?"

"All I'm saying is that being here is a part of a larger game."

Sean wasn't having it. "No, you're saying this is bullshit."

"I didn't say that. What I'm saying is everything here ain't exactly the way it looks — word to the wise." Vince looked like he'd just scored the game winner in a beer league.

"If the counsellors hear you talking like this, you're toast."

Vince was now sure of his new invincibility. "Are you gonna do me the favour of rattin' me out?"

Sean shook his head. "You're a bigmouth; you'll do it yourself." He made a short circular wave with his right hand. "The next time I do that will be when you're on the way out the door. It'll be my way of saying I told you so!"

Tom didn't agree with Vince, but he thought Sean was being confrontational. Tom was going home on Wednesday, and as the senior guy in the house, he felt an obligation to try and reconcile the two combatants.

"Why do you care what this guy thinks?" he asked Sean.

"He can think and do whatever he wants. But I'm not gonna let him get away with saying this place is bullshit. Maybe the rest of the world is, but not here. Don't ruin this. If you don't like it here, be a man and say so."

Vince rose to the bait. He wouldn't have minded a little jostling. "If you wanna fix people, why don't you get yourself a mechanic's licence and set up shop?"

Sean didn't flinch when Vince jabbed a thumb into his chest. He grabbed Vince by his thick wrist and got right in his grill. "I don't need to be a mechanic to let the shit out of a windbag like you."

Czombo gave Sean a dirty look and took Vince by the elbow. "Let's get a coffee, buddy."

Larry was wary of asking Sean anything when he was in a temper. But his curiosity would not be denied. "Why did he make you so mad?"

Sean didn't know. But he didn't say so.

Chapter 24

Kaiser made a great show of setting the pot to steep under the cat-shaped tea cozy. In a place where tea was generally a single bag doused in tepid water and served in a chipped mug, this passed for elegance. As a final touch, Kaiser put out a box of the biscuits he kept for afternoon tea. He'd commandeered Doug's office for this meeting. Now he leaned back in the boss's chair and smiled at Channing Hart like a Dutch uncle. "So what did you make of my three questions?"

Hart was occupying the natural space that separates flattery from embarrassment. After all the dislocations he'd gone through since he woke up in jail, being treated decently made him wary. He could hear Prison Bob pronouncing the magic word: *shtum.* Was this a flat-footed apology for the savaging he'd taken from Reg? If it was, it didn't sweeten his mood any. What he saw when he looked at Kaiser was a pushy salesman thrusting his expensive ballpoint pen across the table.

He hoped to unsettle Kaiser by being rude. "Riddles."

Kaiser smiled, easily detecting the ploy, and asked playfully as he turned his head theatrically to the side. "Too scared to go there?"

An odd thing happened. For a second, Hart felt as if he were at home hearing his father come through the door. He was far away in the future, knowing how everything worked out and wondering about a moment so long ago when he was confused by something that, in hindsight, was painfully obvious. He blinked and the feeling vanished. But the taste lingered on the side of his tongue. He turned his attention once again to the three ancient questions. They hadn't changed. He looked up at Kaiser the way a dying kid in a hospital bed looks at a clown who has come to visit.

"I feel sad when I read them." He groaned. "What's the point? Why all this nonsense about choosing. There are no choices. There never were. I'm going to jail. I've lost everything. Beer is my master. I'm a drunk and that's never going to change. I don't even want it to. What I want is to be out from underneath all this crap. I would happily go to jail for the rest of my life if they'd let me drink there."

"Fair enough," said Kaiser. "But even so, answer the three questions."

Hart had thought about the questions a lot, and they floated through his mind briefly before he delivered his answers. *If I'm not for myself, who will be for me? But if I'm only for myself, what am I? And if I can't change this behaviour now, when will I?* He glared at Kaiser.

"I'm a monster. A selfish monster. They should put me on display to scare the kids. The only people willing to help me are the jerks who work in the treatment centre, and I don't want the life they're pushing at me. I don't care about other people because they always let me down, and nothing is ever going to change that."

Kaiser started pouring the tea. "Hmm … you finally tell the truth and you're still a liar. This is what I see. You live in your head. After you've had a couple of good stiff drinks, the line between reality and fantasy ceases to matter and all your bullshit starts to make perfect sense to you. You think about slapping the hell out of that boss of yours and, wonder of wonders, the booze makes you feel like you've actually done it. Of course, the next morning you look at the boss and you're full of fear, but that doesn't matter. You're hooked on a blend of sensation and fantasy. It's become the centre of your universe and it's all that matters to you. That's why you're whacked."

Hart looked like he was eleven years old.

"You don't have the nerve to ask for what you really need. So you pretend for a while, then you get mad at other people for letting you down, and finally, when you can't stand the way you feel for one minute longer, you numb the pain with alcohol. And here's the part you don't know yet: Everyone knows you're a butthead. Have you ever wondered what people say about you when you're not in the room?"

That jab got through. Hart's thoughts flashed to the big table at Clancy's the morning after the crash. Everyone tucking into the morning-after breakfast with all four newspapers spread out over the top of the Formica table. It was the ritual after any event of note. "Nope, and I don't want to know."

Kaiser sounded like a history teacher making sense of a battle fought long ago. "That whole cockamamie scheme worked as long as you had enough booze to dumb you down. But now you're going somewhere you can't drink. You have the prospect of five wonderful years to feel all your feelings straight up, in a place where you don't love anyone and no one loves you. Then it's back to the bottle and extinction. Are you ever going to tell someone who you really are?"

Hart had heard enough. "I really am beginning to hate you."

Kaiser showed him a crooked smile. "Well, it's a fair question. Hart, even if you did tell us the truth, it would still be a lie. You have this invulnerability thing going on. You're a law unto yourself. The rest of us are a distraction. Is the real you ever going to put up a fight? Are you going to take a stand and meet this addiction head-on or are you going to wuss out, do as you're told, and run out the clock? I know how I'm betting my money on this one."

All that was missing from the performance was Judge Sullivan's black sentencing cap. Kaiser picked up a Peek Freans biscuit and bit into it with finality. He'd said his piece and he was satisfied.

The two men sat in silence, sipping their tea. The quiet and civility were horrible for Hart. He had a vision of his new life, one ordered by cold water shaves and servings of brutal institutional tea. For the first time, he let himself feel the full horror of what lay before him. He really was going back to jail. And this time there would be no hope of escape. Five frightful years of feeling exactly the way he felt right this very moment. His gut tightened.

"Are you on the list to see Father Phil?"

"Right after I finish here."

———

Father Phil was trying to move the list along. He had a board meeting at 6:00 p.m. and he'd arrived forty-five minutes late, which, of course, meant he'd be right in the teeth of rush hour when he tried to make his escape. The temptation was to make up the time he'd lost by listening quickly. The first three clients had cooperated by not knowing why they'd signed up to see him.

While he waited for client four to arrive, he had a look at himself in the mirror. Phil was built like a fullback with a powerful torso and a huge head supported by thick neck muscles. He was the sort of fellow you would expect to see step out of a Viking longboat. He wore expensive tailored suits that the diocese got a deal on, but he betrayed his plebeian roots with his choice of footwear: black leather-topped cross-trainers. The other Franciscans always joked that this choice alone would keep him out of the Vatican.

His face was well fleshed and fair. He had pale blue-grey eyes and a full head of thin, wispy not-quite-grey hair. He could see where he had missed a spot shaving this morning. His eyesight was going — no doubt about that. Still, it was a good face. One he was proud of. The kind of face he would like to talk to if he was at odds with the world.

Hart was the fourth and final name on his list. As the younger man entered the office, Phil gave him a friendly welcome. "So, young man, what did you want to talk with me about?"

Hart's face radiated shame as he settled himself into the armchair. His look said judgment day, disgrace, and the gallows. Kaiser and Reg had prepared him for this moment. Phil looked at the young man with some alarm. *This guy's ready to jump out of his skin.*

Hart's sigh made the rest of his introduction unnecessary. "Do you know who I am?"

Phil tried to make himself comfortable in the hard-backed chair. "Yes, the other counsellors were talking about what happened to you. How are you holding up?"

Hart started to cry like a disgraced evangelist facing the camera for the last time. "I'm sorry … I can't … It's the not knowing…"

Phil pushed the box of Kleenex across the table. His gut told him dinner had dropped off the radar screen.

When God cast Phil in the role of confessor, He gave him a face that let him break down walls. Phil had a preternatural calm and acceptance in his eyes and the most compelling resonance in his deep, quiet voice. "Take all the time you need. I'm not going anywhere."

Hart was wrestling with the angels on both sides of his nature. Try as he might, he couldn't separate them or settle their quarrel. Each would gain mastery for a moment, but neither could keep it. Hart found himself first in one baggage train and then another, going back and forth between hope and despair like the spoils of war from an unlucky village continually changing hands — crushed between two armies mutually bent on annihilation.

He hated himself for grabbing a Kleenex and dabbing his eyes. The honk that inevitably followed diminished him even further in his own estimation. His resolve was betrayed so easily by his unconscious responses. *Tears are for fools and weaklings*, he thought. But all of that faltered when he looked into Phil's eyes. They took the sting out of it.

"I'm so tired of this … all of this pretending … it's too much." Hart's head went up and to the left. The tone of his voice changed from forlorn to engaged. Phil noticed the change but couldn't work out what it meant.

Hart relaxed and leaned back into his chair, letting his elbows rest on the arms. His index finger pointed toward heaven. "Do you know what it's like to have a parody of your life on public display? A work of fiction, something done by a horrible little shit who despises you? Everyone thinks they know who I am. Killing a mother and crippling a child — that's what I'm all about. That's the lens they see me through. Flip over those two cards and you can see exactly what kind of lowlife scumbag I was, I am, and I always will be. Nothing private anymore, nothing lovable, nothing noble, and certainly nothing worthwhile. All of it rationally explained by psychobabble and police double-talk. The fact that no one really knows what happened that night doesn't bother anyone. They have their man. Forgive me, I don't know whether I'm blithering or blathering anymore, and it hurts…" He took another Kleenex from the box and dabbed his eyes. A good honk set him right again. He looked at Phil for some kind of reaction. He got what he needed and continued.

"I'm trying to sell the whole world a lie. If I lose my balance, if I stray off the path, I'm doomed. My gut tells me something different. I'm a high-wire performer. I put one foot in front of the other, going where I don't want to go, trusting people I don't trust, with no way to turn around, and all the time knowing I'm about to lose my nerve…" There was a very long pause and a barely audible whisper: "Sometimes I want to fall." He raised his eyes warily, afraid that he'd offered offence. But then his head went down, and two angry fists took up their station on either side of it.

His frustration punched out the words: "I've done something no one will admit they're capable of doing. I have to hate myself more than they do because if I don't, then I'm not only a killer, but one who was shown compassion and still fucked it all up."

He punched the box of Kleenex across the table. Then he lifted his head and took on the character of his attorney. "Look sad and cry, make eye contact with the judge, show her how sorry you are for what you did, how you'd do anything to take it back. Show 'em you're sick at heart. Give 'em that haunted look." He made a face like a punch-drunk fighter.

A still sharper edge of anger was now present in his voice. He was pushing back with all his strength for the first time. "But sometimes I'm not sorry. It's not enough for these pricks that I have to lose all my money, my friends, my freedom and go to jail for who knows how long. No, I have to be a good sport about it too. I have to be grateful for this chance to lie my face off." Hart took a breath. He was shocked by what he'd said. He instinctively lowered his voice. "I'm afraid of prison. In jail, I lucked out and found a cellmate who protected me. He showed me how to act, taught me the fundamentals of a very dirty game. Without him, my head would already be in the noose. Not just him, but that bullshit lawyer of mine too." His passion caused him to lurch violently to the left, lifting two of the chair legs off the floor and landing them back down with a thud. "Your first night in jail, you learn there's no truth and there's no justice in the world for you anymore. My life hangs on one point: How well can I tell the lie they wrote for me?"

Hart felt alone and exposed, like a man who'd said the worst possible thing into a microphone he thought was turned off. The silence in the room screamed disapproval in his ear, but the truth that had fought its way through his defences to the surface would not be denied. He paused for a second, as if he were deciding whether it was safe to say what he really felt. He was still thinking about what to say next when, suddenly, new words came pouring out of him.

He spit his venom into the faces of his absent tormentors. He'd have beaten Levy or Summers with his fists if they'd been in the room. "I don't give a shit about that woman or her brat. Oh, I cry all right. But it's me and my loss that I'm crying about."

His defiance and rage illuminated his face. He looked alive and fully present for the first time. "All I want to do is get my hands on a bottle of rum and stay drunk in a hotel room until I die."

What satisfied as a feeling went nowhere as a thought. It spontaneously found a more promising direction. "I'd do anything to be able to shoot it out with the police. I get it now, how a person feels when they take on the cops. No explanations, no wallowing in your own shit — stand up like a man and blast away. How do you feel, Father, being in a room with an unrepentant murderer who would gladly do it all again if he could get his hands on a drink first?"

He looked Phil straight in the eye, expecting to see something awful. A look so contemptuous that it would confirm the loathsome opinion he had of himself and unite his past and present forever into a new marriage of horror and self-hatred.

Phil put his right hand gently on Hart's forearm. The touch communicated grace in a way that no word could. "You're mining the hard shale. It sounds like the world has you boxed in pretty good. You want to tell the truth, but you don't know what that is, and the people who should be looking out for you have got you deeply involved in a lie that you can't take back. Is that the centre of what I heard you say?"

Hart looked up at Phil the way a child looks at a conjuror. Someone had finally heard him. As bad as it was, at least now it was out there. "Yeah, that's the problem, all right."

Phil leaned back in his chair with a look of perfect peace on his face. His eyes said he was remembering something. His demeanour spoke of intimacy; it said, I feel comfortable with you and with what you said, and now we're going to share deeply on this subject in peace and privacy.

The storyteller emerged. "Do you know *The Strange Case of Dr. Jekyll and Mr. Hyde* by Robert Louis Stevenson?"

Hart was a little surprised by the direction Phil was taking. He was expecting the usual whirlwind of clarifying questions and off-the-top-of-the-head advice that people felt compelled to share with him. The same crap he'd been hearing for months. Against his better judgment, he felt himself being drawn in the direction Phil was taking.

"I saw the movie. But that was about split personality, wasn't it?"

Phil leaned back in his chair. "Would it surprise you to know that Stevenson was an alcoholic? That story was his way of trying to explain to people who don't drink what it felt like for him to be an alcoholic. That's why I love fiction — it lets you talk about your feelings." Phil smiled. "Do you remember the story? Dr. Jekyll was practically a saint. His patients were the poorest people in London, people who couldn't pay him for his services. And they had the most horrible and debilitating diseases — typhus, cholera, tuberculosis — all communicable. Jekyll was risking his life when he worked with them. In your more reflective moments, you have to ask yourself why he had no regard for his own safety." Phil stirred in his seat and found a more comfortable position.

"But at five p.m., he knocked off work and went down to the lab, where he poured himself a little drinky. Stevenson describes the creature he turns into as a drunken, violent, brutish whoremaster named Mr. Hyde. A young friend of mine read the book recently and suggested that nowadays we might characterize Mr. Hyde as serial killer. So my question to you, my friend, is this: Which one of these characters is the real Robert Louis Stevenson? Is it Jekyll, or is it Hyde?"

"I never thought about the story that way."

"Don't think about it, feel about it. Are you a Mr. Hyde when you drink?"

Hart shook his head vigorously. "The counsellors here think I am. They all keep prodding me. They say they want me to get real. They pick fights with me, try and make me mad. I don't see the point of it. What the hell is *real* anyway?"

Hart was squirming in his chair. He had so much anger pushing for the release. "Same thing with the cops! They say, 'It's time to man up and take the rap.' They say, 'You like to get lit up and you don't care what happens to other people when you do.' Well, I'm not like that. What they're saying is that Hyde is the real me, and Jekyll is the front. But that's not it. I don't hurt people even when I'm drunk. I never even punched someone in the face. I can't bring myself to do it."

Phil's voice was that of a friend. "But Channing, that woman is dead…"

Hart had truly thought about what had happened. He slowed down and enunciated each word. "I admit I like to get drunk. I feel the way I want to feel. No one can hurt me. I feel safe. I make sense to myself, and I understand how the world really works. I may look — and act — like Mr. Hyde when I'm pissed, but I'm not him. It's not in my nature to harm another person."

"Why does it have to be Jekyll or Hyde? Why can't it be both?"

To Hart, Phil's voice sounded as familiar as his own thoughts.

There was a hollow bump that came from the window. Hart sat up in his chair. A cardinal was sitting on the windowsill, warming himself with the air that was exiting the room. Hart ignored it. "I don't see how that helps."

"Well, you're saying that everyone wants you to admit to being Mr. Hyde. It makes it easier for them. You become a monster. You lose your humanity. You become a thing. It's easy to shoot a mad dog."

The bird tapped his beak on the glass several times and then flew off. Hart didn't notice. "Am I a monster? Do I deserve to go to jail for the rest of my life? Have you ever been to jail? Any idea I ever had about fairness or rehabilitation or even common decency vanished the first night. I was caged like an animal with men who really are monsters. The whole Hyde clan. I'm not like those guys. They like to hurt people. All night long, it was one bullshit story after another — their whole world was about crack cocaine and robbing people. Those guys are worse sober than I ever was when I was drinking." Hart paused and his face went blank remembering the broken voices, the odour of confinement. He shuddered.

Phil heard Hart's justification beginning to splinter. He pressed on, hoping for the truth. "Of course, all the courts care about is the body count. Does it matter why you did what you did or only that it happened?"

With his defences down, Hart took the full force of the blow for the first time. He'd always made sense of what happened in terms of a lucky escape. He'd plotted and schemed a thousand different ways to explain away what happened. The thought that he'd actually taken a human life was too much for him.

"I'm going to vomit." Hart grabbed the wastebasket and brought it close to his head.

Phil put his hand on the back of Hart's neck. He closed his eyes and offered a silent prayer.

"I'm having a heart attack."

Phil was calm and in no hurry now. "No, you're not. Breathe. That's it, in and out, in and out. Can you sit up for me? Not yet? Okay. Just breathe."

Hart heard himself whining like a child, powerless and afraid. "How did I ever get into this mess? This changes everything. Every good thing I ever did is bullshit. The only real stuff now is the bad stuff."

"Now you do sound crazy." Phil smiled and rubbed Hart's back as his head came out of the wastebasket.

Hart sat back in his chair and searched Phil's face. He was ready to hear the truth.

"I want you to take a breath and consider an idea with me. You have a bad case of black-and-white thinking. It's what the psychologists call a thinking error. You see yourself as being irredeemably evil or irreproachably good. You're neither. You're human. A mix of good and evil. Some days the mix is fifty-fifty, other days it's eighty-twenty. Do you follow? You'll never be entirely rid of either Dr. Jekyll or Mr. Hyde. All you can do is change the proportion. The point is you get to choose."

Phil had tiptoed around the confrontational impasse. What passed between the two men was only for them. Hart could listen for the first time without hearing PB or hating Levy or wanting to hurt Summers. It changed everything. "Let me tell you a story. I've been sober now for about thirty years. About five years ago, I was under a lot of stress. Things were not going well, and the tension was becoming unbearable. Then I caught a break. In the dead of winter, I got an invitation to go to a conference in Las Vegas. Hot dry weather — what more could you ask for in the middle of a wet, cold Toronto winter? So the next thing I know, I'm in Vegas with about two hundred other priests. We're having dinner in this huge restaurant, all of us dressed the same and talking a mile a minute. You can imagine what a task that was for the waitress."

Phil's face always lit up when he told this often-repeated tale. He got a glint in his eye and a mischievous smile crossed his lips. He was enjoying himself, certain he was on a winner. Hart felt a connection to this man. The wherefore and the why didn't matter. This was real, and real was rare.

"I ordered a soft drink, and when it came, I was thirsty and gulped it down. I was halfway through the glass when I realized it was a mixed drink. I felt like someone I loved had thrown a drink in my face. And I wanted to stop, really, but it was too late. Before I even put the glass down, I had a plan. Mr. Hyde was loose. I knew where to get the bottles and the girls and how to duck out of the rest of the conference. It was all there in my mind in an instant. It was like I'd never been sober."

Hart was surprised to hear this. "What did you do?"

Phil smiled and settled his shoulders into the back of his chair. There was no edge or con in his voice. "I took a couple deep breaths and took inventory of what I was feeling. I wanted another drink pretty badly. That surprised me. After all the time I'd been sober, I thought I was well beyond that. I looked around at the people I was with. They were all laughing and talking and having a wonderful time. That got me thinking.

"The priests I was with didn't know me very well because they were from all over North America. They wouldn't be shocked to see a Franciscan in his cups in Vegas. So I finished my meal — not with much appetite, but I got through it — and then I went back to my room and got on the phone with my AA sponsor. We had a long talk, and then I went to an AA meeting and told them what had happened and how I felt about it. They listened and shared a few stories of their own. They cared and they knew what they were talking about. Under an assault like that, my cravings withered."

Phil's face radiated calm and acceptance. He was comfortable talking about this. "So I thanked them and went about my business."

It can't be that simple.

"Channing, a big part of what's troubling you is that you're an alcoholic being judged by people who aren't." Hart was listening intently. This point of view was new and different. It was the lack of remorse. *How in the world did he ever get there, past all these feelings?*

"Try as they might, social drinkers can't get their heads around what happens to alcoholics when we drink. Our truth sounds like nonsense to them because our reaction to alcohol is so fundamentally different from theirs. But everyone makes the same mistake. We all automatically assume that our experience of alcohol is universal, but it's not. Everyone maps their experience of alcohol onto the other person's story, and when the stories don't match, they assume it's because the other fellow is lying.

"Normal drinkers can stop drinking whenever they want to, and they can't understand why you and I can't. That's why they have no sympathy for us. They think, he's a grown man, he should know better; he knew what could happen and he went ahead and did it anyway, and that's what makes him dangerous; he doesn't care who gets hurt as long as he can have his fun. Is that what you said earlier? Was that the criticism you heard?"

Hart was beginning to see, for the first time, where the real heat was coming from. The big shock for him had been the experience of being abandoned. He couldn't understand why everyone had automatically assumed he was guilty and run for cover. This insight helped, but it still wasn't enough.

"Yeah, they all said I was putting my pleasure ahead of the safety of others. But I don't even own a car. I have a licence, but I haven't driven in years. This ... this ... this is the shit part for me. I don't know if I did it!" He closed his eyes, pursed his lips, and blew out a pulse of air. A soundless whistle calling out in distress to God knows what or where. "One minute I was sitting in the booth at Clancy's having a good time, and the next thing I know I wake up in a jail cell. The cops found me unconscious in the front seat of the car and, through the miracle of cop logic, I'm guilty."

The shape of the puzzle changed as he spoke. What had been settled came unsettled, what had seemed certain no longer appeared to be so, and more than that, Hart was beginning to take Sean Miller's point. The agreed-upon version of events that underpinned the court deal was far from transparent.

Despite his new misgivings, he soldiered on, trying to work it out. "Well, maybe I am. But I could just as easily have accepted a ride from Connor." For a second, he was back into his imaginings, but he didn't stay there this time. The ray of hope offered by the *what-if* receded like a cloud passing overhead.

"But he has witnesses who say he was at the bar the whole time." It was so painful to go over it all again with no hope of relief. "Who knows?"

Phil had gone as far today as he was going to go. Hart needed some time to work all this new information out. "I can see, though, why this would be easier for you if you actually knew. If it were true, it would be painful, but at least there would be no more what-ifs. Did your lawyer tell you to plead guilty?"

Hart's face became unsettled, like he was hearing something for the first time. "Yes. He says we're playing the mercy angle. He says if we try and fight the science and we lose, I'm screwed. I suppose he's right. He must know his business. Boy, I could use Paul Drake and Perry Mason right about now."

Phil looked playful. "Let's talk about the Perry Mason stuff: a good what-if. What if, at the last moment, someone gets caught in a lie, and it all comes out that you were not the driver? Mason cracks somebody on the stand. The news shows all get wind of the story. You're set free." He waved his arms in triumph. "A well-deserved, dramatic happy ending."

His voice moderated as he let the story unwind. "So you go back to your old bar to have a celebratory drink, but everyone there is uncomfortable around you. You put it down to this: Maybe they still think you did it or were part of it somehow. In fairness, you were there, and you don't remember what happened. Maybe they don't think you're good enough to drink with them anymore. Maybe they're worried you're looking for some kind of revenge, or maybe they're ashamed of themselves, embarrassed at having judged and abandoned you." There was a pause as the faces at the big table first came into focus and then took on the character Phil was attributing to them. Clancy, Bill the Thrill, Connor, and Cap, all in their regular seats looking — what? Let down, hurt, and maybe just a little ashamed.

"Well, that's their loss," Phil went on, dismissively. "So the next day, you phone your boss to get your old job back and ... well, they had a restructuring last month and everything changed. They didn't think you were coming back, and they don't have anything for you right now."

Phil's energy flagged as he made a face. "You say okay and you ask for a letter of reference. They say okay, but when you get it, it's lukewarm. And when you really stop to think about it, you wonder why they wanted you to pick it up after four thirty. Are the people in the office embarrassed? It makes you wonder what your co-workers think.

"So you stop by the loading dock on the way out to see if anyone is still hanging around, and suddenly it's clear that you don't belong there either. The guys look at you like you're a stranger. In a perverse way, being innocent makes it worse. You're not being shunned for what you did, you're being shunned because of what you're going to do. The fact that you were there, passed out in that car — well, that's the smoking gun for them. You try and understand. You ask yourself if they think you're guilty and somehow found a way to wiggle out of this mess? But that's not it. They know something you don't — it's an instinct. You're dying, and you're going to take anyone who's too close down with you."

Hart's face was a study. A moving death mask. He'd left his body and embraced an idea. They danced together in his imagination. Nothing mattered but the thought. It was everywhere, always, and everything.

"Channing, how would you benefit if you were found not guilty? Could you go back to the same old bar and crow to the boys? Would you even want to see those guys again? Would you go back to the same job? Could you face the stares of the people you used to work with? Would you have nightmares about car crashes until you couldn't sleep without pills?"

For several minutes, Hart sat stone-faced. Mary's reaction in the apartment lobby made sense to him now. The way she had turned away from him. Her look of fear. She was afraid of him. Her of all people. Words couldn't begin to carry the weight of the feelings bearing down on him. After a few minutes, his vacant look gave way to an expression of fear and then shame. His face coloured ever so slightly, and he put his head down and looked to his left at the floor. It was a triple hit: head, heart, and gut. He blew a long, slow breath out and shook his head from side to side. A small tear formed in his eye but lacked the volume it needed to run down his face, so it stayed in place like a contact lens, forever changing his perspective.

"I can't drink anymore, can I?"

"Nope."

"Part of me still wants to."

"Yup."

"My whole life has been bullshit. I wasted the whole friggin' thing. I don't have a real friend in the world. No one loves me. That's what you're telling me, isn't it?"

"I love you. God loves you. And that's not nothing."

The two men sat in silence.

Chapter 25

John didn't see Peter again until later that afternoon. He'd spent an hour thinking about what had passed between them. It didn't add up. It was only half a story. John came away from his meditation with the feeling that he was being played with, motived to go on some lunatic crusade of Peter's choosing. He wasn't having that. He let fly as Peter made his way down the centre aisle to his place by the window.

"Peter, you didn't tell me the whole truth this morning. Something else happened. I could see it in your face. There was something you wanted to tell me, but then, in an instant, your face changed; I saw fear in your eyes. Why are you keeping secrets?"

Peter was keeping secrets, and until that very moment he thought he was doing it well. "What? Whatever do you mean? The whole truth has been spoken. I didn't leave anything out."

John knew he was lying. "You did it again! You're deliberately leaving something out. Your face went sour there, exactly as it did before, you're afraid…"

Peter was too flustered to think, he waved his hands in the air and looked for all the world like a toddler expressing heartfelt revulsion. "It's nothing. It was an aberration, a trick of the light."

John had him and he knew it. "Cut the crap. We both know what a trick of the light means. What did you see?"

Peter turned away from John like a wounded animal, unsure if he could continue the fight. He was apoplectic. Dark rings John had never seen before were visible under his eyes. "Very well, if you must know, when I looked away from the young couple, I saw a crocodile. A dirty beast. He didn't even have a proper tail. The fat, saucy bastard was leaning up against the black rail fence right at Madison and Bloor. He was wearing a double-breasted topcoat and smoking a cigar with a smug look on his face. He laughed at me and said, 'Sorry, pal, that ship has sailed, sunk, and settled on the bottom. Your days of romancing are over. Naff.'"

"That's it? That's all he said?"

That's all you're going to hear.

Chapter 26

Sean was daydreaming on his bunk while he waited for Hart to return from his session with Father Phil. He was thinking about Kaiser's three questions and Reg's admonitions about minding his own business. He was pretty sure he knew what Hart was going to do. He'd head straight to his bed, looking neither left nor right, and then turn his face to the wall with a groan — another hour of agony in the dentist's chair.

Why does he do that? He should be over at Clancy's beating the supreme piss out of that lying bag of shit, Connor.

He heard familiar footfalls and looked up to see Hart hanging up his coat. Sean slyly pulled a cigarette out of his pocket as his roommate passed. "How did it go?"

"Great..." Hart flung himself down on the bed.

Sean walked out of the room with the smoke in his mouth. He opened the fire door in the hallway that led to the stairs but didn't walk through. When it banged shut, Hart had the illusion of privacy. Sean stood outside their room and listened.

Hart kicked off his shoes and draped the blanket over his head. What a verdict. Five years of misery and then back to the bottle and extinction. He hated Kaiser for saying that. That was when the ground under his feet started to give way. Then Phil, hot on his heels, pulling apart all his daydreams about going back to his old life. He had counted on that. Without that he had nothing.

Sean walked silently back into the room and sat down on his bed. He reached across the space between the bunks and gave Hart a little nudge. Hart rolled over on his side, desperate to hide his vulnerability.

"So this is how you take care of you?"

"Please get out."

"Nope, not this time. You're going to do something about this, whether you like it or not. You understand me? You need to man up."

That was the wrong choice of words. Hart sat up in his bunk and flung his pillow at Sean. "I heard that one from the cops."

Sean wasn't deflected. "No, you idiot. The cop version is that you need to do something that's going to help them screw you. It's an invitation back to jail and the settled life. You need to go down there and settle up with Reg."

"Why? Do you want a new roommate? Go away — you're crazy!"

Sean had no idea where the words came from. He'd planned to say something, but not this. There were lots of words down there, all of them scrambling to get out. He had the oddest impression that someone else was talking. Someone who knew everything. "He's a big bag of wind! You're cowering in front of this guy like a kid. Kick his ass! What's he gonna do? Double up on your chores? Tell you off again in front of the guys? Throw you out? You stood there and let him humiliate you in front of everyone!"

Hart's nostrils started to flare and his mouth curled up on one side as he leapt out of bed. He looked ready to throw a punch.

Sean wasn't concerned. He'd been punched before and would be again. He almost had him where he wanted him. He dropped his arms to his side and invited a blow by thrusting his face right into Hart's line of sight. As Hart tried to turn away, Sean pivoted on his heels and followed him. "You're going to jail for something you didn't do. Why the hell are you worried about Reg? For the good of your soul, get down there and tell that son of a bitch where to get off. Close the deal."

There should have been an audible click. That satisfying sound that's heard when a safe cracker hits the final number after hours of trial and error. Or a visible change of some kind. Perhaps a light shining through the window and illuminating Hart in profile, because the fear that had always moved him to the left, now, for the first time, morphed into action and thrust him to the right. Doubt vanished. He heard Phil and Reg and Kaiser and Prison Bob all blathering away in the back of his mind, like a choir gossiping before they sang. They'd had their say. They didn't have the answer. There was a new song to be sung. Hart got to his feet, wiped his face with a cold washcloth, and checked his appearance in the mirror. He turned on his heel and left the room without saying a word.

Sean had a bad moment. He'd expected an argument. When Hart left the room, he was suddenly seized with feelings of doubt and fear. *Is that what a guy looks like the moment before he kills someone? Why did I say that? Where the hell did those words come from?*

Hart descended the stairs four at a time and came to rest one level below where Sean was dithering. Hart briefly considered kicking the office door open but thought better of it. He looked through the window and saw someone he didn't recognize sitting with Reg. The two men were smiling and obviously enjoying each other's company. Not the set-up he'd had in mind for this gunfight as he'd made his way down the big oaken stairway.

Insight was harnessing the anger in Hart's soul, using it to process pig iron into burnished steel. Looking through the office window, all he could see was one fallible man speaking with another. Without the distraction of words and feeling and misremembered history, all that was left were the faces. They wouldn't have looked out of place holding a lantern in Rembrandt's *The Night Watch*.

There he stood at the door. His heart hammering in his chest. Blood pounded in his ears. But then an eerie calm and sense of certitude overtook him. Time slowed down and silence overtook him the way white noise overtakes the weary sleep seeker. He found himself once again trapped by Reg in the classroom. No sound this time. Only the eyes. Reg had egged him on. He was an actor on a stage, reading words that someone else wrote, pretending to feel something. That made two of them — a matched pair.

It all came clear to him. He heard a growl of thunder and, looking skyward, imagined a thundercloud as it rose. He marvelled at its beauty and purpose. He could feel it. In his own chest. Whirling through his ears and nose and lungs. He was the storm.

He grabbed his phone card and picked up the payphone that hung on the wall right outside the office. He rang Clancy's Tavern. Clancy, the barman picked up.

"Clancy, it's Hart."

The old publican wasn't sure what to say. "How you doing, buddy?"

"I'm okay. Listen, is Connor there?"

There was a pause. "Yeah, he is. Are you sure you want to talk to him?"

Hart's voice left no doubt. "Put that bag of shit on the line."

Clancy shook his head as he left the phone dangling on its cord. Hart heard him say, "This should be entertaining."

Then he could hear the message being relayed, muttering voices, and furniture moving. Hart imagined Connor gulping his drink to fortify himself before he took the call. Maybe he gave Clancy a hand signal telling him to pour another one, a strong one this time. Big eyes were on him, and he knew it. Hart could see Clancy giving him a little push behind the bar and toward the phone while Bill and Cap exchanged worried looks. They all knew how big this was.

While he was waiting, Hart did the math. Connor would be half in the bag. Worse, he'd be caught unawares. His heart would be racing. Hart strained to hear the timbre of his voice. That's where the truth would be, not in the words.

He heard someone pick up the phone, but they didn't say anything, they were listening. Hesitation invited aggression, and Hart bloodied Connor with his opening salvo: "Listen, you piece of shit. You're going to come clean about what happened!"

People in the living room heard Hart's loud, angry words.

"Who is this?" said a voice desperate to hide its fear.

"It's Hart, you son of a bitch. I didn't realize your lies sent more than one man to prison. You gotta couple of us on the go?"

Connor's brain was spinning. He was drenched in flop sweat. Was this being taped? Had Hart gotten the cops on his side? Connor could see the long, earnest faces of the detectives as they strained to hear every sound from their earphones. Running his words through an oscilloscope. He imagined himself sitting helplessly at the defence table, listening as this tape was played in court. The next words out of his mouth would save him or damn him. He was so upset, he couldn't think. "I-I don't know what you're talking about."

Words and purpose found congruence. "Well, here's the thing. I know you're guilty, and I'm gonna make you pay. Every time you walk somewhere alone, you won't be. I'll be there. A possibility waiting to become a fact."

Hart slammed down the phone. He stood with his back to the wall and slid down to a sitting position on the floor. "Shit, that felt good."

At the bar, Connor stood with the phone still in his hand like the conversation was ongoing. The crack of the receiver being slammed down had genuinely terrified him. He was reeling. His gut told him he'd blown his whole life. *Why did I answer the phone?* Everyone at the table was staring at him. He tried to remember what he'd told them. What was he going to say now? He'd been cleared; everyone knew that. He'd been cleared. They couldn't take that back. He felt a sick, cold fear run over him like a freight train. He turned for a second to face the wall and thought about pretending to tell Hart off. But the words wouldn't come.

At Punanai, Hart rounded the corner to the now open office door and plunked himself down on the chair opposite the desk where Reg, now alone, was writing.

"I just phoned up the guy who got me into this mess."

Reg was a little surprised but otherwise delighted to be back on speaking terms with Mr. Hart so soon. He'd been expecting at least a week of silence for his sins. "That needs a word of explanation. I thought *you* got yourself into this mess."

Hart shook his head. He looked like a man who was in possession of letters and tapes that could send the prime minister to prison. "No. It was Connor, the bastard who lied to the cops. I called him at the bar. He's guilty, and now I can prove it!"

Reg smelled real trouble coming. "Take a breath. You're over the top here. Why did you phone him?"

Hart was still on a high. "The bastard lied to the cops about me and I'm not going to let him get away with it."

Reg was very afraid for Hart. Maybe the young man didn't realize what he'd done. "Channing, you could make your situation a lot worse making calls like that. How did the call prove he was guilty? Did he confess?"

The feel-good chemicals wouldn't leave Hart alone. "No, of course not. But I could hear it in his voice. He was scared. I told him I was onto him and that I was going to get him."

"Channing, did you threaten him?"

Hart looked at Reg like he was an idiot. *How can this guy be so slow?* "No, I told him I'd be on his mind whenever he was alone or in a dark place, and that one day I would stop being a possibility and then I would get even."

Reg was starting to see the outline of what had occurred. At least he thought he did. "If he calls the cops, this could be bad for you."

Hart was way out in front of this one. "He isn't going to call the cops. He's got guilty secrets."

Reg had never seen Hart so animated, and though he liked it, he was a cautious man at heart. "Channing, this doesn't change anything. You've already pled guilty, and the Crown and your lawyer have agreed to a sentence. Even if this guy goes to the media and confesses, which he won't, you're still on the hook."

Nothing could dampen Hart's joy. "Well, maybe you're right about that, but let me tell you this: Goddamn it, it felt good to call that son of a bitch a son of a bitch." Without missing a beat, and with a smile on his face, he moved on to his next task. "And while we're on the subject, I gotta say I didn't appreciate the talk we had the other day. Who the hell do you think you are, talking to me that way? I treat you with respect. Why don't you treat me the same way?"

Reg found the confidence with which Hart delivered the line unnerving. But long practice had given him the gift of grace under this kind of onslaught. "I do treat you with respect, Channing. I tell you the truth."

"Well, I didn't like it."

"Nobody likes the truth." The right thing to say finally occurred to Reg. "Are you going to be able to calm down? Or are you going to go on a rampage and tell off everyone who has ever made you mad?"

Hart's look said that he might very well do that.

Reg wondered for a second if Hart was high. That would explain all these new behaviours. "Channing, you're in treatment. You're not the only guy here. If you can't settle down and behave yourself, I have to call the cops. I'm responsible not only for you but for everyone else in the house too."

Hart looked pained at the suggestion. He made a face and shook his head. "Don't worry, I'll obey all your stupid rules. But let me tell you something. I'm not taking shit from anybody anymore." With that, Hart slumped back in his chair with a big smile on his face.

Reg looked at his watch. "Okay, so let's make a deal, man to man. I have to ring the dinner bell in an hour. Go on down to the coffee shop and savour the moment. Try and walk off some of this energy. I'm not sorry that I told you off in front of the guys. That was long overdue. I was hoping that something like this would happen. It doesn't always. Sometimes guys hate me forever when I do that. But you have to admit, there's been a change for the better in you."

Hart was dumbfounded by the arrogance of this little man. "Oh, so now you're taking credit for this?"

Reg smiled and slowly got to his feet. "No, I'm not even sure what's happened to you. But I do know one thing, my friend. I like what I see!"

Hart bounded down Madison Avenue like a colt prancing in the walking ring before a maiden race. He was still elated. His muscles and joints felt warm and powerful. Nothing hurt and nothing held any tension. He was a big fluid animal, rolling effortlessly over the land. What a glorious feeling! One he hoped would never end. Where was that nosy old lady now? The one who had given him the evil eye and spat when she recognized him. She lived in one of these houses. He'd show her what the evil eye looked like and then laugh in her face for good measure.

This was better than any high he ever had in a bar. He stopped outside Tim Hortons, but he couldn't bring himself to go in. He headed for the park instead and sat on a bench. The cool, dry air was cleaning his lungs with each breath. The squirrels were fat and sleek and running around to stay warm. The sun was going down without putting on much of a show, but for Hart it was glorious. The failing light looked like the coming of peace to him. Could this even be the same body he woke up in this morning?

He looked at his watch, and as he got to his feet, he heard trotting footfalls behind him. It was Sean. "What happened to you? You disappeared."

Hart's feelings of power and wellbeing were beginning to give way to a profound relaxation and sleepiness. "I don't know what's happening with me, but I like it. I phoned that asshole Connor and told him I was going to kill him, and then I told Reg off, and now I'm going to have dinner and go to a meeting. I haven't felt this good in years."

Sean's pet viper had killed the neighbour's cow. *I didn't think he had that in him! That's what I would've done.*

Hart spread his arms wide and spun around slowly in a circle. "I'm on such a high right now, and I haven't taken a thing all day. If this is sobriety, I could get used to it. Reg apologized to me. How sweet is that?"

Sean looked at his watch. "We're up against the clock here."

"Then let's trot!" said Hart, setting a lively pace.

Sean ran like a smoker and had a hard time keeping up. He was just able to say, through frantic gulps of air, "Okay, but after dinner you're telling me the whole story!"

Hart stopped and jogged on the spot while he waited for Sean to catch up. "Nothing would make me happier than to relive the entire experience."

———

Reg was counting noses in the dining room. The guys were all talking at the same time at their tables. Reg was stalling. He knew who was missing, and he wanted to give them a minute's grace. Ordinarily, two fellows coming in late for dinner would earn themselves a very public put-down, especially since it had also happened at lunch, but Reg was so damned relieved to see them back that he gave them a pass. Elation and short-term sobriety are dangerous bedfellows. He called the room to order.

"All right, fellas. You're going out for a meeting this evening. You can leave as early as seven p.m., and you have to be out of the house by seven thirty at the latest. I have some girls coming over."

That line always got a laugh.

"Now remember, you need to take the new guys to the meeting, and even more importantly, you need to bring them back. Got it? So for you new guys, you have to go to the meeting with someone and come back from the meeting with that same person. I'll be at the front door, waiting to check you in when you get back. Any questions? Good. Now will you please join me in saying grace?"

Chapter 27

Hart wanted to talk to Sean about what he'd done, but his friend wisely silenced him. "Not here," he said, looking across the table at Vince and Czombo. They were inseparable now. They would make trouble if they got something to work with.

Sean didn't like Czombo or the fact that he could never look anyone directly in the eye. Czombo's eyes were always all over other people's faces, looking for little clues about them that he could exploit, but he never sought a moment of connection. He had the unsympathetic face of a prison guard — someone forced to watch a world he despised for ten hours a day on a flickering television screen.

At first, Sean put Czombo down as a fugitive from the mental health system. Another derelict taking up space in a treatment centre simply because he had nowhere else to go. He read his expression as a combination of fatalism and boredom. Why wouldn't a guy who had no intention of getting sober tune out people talking about recovery?

But that cut both ways. Sean had been perfectly content to ignore Czombo until he noticed Czombo watching Larry Lorne. Sometimes it was like the rest of them weren't even there. Sometimes there were little exchanges between Czombo and Larry. Sean kept telling himself to mind his own business, but at the root of his psyche he knew that what he was seeing was wrong, and maybe even dangerous.

Czombo was a welcome distraction for Sean. Another puzzle to be solved. Like Connor and Hart, Czombo was someone who had to be dealt with before he could turn his attention back to his own problems. Larry Lorne and Czombo made no sense together. Sean itched to know what the connection was. They were up to something, and they were up to it on his turf.

———

After they finished a delicious dinner, one that featured Sylvester's famous pork chops with secret sauce and rice, Hart and Sean headed out to the park, where they could talk without the other clients butting in. The air was cool and fresh, but the park bench was moist from the mist in the air. Sean picked up a newspaper that was lying on the grass and used it to wipe the bench. It came away with a dark streak of city grime. He tossed the paper in the garbage and they took their seats.

Sean was struggling with the new Hart. The old one was lovable but lame, and the new version was trouble writ large, too preoccupied to notice his hair was standing on end or that freezing drizzle was starting to fall and he needed to button up his coat. Hart's focus was definitely elsewhere.

Hart was still on a high. "I put the fear of God into him. Oh, it felt so good. I almost never do that. I'm always afraid that if I lose my temper, I'll go crazy and kill someone."

Sean was once again on firm ground. "You got the size, but you lack the inclination. You have no idea what kind of mess you've made for yourself do you?"

Hart was still working on the rewrite of his life script — the one where he didn't go to jail. "You know what Connor's doing, right? Freaking out. He's feeling the way I did when I came to in that cell."

That's a stretch.

Sean tried to push him back on side. "I've seen a lot of alcoholics get bad news in a bar," he said. "The thing he's doing is drinking. He's replaying the tape in his head over and over and getting angrier and angrier about it. This is a power drinking occasion. Where's Clancy's?"

"In the mall at Islington and Bloor, near where I used to work. This is so great! I've never felt this way before. Things are really going to be different from now on."

Hopeless, head right up the ass.

"What meeting are you going to tonight?" asked Sean, seeming to have moved on.

"The AA meeting down the street. You?"

"The CA meeting." Sean looked at his watch. "We need to be getting back."

They got off the bench and started to walk, their coffees in their hands. Sean was keeping his thoughts to himself. Hart kept working variations on the theme that now his troubles were over. In the high of the moment, his better judgment was overwhelmed by fantasies of a long overdue rescue. Sean let him talk. His thoughts were taking a darker turn.

On his way past the front desk, he popped his head into the office. "Reg, have you got a map of the TTC?" There was a stack of them on the shelf. The guys were always consulting them before they left for the more remote and exotic meetings.

Sean took the subway map and laid it out on the coffee table. A plan was taking shape. He figured he could disappear for ninety minutes this time of day without getting caught. *Lucky Clancy's is on a subway route.* He wasn't sure what he was going to do when he got there, but he needed to take the measure of this Connor guy.

He grabbed a bag of garbage and slipped out the side door to where the bins were lined up. He stood still for a minute, looking around to see if anyone was watching him. He slid over the top of the brown wooden fence and walked down the neighbour's driveway, which was wonderfully concealed first by the fence and then by the hedge. He was out with no one's eyes on him. He pulled his hoodie up over his head and walked north on Madison. He deliberately walked with a limp so that someone seeing him from behind would not recognize him. He didn't want to use the nearest subway station at Spadina because the other guys were always hanging around there, drinking coffee and using the payphone. He ducked into the Dupont TTC station, and twenty minutes later he was standing outside Clancy's Tavern.

The sun had been down for quite a while, which made sneaking around a whole lot easier. His hoodie helped too. He helped himself to a *Real Estate News* from the box on the sidewalk and went inside the tavern, where he bought a cup of coffee from Clancy.

He looked around the dark and dingy room. It didn't look like the home away from home that Hart had described. They had a menu on the wall, but the room smelled like stale cooking oil and disinfectant. This was a bar.

"Cold out there," he offered as he paid for his coffee. This was his first time in a bar since he got sober, and it felt like he was deep in enemy territory. He chose an empty table three down from the big booth where some bad boys were talking loudly. He could see only half of the booth from his vantage point, but he didn't want to move closer and risk being noticed.

Sean sipped his coffee and pretended to look at the rental ads. Why not? He'd be needing a place in a week's time. The conversation at the big table was all about ego and hurt feelings, even though the topic was hockey. Sean was listening intently for a name while he watched the guys in the booth.

"Those clowns are figure skaters — no heart, no balls."

"The biggest mistake they ever made was trading Randy Carlyle."

"Connor, if you got no goalie, you got no chance."

There it was. The magic name. Sean glanced over and his eyes settled on the fattest guy, who was also the drunkest and loudest. His gut told him this was Connor. And so did the haunted look on the guy's face; he looked like something serious was eating at him. Sean's knuckles showed white around the dark coffee cup in his hand. Maybe Hart had done the right thing by confronting this douche when he was half in the bag. Maybe Hart knew how he'd react. This boy was getting shit-faced and sloppy. If he had any sense, he'd be at home or talking with his lawyer. This was neither the time nor the place to drink too much. This was a time to get sober and make sure the trail that led back to you was cold. Connor hadn't done that, and that told Sean what he'd come here to find out. This guy was a loose cannon, and the deck was heaving in a gale-force wind.

After observing his quarry for several minutes, Sean lost his fear of the man. Connor was big, but he was more fat and hot air than muscle. His voice had an annoyed, self-righteous anger no matter what the subject was. He hadn't been anywhere but a bar stool in quite a while.

Connor got to his feet and gave himself a mighty tucking in. He was so big that when he leaned to the left to tuck in one side of his pants, his movements unstuck the other side. It gave him a comical appearance. When he finished his protracted self-grooming, Connor headed off for the gents.

Sean pushed away his now empty coffee cup, gathered up his stuff, took a cigarette out of his pack, and put it in his mouth. It was the international signal for *I'm going for a smoke.* When he got into the hallway, he looked around to see if anyone had followed him out. They hadn't.

He followed Connor into the men's room. They were alone. Sean chose a urinal a respectful distance away and pretended to relieve himself as he tried to make up his mind about what to do. Connor, like all men, pretended the other guy wasn't there.

Should I do this or not?

Connor finished his business and was back to the lopsided ritual of tucking in his shirt. His beer gut looked like an enormous tongue peeking out from under a tent. Being drunk and wobbly did nothing to improve the look of the man. Connor was set up perfectly for what Sean had in mind.

You fat shit — you ruined his life and now you get yours.

As the big man turned to walk out, Sean closed the distance between them silently and tripped Connor with his right foot as he violently directed his head into the wall. There was a horrible thud. Connor was so taken by surprise that he didn't even tense up. Sean had expected that he would, and as a result, Connor hit the wall with far more force than Sean had intended. The impact opened a long crease on Connor's forehead.

Shit ... too hard.

Connor was stunned by the blow and lost consciousness a second later, just as Sean grabbed him by the scruff of the neck and eased his bulk to the floor. Connor was still breathing. Sean pulled his shirt up over his enormous girth to stage him in the most unflattering light possible. Whoever came in next would be set up perfectly to connect the dots in a way that would diminish Connor from a person to be feared to a drunken clown.

He went to the sink and got a handful of soap that he mixed with water and then threw onto the floor. It made the floor as slippery as oil. He made a quick survey of his work, then pulled his hoodie over his head and vanished into the night.

He double-timed it back to the subway. As he lengthened his stride, he gave way to a moment of fear. *I hope I didn't kill that prick.* Going back wasn't an option. He sucked in his doubt and did his best to avoid the cameras at the entrance to the TTC.

He got off the subway at Dupont and walked the long block down to Spadina and Bloor. He waited at the corner until some of the guys from the house showed up, and then he acted the fool with them for a couple minutes. As they headed back to the centre, he pointed to the public phone. He had his hoodie up, just in case. He dialled the police. He sounded as drunk as he could.

"There's a big guy named Connor drinking his face off every night at Clancy's Tavern at Bloor and Islington. Then he jumps in his car and drives home like a madman. He's going to kill another old lady some night if you lazy bastards don't get up off your asses. No, I don't want to give you my name. This guy is dangerous, and if he knew I was telling you this, he'd punch the supreme piss out of me. That's right, he threatened all of us with death and damnation if we talked. If you don't believe me, send a car to the parking lot and see who comes crawling out of there at closing time. Do you think you can handle all that, Kojak?"

Sean hung up the phone with a sense of considerable satisfaction. *That should keep Connor on the defensive for a week or two. Let's see if all that pain and embarrassment doesn't get Hart off his mind.*

He jogged up Madison until he caught up with some other guests returning to the centre. Reg was never going to notice that one more bunny had joined the hop. It had taken him less than an hour to do the round trip.

Chapter 28

Reg woke the house at 7:00 a.m. The weak winter morning sunlight was beginning to show more grey than pink on the horizon. It was easy to roll over and go back to sleep at this time of year. Doug's predecessor and mentor, the first manager of Punanai Centre, was the storied Major, long since gone to the grave, who forever set the tone for waking the guests by walking through the house beating a metal garbage pail with a stick. It took negotiation right off the table. Kaiser, when the evil spirit was upon him, would wake the men by walking into their rooms, seemingly confused, asking if they had seen his mother. Reg was more of a humanist.

He knocked politely on the door with one of his canes and asked if they were awake. Then he flipped on the light so they wouldn't trip when they got out of bed. Hart was in a very deep sleep when Reg knocked.

"You up?"

Sean had spent a conscience-stricken night and was wide awake, waiting for his turn in the shower. "Yeah, we're good."

Hart stuck his nose out from under his blanket, not sure for the moment what annoyed him more: the light or Reg. The warm bed counselled against leaving its protection.

"Do you want that off for a couple minutes?" asked Sean after Reg left.

"Thanks, that would be great."

Sean slid out of bed. As he flicked off the light, he saw someone come out of the shower down the hall and he made his move.

Hart was alone in the dark. He didn't want to get up. A part of it was depression, but mostly it was the fear that today was going to bring him more sorrow and disappointment. He'd crashed from his high when they'd called lights-out. As he lay in bed trying to fall asleep, his feeling of power and control started to subside, and he began to imagine what the future was really going to look like for him. He wasn't thinking about a happy ending this morning.

Imagining something that isn't true is hard work. It was like the job he had at Woolnot's. Not always, but sometimes he hated the place, and sometimes he even hated everybody there. And when he felt that way, it made him sad to think about it on his own time. So he invented a rule for himself. He wouldn't think about work unless he was on the clock.

He'd done the same thing with prison. To worry about prison was to already be in prison, so he put it out of his mind. His sentencing was coming up, and he knew what that meant. Lots of the guys at Punanai complained about the rules — they had no idea. Jail was a rule factory. The guards made rules, the prisoners made rules, and every new prohibition dined on your sense of self-worth. The whole morass of contradictory commandments was dehumanizing, psychotic, and mandatory. The only way to feel fully alive was to know that you were breaking the rules and getting away with it.

Was there ever going to be a day when he was back in charge? That didn't feel like a possibility this morning. He rolled over on his side, hoping to die while he catnapped.

Sean burst into the room fresh from his shower and finished dressing. He turned on the lights again and gave the bed a kick. "Up and at 'em, sunshine! I'm going for a smoke. Don't you dare go back to sleep."

Why not? What are they going to do, shoot me? This could be my last chance to sleep in for the next five years.

He sat up and pretended to be stirring until Sean left the room. Then he got to his feet, closed the door, turned out the light, and got back into bed. He rolled over on his side and pulled the blankets up over his head.

I don't care what anyone wants anymore. Beat me if you want to — the pain will help pass the time.

Reg was serving breakfast when he noticed that Hart was missing. This was three meals in a row. When the last plate was delivered, he sat down in the courtyard to see if Hart was going to show up to do his chore. When he didn't, Reg took the elevator to the third floor. He wanted to catch Hart in bed, so he stealthily pushed the door open. There he was. Not the world beater he'd been twelve hours before.

Reg walked over to the venetian blinds and raised them to allow a flood of light into the room. Hart was awake but he didn't stir.

Reg sat down on Sean's bunk and gently poked Hart with his cane. Hart wasn't happy being found out this way, especially by Reg.

"While you're up here feeling sorry for yourself and blaming the world for your troubles, your partner is downstairs, doing the dishes by himself, trying to cover for you."

With that, he rose painfully on his canes and left.

Chapter 29

It took a long time for Peter to calm himself. The two ghosts sat in silence in the now empty chapel. Everyone else had gone home, but then they had homes to go to. The sun was going down when he finally settled. There he sat in the pew, shaking and looking blankly at the stained-glass window of St. George slaying the dragon. Maybe he could turn his hand to crocodiles. His breaths sounded like the exhalations of an angry bull. After a while, he began to rock back and forth slowly like he was coming down from some fearful trauma, trying to soothe himself as best he could.

John was terrified. Crocodiles in suits and doe-eyed girls — it could only mean one thing. John had seen ghosts get angry and frustrated or so insane that they forgot who and what they were. Yes, ghosts could and sometimes did exert themselves to act in the human world. But at a ruinous cost. How useful was it in the grander scheme of things to push over a potted plant or send a bookcase crashing down a flight of stairs? That kind of excess landed one in the poltergeist camp all too soon.

Those white patches that kept coming and going on Peter's forehead were a vital part of this. But John couldn't work out how. He wasn't even sure if should tell Peter. Is Peter messing with the material world, up to something behind my back? If he is, that's bad news writ large. What's he up to and why won't the great blabbermouth tell me about it?

The fat spectre sat motionless, reeking of despair. He was changing right before John's eyes, doing things that no ghost had ever done before. What were his dry tears all about and did they have something in common with the white patches on his skin? They looked like frost. But that was impossible. Ghosts were as dry as gunpowder!

John had to move. He got to his feet and walked the length of the pew several times, pretending to be a high-wire artist. Peter ignored him. Is this how things are going to end for me? In a hissy fit? Is some theoretical abstraction going to send me over the edge into a tantrum and, from there, into the waiting arms of whatever the light turns out to be? Is there a frost patch on my ass that I can't see?

Chapter 30

Reg was leading the census meeting. He'd been the eyes and ears of the franchise since 7:00 a.m. yesterday. He needed a shave and a good night's sleep. The perfectly appointed suit he'd put on yesterday morning had sagged; his bow tie was in his shaving kit, ready for the trip home, and the shine on his shoes had dulled only slightly more than the fire in his eyes. When Reg finished this briefing, he could go home and have a nap and then play his music and fool around with his manuscript. But he wasn't there yet, one more meeting before he could say après moi le deluge.

When he'd settled himself and arranged his notes at the table, he was surprised to see Paul writing in the official treatment record. It should have been Kaiser getting ready to begin his twenty-four-hour shift. He had to ask: "Where is God's anointed this morning?"

"Sprained his ankle on a stumbling block," said Paul with more than a hint of disbelief. "He's on the way in."

More like on the way out, thought Reg uncharitably.

Reg turned to Paul and smiled. "You have big shoes to fill this morning, my friend. Do you feel equal to the task?"

Paul's eyelids fluttered. "I'm no Emmett Kelly, if that's what you mean…"

Mike, who had a lot of work to do, was annoyed and wanted them to get on with it. "Who the hell is Emmett Kelly?"

Reg loved Paul's very dry humour, and he especially loved the small shy smile he reserved for occasions when he'd truly put one over on the world. Doug wasn't listening to the chit-chat at the table. He was elsewhere in the cosmos. Reg turned to the business at hand. "We had a good night last night. The guys were well behaved and they got out to their meetings on time." He stopped and waited with a theatrical flair, daring someone to spot the contradiction.

Paul piped up. "It says here that Vince got drunk."

Reg didn't want to stop his monkeyshines, which he was, apparently, sharing only with Paul. "I didn't say they all came back from the meeting now, did I?"

Doug landed with both boots in the middle of the conversation. "Vince was mulling things over with a mickey at the AA meeting last night. One of our alumni phoned me at home. We had a chat and he agreed not to return to the house intoxicated. He promised me he was going to take a cab home and come by this afternoon to collect his belongings and discuss the matter. Which may or may not happen. He was happy to go. He didn't like it here."

The door opened and Kaiser walked in with a cane and a top hat. He had an improbably large tension bandage on his right ankle that screamed *this is a scam*. He looked for all the world like he'd attended a costume party the night before dressed as the banker of Monopoly fame and hadn't been home yet. He made quite a show of hanging up his coat, removing his ridiculous hat, and limping painfully across the room toward the table.

Paul leaned into Reg's personal space and whispered, "Is that limp an unlicensed parody of your intellectual property?"

Reg looked his rival up and down. "It looks like fair use to me."

Doug had to say something. He wasn't going to let Kaiser get away with whatever all this nonsense was about to become. He keyed on the hat. "Well, look who's here at last, our own dear Kaiser, looking like a slightly dishevelled version of a super villain. You must tell me sometime exactly what it is that you get up to on your time off."

Paul slid the treatment record across the table toward Kaiser as the large man took his seat. Kaiser looked first at the treatment record and then at Doug, prepared as always to give as good as he got. "I appreciate your concern," he said with a smile. "It takes the sting out of my injury."

Mike chimed in. "All right, children. We're all here now; time to quit the clowning."

Reg was fascinated by the look on Kaiser's face. He'd never seen him this way before. There was a heightened awareness of possibility about the man, if such a thing could actually exist. No, that wasn't it. Perhaps the look suited a blackmailer whose first cheque had cleared. Yes, that was better but still not right.

Reg gave way to a smile. This was really one of those moments. He was tired and ready for home, but he was happy. He and Paul were making high-level jokes that went way over the boss's pointy head, and now here was Kaiser, step-dancing like a puffin.

Can't you smell the change in the air? The turning of the season? Oh, little flightless bird in your tuxedo and top hat. With your silly bandage and vaudeville cane. Don't you know that you have been supplanted? Has no one told you about Reg the torpedo?

Paul, too, was struggling to contain a self-satisfied smile. He loved the cut and thrust of census meetings. He got to his feet slowly, so as not to attract undue attention to himself, and made his way over to the coat rack. He picked up Kaiser's top hat and fingered the brim with a highly critical and unhappy look on his face. It was well made. The black felt had held it look and shape for quite some time now, if Paul was correct about its age. He placed the hat over his chest, took up Kaiser's walking stick in his right hand, and proceeded to do a little soft-shoe. He was actually quite good at it. Only Reg saw him; he thought this was the most wonderful thing he'd ever seen. As Paul returned to the table, he offered an opinion as if nothing had happened. "I think the house will improve now that

Vince is gone. He was bringing everybody down. It was hard to teach with him smirking." The word *smirking* almost caused Reg to laugh out loud.

Kaiser spoke up, oblivious to the fun going on at his expense. "Having him gone will help. But I'm expecting this place to really start percolating. I gave our Mr. Hart a good going-over and he responded brilliantly. He was out of the dumps and full of hope when I left, and I expect that from here on in he's going to be a good influence on the rest of the guys."

Paul couldn't help himself — the shy little smile was back. "So that was all your brilliant work?"

Kaiser didn't even break stride. "I knew I was the only one who could help. Needed a special touch. A lot of repressed anger. I gave him a new way of understanding himself."

Doug picked up on Paul's comment with his own wry smile. "But does he know that he has you, and you alone, to thank for all this?"

Kaiser opened his palms and cocked his head to the left. He did sociopath with the same panache that the Toronto Symphony Orchestra brought to Gershwin. His was a perfect parody: all smile and unconscious bluster. "Doug, I'm like the Lone Ranger. By the time the little girl has finished her speech and curtsied, I'm gone. She has no one to hand the flowers to."

Paul turned to Reg and asked, "What should we write in the book?"

"Doesn't know who he is or how he fits," Reg replied.

Paul laughed. "No, I mean about the client."

Doug smiled ruefully — he wasn't convinced by any of this nonsense. "Mr. Hart has a couple more days with us. Let's try and make them memorable. Does anyone have anything to add?"

Reg thought about bringing up the phone call to Connor and catching Hart in bed, but he let it slide. They really had done everything for Hart now that they could do. Pretending they could do more would be foolish. It was up to him now.

Doug turned to Mike and asked, "How's Mr. Hutton?"

"Ah, Jabba the Hutt," said Mike, sitting up and taking notice for the first time. Mike had been trying to shoehorn this guy into treatment for a month, and he was already fed up with his bullshit.

"Since when do you come up with the nicknames around here?" asked Paul.

Mr. Hutton — never Jacob — was a huge, fat, mushroom-shaped person who smelled of gin, self-hatred, and pee.

Mike grimaced. "He's haunting the best room in the house because he always pays cash for his babysitting, and all he requires to sustain his existence are his benzos and his delusions of grandeur."

"He's back? We just got rid of him last fall," said Reg.

Mike looked resigned. "Yup, he's back, but maybe not for long..."

"I'll say..." intoned Doug as a rather sad look crossed his face. He ran his fingers through his hair and bit his lower lip. "Dr. T. got his blood work this morning, and she's sending him back to St. Joe's for some more tests. Jabba is maybe not going to make it this time."

That didn't sit well. There was silence broken only by Kaiser writing in the treatment record.

Doug decided to have a little fun of his own. "What about Daniel Philips? Reg! I hear from him that you lack tact, empathy, and human decency."

Reg looked unconcerned. "I asked him in an offhanded way if he'd kill his mother for a drink. He took it badly. Did he pursue the matter further?"

"He came and saw me this morning. He thinks you like to hurt people."

Reg left it behind him like the wake of a torpedo. "I'll bring it up with my spiritual director."

Chapter 31

Sean and Hart were crossing the living room on their way for a smoke when Hart came to an abrupt stop and turned to face the man who'd just come through the heavy oaken door. The man had a familiar face.

Sean stiffened, getting ready for real trouble. *Oh shit, it's Connor. Here we go.*

The fat man pushed his way through the door and took a moment to adjust to the lower light inside the living room. An enormous crease on his forehead was held together by some dark stitching and a bandage. His right eye was swollen shut. He had a classic black eye that had stained his face black at the eye, blue in the cheek, and yellow and brown on his chin.

Shit! I guess I didn't hit him hard enough. How the hell did he put it all together?

Hart moved decisively toward the man before Sean could restrain him.

"Bill, what are you doing here?"

Sean was struck with the wonder of it. *Bill? Who the hell is Bill?*

The mangled man smiled. "Hart, I thought you were in jail."

"I will be soon enough." He pointed at Bill's face. "When did you take up mixed martial arts?"

Bill grimaced. It was a bad idea. His face was so swollen that it hurt. "I didn't. I got drunk and fell in the john at Clancy's. Quite an eyeful, eh?"

"But what are you doing here?"

Bill lowered his voice. "I got an appointment for an assessment, and if that all works out, I'll be staying. I sell real estate. My boss told me I couldn't work looking like this. I told him we could say that I got hit with a puck. No dice. He told me he was fed up with me coming into work smelling like a brewery. I don't know if he's really fed up or figures no one sells diddly this time of year."

The counterpoint of Hart's happy welcoming face and Sean's guilty sideways glances confused Bill. But he soldiered on. "We've gone back and forth about the drinking lots of times, usually in a pub. It always ends with both of us half in the bag, loving each other and agreeing that I'm going to cut back on the booze a little bit. But look at me! It's not only the eye — I'm a mess. I gotta do something. Since I'm off work for three weeks anyways while my face heals, I figure I might as well come in here."

Sean was dying to know everything there was to know about Bill and Connor and Clancy's. But he wisely shut his mouth and let Hart handle the introductions.

Hart beamed as he presented his friend to Sean. "This is my buddy Bill. We used to drink together at Clancy's."

"Sorry about your eye there, big guy," Sean blurted out.

Only the angels caught it. "Don't be. It wasn't your fault."

Sean stood by the fire door that led from the living room to the smoking deck, watching as Hart introduced his friend Bill to the rest of the house. Sean needed a moment alone. He was still trying to figure out where he'd lost his way. He'd been certain that Bill was Connor. He'd heard the other lout say Connor's name and then look directly at Bill. There were only four guys at the table. How could he have gotten the wrong guy? This was serious. He could see now why Mafia shooters always went for the driver's licence.

Sean took out his cigarette lighter and started working it with his hand. It was cool to the touch and felt heavy and reassuring in his palm. It gave weight to his hand but more than that, it gave weight to his deliberations.

What am I going to do? I can't go back to Clancy's. Some sharp-eyed barfly is bound to notice that every time I show up, another loser gets clobbered. It's a good thing that Bill didn't get a good look at me. Besides, Connor hasn't come after Hart, so maybe the whole thing wasn't a waste of time. That telephone call might have done the trick. Wouldn't that be something, seeing the cops in your doorway after you've stamped Case Closed on the whole business. Almost feel sorry for the prick.

Hart had finished introducing Bill to the boys, and the duo were making their way back to the living room. As Sean watched their progress, he started to turn his Zippo end over end in his hand. It felt good to have something to do. He flipped open the lighter and spun the gritty flywheel. A second later, it burst into flame with a pleasant smell of naphtha. *Bill is my man. He was at Clancy's when the shit went down. He'll remember what they said when it got talked about the next day over ham and eggs. This guy knows everything that I don't.*

Sean turned on the charm and took up his role as group leader. He got Bill gently by the elbow and started chatting him up. "Are you coming in today?"

Bill took the damp cloth away from his face. It helped with the soreness and swelling. "Yeah, they've had me in the detox for a couple days. What a place!"

"I spent some time there myself — not much in the way of good conversation."

Bill kept dabbing gingerly at his swollen face. "I didn't expect it to be so rowdy. Imagine me not handing out a business card for three whole days."

Sean smiled. "That would be my group: the crackers. Even when we're hurting, we're high energy. Listen, would you mind if I asked you a question?"

"No, go ahead." Bill was glad to have someone to talk to.

Sean extended his thumb like a hitchhiker and flipped it back and forth between himself and Hart. "Hart and I are roommates. We've been talking a lot about what happened to him. But there's so much he doesn't know. He doesn't remember the crash or what happened after, and no one from Clancy's ever came to see him. What do people at the bar think? It would really help if they were on his side."

Bill took the cloth away from his face and examined it minutely, looking for blood or discharge. Then he looked Sean up and down. There was something familiar about Sean, but who knows, maybe he had one of those faces. Besides this was an area of expertise for Bill. It felt good to have something important to say. He motioned Sean into the coffee corner. They had a bit of privacy there.

He put the middle three fingers of his left hand over his mouth before he spoke. "The night of the crash was crazy. We were bombed. Figured Suzie musta been shortenin' up the time between the rounds or somethin'. Who knows? Maybe she took some diet pills so she could look good for her boyfriend. All I remember was, we were done in long before closing time. We got the news over breakfast on Saturday. We always meet back at Clancy's to read the papers over scrambled eggs and get our bets down for the weekend. There's a kiosk in the mall that carries all the sports papers. Hart's face was everywhere."

Sean was learning from the counsellors. He asked another open-ended question. "What did you guys think when you saw the pictures?"

Bill got defensive. "Connor told us what happened. It was on the news. We didn't see any reason to bet against the spread." He went from thinking to feeling in an instant. For the first time, he considered the possibility that his friend could be innocent. That didn't feel very good. He blushed — not that it made much difference to the overall colour of his cheeks. "Are you saying he didn't do it?"

Sean bit his lower lip with his top row of teeth as he slowly nodded. He instinctively took out his lighter and lit it. "Hart couldn't have done it; he was too drunk."

Bill couldn't see it. "He was in the car."

Sean had no time to walk him through the process. "What about this guy Connor? What's he like?"

A big smile crossed Bill's face. "You know the type. One of these guys who always has a thousand dollars in his pocket. Has some kind of technical-support job, but he only seems to work one or two days a week. Lives at Clancy's and sleeps in a three-floor walk-up that he hates."

"He drives home every night, doesn't he?"

"Not anymore. That Mustang was his pride and joy. It got totalled. And he's been different since the accident. Keeps to himself now."

Sean lost all interest in Bill as the dominoes in his head began to tumble. *It's the car, Billy Boy. It's all about the car. Who'd look twice at a guy having a smoke in his car on a cold winter's night or taking somebody for a spin in a classic like that? Oh shit, that's how it happened.*

Sean saw the overturned Mustang in his mind's eye. He could imagine the panic.

Bill was having a moment of his own. *Shit, I should have gone to see him. He's going to think I let him down. I did let him down. Now I'm stuck here for a month. This is going to be bad.*

The two men looked at each other, both a little embarrassed after their coincidental time outs. "Tell me some more about Connor. You said he changed after the accident."

Bill grew reflective as he considered his answer. He turned and rested the small of his back on the reassuring counter of the coffee corner. "He was scared. The cops were brutal. They were very interested in why he drove his car to a bar. He told them he never drinks and drives, but that the owner lets him park it there overnight when he drinks. He was coming back anyways the next day for breakfast, so where was the harm?"

Sean made the intuitive leap. "Conner sells dope, doesn't he?"

Bill's eyes registered discomfort. "What makes you think that?"

That has to be it. He kept the dope in the car. He had to get rid of the dope. That's why he left the scene. He stashed it back at Clancy's. He couldn't take it home. Sean pointed at his nose. "I have a wicked sniffer."

Bill looked increasingly uncomfortable. "He does more than that…"

"Like what?"

"He makes the book."

"So everybody there owes him money?"

"Well, yeah, but he doesn't just take bets. He lets us run a tab."

"So you wouldn't want to see him go away?"

"Some of the guys would. A couple of them would be overjoyed if he did."

Chapter 32

Reg sat at the occasional table in the reading room waiting for Hart. A chat like the one that Reg had in mind needed the right backdrop.

Hart needed to stop drinking. It was a no-brainer — and therein lay the problem. Why was he the only one who couldn't see it?

It was a perceptual problem. Reg had heard doctors use the word *awareness*. Hart could look at another person in his situation and come to the right conclusion, but he couldn't make the math work for himself. There was a curious paralysis of analysis that crept into the thinking of an addict. It was conditioned by the use of the drug. Years after someone recovered, they looked back at the choices they made and they experienced a complete disconnect. They couldn't recreate in sobriety the world picture they relied upon in addiction. What looked at the time to be high-altitude physics turned out to be simple arithmetic.

Reg couldn't simply give him the answer, because that would be interpreted as imposing a solution, which, in turn, would occasion a power struggle, and no alcoholic ever lost one of those. This new insight had to be his own or it would prove worthless. Hart had been sober long enough for his perceptions to improve, but this was still rushing things. He wasn't ready for this. But they'd run out of time. The courtroom loomed in his future. This was the best they could do.

This knitting together of experience and insight was Reg's long suit. Reg the torpedo was a daydream. Reg's superpower was his ability to get right down there in the mud and brawl bare knuckled for a soul. The crucial thing was to not muddy the waters. Every addict had an origin story. It was where they went when they were asked why they drank. They imposed meaning on events where there was none. It was never a question of recognizing that they were doing the wrong thing and deciding to change. People who used highly addictive substances over time became addicts. That's really all there was to it. But that kind of clarity still eluded Hart.

Reg glanced up as Hart pulled out a chair and sat across from him. Reg looked his quarry up and down, hoping to spot something to give him an advantage or a way into the conversation. "Have you thought about our last chat?"

Hart was still feeling like the offended party. "You mean the mugging?"

Reg smiled and put his right foot up on the table and gave it a brisk rub. "I'm not getting a card on my birthday this year, am I?"

"Nope."

Reg hauled his swollen and painful leg back down to the floor. He sat up in his chair and leaned forward, using his canes as a chin support. His broad smiling face was perfectly supported by his choice of bow tie. He looked less the grand inquisitor and more the father of the bride. "Well, you're going home tomorrow, and the boss says I have to waste another hour on you. Do you want to talk or have a game of backgammon?"

Hart was sad to be leaving. He was going to miss this place. He couldn't have explained why, because he hadn't gotten quite that far yet. There was a lot of rubble that needed to be bagged up before he could start rebuilding his bombed-out capital city. A wise man would sift through it carefully. No addict with an itch could summon that kind of patience. "I want to have a crack at your three questions again."

Reg feigned surprise. "You mean the ones that Kaiser stole from me?"

"Yes."

"You mean the ones that I stole from Rabbi Hillel?"

"Yes."

"You mean the ones he stole from the other rabbis?"

Hart took a turn at being the adult. "Will you stop?"

Reg was smiling broadly. "Suddenly, you don't strike me as being completely crazy, merely moderately so."

Hart liked that kind of teasing, but he was in the mood to be serious. "I've been talking to other people and thinking about what you said and about what they said. I really hated Kaiser for telling me I was going to do five years in jail and then become the new resident bad boy at Clancy's. That broke my heart."

Kaiser, I could kiss you.

Hart leaned back in his chair and put his hands behind his head. Reg had the good sense to do the same. "If I went to jail and got out and nothing had changed, then I'd be right back at Clancy's, lying my face off about what happened and bragging about where I'd been." There was a pause as he imagined himself taking his regular seat at the big table. He didn't want to be there. His voice weakened. "Where else could I go? What else would I have?"

Reg put his canes down on the table. "You got it."

"That happens to guys, doesn't it?"

"Yeah, and after a few years of that kind of rough stuff, it's really hard to reach the human part of them. They get hard and cynical, like your pal Sean."

Hart had to laugh. "You're wrong about him. But maybe that's why I like you a little bit. You just put what you think out there for anyone to take or leave as they see fit."

"Careful, it's trademarked."

"No, really, the thing I like about you is that you're wrong most of the time. Which means that I can't rely on you to make my decisions. I gotta take what you say, and then really think about it."

Reg was intrigued. "Where did you ever get the idea that you didn't have to do that?"

"My mother always thought very deeply about things and then did the best she could. It seemed pointless to me as a kid to do all the heavy lifting on my own when Mom was going to present the whole thing to me, gift-wrapped and on a platter."

"You got lazy in the head."

"I guess I did."

"Now you're back on the job, how do you feel about what's happening?"

"Well, I was thinking…"

Reg held up his hand and smiled. "Hart, don't think about this yet. We'll get there, but let's lay the groundwork first. Let's get all the information that's percolating around inside you on the table. *Feel* about it first. Let your gut inform your head."

"All right, I'll try. I feel like I'm going to be okay. I feel like I'm alive again for the first time in years. I feel like I've been screwed around by a bunch of bullshitters and I feel like it's my fault because I let them do it. I feel sorry for the Gibsons. I feel sick about Alice being crippled and I shrivel up inside when I think about Margaret lying dead in her grave with that little girl still needing her. I keep seeing that whole family, standing around in new clothes, crying."

That cost him something. Reg let a moment pass. Outside the window, the sun scudded in and out of the fast-moving clouds. Light and shadow were playing on Hart's face.

"That was a good beginning. Now I want you to let all that feeling inform your head. Imagine your feelings are children: They've been playing downstairs, in another room, and they've seen and heard things the adults don't know about. Imagine them tiptoeing up the back staircase to the kitchen, where the adults are having an argument. They want to tell what they know. They want the adults to make sense of what they've seen. But they're afraid of the adults' anger and certain they're going to be scolded and sent away."

Hart's head started to nod. "That's a lot of premise. But okay, I'll try."

Reg's left hand came up like a father's supporting the back of a child taking his first solo ride on a two-wheeler. "Shoot from the hip. Don't think about what you're saying. Don't give the power to the adults. Let the children find their voice."

Hart struggled with the instructions, so Reg reframed the proposal. "Ask the children who's looking after them?"

"It feels like no one is. But I know that's not true."

Reg tried to push him back into feeling. "What do the children mean by that?"

"They don't know what to do."

Hart couldn't stay with it yet, so Reg reframed the question again. "But if you're only concerned about yourself, where does that leave you?"

"Scared and lonely. I only had myself to please, and I couldn't even do that."

"When is this going to change?"

"When I get a break, which is never going to happen."

Reg sat up in his chair and tucked a single cane under his chin as he prepared to give his actor some notes. "Now take a very deep breath. You're still running your feelings through your head."

Hart's upper lip covered its companion. "But that can't be right…"

"Humour me for a second. Hart, you can't fix yourself. If you could, you would have. I want you to go deeper. I want you to answer the three questions again, but this time I want you to pretend, if that's what you need to do, that you're a child talking to a parent, someone who's willing to help you with this problem, someone who's in a position to put things right. Pretend that one of the adults wants to hear what you have to say."

"Wait a minute, hang on — that's nuts."

"We're not signing legal papers. Try this. Sometimes it helps."

"I wouldn't know how to begin. This feels so awkward."

"You're thinking about your feelings. Everyone with an addiction does that. It's the way we justify all our nonsense. Our feelings have a much better grasp of what's going on with us than our thoughts do. Our thoughts are like playwrights on opium. They keep writing happy endings. It's our feelings that know we're damaged. All you had to do was look after yourself and look at the mess you made. Thinking can't solve this problem. If you let them, the adults will spin out this conversation without a resolution until you die, while the children stand outside the room, hoping for a chance to speak."

Hart's mouth was open and his eyes narrowed almost in wonder. "But when I go to my feelings, I keep thinking, crap, I did it again. I keep landing on Margaret. I feel sick when I think … no, I feel sick when I imagine what that must have been like for her."

Reg kept pushing, with the lightest possible touch. This was a guided meditation that would never be forgotten. "You described that feeling earlier as *despair*. Let's start there instead of at *I'm going to be all right*. You're not all right. Put yourself in Margaret's place. What would it feel like, being all busted up in a car crash, sitting there stunned, trying to make sense of what had happened?"

He let a little time pass before he took up the narrative again. He knew full well that Hart knew exactly what that felt like, even if it had happened to him in a jail cell. "Hoping you were going to be okay but then feeling a wave of pain move through your body, pain so bad you didn't think you could bear it." Again, a silence dreadful and deep. "Your first instinct would be to reach out, to see what was going on with your daughter, only now you discover that your body won't move. You hear a horrible wet sound when you breathe. You panic when you can't draw air into your lungs. It's like when you were a kid and someone would sit on your chest."

Beads of sweat began to form on Hart's upper lip as his complexion grew ashen and his lips began to quiver.

"Then the horrible thought — maybe your daughter is dead. When Margaret cried out in pain, who was she worried about, herself or her daughter? She knew she was hurt bad enough to die. Did she cry out for help?"

"I don't ... I can't..."

"Hart, we're swimming around in the deep end of the pool here. We're talking about whether life has any meaning. We're talking about finding a reason to live. There's always a vital source of hope available to us, even in the shark-infested waters that we swim in. Can you feel that woman's despair?"

"Yes ... it's choking me." He was back in the cell. Barefoot, shivering and wishing that he could die simply by closing his eyes.

Reg let him sit in that for a count of one hundred. The only sound to intrude was the muffled drone of a distant radio. It had been there all along, but they hadn't heard it until now. It drew some of the pain away from Hart's eyes simply by being a sound. "Good. Now can you feel your own?"

There was a horrible, protracted silence that ended when Hart gasped.

"Knit them tighter. Connect with Margaret."

Hart groaned. His body shrank in the chair as he cocooned himself, wrapping his arms around his knees and resting his forehead on the flat space thus created.

Reg was speaking in a whisper that landed like blows from a middleweight. "Sit there in that blackness. Margaret had to, and now it's your turn. Would she have saved her life if she could have?"

Hart stared past Reg into the distance. He knew that if he looked Reg in the eye, he would weep.

Reg's voice was calm and certain. "Where was justice for Alice Gibson, huh? Tell me that. She was innocent. Where was mercy for Margaret? Did she have that coming? Hart, they were both innocent and they both got hurt. And I'm going to cut you a break here and take it as read that you were not driving that car and that you're as innocent and cut up as they are."

Hart forced himself to look at Reg's chin.

"The point is that you're powerless. You can't fix this. That's what your feelings have been trying to tell you. This is the point your thinking never lets you get to. You know, somehow, if you feel all those feelings of despair rolling around inside you, you're going to die. But that is the very thing you need to do. You can't get to the hope in that darkness until you pass through the despair.

"Nothing you do, and nothing you avoid doing, can cure your addiction. Most drunks get that after a couple of bad beatings. But here is the new horror for you: You cannot compel God to take away your addiction any more than you can force God to restore the Gibsons to life and health. It's not yours to give life and death. Stop acting like you had God in your watch pocket."

Hart lurched forward in his chair. "You're making this shit up; there's no way you can know this!"

Reg didn't give an inch. "These canes have made me a wicked observer of the human animal and the one-dimensional world you live in. I'm a proper sounding board. I amplify the little voices of conscience that you would rather trample underfoot. I am those voices. You tell me who you are the first time you look at me with pity, contempt, fear, and avoidance. I'm here. I'm real. I matter. I exist. You have to deal with me. I won't be pushed into the background."

The face, the voice, the body language, and the eyes — especially the eyes — said, *I know*. The children were his children. Their confidences and wellbeing, his concern. Hart went with Reg, bow tie and all.

"The despair that woman felt at the moment of the accident, that minute when she realized she was dying, that's the human condition. You used booze to mask those feelings. Booze told you that you were above all that. The mask was so powerful and so persuasive that you forgot it was a mask, and then you forgot you were even wearing it, and then you even forgot why you put it on in the first place. Then you said you never needed a mask at all. Well, life has a way of reminding us that our foolishness is just that. Look at me, Hart. I'm what you look like inside, without your mask."

There was nothing to be done. No handkerchief, no glass of something, no hug, no reassuring touch, no quote, and certainly no word could take this away. Hart remembered the sound of the pipes at his father's funeral and felt the sound move through his entrails unimpeded once again. "I feel so empty."

"Hart, you came that close to dying. But there's more to dying than just the death of the body. You killed your spirit with booze. The only reason you were in the car that night was because of your addiction. It doesn't matter one bit if you were driving or not — that's the accidental part. If not that night, then another. If not in that place, then any place. You were aching for it to happen."

Hart started to rock without realizing it. Reg's words had a narcotic effect. The wound was still fresh, but the pain and fear were in abeyance.

A leg cramp straightened Reg up in his chair. The pain showed on his face. Some panic too, as he lifted the offending limb up onto the table and tried to knead out the cramp with his fingers. But he didn't miss a beat. "You never grew up. You have a deluded sense of your own power and importance. Now there's blood on the floor and maybe even blood on your hands too, all because you were playing with fire. Has all this suffering taught you nothing? Here and now, in this room, your ability to choose has been restored, if only for the moment. It may not last. The feelings that are trying to draw you back into darkness are powerful. They revel in shame and feast on disgrace. But now, this instant, while you still can, while they're at the low ebb of their power, draw a line in the sand and say, *Not one inch further*" — Reg paused in midsentence, the way a vocalist takes a half step away from the microphone. Not needed but not done. His voice was devoid of hope and his eyes sad and moist as he concluded — "or say, *Take me because I am yours*. It's time to choose: Are you going crawl out of the wreckage? Because that is the only power you have. You can choose to try."

Hart was still fully in the moment. He imagined the blood running to his head as he hung upside down helplessly in the wreck. He could smell gasoline and see the upturned world through the blank space where the windshield used to be. It took him five minutes to regain his words. "There's no way back from this. I'm glad I'm going to jail. That's where monsters belong. Everyone hates me. This pain is going to last forever."

Reg didn't rush his reply. He eased his bad leg back onto the floor and give it another going over. "No, it's not. It's like a kick in the nuts — it just feels like forever. What you're feeling, my friend, is the cold, lifeless blood draining out of the corpse of your addiction."

That went straight over his head. "Reg, I don't know what I believe anymore. This last year has unhinged me from everything I ever counted on, everything I thought was real. What if there's no God? Where does that leave me?"

"Then we're all screwed. If there's no God, then there's no recovery. Most people are like you. They're head lazy. They let other people tell them what to think, and then they lose what little faith they have when things don't work out exactly the way they think they should. I know there's a God, but I don't know much more than that. And in this job, I've learned not to pretend I know something when I don't. So let's talk about the stuff that we can know. Do you suppose Margaret would've climbed out of that wreck if she could have?"

"I know she would have. She had a life."

"So why don't you embrace her despair — and maybe your own too — and start clawing your way out."

"I still don't feel right about this. It's not right that she died and I lived."

"Stop. That's not your call. Don't put a bandage on her corpse because you feel bad about yourself. That won't help you and it sure as hell won't do her any good. Reach out into that darkness and take her bloody hand in yours. Join your fingers. When you want to crawl out of that car as badly as Margaret did, then I'll have some hope for you. And if you're smart enough to ask for some help, I might even start liking your chances."

Chapter 33

John and Peter were heading back to Flannerman's after taking in a movie. Peter was coming out of his funk. Films always made him feel better. They took him out of himself. John usually turned down Peter's invitations to the theatre, mostly because the fat ghost always chose a film that he alone in the wide world wanted to see. But he'd gone along this time because he was unsure if Peter could find his way back on his own.

That assessment proved too harsh. Peter found his way to the theatre without prompting and was able to carry on a conversation. He even took it upon himself, without being asked, to explain the subtle meaning of the film to John as they stood waiting for the train. John now put his recent peculiarities down to something like shock. That she-devil-little-lady taking the shape of a talking crocodile would put any ghost off his fodder. But now there was another problem. He spotted Barry standing alone at the far end of the subway platform. The last thing John needed was to run into Chairman Butthead. He had no desire to be anywhere within earshot of Barry ever again.

John tugged on Peter's sleeve to put a stop to his film review and direct his attention toward the far end of the platform and Barry. "You can go and talk to him if you want, but I'm going to duck behind this pillar and stay out of sight."

"We're being a little childish, aren't we?"

"No more than watching where you step on a sidewalk covered with dog dirt."

Peter made his way down the long platform under his own steam. It wasn't busy. If he'd waited, he could've button hooked someone, but he was afraid that Barry might get on the train before he could reach him. His other big worry was finding himself with nothing to hold on to if one or both trains entered the station. God alone knew where he'd find himself when the whirlwind dissipated.

Peter was out of breath and out of sorts again when he arrived at the far end. After such an effort, he expected a warm greeting, but Barry was as sharp as a flint and came right to the point. "Did you talk to John?"

Peter looked at Barry, who was very careful to keep his back up against the wall. "We spoke and I explained our dilemma to him in the most lucid terms."

Barry was still thorny. "What did he say?"

Peter sighed. Did he really have to take Barry line by line through that very disappointing conversation. He resolved to move Barry off the subject of the intransigent John and on to something more productive. "John is losing it. I explained the situation to him in detail only to have him respond by staring back at me blankly."

Barry was agitated. His foot was bouncing and he was biting his index knuckle. "That was it?"

Peter was growing wary. "Well, he looked like he wanted to say something. He kept pointing his finger like he wanted to butt in, but then he sputtered and said nothing. I think he's hopeless. He'll be of no use to us. He's well past his best-before date. He even came to the movies with me ... he never does that." *He left out the other strand of the narrative, which was that John wouldn't lift a finger to help Barrie but that he'd use the last of his strength to sandbag any project that the chairman of the board hoped to get off the ground.*

The interrogation continued. "What about the girls?"

The tone of that question irked Peter. He took a step closer to Barry and thought about giving him a shove. "They're gone and so are the Baileys."

"That's a lot of ghosts for you to lose in a single day."

Is he saying that was my fault? Peter vented his irritation by asking an awkward question of his own. "You're the head of the council. What are you going to do about this?"

Barry's energy dropped to zero. He stopped chewing his knuckle and let his eyes drift down to the floor. As the eastbound train entered the station, the two ghosts instinctively got a death grip on the garbage pails. The force of air from the train lifted them both off their feet for thirty seconds and the noise made conversation impossible. They glared at each other in silence. As the commuters exited the train and made for the elevator, their feet slowly drifted back to the ground. Barry clasped Peter by the elbow. "There's only you and me now."

That didn't make any sense to Peter. "What about Jack?"

Barry looked at Peter in disbelief. "You know who Jack was when he was alive?"

"No," *said Peter.* "All I know about him is that he gives me the shivers."

Barry spoke in a whisper. "Jack is the Rosedale strangler."

"Why didn't you tell us?"

Barry looked ashamed. "Maybe I should have. I was afraid of the guy, and he didn't want me to tell anyone."

Peter made the connection. "That's how he came up with button hooking, isn't it? He was trying to strangle people."

Barry put his head down, shut both eyes firmly, and began scratching his forehead with both hands, palms up. The gesture brought him no relief. "I kept his secret because I figured he couldn't hurt anyone anymore ... I didn't know..."

Peter felt some compassion at last for his failed leader. "You look so discouraged, Barry."

Barry's hands came up again in a theatrical gesture that was unfortunately discounted when he turned his back on Peter to expose his white boxers and split suit coat. "The entire council died on my watch, Peter. I don't want to do this any longer." *He turned and grabbed Peter roughly by both elbows.* "It's time for us to go. Our day is done. The task force was our one hope."

Peter tried to pull away. He suddenly detested this little man. His very touch was a violation. "What are you talking about?"

Barry held Peter's coat with his right hand and began to search for something in his pocket. "It's over. All that's left for us is the suffering." *Barry produced a waterproof wooden match. Peter was aghast.*

"It's better this way. I can't leave you on your own."

Before Peter could act, Barry struck the match against the painted brick wall. But all he got was a spark. The soft paint on the wall fouled the match. It was useless. Barry flung it away and fumbled in his pocket, looking for another.

Peter was furious. "You lunatic! Let go of me. You could've killed us both."

Barry's grip seemed unbreakable. "We're dead, Peter — there's nothing left to be done."

"Says you!" *Peter wrenched himself free and stumbled away from him.*

Barry looked surprised. The despondent ghost had become too focused on finding a second match to keep Peter in his clutches.

"Don't..." *Peter said.*

The terrazzo floor was a much better scratch pad than the painted wall had been. Barry vanished like a sheet of flash paper before the flame from the match reached its maximum flare.

Peter recoiled in horror as the still flaming stick landed on the floor only to be trampled underfoot by a commuter walking briskly down the platform.

Dry as gunpowder, they say ... dry as gunpowder, he proved.

Peter was shaken to his core. That was too close. Too damned close.

He looked down the platform instinctively and saw John rushing toward him. He was still a long way off, but Peter could tell he'd seen everything.

That could've been it! The past, the future, Terri and I trapped forever in a man-made glacier. How could I have been so careless? Ghosts don't murder each other!

He shuddered when he thought about sitting next to Jack at the meetings. The detestable little man was always playing with wooden matches — shaking the box, smelling the sulphur, and arranging the sticks into letters and sentences. Always complaining about some obnoxious poltergeist or another who needed fixing. Is that where they all went? Did they step into the frightening light the way Barry had? How was I so blind?

This put the subject of the light in a whole new perspective. The portly ghost looked around, but there was nothing to see but the tired and disinterested faces of the workforce, rushing forward, hoping for a seat on the subway and the thin spectre of rescue coming too late. I need to talk to someone sane. I need to get these lunatics out of my head.

Chapter 34

Weekends at Punanai centred around two events: family visits on Saturday and the Straight Up meeting on Sunday. These two activities afforded the weekend counsellor a rare chance to peek behind the mask. Alcoholics vetted the flow of personal information with the same assiduous attention to detail that they applied to husbanding the supply of intoxicants. Paul understood that he could never really know any of the clients until he saw them interacting with their family. He also knew that nothing glossed over sore spots on a resume better than self-reporting.

He always took advantage of the chance to speak with family members when they came to visit on Saturdays. He loved to put pressure on the clients' versions of events and to judge for himself if the accounts of home life were real or fanciful.

Wives and mothers were always the most forthcoming with the insightful questions and comments that pulled back the roofing tiles to reveal the rotten plywood hidden below. They would say things like "Has his girlfriend stopped in yet?" or "Things are so much better at home since he stopped playing cards."

A dumbfounded look on the counsellor's face usually prompted the obligatory question. "Oh, he didn't tell you about that?"

Paul had been meeting and greeting family all afternoon. He had a flair for it. He possessed the skills of a political candidate, but he'd yet to find a political party that he approved of. It was his face that carried the freight. Handsome, inquisitive with a warmth around his eyes and a slight disapproving frown that made you want to try harder with him. That and the grey around the temples put the product in an intriguing, hard-to-open box.

He was sitting alone in the office, recording a few of his impressions and formulating a few questions that he'd like to pursue the next day, when Jenny from the lab called. He almost didn't pick up because it was time to ring the dinner bell. But when he saw her name, he couldn't resist.

"Hey Paul, you working all alone?"

"Yup, nobody loves me."

"I might start to like you a little bit, but first you'd have to do me a favour."

"Jenny, for you? Anything."

"Can you look up a file for me?"

"Which one?"

"Michael Eustice Czombo."

Never heard him called Michael before. What's up with that?

Paul laid hold of the file. "Got it right here. What do you want to know?"

"Look in his drug history and tell me if he has ever done benzos."

Paul leafed through the file. "It doesn't say so here."

"That's weird. His first urine sample showed no benzos, but now it's showing benzos at a very low level."

"Could he have popped one this week?"

"Nah, the reading would be much higher. This reading is consistent with someone who's been off them for a while. It might be a lab error. I'll get them to check their settings. Sometimes a little bump makes the results wonky. I don't want to overthink this — let's wait and see what we get from him on Monday."

———

At 7:00 p.m. Paul pushed the guys out the door for the Saturday evening meeting. He had the place to himself. He was getting rocky after twelve hours of listening, and the prospect of putting in five more before his head finally found respite on a pillow was discouraging. A touch of sadness tinged the room, but he was too tired to work out why. He turned on the radio and sat at Mike's desk to better hear the music.

These long shifts took the mickey out of everyone. He needed time to reflect. He'd picked up a lot of new information and insights by talking to the visitors and watching the clients interact with their loved ones. He'd made some valuable connections and wanted to commit them to paper before they vanished.

The phone rang. The display registered a familiar name: Aaron Johnson, who had forgotten to collect his bottle of Buckley's when he left.

A woman's voice sounded eager to talk. "My name is Ella. Someone named Paul called this afternoon and wanted to do a follow-up call with my husband."

"That was me. I'm Paul. How's Aaron doing?"

"He's out of town, working on a bridge near Peterborough and living in a camp, so I thought I'd better call you so you wouldn't worry."

Paul selected the file from a stack by the phone and opened it to make a note. "Well, thank you for that. We usually like to talk to the client, but we take what we can get. How's he doing?"

There was a pause and then a rush of good feeling. "You guys are miracle workers!" In his mind's eye, Paul could see the happy tears welling up. "Aaron didn't want to go to your program. We had a hell of a fight about it, if you want to know the truth, but I told him it's go or get out. He knew I meant it this time. Well, you know what that's like — you hear the stories. He went for treatment once before, you know. And he was drunk when he came home from it; got himself a bottle to celebrate with on the bus. Was so proud of himself for going three weeks without a drink."

Paul began to wonder where the gush was going. "So he's sober and going to meetings?"

You could feel a storm cloud rising on the horizon in her voice. "Well, I don't know about the meetings part. They're living in a pretty rough camp at the bridge. They work for ten days and get a week off. May not be any meetings where he is. But he's sober and that's the wonder of it."

Paul was relieved by her certainty. "Well, that's the main thing." He did a little reaction formation with his next comment. "He can start the meetings again when he gets home."

She didn't want to give up the feeling. "It's hard to believe he's the same man. Last week, he took me dancing. We haven't set foot in a club for years. We danced until we couldn't dance anymore. It was wonderful. He's not like he was. He sips his drinks now. And when he's had enough, he just goes for a little lie down. No more fussing or cursing or fighting. It's a miracle!"

Paul gave his head a little shake. "He's drinking?"

The voice registered mild surprise. "Well, yes, he's always been a drinker, but now it's different. He's drinking like a gentleman, and we're all so grateful to you for teaching him how to do that."

With that, the phone line went dead.

Paul resisted the impulse to write *Living under a bridge in Peterborough* in the area reserved for comments and instead judiciously marked the file *Drinking, no meetings*.

His curiosity about the Johnsons' homelife was piqued. He flipped through the file until he found the family counselling page. There was a useful note. Aaron had declined to invite his wife, Ella, to the family care program. He said her wheelchair made it too difficult for her to travel. Clearly there had been a spate of miracles this winter in the Peterborough area.

Chapter 35

Czombo was finding it harder to wait until 10:00 p.m. for his nightly excursion to the garage next door and his very special bedtime treat. He reported to the staff that he'd reserved this time slot for a daily fifteen-minute guided meditation, but he left the details vague; they didn't need to know that his forays into mysticism took place in the wonderfully faded blue leather La-Z-Boy chair in which he found himself now. He took in the view of the smoking deck and the manager's office from his perch as he rolled up a reason to get excited, forming his inspiration into a tight, well-packed tube.

He prudently turned the old fan on to its highest setting and wrapped himself in a blanket while he fumbled for his lighter. He kept the joint as far away from his body as he could. He'd been lucky to find a cigarette holder in the head shop on Bloor. The adapted device undoubtedly wasted some of the precious smoke, but it left his fingers unstained and his person not smelling of bud.

He inhaled the first fruits of his labour and held the breath until he gave way to a fit of coughing. As he waited for the spasm to pass and his eyes to clear, he looked at his surroundings. The garage was a dump, but a very nice one. Everything that occupied the space between not wanted but still useful took up residence here until its final disposition was decided by the supreme arbiters: rust and rot.

This is death row for things, he thought as the magic gathering strength behind his eyes began to break forth and illuminate the world. *No* — he discovered a more compelling direction — *this is the unconscious. Jung would love this place with all its smells and wear marks and associations and memories.*

There was no order to the contents of the garage. Objects that had fallen out of favour were brought, stacked, and forgotten. The building itself was originally constructed to house a carriage and possibly even a horse or two, and, in the roaring twenties, it had hosted a series of rather fine touring automobiles. But it was too small for modern cars. The gabled roof and the beautifully executed wooden lattice that stood out so brilliantly against the brickwork was widely regarded as adding character to the property. No one had the heart to tear it down, but opinions about what to do with it differed widely, and so its purpose began to vary as a series of owners came and went.

Czombo's lungs made their peace with the healing vapour. He was able to get a couple of real good ones into him. He held on to that richness with all his might as he stubbed out the joint. He needed to catch his breath and he didn't want to waste any of the smoke. Things began to connect and make sense to him in a new way that justified all the time and expense that the drug demanded. He looked at the world around him with wonder.

This is a jumble of time and a tangle of things. It's like a road map to the past all balled up and stuffed every which way. If I had a photograph to work with, I could resurrect an entire living room from the nineties simply by digging to the bottom of this pile. All this good stuff packed in here because someone got bored with it. Why do they hang on to it if they can't stand the sight of it?

He sparked up the joint again and took three major pulls in rapid succession. His eyes took on the look of a slot machine announcing a winner.

Czombo started to experience a fit of the giggles. They were too much fun to resist and so he went with them willingly. There was enough joint left to be worth the effort needed to light it. He took it in and held it until he'd extracted all the wisdom it had to impart.

I'm going to write an article about this for Rolling Stone. *The garage as a metaphor for the unconscious: insights into the ever-changing nature of wanting and being bored.*

He glanced at his watch. He needed to get back. But to accomplish that he needed to stay invisible. This was a sweet set-up and he had no intention of messing it up. He turned off the fan and removed the blanket. He took a long, slow look out the window to make sure there were no prying eyes and no one coming with a bag of garbage from the kitchen. The way was clear. He pulled his hoodie over his head and slid out the door, keeping low to the ground with this back in the shadows.

He had to walk around the block to avoid detection. There was no safe way to cross the property without being noticed. His completed circle brought him at last to the seldom-used south fire door that he'd carefully taped so that it could be opened from the outside. Once he was inside, he collected himself. He smelled his hair and his hoodie until he was satisfied he was odour-free.

The pot had made him fanciful. Being stoned should have been all the reward he needed. But being stoned in a house full of addicts who were sober against their better judgment and almost certainly against their will — well, that was special. He started to think about all the things that still needed to be done as he quietly descended the stairs to the now-deserted kitchen. He helped himself to a glass of juice that would justify his presence on the lower level and then took the elevator to the third floor, even though he'd been told it was only for the people who couldn't climb the stairs. As the door opened, he could see a line of men waiting for the shower.

All addicts carry within them the seeds of their own destruction. To the outsider, what looks like disdain or recklessness is really a kind of drug-induced divine authority. People in the know often say that, when they have the right amount of their drug of choice, they feel like the smartest person in the room.

It shows up on a brain scan as an area of hyperfocus — a little red dot of frantic activity that goes on in the midbrain, while the rest of the thinker lies dormant. An addict in this condition can concentrate on one thing and exclude everything else. This intense focus sets up the belief that they really are above and beyond the dialectic of their tribe. And it's always their undoing. It's what's going on when they decide to insult the boss's wife or confound a police detective with a blazing display of logic in an interrogation room.

Czombo's impressive list of recent successes had gone straight to his confidence. He fancied himself the only sighted man in the land of the blind, unable to articulate his advantages to his less able companions simply because of their limitations. He was so far out ahead of the curve that he felt safe enough to taunt his opponents. In fairness, it'd been quite a run. With a simple anonymous phone call, he'd gotten that pious little turd Arthur thrown out of treatment. But more importantly, the act had done more than remove an irritant, it had transformed shared accommodation into private space. Larry, his willing and flattered acolyte, was passing mountain fresh urine for him. He'd found a secret lair where he could smoke a joint at bedtime, and his Employee Assistance Program worker, Jeffy Poo, was buying up his bullshit by the metric ton.

All these accomplishments were top of mind when he looked up from the elevator door and saw that toad Sean Miller standing with his back to him, waiting for the shower.

I really shouldn't. This isn't going to do me any good. Oh, what the hell. This guy's got it coming.

He didn't exactly shove him — that would've been over the top — but he gave him the best nudge he could offer and a quick apology as he passed.

The guys were outside, smoking furiously before lights-out and huddling in a tight circle for privacy and warmth. The light that generally illuminated the space had burned out, rendering the smoking deck mysterious. The darkness offered no barrier to words, but it disembodied their voices.

"Did you guys see Czombo give Sean a shove?"

"Yeah, that looked odd."

"He apologized."

"That makes it look even worse, far as I'm concerned."

"You guys are missing the point. Didn't anyone else smell it? The sweet smell of bud coming off the prick?"

The final canary fell over dead. That made three of them.

"He's smoking?"

"So that's what he's doing! I saw him the other night, skulking around that garage next door. I wondered what he was up to."

"The suits are gonna get mad about this."

"Someone should tell 'em."

"I'm no rat."

"Someone's gonna get triggered, then the shit's gonna hit the fan."

Larry Lorne was frozen in the moment of discovery. The darkness that unyoked voice from identity gave power to the disembodied words. Without affect and gesture, the words took on the force of private thoughts. They cut hot and ragged like a saw blade. They knew. Everybody knew. He felt a sickening fear rise up his windpipe. He sucked in a huge lungful of frigid air and slowly exhaled it, puffing his cheeks as he did. The fire in his gut matched the unseen colouring of his cheek.

"Well, let's sleep on it, boys. Nothing to be done tonight about this."

"It's lights-out in sixty seconds."

"How can you tell?"

"Easy! Here comes Maurice. You can set your watch by him."

"What does he care if we're five minutes late for bed?"

"I don't know — maybe he likes to watch *The National*."

They all laughed and scurried through the fire door.

Larry followed them at a distance up the staircase and across the landing, still feeling numb and shaky. He fancied himself a man who'd swallowed poison out of spite and now had to decide whether to call the ambulance or wait to die. He carried on across the living room and up the oak staircase to his room. He didn't bother with the light and just flung himself down on his bunk.

I'm gonna get caught. No! There's no way he's gonna squeal on himself and even if he did, all I'd have to say is that I didn't do it. Why did I ever agree to do this? I could slip a note under the counsellors' door. No, that's suicidally stupid. The thing to do here is to do nothing. How could that prick let me down like this? That fucker wanted to use, and he used me to do it. Yeah — no, wait. Think about this again. No one could possibly know what we were up to except Czombo and me. He won't tell. I'm gonna carry on doing what I've been doing and wait for the other guys to squeal, then stand around and look surprised. It's all I can do.

He rolled over on his back, firm in his resolve, and felt, if anything, worse than before. *Why does this keep happening to me? I was finally getting somewhere!* He shifted again, lying face down in his pillow, and weathered the long, cold sea of despair.

Larry rolled over and looked at the clock every fifteen minutes until the sun finally came up. He was the first one out the door, ostensibly looking for a coffee, but what he really needed was a place to sit and process his horror. Even at this hour it was hard to get a table at Tim's. He got the least desirable one by the front door. The table wobbled, the lineup for service crowded him, and every time the door opened, he got blast of arctic air. A part of him wanted to throttle Czombo on the smoking deck. But Punanai was starting to make some inroads into his psyche. He was looking at his part in this debacle. This was new territory.

I didn't have to do what I did. I coulda said no. But I felt sorry for the guy. He was trapped. I know what that feels like. That time I put the bad cheque through the bank machine — the second that envelope disappeared down the rat hole — I knew I couldn't live with it. They believed me when I said I was drunk and confused. But the way that lady looked at me from behind the glass told me she wasn't fooled. She wasn't gonna say anything this time, only the look. But what a look!

He blew out a puff of air and then sipped his coffee. *I had to smoke a lot of shit to blank that look out. Makes me want to use every time I think of it.*

A thin figure hovered over the table. Larry assumed it was a beggar, but the voice was familiar. "Can I join you?" It was Daniel Philips.

"Sure. Sit down, there's plenty of room."

The tall young man set his tray with a breakfast sandwich and a mug of coffee on the table, then took off his parka and long, ornately coloured, hand-knotted scarf. Larry didn't realize that you could still get coffee in a mug.

When Daniel settled, he looked at Larry and smiled. "You've been here for a while?"

Larry began to forget about his troubles. "Yeah, I'm getting to be a real old-timer."

Daniel was hunched over his sandwich, trying to remove the wrapper without much success. He turned his attention first to his coffee and then to his newfound companion. "Well, I don't know why I'm talking to you about this, maybe because I like the way you handle yourself in the group, but I'm worried sick about the Straight Up meeting this afternoon."

Larry knew where this was going. He moved the heavy metal chair, trying to find a more comfortable angle, but all he produced was a rather annoying screech that caused a sleeping vagrant to lurch for a second before his head slumped again. "Does the name put you off?"

Daniel looked helpless. "It makes me squirm."

They both laughed. "I didn't like it much the first time I heard it, either."

Daniel's fingers finally found a way through the steaming wax paper, and he was rewarded with his first bite. "Do people really talk about their stuff?"

Larry shook his head. "You gotta judge that for yourself. All I know is when I stood up, the whole room changed. It was fine until I spoke, but when everyone's lookin' at you, things change ... for the worse."

Daniel had a funny look on his face, like he was simultaneously disappointed and relieved. "I hate being singled out."

"No one likes it, but the suits are all agreed, this is good for us."

Daniel's eyes grew merry. "They think not drinking's a good idea too."

Larry gave his companion a smirk. "Still unconvinced?"

Daniel looked defeated. "I like my booze." He dropped the half-wrapped sandwich onto his tray. "I hate where I end up most of the time, but that's when it really helps. When they're all staring at you like you're a monster." He looked at Larry to see if he was on the same wavelength.

Larry laughed. "It's perfect, isn't it? Booze makes you do something that embarrasses you so much you can't stand it, and then a moment later you take a swig, and it all goes away."

Daniel took a sip of his coffee. "One of the guys on the deck says you can pass if you don't wanna talk in the group."

"Yeah, but all it does is put off the inevitable. If you don't talk, they get you to do a one-on-one with a counsellor on Monday, where they work you over so good you promise to squeal on yourself next Sunday."

Now Daniel was really bothered. "So there's no way out."

"The best you can do is a one-week reprieve. But the guys say when that happens, you spend the whole week obsessing about it, and by the time Sunday rolls around, you're a raving lunatic."

"That's the way I usually handle my shit."

"Me too." They both laughed.

Daniel picked up his sandwich and took a big bite, then offered up a line that he hoped would give him time to chew. "So what's the deal with you? The guys on the deck call you Batman."

Larry didn't like the sound of that. "Batman?"

Daniel chewed and swallowed hard. "You know, a secret identity. Vince told everyone you were an undercover addictions counsellor working for the insurance company."

"I didn't know they talked about me."

"They talk about everyone. Not in a mean way — they're trying to figure everyone out." Daniel cupped his mug in his hands and put his elbows comfortably on the table. "What are you gonna say this afternoon?"

Larry smiled as he ran his fingers through his hair. "Yeah, my plan is to look horrified and hope they let me go last so I can blurt out something that sounds like the truth and then go hide in my room."

Larry fell into a funk hole at the thought of having to speak. What could he possibly say? He wanted to tell the truth, but he couldn't without getting kicked out. Should he try and make something up or shut his yap and take his chances on the one-on-one with a counsellor. As he agonized about what he was going to say, Larry forgot that Daniel was sitting opposite.

Daniel sensed that Larry was rebooting. He searched the other man's face for clues. They were the same age, but they came from different tribes. It was easy to deconstruct Larry by observing his choices in footwear and grooming. A jock. Larry looked worried. Almost guilty. Daniel wondered if they had more in common than the addiction. That was wishful thinking. Larry was a friendly guy destined for the altar and a life that revolved around buying a new pickup truck every three years.

What does a big, strong knucklehead like you have to worry about?

Chapter 36

Hy Campbell was a good-looking woman in her prime with a beguiling sense of self-confidence. She kept herself busy with different jobs on weekdays, and on Saturdays she preached the gospel to a faithful band of Seventh-day Adventists in a space they rented in an industrial plaza. Sunday was her well-deserved day of rest.

Hy had been keeping house for both Kaiser and Reg in the boarding house she inherited when her mother died. The arrangement worked well for Kaiser, who couldn't abide disorder in his surroundings, even though he thrived on chaos in his personal and professional relationships. He made a point of not being around when she came upstairs to do her work. Kaiser had a good stereo and she loved cranking up the music and reviewing his records while she cleaned. Today was an exception — a remarkable day all around. Kaiser was off work with his ankle sprain and desperate for a little distraction.

He'd made a pot of coffee and put out some cookies for the two of them when he heard a buzz at the front door. His postman had a parcel for him. It was heavy. With considerable difficulty, he limped his way back to the kitchen table and began to open it up as Hy looked on.

"What do you suppose it is?" she asked.

"I hope it isn't more bees."

Hy picked up the discarded wrapping paper. "Oh my, it's from a lawyer."

The package was wound tight like a mummy with metres of brown butcher's paper. "Whatever it is, they don't want it getting loose," Kaiser said.

Hy picked up a letter written on expensive paper and gave it a wave. "There's a letter."

"You read it; I'm having too much fun."

She put on her glasses. "It's from the legal firm of Dover and Gregg in Lakefield. Mr. Dover says a Mr. Ian Spraklin died and named you the sole beneficiary of his estate."

Kaiser stopped what he was doing. "Who did you say that was?"

"A Mr. Ian Spraklin, late of the town of Lakefield."

"I kind of know his name. I'm sure he isn't a relative."

Hy kept reading as Kaiser burrowed toward the centre of the mystery package. He was just about there when her voice startled him. "Stop! These are Mr. Spraklin's mortal remains."

Kaiser stumbled backward. "What? What kind of asshole sends *mortal remains* through the mail? Aren't there laws about this?"

Hy took a seat at the table and helped herself to a biscuit. "This came up in my minister's course. It's legal but oh so very undignified." She smiled at Kaiser. "You know what happens to funny old gentlemen like you. They don't marry, they don't have kids, and one day they disappear into the mist. First time I ever saw one get boxed up and mailed somewhere. Probably won't happen to you, though. Damn shame too, with all those good-looking widows in my congregation dying for a second chance at love."

Kaiser was hardly listening. "Spraklin, Spraklin, Spraklin … who the hell is Spraklin?" He took the letter from Hy and began reading. He ran his eyes up and down the page looking for a dollar figure, but he couldn't find one. With his eternal hope for quick cash dashed, he began reading again, this time more slowly. "Listen to this: Ian Spraklin owned a small mixed-use farm outside of Lakefield. There's forty acres of pasture and woodland and a barn, a tractor, and a farmhouse. Oh, look, no mortgage and nothing owing on the farm machinery. This could be worth some money."

"So why in the world are they shipping him here, to you?"

"My God, he has bees — thousands and thousands of bees. He's the lunatic who's been sending me dead bees. Mr. Dover wants to know what I'm going to do with the bees."

"That's why I know the name!" Hy went to the cupboard and pulled out a dusty old jar of honey. "Spraklins' Honey, RR2 Lakefield, Ont."

Kaiser could finally picture him: the quiet old man who would talk to him only while they were playing checkers. *Did our talks mean that much to him?*

"So what about the remains?" Hy asked.

"I'm getting to that part. Legal mumbo, legal jumbo, and … here we are — oh shit, he wants his ashes scattered at Punanai. He said he found God there and that's where he wants to find his rest."

Hy frowned. "That's illegal. You can't be scattering the ashes where people live. It's not right."

Kaiser was still focused on the letter. "It's only dust. I'll use a teaspoon. A little here, a little there. No one will ever know."

Hy wasn't having this. She put on her preacher's hat. "Remember your scripture: From dust we are created and to dust we return. You mess with God's dust at your peril. I don't worry about the dead. They don't have power. But God can make the dry bones dance. You need to worry about God here, Kaiser, not the law."

He wasn't interested in God or the law, only the money. "What harm is there in scattering a few ashes here and there? As long as it doesn't clog the vacuum."

Hy was horrified. "Think this through. Dust gets gathered up into a bag and dumped in a dumpster where it goes to a landfill. No one wants to spend eternity in a stinky old landfill. It's an indignity to one of God's creatures and, by extension, to God Almighty himself."

Kaiser kept reading. "It doesn't say precisely where he wants to end up. I guess that part is up to me. I could mix him with some potting soil and put him in the garden. That might do the roses a power of good." There was a twinkle in his eye.

Hy missed the joke. "That is not a Christian burial, and you know it. Kaiser, this is important. This man was caught up in the sin of Adam. The image of the creator has been distorted in him by his sin. The poor man is so disoriented, he's wasted his opportunities for life, and now in death and despair he's sent his body to be burned. He thinks that because his mortal life is done, his spiritual life is over too. Did no one ever talk to him about the possibility of repentance and the power of God's love?"

Kaiser took a sip of his coffee. "Hy, I don't think he believed in God in any traditional way. If I remember him right, he was a freethinker. He was always talking about his bees. He was fascinated with bees. In fact, I think he was nuts."

Hy could see she was getting nowhere. She put her head down and said a prayer. "Oh Lord, in your mercy ignore this provocation made in ignorance and desperation. Send your ministering angels to care for this poor deserted man, and while there's still time, bring our poor brother Kaiser to a new understanding of your love. Amen."

When she looked up, Kaiser was gone. She finished her coffee and gathered up the dishes in the sink. She looked over her shoulder when she heard a footfall in the hallway. Kaiser had put on his best suit and was taking his topcoat out of the hall closet. "Where are you going? You're supposed to be laid up."

"I'm off to Lakefield. My bees need me."

——

The old grey Toyota sprung to life on the tenth try. The starter engine was going. The body had rusted through, and the car continued to run for up to a minute after the ignition was switched off — all of which indicated a problem with the solenoid. The vehicle had originally been Uncle Oren's retirement car. It came to Kaiser as a gift when a doctor took Oren's licence and then whisked the old man into the Granite Glen Nursing Home.

Oren had run up eleven thousand kilometres in his decade of ownership. That was twenty years ago. Kaiser had been using it as a grocery grabber and it had given him good service, but his last emissions test had put the old bus at the top of the endangered species list. It was running fine today. There were yellow warning lights all over the dash and the heater didn't work, but at least the air conditioning didn't come on when it wasn't wanted.

Conditions were perfect for a winter drive. The roads were bone dry and covered with a rime of salt. The hum of the tires on the cold, hard flat-top of Highway 115 made a lovely counterpoint to Kaiser's mulling over the facts. The drive north gave him a chance to try to recreate in his imagination a relationship that was, at best, incidental to him. He couldn't even remember his benefactor's face. What he did recall was the plaid shirt that Ian Spraklin wore daily and slept in nightly. He must have had ten of them.

Kaiser smirked when he thought about that. *What a funny old bird.* Dr. T. told them he had Asperger's, and the counsellors had to be careful what they said to him and to not be too upset about what he said back.

As the miles rolled by, Kaiser saw once again the frail-looking old man bulling his way into the office with his checkerboard under his arm. Kaiser remembered once when he'd been on the phone and didn't want to be bothered, Ian had ignored Kaiser's frantic arm movements warning him off. When he put his hand over the receiver to berate him, Ian had looked at him blankly as if he was yelling at someone else. He'd sat down at the conference table and began setting up the board.

It didn't matter if he won or lost, Kaiser remembered. Ian had been endlessly fascinated by the movement of the pieces. *How the hell does a guy like that end up with a piss-pot full of money? And why the hell would he leave any of it to me? I have to read that letter again.*

Kaiser made it past Peterborough with no trouble and was looking for the exit to Highway 28 to take him into Lakefield. A dump truck overtook him and gave him a good shaking as it passed. Kaiser wisely let the letter slide back down onto the passenger seat. *I'll figure it out when I get there.* A red light started to blink on the dash and then vanished. "If I get there," he said.

He was close now. He started looking for a landmark. The image shown on the Google map had been taken at the height of summer. Now, in January, the last stubborn handful of leaves was all that remained of the deciduous canopy.

He saw the turnoff for Lakefield and ten minutes later he spotted the Dover and Gregg logo on a sign over top of a strip mall. He parked at the far end of the nearly deserted parking lot. He didn't want the lawyer or anyone else to hear the Toyota's smoker's cough.

It felt good to get out of the car and stretch his legs. His ankle was still stiff and swollen, but he wasn't planning to walk very far. He lit up a smoke and did a final review of his options. He looked through the tinted window of the lawyer's office and, to his great relief, a figure was seated at a desk. It was almost 3:30 p.m. He needed to pick up the pace.

The office looked like a college library. Legal books lined the walls as far as the eye could see. All of them looked immaculate, as if they'd never been read. They were housed in a glass bookcase made of some kind of hardwood stained dark. The room smelled agreeably of old books, leather sofas, and, yes, there it was, fresh brewing coffee. He might be able to finesse a cup if he smiled a little.

The woman behind the desk looked up at him.

"I'm looking for a Mr. Dover."

"May I ask who you are?"

"My name is Kaiser. Mr. Dover sent me a very strange package in the mail this morning, and I came right over when I got it."

She tried to make sense of this insight but couldn't. "Is this about the Spraklin estate?"

"It is."

She nodded and gestured toward a pair of armchairs to her right. "Please make yourself comfortable. You can hang up your coat over there. Can I bring you a coffee? It's freshly brewed."

Kaiser was still reconnoitring, trying to size up the legal fitness of Dover and Gregg, and so he kept his manners to the fore and his smart mouth in reserve.

"Could I see Mr. Dover this afternoon? Perhaps I should have made an appointment."

"He's in the back somewhere, cleaning up some old paperwork. He'll come out when he hears the coffee machine stop hissing." She smiled. "I'm Kate, by the way."

"Pleased to meet you," Kaiser said, somewhat more formally than was his custom. There was something about this office and about this Kate that reminded him of a British comedy of manners. The Lakefield he knew and loved was a much rougher place, with hockey games, poutine wagons, and earthy country pleasures. Mr. Dover's assistant would've looked out of place chewing on a corn dog and cheering on the Peterborough Petes. She was refined and well dressed without being overtly sexual. She wore her blond hair short in an easy-to-manage style and had an otherworldly look about her, as if home and hearth were the centre of her world and this employment was a necessary distraction from all that.

He was going to say something smart when he heard his dark angel's voice. *Keep your yap shut. These two have your cash in their strongbox. Smiles and good manners may be all it takes. Nah, they're gonna try and rob me. This lady looks like she plays the organ for the Anglicans on Sunday; she won't be a problem, but what about the lawyer? Is he a crook?*

Kaiser heard an exchange of words from behind a partition, and a moment later Kate presented him with a cup of coffee on a silver tray. There was even a sugar bowl and a small pitcher of real cream. These guys did things right. "Mr. Dover will be out in a moment."

Kaiser smiled and helped himself to the coffee. It smelled good. A cigarette would've made this special, but he didn't smell stale tobacco or see an ashtray anywhere, so he assumed smoking was off the menu here. Out of the corner of his eye, he caught a glimpse of a man putting on a suit coat and straightening his tie in a mirror.

Francis Dover — barrister, solicitor, and notary — was of middling height. He looked fit but not trim, which wasn't out of place for a man who Kaiser placed in his early sixties. His hair was dark brown and as thick as a beaver's hide. He had deep laugh lines in his face and a beautiful smile. Oops, there was the tell: He hadn't thought to dye his eyebrows. They were thin and grey. In the poor light of the office, the toupee hinted at strength and vitality, but at close quarters, it suggested a sadder, diminishing truth.

Kaiser acknowledged their common struggle against the sands of time with a grin. Did Dover hate the sight of himself coming out of the shower with the same intensity that Kaiser did? Was he, too, seeing vital flesh driven from its rightful place in his arms and chest only to find a cowardly exile around his waist?

He dresses like he has money, but then, so do I.

Kaiser had been living one paycheque away from disaster for his entire adult life. Even when he had high-paying employment, everything went out as fast as it came in. He didn't care about money, and he sure as hell couldn't manage it. People who could balance a chequebook or, worse still, people who talked about money as if it were a person or a thing of great beauty, brought out the worst in him. He had a hard time imagining his life without financial pressure. Could his whole life change from tragedy to triumph at the turning of a single card?

Dover helped himself to a cup of coffee and settled back in his big comfortable armchair. He took Kaiser's measure on the sly as he shovelled four heaping tablespoons of sugar into his brew.

Sugar junkie, is it? Hooked on the white death. What evil little secrets does the sweetness keep at bay, Mr. Lawyer Man?

"So what brings you in to see us this afternoon, Mr. Kaiser?"

It was too much to resist, his tone was Girl Scout earnest. "Well, it's not every day that someone sends me a body in the mail."

Dover and Kate exchanged horrified looks.

Kaiser brightened. "You did a lovely job wrapping it though."

There was a pause and a further exchange of looks. "Mr. Kaiser, we have just met and so I don't know how to take what you're telling me. You say you received a body in the mail? How is that possible?"

Kaiser had their attention and he intended to keep it. So he started to walk back his original claim. "I received an urn containing the ashes of a Mr. Spraklin and a letter from your office."

Dover was caught unawares but didn't seem overly concerned. "Well, this is a turn around. May I see the letter?"

Kaiser produced it with a flourish.

Dover's sober eyes sparkled as he examined the document. "Oh, dear Kate, I do believe that Chester had a hand in this."

Kate made a face that suggested she knew something was in the wind. "He was in the other day all excited about something, but I couldn't make sense of what he was trying to tell me."

Kaiser smiled. "And Chester is...?"

Dover put down the letter and took up his cup of coffee once again. "He is Mr. Spraklin's younger brother. He owns the other half of the property that Mr. Spraklin left to you in his will."

"Is he crazy?"

"I don't think so. Like his brother, he has certain social deficits that have made his life a damn sight more difficult than was absolutely necessary."

"So you think he sent me the urn?"

"Undoubtedly. He had it on his kitchen table last time I saw him."

"Why would he do such a thing? Is that even legal?"

Dover pressed his lips together, trying to find the right tone. "The legality of the thing would never occur to Chester. He obviously thought that you were the person best qualified to carry out his brother's wishes."

Kaiser raised his left eyebrow and sat up straighter in his chair. "In the letter, he said he wanted to have his ashes cast about the Punanai Centre."

The lawyer's head tilted in disapproval. "Which is undoubtedly private property and so it cannot be done without the consent of the owners."

It was unusual for Kaiser to want to be helpful, but there was something about Dover. "Punanai is a treatment centre for alcoholics and drug addicts, and as such it's supervised by the Ministry of Health. They would never give their permission."

Dover looked over at Kate. "I tried to explain that to Mr. Spraklin when we drew up the document, but he insisted. He was never capable of the level of abstraction necessary to separate what he desired from what was right. In his mind, they always went hand in glove."

Kaiser probed, hoping to refresh his memories and test them against a reliable source. "And his brother, Chester…"

"The same problem but at a more frustrating level. Ian looked after Chester for most of his life. I'm not sure Chester can stay on the farm alone. I'm afraid he'll starve to death."

Kaiser saw that as a plus. "Is he that badly impaired?"

"He can't get anything done, save on the one subject."

"Bees?"

Dover actually smiled. "How did you know?"

Kaiser was off and running. "I'm guessing here, but I think that Chester's the one who has been sending me dead bees and honeycombs and rambling, unsigned letters for months now."

Kate looked concerned. "It must have been important to him. Chester has to walk five kilometres to mail a letter."

Kaiser turned to include her in the conversation. "Bees were the only thing Ian ever wanted to talk about when I knew him. Did he stay sober after he came home from treatment?"

Kate and Dover looked at each other like two friends worried about picking up the check. "Mostly he did. He went to the AA meetings, but he had a hard time fitting in. They always wanted him to get up at the front of the room and talk. He hated that. He told me once that he went out and got drunk every time they asked him to speak and they very quickly got the message."

Kaiser put down his empty cup. "So what do I do with the ashes?"

"Keep them safe for a week or two. There's no hurry. We have eternity to work with. Let me try and have another talk with Chester. There has to be a solution that is legal and dignified, something that is going to accommodate everyone's needs."

"You mean Chester's."

"Yes, you have it exactly."

"Forgive my bluntness, but Ian Spraklin was a client of mine at Punanai and inheriting his estate is going to cause me some real problems."

"Ethics?"

"That and gossip. Someone is going to cry foul. Why leave it all to me and not to Chester? I barely knew the man."

Dover smiled sagely as Kate laughed and took up the tale. "Because Chester didn't import his bees from Scandinavia. He used local bees. Chester's corn cobber's kept mating with Ian's thoroughbreds and submerging all of their finer qualities. If he'd let them, Chester's bees would've destroyed everything Ian was trying to accomplish."

Kaiser watched Kate wiping the tears from her eyes. "I never thought I'd laugh at that. Mr. Kaiser, I can't count the number of times I've been harangued in this office by the late Mr. Spraklin about his brother's failings as a beekeeper. He'd bring in petitions for us to sign, and a couple times he wanted to institute legal actions on behalf of the public to protect them from his brother's odious practices."

"Did he sue?"

Dover leaned forward in his chair. "No. I told him that the case law was against him. The research alone would cost over two hundred thousand dollars, and I would need a retainer in that amount before I could even begin my efforts." Dover looked over at Kaiser. "The word *bullshit* is on your lips, Mr. Kaiser. Go ahead and say it."

"The old razzle-dazzle?"

"The game wasn't worth the candle. I took the view that Chester should raise his bees in his own way and allow Ian the same liberty."

"But they weren't buying it?"

"Family struggles for power frequently end up before the courts. Lots of common assaults, frauds, arson, vandalism, and even murders are the result of people who have been quarrelling for so long that they can't let go. These people end up in the courts because they cannot govern themselves. As a people, we believe in judgment day, my friend. We believe that someday an outsider is going to judge both us and our families and find heavily in our favour."

"What about Jesus?"

"That is another strand of the same narrative, another one of the possibilities. But here is a fact for you to consider. The law will never bring you justice. It cannot, because such a thing can never exist. Lawsuits can bring you revenge, offer you hope, and put the fear of God into the people you despise. But mostly it's an exchange of letters between two attorneys."

"Very expensive letters."

"It's often a question of what lasts longer: your ill will or your cash."

"But why are you telling me all this? Surely this is the kind of insider stuff you talk about with your cronies over drinks."

"Mr. Kaiser, I put myself in your position before I wrote that letter. But I did not send it. The original is still on my desk. The letter you received is a copy that I showed to Chester. I can only assume he sent it and Ian's remains. Chester has agreed to look after Ian's bees until such time as you can find your feet as a beekeeper."

"What if I don't want to?"

"Indeed, why would a professional man in the middle of his career chuck it all for a broken-down bee farm in Lakefield? You see such an obvious objection would never occur to either Ian or Chester. Bees are life. What fool wouldn't want to be in the thick of it?"

Kaiser shuddered and wondered why.

"You have to understand, too, that the Spraklins built this town. Their name is on the original land grant for the area, and if you examine the church yard and the sanctuary, you will find their name preserved everywhere you look: on tombstones, engravings, stained glass, and brass plaques. It's hard to talk about the history of this place without engaging this remarkable family."

"Are they the last two?"

"In town, yes. Most of the family moved to Toronto at the start of the twentieth century. They now number in the hundreds, but the local variety of Spraklins are a dying breed."

"Why not leave the farm to one of them?"

"They, too, are the enemy. They wouldn't sign the petition or mortgage their homes to come up with the money for the lawsuit, and so they get nothing."

"Mr. Dover, this problem feels very familiar to me."

"How so?"

"All of my clients are as self-righteous as Old Testament prophets. They all want something they can't have. In order to get it, they're willing to make everyone around them miserable, and they expect to be treated like heroes. They believe their own lies, and anyone who stands up to them and calls them on their selfishness is a rat bastard."

Dover liked what he was hearing. Perhaps Ian's choice of executor was going to work out after all. Here was a man who said what he meant and meant what he said.

"There's a condition in the will that is going to give you pause."

Kaiser heard a heavy truck speeding by on the highway outside the office. It reminded him that there was more going on in the world than this conversation. The outside world would never let Kaiser win. Of course there was a catch.

I knew it.

"In order to inherit fully, you need to bring three crops of honey to market in the next five years."

"Why five years?"

"Ian figured you would kill most of the bees the first year and you might have some bad luck after that, so he gave you five years."

"Why would I do such a thing for forty acres of farmland?"

"It's only farmland because the Spraklins won't sell."

"What's it really worth?"

"I have an offer on my desk worth two million dollars."

Kaiser felt his heart set to work. "That's nuts!"

"The local golf course wants to expand, and the Spraklins are the only ones not willing to sell. The golfers are waiting for the old boys to go, and they're hoping that the heirs will see things in a different light."

Dover gave Kaiser a look that said their business was finished for today.

Kaiser obligingly looked at his watch and got to his feet to go. He forgot about his ankle, and a spark of pain crossed his face when he stood.

"Are you unwell?"

"An ankle sprain."

"Good. Beekeeping isn't heavy work but you have to be fit."

Kaiser looked first at Dover and then at Kate. "So you think I'm going to do this?"

Dover got to his feet to see his guest out. "If I were you, I'd go home and discuss it with those near and dear to me over the weekend. Then, if you like, come back next week and I'll drive you over to the Spraklin farm and introduce you to Chester."

Chapter 37

Paul always took great pains to make sure the Straight Up meeting was given a chance to work its magic. His colleague Greg played music and asked everyone to reflect before he led the group, but Paul got the guys to sit in a circle and pay attention to their breathing with their eyes closed for a few minutes before they started.

The guys had a hard time with meditation. They were still too jangled by their years of abuse and sudden about-face into abstinence to get the full benefit from it. Meditation required a healthy body and a sound emotional state. Still, they had to start somewhere. One by one, they gave up on their breathing and turned their attention to Paul.

While he was waiting for the group to find its focus, he reached into the pocket of his decades-old tweed jacket and took out a cloth that he used to polish his glasses. As a photographer, Paul had a deep appreciation of and reverence for the lens. The right lens could make any difficulty manageable.

He began his analysis by taking stock of who was sitting with whom for this installment of the family portrait. Fifteen bodies: He knew ten; the other five remained a mystery. Hart and Sean were sitting side by side, facing the window. Prime seating as befit their station. When someone was being boring, the window offered an easy escape into the past or the future or sometimes even fantasy. Czombo was sitting alone this week and he'd moved as far away from the others as he could. His wingman, Vince, had gone back to the bar and, clearly, Czombo and Larry Lorne were now on the outs too. *How are you going to behave now without your posse?* Larry was sitting beside Daniel Philips. That could be a big positive. Maybe he was starting to buy into the process. Bill was sitting alone near the kitchen door with his now purple face half hidden by a cold compress.

Paul's voice was warm and comfortable. "In a minute, we're going to start. What gets said here stays here. This space is sacred. Nothing you say here is going to be used against you. This is your chance to get outside all the clutter going on inside your head and speak your truth aloud, maybe for the first time in many years — and not to strangers or people who are angry with you, but to a group of men who are all struggling to understand their own addictions. Don't miss this chance."

He looked around the room, trying to gauge who was up for this. The newest recruits were all checking out their neighbours for a reaction, wondering if this could be true.

"You can talk about the moment you realized you had to come for treatment, that moment when you finally knew you had to do something about your addiction. Or you can talk about some experience or insight you've had since you got here, something that has maybe given you a little hope that it's possible to recover. Now I want you to nod to the men on either side of you, let them know with a look that you're on their side. And, even more importantly, I want you to notice that there's an empty chair in this circle. That chair is there to remind you that whatever's sacred to you is on trial for its life in this room. Don't let that part of you down. So who wants to start?"

Czombo and Hart had their hands up. That surprised Paul. If Czombo came from an authentic place, that could really make the meeting. Paul thought about that as a realistic possibility for a second and then shook his head. Czombo was going to pour poison into the punch. Paul knew he had a winner in Hart. "Channing, why don't you start?"

Czombo fired an angry look at Paul and then examined the room, looking for signs of support. His face was red and his right leg dancing. He kept his hand up like an angry schoolboy with a righteous point to make.

As Hart began to speak, he looked around the room, making eye contact with as many of the men who would have it. They were comfortable with him now, over the shock of seeing someone on the news in the room with them. They were interested in what he had to say. "I think I know you all now, at least a little bit. Some of you guys are new friends and one of you, that would be Bill over there with the hockey eye, is a guy I drank with. No one bothered to ask me if I wanted to come here. I was ordered to by a judge. On Monday, my time here is done, and next week I have to be back in court for sentencing. I don't suppose any of you guys know what goes on in the Don Jail."

That got a laugh.

"I didn't think we had places like that in Canada. I was there for almost three months." For a second, he found himself back in the Don, playing cards on the range with his doper pals while PB fretted the comings and goings of everyone. He touched his sleeve, greatly relieved not to feel the orange jumpsuit that marked him and the others as less than human. What a counterpoint to this group. It felt safe to say what he wanted to for the first time.

"I was desperate to get out. I wanted to have a bath and go to a movie and eat in a restaurant — all the things that are still off the menu. I wanted to live my old life again for a few more days and pretend, if that's what I had to do, that nothing bad happened. That everything was the way it had been before." The words ground to a stop, but the pain that clouded his eye said he wasn't finished. The only sound was the gurgle of the water cooler.

Bill had a tear in his bloodshot black-and-blue eye. His response was infectious. There was a groundswell of support for Hart. If only they were the jurors.

Hart smiled an embarrassed smile. It wasn't the words that were the problem. It was the display of emotion. The underside of the leaf. Stark, veined, and paler in colour. Never intended for public view. "I shouldn't tell you this, but I'm kind of psycho with telling the truth these days. An hour after I got out of the Don, I walked into my apartment, opened the fridge, and drank a beer. I was halfway through the second one before I realized what I was doing. The next day, I had to be here, clean and sober for seventy-two hours, and there I was guzzling beers."

The guys all laughed. That was a universal experience. Even Czombo's head popped up and he went so far as to lower his hand.

"People went out of their way to give me a chance to help myself before I got sent away and that was how I was acting. I was on autopilot. I didn't even know I was drinking a beer. It coulda been a glass of water."

Larry Lorne flashed back to the moment of discovery on the smoke deck when the final canary of his faith in Czombo fell dead at his feet. Daniel Philips was knocking softly on the crack-house door, feeling the weight of gold coins in his jacket pocket. The two new friends exchanged a look that fully engaged Sean Miller's curiosity.

"That was the moment. I poured the beer down the sink, piled all the bottles back into the case, and got rid of 'em. That was the first time I let myself feel everything that was going on. You can't do that in jail. The first time I let myself feel how — how broken I was..." He found himself back on the cold floor of the holding cell, barefoot. His throat parched and his neck throbbing in pain. He was stunned the way people so often are in the recovery room when they come out of the ether. Full of benzos. Blacking out and coming to. Full of wonder at this new reality that came and went in alternating fits of florescent light and interior darkness. There was a very long pause. A new thought came to him, and he spoke it into the room. "That should have happened when they told me I killed Margaret Gibson ... but it didn't."

That was too much. The chairs all started to move and make sounds. The men were squirming as they recalled their own close calls and near misses. Paul looked over to where Czombo was sitting by himself, expecting to see him tearing pages out of a Bible or setting fire to loose threads in his pant cuffs. Czombo looked calm except for his unrelenting restless leg syndrome. He was pointing in the direction of the hallway with his index finger, but Paul didn't care. He had no time for his distractions.

Hart noticed the sea change in men's moods, but he wasn't put off. "Don't get me wrong, everything was different after they told me she was dead. How could it not be? But I wasn't. I was still me, in trouble and desperate to get out." Bill thought about the Saturday morning breakfast. How easily Hart had changed from friend into other. A tale told twice has to be true. A media assertion becomes proven science when no one has the stomach to continue thinking about the horror of what happened. When obliging blame was so near at hand, ready and willing to whisk it all away.

"In jail I met a guy who called himself PB, Prison Bob. He was all about beating the rap. Showed me how to take care of myself in jail for the price of a

Mars bar and a Coke. I asked him once why he called himself Prison Bob, and he told me he was a different man when he was free. I didn't get that then. I don't know what you guys would make of Bob if he was here with us this afternoon. He was small and had bad teeth, a straggly beard, and a bald spot, but that didn't matter. I needed a friend pretty badly. I listened to him. I let him be my guide."

The point was not lost. Even the new guys were nodding.

"When we're in trouble, we take care of ourselves, even if it means doing the wrong thing. I get that, and I can live with it but not with the way it hardens us. I can forgive myself for behaving badly in the Don. A saint would. But there's no excuse for behaving badly now that I'm free and sober. I can't let anybody take that away from me again. That's the thing that changed for me while I was here. That's what I see when I look over at that empty chair. I didn't have that in jail." He thought about Levy and Summers and the big lie and that poor family until it all became a pill that was stuck in his windpipe. All eyes were on him but in a good way for once.

Sean was thinking about Kaiser's three questions and Reg's advice. Was this the medicine he had ordered? This felt like betrayal and cowardice. Leaving his friend to swing in the wind. In that instant, he saw his mother's face as she uncomprehendingly watched his descent into addiction. She was in that damn chair. She was dead too. No way to get her out of it.

Hart swallowed the pill and found his voice again. He felt gratitude, which seemed wildly out of place. "This place is rough, even borderline psychotic at times, but it's exactly what the doctor ordered. See, I was already doing a life sentence, I just didn't know it. No one ever gets outta this place without being confronted with the truth about themselves. So for you new guys, you can take it from me: These impossible, infuriating, full-of-themselves suits know what they're doing. They know you can change, and they'll be there for you to lean on and learn from while you do. This isn't the end the world — it feels like it most of the time, but it's not."

The guys were all nodding. Hart had made his case. There was only one holdout: Czombo. He was waving his hand frantically in the air again. Paul pointed to the far end of the circle.

Larry Lorne spoke next. His confident appearance didn't match what he was feeling. "This is my first time speaking here. I don't like myself very much these days." He had to fight the urge to turn and stare at Czombo. He wanted to punch him, but he knew better. "I'm depressed. I don't wanna do anything. I hate getting out of bed in the morning and the only thing I have to look forward to is sleep. I can't stand thinking about my life because when I do, these awful feelings of fear and failure…" The words petered out as his shoulders gave way under the weight he was feeling. *How can Hart tell the truth about killing someone and I'm afraid to talk about a piss test? I am a coward and a fool.* "I don't mean to cross talk, but I really wonder how I'm ever going to get from where I am to where Hart is. I had a talk with Paul, and he encouraged me to tell you guys who I really am and what I really want, but I can't find the juice. I don't have the words to do that today. So I'm gonna stop now and hope for better things next week. I care about this, but I just can't pony up."

All the guys nodded, except for Czombo. He was bouncing up and down on his chair with his hand up. He looked like he was going to burst if he didn't speak. Paul took enormous pleasure in ignoring him.

Daniel didn't wait to be asked. He looked over at his much bigger friend and sighed. It was hard to tell why. Larry sat with his head down, looking beaten. "I guess it's my turn now," Daniel said. "I'm a mess. Changing is hard. Some mornings I wake up and I feel good, you know, kind of positive, like — I don't know — like it would be fun to hop in a car and go for a drive. I think about the future and what I want to do, and it all seems doable and maybe even a bit exciting. You know, like, I could get lucky and find someone, someone who understands. An hour later, it changes. I think about all the things I did wrong, all the things I did to hurt and disappoint the people who care about me, and all the lies I told to cover my tracks. I don't think there's a way back from that. Even if there was, I'm not sure I'd want to go back. When I tell people who I really am, they don't like what they hear."

There was a disconnect between the fastidious, well-behaved speaker and his words. One had to wonder. What could this young man, barely more than a boy really, have done to make the world shun him and to make himself so miserable?

Daniel sat up in his chair and squared his shoulders. It didn't help. "The thing I understand now that I didn't know when I got here is that the drinking is just the symptom. Alcohol and drugs are where I go when I can't stand the way I feel. I'm not saying I don't have a problem. Hell, my emotions are back and forth at least once a day. If I wasn't here, I'd use. That's a good thing, you know. I'm not using here. This is the only place in the world I've ever been able to stay sober. There's something wrong with me, and I don't have the words to tell you what it is, but even if I did, I know I'd be too afraid to."

His head went down. He put his palms face down on his knees. In the silence, a few whispers of encouragement were heard. Larry made a fist and gently tapped it like a gavel on the back of Daniel's hands.

Czombo had kept his hand up all through Daniel's share. Paul had motioned for him to stop, but Czombo ignored him.

Paul grit his teeth. *I have to let this jackass speak sooner or later. He's making it hard for the guys to speak. I'm not gonna let him ruin this. When he says something stupid, I'll tell him to shut up and ask Sean to speak next.*

Paul nodded at Czombo. "I don't wanna talk," Czombo said. "I need the bathroom."

Paul couldn't say what was in his heart. He watched as the thin young man with the shoulder-length green hair and the bathtub plug around his neck got up and left the room, and it took his breath away. *Raised by wolves and aching to have a litter of his own.* Paul couldn't say that aloud, so he let a look of contempt speak for him. Doug didn't throw out the kids. No matter what they did. That was probably the smart move. Even if it didn't feel like it this afternoon.

Czombo sprinted upstairs to the big, oaken front door. Outside on the patio, a thin woman with red hair was shifting uneasily from foot to foot, smoking a cigarette and fooling with her phone. It was Darlene, the lady who sold drugs out behind the 7-Eleven. She must have been out of product. She badly needed something to steady her nerves.

Czombo opened the door and let her in. "I can only give you five minutes of my time."

Darlene was angry. "I'm freezing. You left me standing out there for twenty minutes."

Czombo gave her an exasperated look as he reached out to take a lock of her hair in his hand. "It couldn't be helped. I was stuck in a meeting."

Taking her cue from him, she put her hand seductively on his lapel. "Let's take care of the money first."

Czombo produced the correct sum from his shirt pocket. "Does it ruin the romance of the thing for you, having to ask for money afterwards?"

She ignored him, dorks always said something they thought was charming when they were embarrassed. "What kind of place is this, anyway?"

Czombo held out his arms in a classic gesture of welcome. "It defies description." He nudged her into an interview room and closed the door.

Back in the dining room, Paul stepped out of character for a moment, as deftly as the author of a play taking off his mask to correct a small difficulty observed in the dress rehearsal. With Czombo gone, he hoped to restore the tone of the meeting to where it had been at the high point of Hart's remarks, to make it safe again to speak the truth. "When I was sitting where you are, many years ago — not in this room, but in our old house — I remember feeling threatened by the guys who were doing well. They intimidated me." He looked around at them all.

This felt more personal to the guys somehow. It was as if Paul was simply one of them, taking his turn at the helm. They wondered what he was up to.

"I was sure the things that had defeated me in life were going to defeat me in sobriety too. Sure, guys around me were getting well, but look at the advantages they had. This guy was rich, that one good looking, that guy over there was really smart. What chance did I have? I felt like they were going to recover because they were better than me. God knows that's a message this alcoholic heard loud and clear — from preachers on high to bartenders and bouncers."

Everyone was grinning. Paul the drunk was a far cry from the poised man speaking to them now. They made a new connection with him. He didn't just know what they did and how they thought because they'd told him. He knew from experience. That took a second to sink in. He was a man with a foot in both their past and their future.

"But I had it all wrong. I can hear the struggle I went through in your stories. People get this because they're willing to change. That's the secret ingredient. A part of it is recognizing that there's a problem, and maybe another part is knowing that other people have come through and stayed well. But recovery is all about authenticity. It's wanting to become who you *really* are. Guys get hooked on other people's opinions. It's hard to take back control of your life after you've made a mess of it. It can set you up to trust the wrong people."

Paul gave Sean a subtle nod that said it was his turn next just as Czombo re-entered the room and took his seat. But Sean had been ruminating on his own thoughts and had missed everything Paul had said. The big smirk on Czombo's face brought him back into the room. The green-haired creep made quite a show of taking his seat and behaving as if his presence had been sorely missed. He turned to the new guy, who didn't know enough yet to keep his distance, and whispered theatrically for everyone to hear. "A personal best."

Sean wanted to take a round out of Czombo right there in front of the group. He looked at Paul and wondered why he wasn't up to the task. Couldn't he see what was going on? Were all the counsellors blind? He was screwing with them, and the question came down to this: Did they not know — in which case, they were pathologically stupid — or did they simply not care — which suggested something quite a bit worse?

Sean scowled. *I'll be damned before I speak my truth into this circle of vipers.* That's what he wanted to say. Instead, a new line was carefully delivered in a neutral tone: "I think I'll pass and have a one-on-one with Paul when this is over."

Bill looked up from his compress with a sad smile. The impasse between seller Paul and buyer Czombo was familiar. The empty chair, an apt symbol for that thing we all long for but are afraid to inhabit. Sean had seen through to the bottom of the impasse. His polite but nonnegotiable time-out saying that this was a charade. On offer, a home — requiring a substantial down payment and a thirty-year commitment. At hand, a motivated seller and a deadbeat buyer. There is a difference between buying a house as an investment and purchasing a home. One you love, the other serves a purpose. This was unfortunately neither. This was pretending writ large. A fault-finding mission that would inform a refusal in the making.

Bill looked over at Czombo. "Do you know the difference between you and me?"

Czombo glared at Bill and struggled to come up with the perfect put-down to shut up this fat old dick.

Paul looked at Bill and then back at Czombo. *It would be wrong to stop this.*

Sean was praying, *Tell the little prick.*

Before anyone could spoil the moment, Bill lifted the compress from his swollen face for effect and pointed at Czombo. "That's what you look like when you're full of shit and don't know it." He jerked his thumb back toward his face. "I'm what's left when you finally figure it out."

———

Sean went looking for Paul after the meeting, as intent on talking to him as he had famously been with Doug when his coat had gone missing. He found Paul in the office, finishing his paperwork and thinking about the extraordinary exchange between Bill and Czombo. The guys on the smoke deck were choosing sides — nothing new there. But there was something else going on.

Paul brightened when he saw Sean staring at him through the window and motioned for him to come inside.

"I want to talk to you," Sean said.

"Please," said Paul, holding out his hand. "I was hoping to hear a lot more from you at the meeting."

Sean kept his anger on a leash but only barely. It had practically dislocated his shoulder. There was a dangerous texture to his tone. "Not happening."

Paul looked Sean up and down. "You're angry. What have you got to be angry about?"

Sean got right in his face. "I'll tell you what I'm angry about. There's a monster loose in this house. He's fucking up everybody he can and making all you clowns here in the office look pathetically stupid. Don't you have eyes? Can't you smell the pot coming off this little fucker?"

Paul saw through to the bottom of things. All the pieces fit. The new pairings in the group. The unwillingness of some of the participants to take a chance and tell their story. He hated it when the guys figured out what was happening in the house before the staff did. But so often that was the case. This kind of problem was disruptive. Still, he reasoned, it couldn't be as out of control as Sean was suggesting, because the Straight Up had gone well. If the men were holding grudges, the meeting would've been two hours of long faces, pained silence, and pointless generalities. He'd seen it before.

"I better shut the door. Can you tell me who's using?"

Sean literally became tight lipped. "I'm not a squealer."

Paul knew enough not to say, *Yeah you are. Finish the job you started.* Instead, he appealed to Sean's better side. "How can I keep the house safe if you won't help me?"

Sean hated Czombo, but he'd played long and hard for that franchise and he still had some feelings for it. Could he give up one of his own? Maybe he was never going to use again, but maybe he was. Maybe this recovery thing was the real deal and maybe it wasn't. Or maybe it wasn't the right thing for him. But that was only the surface. What he wanted was for Paul to get up off his ass and go find the little fucker and set fire to his tail feathers. The thought *Show me you believe in this shit* was more diplomatically delivered as *Look here, super sleuth. There are fifteen guys in the house, and one of them is smoking dope and beating you for all you're worth. If you can't catch him at it after what I told you, you really are a mutt.*

Paul was about to make a point when Sean bolted out the door.

———

The guys departed at 7:00 p.m. for their community twelve-step meetings, leaving Paul alone in the house. He locked the door and made his way directly to Czombo's room. Paul still hadn't settled on a nickname for Michael Eustice Czombo. *Why would he foreground Eustice and hide the Michael?* Paul was going back and forth between monikers. The most apt description was *jolly green indigent*, but he had to admit in his heart of hearts, he favoured *useless*. Neither fully satisfied, but perhaps a third possibility would occur to him.

Some of the counsellors made a point of leaving signs of their passing when they searched a room. Not Paul; he didn't want to spook his quarry. He shut his eyes and smelled deeply. It smelled of strong cologne. Paul opened Czombo's drawers and looked through them, but he knew there'd be nothing. He checked the window, looking for transparent fishing wire but found none. Lots of contraband was stored outside the building, within easy reach, using this technique. You had to feel for it because it defeated the eye. He examined the elbow joint beneath the sink to see if it had been moved recently and ran a blast of water down the drain to rule it out as a possible hiding place. He searched for traces of pot in the coat pocket of the jacket hung in the closet but found nothing.

So much for the easy stuff. He widened the scope of the investigation. Czombo's room had a sink but no toilet or shower. He went across the hall and turned on the light to the shared bathroom. He let his eyes adjust to the illumination as he slowly scanned all the surfaces. Nothing looked out of place. The ceiling tiles offered the best hope of concealment. They spoke to the addict of both convenience and deniability. How could you say that dope found there belonged to anyone? One tile was ever so slightly out of true. Paul went to the maintenance office and helped himself to the ladder. The moment he ascended the top rung, the doorbell rang. He got down and made his way to the front door. A thin red-headed woman was standing shivering in the cold. She had tried to hide a black eye with makeup but it had smeared. She was jonesing. The wild look in her eye made that abundantly clear. Paul opened the door a crack. His body language said that he wasn't going to let her in.

"Is Czombo here?"

Paul recognized her but didn't let on. "I can't tell people who's here."

There was a sudden edge of anger to her voice that wasn't hard to figure out. "Well, he was here this afternoon!"

"What you can do is leave a note, and if he's here, I'll give it to him. That's the best I can do."

She suddenly went limp. "I'm broke, and I was hoping he could, you know, help me out again."

Paul wanted to ask, but he didn't. His silence would have been rude in any other context.

"I'll come back later."

"I can't let you in. This is a treatment centre for men."

Her look was priceless and practised. "Oh, is that what it is?"

Paul had a hard time not calling bullshit. *You sell dope to the guys. How can you not know?*

The hustle was lame. The words ran out. Darlene looked at Paul helplessly. "I'll do you for twenty dollars. Please. My baby is sick, and I need to get home."

Chapter 38

Kaiser was tired after his trip and grateful that Uncle Oren's Toyota had come through death's dark vale one more time. Hy had placed Ian's remains front and centre on the kitchen table beside a Christ candle that she'd left burning. The phone rang as Kaiser was tenderly removing his shoe from his now badly swollen ankle. The swelling that had started to subside was back with a vengeance. Kaiser looked at the phone and recognized Reg's number. He put him on speaker. "Hey, bonehead! What you doing?"

Reg's cheery voice filled the room. "Well, if it isn't the invalid. How's it going, hop-along?"

Kaiser was fixated on his ankle and consequently blunter than he intended. "Something's come up. We need to talk."

Kaiser never came right to the point. He liked to play before he pounced. This departure whet Reg's appetite. "Well … talk."

Kaiser put some weight on his foot and winced. The pain registered in his voice as annoyance. "Not on the phone. I'll pick you up in an hour. We're going to Billy's."

Reg wanted to talk now but knew that he'd have to wait. "Sounds good. Pine Rock is tonight. You can take me there afterwards."

"I hate that group."

That's why I joined it.

———

Billy's Pho was always jammed. It was cheap and cheerful with ample parking and a menu that never got tired. If Kaiser had his druthers, they'd be eating at Swiss Chalet. If Reg was paying, they'd be meeting at the Tartu on Bloor Street. This choice beautifully split the difference between location and entrées right down the middle — the same way that Kaiser was hoping they were going to settle the bill, even though it was his turn to pay.

Kaiser wanted to talk over Dover's advice, but he didn't want anyone to know what he was up to, how much trouble he was in, or how beaten up and alone he felt. This was going to be a conversation in the abstract.

As the waiters approached with the steaming hot bowls of pho, Kaiser looked across the table at Reg and asked innocently, "What would you do without me?"

Answering a query like that from Kaiser was like diffusing a bomb. Best not to cut any wire or answer any question until you understood its purpose. "In what sense?"

The waiters set the food down. Kaiser ignored them, but Reg gave them a smile and a thank you. "Well, if I went away?"

Reg was wary but amused. "Custodial sentence or witless protection?"

Kaiser frowned and started dumping vegetables and mint into the boiling water and then set about giving the whole thing a good stir with his chopstick. A lovely waft of fragrant steam rose from the bowl. "Very funny. What if I upped and left, disappeared off the face of the earth?"

This was a matryoshka doll. The harder you worked, the smaller the prizes got. It was the classic set-up for a Kaiser sandbagging. "Something in what you're saying is prompting me to ask, Kaiser, how are things at home? Are any of your little playmates having a problem?"

Kaiser stared at his dinner and the implements available to him for some time before he picked up the spoon. He pointed it at Reg. "Put your counsellor's diploma back up on the wall. Tonight, the question is simply the question. Nothing hidden, nothing psychological, straight up, how would you feel if I vanished?"

"You and DB Cooper are gonna go and pick up the airliner money, aren't you? That's why you've been hanging around here all this time."

"You're stalling."

Reg opened up and carefully placed his napkin on his lap. "I can't answer the question in the sure and certain knowledge that you're laughing at me."

Kaiser couldn't get real, so he stayed with bully tactics. "That's the bonehead in you coming out."

Reg didn't want to fight over dinner, but he wasn't going to take any nonsense either, even if it meant having to slog his way home on the TTC again. "Kaiser, you love to sandbag people, you deliberately embarrass them, you find ways to make people look like idiots. Okay fine, that's a useful skill in a treatment centre. But you do it everywhere, and that's not right. I'll grant you, most of the people you jack up are in the wrong and they need to be called on their stuff and mostly they even want to be. But you give them such an easy out by being so outrageous."

Kaiser was the very picture of impatience. "And—"

Reg held up a chopstick. "Not done yet. Likewise, you can't pretend to be innocent. You do this all the time. The question is neither simple nor straightforward. It's a jack-in-the-box and I don't know when I turn the crank if I'm gonna get an expensive cigar or an exploding one."

Reg had deftly stopped the advance of Kaiser's armoured column with this dazzling display of defensive artillery. Kaiser sent skirmishers to try and outflank him. "Let's step one floorboard to the left then. If I disappeared, what would the people at work say?"

Reg was using his chopsticks with great skill. He was able to talk and eat at the same time. "Half of them would think you were drunk, and the other half would think you finally pranked a serial killer."

That was the answer he was looking for and he was satisfied. *So no one would be checking out monasteries or refugee camps in Africa looking for me. Good to know.*

Reg mistook the look of satisfaction on Kaiser's face for arrogance and he sighed. "Kaiser, you're a hurricane. Full of menace, then destructive, until you finally peter out into a gentle rain ten thousand miles from where you started. I worry about you. If you vanished, I'd be sad and I'd miss you. But I'd know it was all a crock."

Kaiser had a fat piece of ginger beef between his teeth. "There really is no graceful way for a goon to retire from hockey."

This struck Reg as an odd direction for the conversation to go in. Kaiser didn't talk much about his hopes and dreams. Reg went exploring. "Kaiser, I'm at the point where I'm ready to hang up my guns and retire. I don't want to be an addictions counsellor for the rest of my life. I had a lot of fun doing it. I learned a lot. I grew a lot, but now I want to turn all of my talents to writing."

There was a pause, a very long, telling pause. Kaiser looked like an infant caught in the moment between a loud crash and the desire to cry. It annoyed him to no end how close Reg had come to the truth.

Reg pushed it home. "Are you thinking about retiring? Is that what we're talking about?"

"Wrong again, bonehead."

Kaiser, why can't you do vulnerability? Are you ever going to say you're hurting?

Reg looked at Kaiser's face for a clue. Kaiser couldn't return his stare. That had never happened before either!

Oh crap, what's he not telling me? They've showed him an X-ray ... the dumb bastard has smoked himself to death!

Chapter 39

Paul resumed the search after sending Darlene on her way. Czombo's girlfriend would've made an excellent witness for the prosecution, but alas, her testimony was inadmissible. Paul knew he had the right man now. He knew what to look for and he knew he had two glorious hours before the guys came back. Back up the ladder he went.

He hit pay dirt on the third ceiling tile. Czombo had been quite clever. He'd put a brick on top of it so it couldn't easily be dislodged. Paul reckoned a tall person like Czombo could stand with one foot on the sink and the other on the bathtub and easily reach what lay hidden. His hand bumped something hard and round. He was confused when a urine bottle came rattling out of the ceiling and onto the floor.

He moved the ladder and took out two more tiles. There they were: a clutch of urine sample bottles. Czombo must have burgled the supply room in the basement. It was supposed to be locked. After tonight it would be.

No amount of searching turned up any dope. Still, half a mystery solved was something. Paul gathered up the urine bottles and put them and the tiles back the way they'd been — albeit, with a telltale scratch on the bottom of each bottle. He went back into Czombo's room and sat on his bed. There was still too much cologne in the air for him to do what he needed to. That was likely intentional. He took the pillow off the bed and a sweater from the closet and walked into one of the empty adjoining rooms. What he wanted was some still air, a place without circulation. The empty top bureau drawer was perfect. He put the pillowcase and the sweater inside the drawer and let them sit for twenty minutes.

In the meantime, he went to the storeroom and retrieved the nasal irrigator. He filled it with saline solution and helped himself to one of the disposable blue nose pieces still wrapped in plastic. It would take a few minutes before the green light came on. He went outside and took in a deep lungful of air. He blew his nose and went back into the bathroom. He took himself to task in the mirror. "You are not going to wuss out!" He very carefully irrigated his nose with warm salt water. It was a curious sensation to say the least. His wife was prone to chronic sinus trouble, and she did this on a daily basis to keep from getting completely blocked up. She'd been the first person he'd ever seen use such a device.

Paul had used her machine once or twice out of curiosity, but he didn't like the sensation or the resultant increase in his olfactory sense. Like most people, he was insensible to the everyday smells of humanity. However, when he irrigated his nose this way, he became hyperaware of his surroundings, to the point where he couldn't stand the smell of the other people on the bus. He recognized that this device would come in handy in exactly this situation. He needed some superhuman smelling power this evening. That was why he'd suggested to Doug that the house spend a few dollars to get one.

When he was ready, he entered the vacant room and opened the top drawer. It was there, the faint smell of pot, coming off the pillowcase and the sweater. He held them up to his nose and smelled them again.

"I can search luggage at the airport now," he said brightly as he put Czombo's possessions carefully back into his room.

———

When Paul returned to the office, he called Doug. He was surprised when all he got was voicemail. Doug always answered his phone. He waited a few minutes and then called again, only to get the same result. It was Sunday night. What could someone Doug's age find to do on a Sunday night? Paul dialled Mike's number and got him on the third ring.

"Boss man, I got a problem."

"Call Doug."

Paul smiled; this was going to be fun. "He isn't answering his phone."

Mike got out of his favourite chair and popped a cigarette in his mouth. He headed over to the balcony door and stepped out into the winter night. The view of Lake Ontario was spectacular, but the air was perishingly cold. The last thing in the world he wanted to do was go out tonight. "Oh, that's right," he said as the work-a-day world intruded into his private space. "He's speaking at a conference in Oshawa tonight. He's probably at the microphone right now."

Paul pictured the horror Mike must be feeling. Caught unshaven and in his comfiest with the prospect of Chinese takeout and the football game about to fall off the radar. If he had to, he'd shave, suit up, and drive across town, but he didn't want to. With that in mind, Paul delivered the news gently. "We have a guy in the house smoking pot."

Mike smiled. "Did you catch his name?"

"It's Czombo."

Mike was full of energy now. "How do you know?"

Paul leaned back in his boss's chair and put his feet up on his desk. "Jenny phoned yesterday and said there was something funny going on with his urine samples. His first sample had no benzos, but his second sample did."

Mike smiled ruefully. "That will take some 'splaining…"

"Then Sean came into the office and told me someone was smoking, but he wouldn't tell me who."

Mike tried to sound indignant. "Fair enough — neither would I."

"So I tossed his room and the washroom next to his, and I found urine bottles in the ceiling."

"Yeah, this is starting to add up."

Paul jumped right to the heart of the thing. "Then Darlene showed up at the front door asking for Czombo. She offered to help me manage my stress for twenty dollars."

That news made Mike sad. She had once been a friend. He covered his tracks with a horrible laugh. "I'll be counting the petty cash first thing tomorrow!"

"I can smell pot on his pillow and his sweater, but I can't find his stash. Shall I ask him to leave tonight or wait for you guys tomorrow?"

Mike was genuinely relieved. He stubbed out his cigarette on the balcony railing and threw the butt into the rusting coffee can he kept for that purpose. Dinner and the game had been snatched from the jaws of defeat, an irritant had been identified and could now be eliminated, and he didn't have to shave and shovel out his car until tomorrow morning. "Good work, Paul. Keep an eye on him. Don't say anything yet; we can talk this all over at the census meeting. Someone else will have noticed something. We may be able to smoke out his confederates if we put our heads together."

Chapter 40

Peter crossed the street from the Granite Glen Nursing Home to Theta Delta Chi under his own power. He could've waited for an hour and put an arm on Bertie the mailman, but his business was urgent.

The sorority house was an enormous nineteenth-century dwelling that had been given over to undergraduates attempting to make sense of themselves and the modern world. Peter knew that Walter had taken up his station on the top landing of the fourth floor, but he was damned if he was going to climb all those stairs. An obliging feline tail took him up the first three flights. He managed the final hurdle by taking the arm of the cleaner.

There he found his friend: the indomitable Walter, looking like a slightly disreputable sleight-of-hand magician. His family had class and dollars, and they had decided they might as well bury Walter in his tux because he looked good in it, and it was hopelessly out of style. It had served him well in the afterlife. He cut a splendid figure as a spectre. No tail feathers showing on Walter.

There were competing versions of how Walter had run aground. Voyeur and tin woodsman were the heavyweight choices. Rosa, who'd known him well back in the day, favoured the tin-man theory — that he'd simply run out of steam and the only reason he'd not been scooped by the light was his remote location. The late Barry had been predictably less generous, landing on lecher. He observed rather acidly that, from his perch, Walter could see the comings and goings of the young residents as they moved between their rooms and the communal shower.

Either way, clinging as he did to the banister with his noble brow and his impeccably tailored tuxedo tails, he looked for all the world like the prow of a once mighty sailing ship.

Peter sighed when he saw him. It was hard to see Walter like this. He'd moved through the afterlife at speed, ignoring all the advice. Peter touched his old pal's sleeve but got no reaction. He waved his hand slowly in front of Walter's eyes and again saw no change. Walter wasn't receiving visitors. He was oblivious to everything save his own thoughts, and Peter wondered, after looking into his vacant eyes, if he even had the comfort of those any longer.

"We've seen better days, you and I," Peter said. "You look like you're napping. Well, don't stop on my account. I was hoping to find you in a better state of repair."

Peter sat down on the stairs to rest and catch his breath. He started to talk to his old friend as if he were in a coma and needed to hear the sound of a human voice to find his way home. "I love that peaceful sleepy feeling. I lived for years in *an apartment right below a woman with regular habits. She worked and kept to a very tight schedule. Every morning at six forty-five, I'd hear her footfalls and then the sounds of running water and chair legs moving across tile. I loved to hear her move around."*

Peter sighed and shifted his weight. "While I was dozing there in the dark, feeling the warmth of the bed and the peaceful feeling of waking up slowly, I would become aware that it was almost, but not quite, time for me to wake up. I knew I had at least an hour until my own alarm went off. I loved that moment of awareness. I'd roll over on my side and find myself wonderfully back asleep again." He glanced sidelong at Walter. "I hope this is what's happening to you. But that's crazy, isn't it? There's nothing going on behind your eyes anymore."

Peter laughed. "Do you know what else I do, Walter? That's right, when I'm not talking to people who can't answer me back. When I go to the cryogenic lab, I always knock three times on Terri's cylinder so she knows I'm there and thinking about her. I hope that she feels my love and it makes her feel safe enough to go back to sleep for another hour. I don't want the waiting to be horrible for her any more than I want you to suffer."

Peter turned his back on Walter and spent a full five minutes looking out the window at Madison Avenue below him. When he was settled, he approached his old friend again. "Walter, the crisis is upon us. We need to act. What I have in mind is unorthodox. I came by today hoping we could discuss it, but I can see you're not up to it. The thing is, what I have in mind is dangerous, maybe even desperate, but it's the only way I can see to get from where we are to where we need to be. I'm going to try and take you with me when I go. But that might not happen. I don't know how it's all going to work out. But I have to try something. My strength is failing. I need to get back in the driver's seat while I still can."

He gave his old companion three playful knocks on the forehead. "Sleep well, my old friend. I'll be back for you soon."

Chapter 41

When the guys came back from their meeting at 10:00 p.m., Paul had a hard time hiding his feelings. When he looked at Czombo, he felt an odd mixture of anger and sorrow. He willed his face to look disinterested as he nonchalantly checked the names of the returning guests off his list.

An email from Hilary Versenken appeared in the counsellors' general inbox at about the same time that Paul was checking the guys in. Maurice, the night man, opened it. It was a grainy rendering of a male figure looking out a window. The text said, *This is the wanker who's been waving his Johnny at my wife!*

Maurice went to fetch Paul, and the two men returned to the office to see what they had. Paul looked at the photo very carefully before he pronounced it a fraud. Point one: It was Sean Miller. But he didn't have his forty-five in his hand. Point two: The angle was wrong. This image had been cropped and maybe even reversed, but there was no way that it could've come from the apartment building across the way, where the mysterious informant claimed to live. The angle was too steep. Paul went outside onto the smoking deck and considered the possibilities. The roof of the garage next door was the source, but that seemed improbable. He wanted to ask the owner for permission to have a good snoop around, but it was late and all the lights next door were off.

––––

At eight thirty the following morning, Paul surveyed the room before calling the census meeting to order. Mike, Doug, Reg, and Kaiser had all benefited from two nights of uninterrupted sleep and some time off work. Paul rose to his feet and struck a heroic pose. "The world is full of mystery and magic, but the greatest mystery of all is the mind of man."

Reg was impressed. "Who said that?"

Paul looked around with a hurt look on his face. "Me, just now. You going deaf as well as blind?"

Mike was impatient. "Will you guys settle down? I want to hear what happened."

Paul leaned back in his chair and smiled broadly. "While you guys were taking it easy, I was busy saving the world."

Kaiser needled him. "Don't be modest, tell us what you really did."

Paul sat up straight. "We had a busy weekend. The lead story is Mr. Michael Czombo. Yes, his real name is Michael and not Eustice. Kind of makes you wonder, doesn't it?" He stayed in character. "I had a phone call from Jenny on Saturday afternoon about his urine samples. His first sample showed no sign of benzos, but his second one did."

Reg pounded his fist down on the desk. "An obvious KGB ploy!"

Doug's curiosity was piqued. "Was he fiddling the urines?"

"It would appear so."

Kaiser attempted to take charge of the conversation. "So we have two malefactors!"

Paul was pretty sure that Kaiser didn't know what the word meant. He did a little probing. "What's a malefactor, exactly?"

Kaiser was on his game. "Fancy name for piss switcher. It's got to be coming from somewhere. How are we going to smoke out his confederate?"

Doug shook his head. "We're not."

Mike tried to settle them down again. "Focus. Focus."

Paul got to his feet and took command of the room, doing his very best impersonation of a prosecutor. "The evidence against the accused is overwhelming. Sean Miller came into the office on Sunday and he was very angry. Said he wasn't going to share anything in the Straight Up meeting because one of the guys in the house was smoking pot and everyone but me knew about it."

"Why didn't you know?" asked Reg helpfully.

Paul ignored him. "When the guys went out to their meeting, I searched his room but didn't find anything. So I went next door into the common bathroom." He turned toward them dramatically. "And that's where I found a selection of urine jars hidden in the ceiling."

"Can we prove they're his?" asked Reg.

"Don't need to. It's not what they say, it's what they point to. The benzos are the canary in the coal mine. A urine sample before he leaves will tell us what we need to know."

The heads all nodded.

Paul wasn't finished. The decision had been taken but the whole story deserved to come out. "Wait, there's more. While I was tossing his room, an old pal of ours came to the front door looking for him. She informed me he'd helped her out earlier in the day, and then offered to do me for twenty dollars."

"A misguided social worker perhaps?" said Reg, feigning confusion.

Paul looked hurt. "Do you want more proof? At ten p.m. there was a photo sent to us by email, purportedly from an English gentleman with the improbable surname Versenken, whose wife keeps seeing a flasher. It was a picture of the perv caught in the act." Paul fished it out of the file and slid it across the table. "It's Sean Miller. And while he's guilty of looking out a window, beyond that, the image reveals nothing to incriminate him and much to rescue his reputation. Look at the angle of the thing. The camera is looking up from near ground level and the angle suggests it was taken from off our property. I think it was taken from the roof of the garage next door."

"That seems unlikely."

"I know but that's what it looks like."

Doug wasn't going to let something like that go unanswered. Nobody got away with putting something over on him. "I'll make a point of speaking to them and having a good snoop around."

Paul was all smiles now. "You guys want to hear the best part?"

Reg nodded. "You know we do."

"This is silly, but I'm so proud of myself. You know that nose gargle kit I talked Doug into buying?"

"There should be one in every home!"

"Well, I used that to give myself olfactory superpowers, and I could actually detect the faintest smell of pot coming off his pillowcase and sweater."

Doug had heard more than enough. "Okay, he's busted. Ask him for a sample and when he refuses, ask him to leave."

"What about Miller? He's still angry."

Doug swivelled in his big leather chair. "Well, calm him down. He's gonna make a big fuss about this if we let him. So someone smoked dope in treatment. It's not like he invented cold fusion. Miller is out next Monday, is he not?"

"Yes."

"Let's see if we can't get his focus back on his own recovery. It'll be a new experience for him."

Paul pulled a printed copy of an email out of a file. "The other piece of news is that Hart's case has been put off for a week. There was a pipe rupture in the courtroom that's buggered up everyone's schedule. His probation officer called, and I worked out a deal. Hart can go home at night, but we need to see him here seven days a week at two p.m. to piss test him."

Reg brightened up considerably. "That's a wonderful stroke of luck; he was worried about packing up his place."

"Well, he has at least a week to think about it now," said Mike.

Reg looked up from the treatment record. "Have we done Hart any good?"

Paul pursed his lips and blew a stream of air through them before he answered. "Maybe. His sharing at the group yesterday sounded heavy — emphasis here on *sounded* — like he was connecting the dots. I still have my doubts. It's all too soon."

"Move along," said Doug.

Paul took up the task. "Daniel Philips sounds as if he's finally settling in. He and Larry Lorne are spending a lot of time together. I bullied him before the meeting a bit to get him to speak in the group, but he froze when it came time to own up — big surprise there — but he was real about how he felt about being asked to speak."

Doug looked over at Reg. "I want you to do a one-on-one with him this afternoon. Get to the bottom of this. If we can't embarrass him, maybe we can pal him out."

Paul landed on the next square. "Day twelve, room six, bed fourteen, Larry Lorne. Still as silent as a tomb. He looked like he really wanted to let loose with something but then it all petered out into generalities. He's been sitting alone ever since, staring off into space."

Doug looked over at Kaiser. "Find out what's up with that."

Kaiser made a note and then asked, "Who do you want to throw Czombo out?"

Doug looked around the room. "Who has the energy?"

Paul smiled. "I think I know what note to strike here."

————

Czombo was holding court on the back patio. He sounded a bit like a quarterback on the eve of his admission into the Hall of Fame. He didn't look concerned when he was invited into the office by Mike and Paul.

He smiled his happy smile and went willingly. *This will be about the shove. We can't be having physical contact of any sort with the other bathers.*

Sean's face showed considerable satisfaction as he gave Czombo the farewell wave he had promised to Vince when they had quarrelled, the one that said, *you brought this on yourself.*

Paul said nothing as he arranged the seating around the big round table in the interview room. He placed Czombo with his back to the window and took a chair facing the young man. Mike remained standing by the door. Mike, as always, managed menace to perfection.

Paul looked over at Czombo. The young man had a peculiar expression on his face: one part curiosity and two parts indifference. "Mr. Czombo, we would like a urine sample, please."

Czombo didn't bat an eye. "Why me? Why are you picking on me?"

Paul's face didn't change. "We're worried about you. We need to keep you safe."

Czombo stood his ground and gave nothing away. "You can't have one. This is discrimination; you have to either test everyone or leave me alone."

Mike shook his head. *I wonder if he really believes that.*

Paul pushed a little bit harder. "Mr. Czombo, one of the staff members smelled pot coming from your person."

Czombo looked confused. He gathered up his long green hair and made a ball of it. He smelled the hair carefully and then pulled his sweater up over his nose to check it for the scent of pot.

"You can't smell anything!"

Mike looked over at Paul. *After a display like that, we don't need to.*

Paul still didn't look fussed. "If you won't provide a urine sample, you'll have to leave. You can reapply in twenty-one days and be readmitted after a counselling session and a urine test."

Czombo jumped to his feet. "You can't do this to me. I have rights!"

Paul remained unfazed. "You used, you got caught, and now you have to leave. What's not to understand? You may very well end up graduating from our program and achieving long-term sobriety. But that isn't going to happen this morning."

"You guys are the worst kind of hypocrites."

Paul and Mike exchanged a look. "This is unfair" and "You don't care" never failed to put employers and parents into a full-on panic. It set up the whole conversation to come about inherent bias, misperceptions, and publicly funded misanthropic institutions.

"We need to go to your room and get you packed."

"You stay the hell away from me."

"As you wish. I can remain in the hall while you get your things."

"Screw you! You haven't heard the end of this."

Czombo pounded up the stairs while Paul walked at a sedate pace behind him. Two minutes later, the elevator door opened and Czombo rolled his suitcase out the front door, pausing only to fire a one-fingered salute at the office.

"That was quick," said Mike.

Paul was smiling. "He was all packed and ready to go. All he had to do was grab his toothbrush."

"And his stash," said Mike. "He wouldn't want to leave that behind."

Chapter 42

Sean and Hart looked like two sailors home from sea. Sean had everything he owned secured in a hockey bag, while Hart had his stuff tucked neatly into a well-used suitcase with a wonky wheel. They left Punanai on a high note — back-slapped, man-hugged, and shoulder-punched. They walked north on Madison and took the subway from Dupont station to Wilson station and then boarded the Weston 165 North, which dropped them off at the front door to Hart's apartment building.

As Hart rolled his suitcase up the long walkway that led from the bus stop to the three-storey brownstone, he sensed a presence. Spooked, he checked his pocket for his keys and his wallet, even though he'd done so innumerable times already. This second homecoming felt forced. Having Sean with him made it easier, but Hart couldn't get past the image of his neighbour Mary Pearson looking backward over her shoulder at him as she hurried down this very walkway, desperate to get away. The look on her face cut as hot and deep as Alice Gibson's tears.

The pipe bursting at the courthouse wasn't a miracle, but Hart was as grateful for that flow of water as the Hebrews had been for the gusher at Meribah. He now had the time he needed to close out this part of his life. It felt like the first break he'd gotten in this whole mess.

Why am I shaking? No matter, I'm almost home.

The instant they opened the door to his apartment, Hart sensed more evidence of bewitchment. More than his plants were dead. The air was dry and lifeless. The odour of hardwood floor was trying to overpower the bacterial choir emanating from the soft furnishings. It was like they were working out a tune. Playing with the harmony. But was their song one of welcome or warning? The dark silence behind the drawn blinds soured his stomach like the first touch of a migraine. A sorceress had transformed his space from something comfortable into something dire.

Everything held a memory. Everything had to be picked up and examined and remembered because once it passed out of his hands, that was all that he'd have of it. If he hadn't gotten bail, everything would've been dumped unlovely into the big green bin that graced the parking lot.

As he looked around the apartment, he recalled reading about the French retreat from Moscow in 1812. How officers and men alike had pillaged the city and loaded heavy furnishings and paintings onto carts to carry back to France with them. Typhus and the cold made other plans. They left their booty and their bodies strewn over miles of sneering frozen road. Happily, this wasn't quite Moscow. But it was more than he could face this evening. He turned on the television — loud enough to drown out his forebodings — and ordered a bucket of fried chicken. Tonight, they'd watch hockey.

———

Sean was still asleep when Hart got up and made the morning coffee. It had been so long since Hart had slept in his own bed that it hadn't felt like his at all. He still had the apartment for another three weeks, and Sean would be sleeping there on a mattress in the corner until the lease was up.

Hart started to eye up the apartment and think about what needed to be done. Almost everyone who went through treatment was on the lookout for a sober roommate and a clean, safe, cheap place to live. Even partners of long standing often had to stay sober outside the matrimonial home while they regained their ritual purity. Hart's belongings would be offered first to the guys in the house, and what remained would be donated to charity.

His reverie was interrupted by Sean's morning hack. Sean attempted to put it right with a cigarette, and when that didn't work, he tried another. That and a cup of black coffee seemed to do the trick. The disentanglers set to work after finishing the last of the cold chicken. Sean went out to secure packing supplies and make arrangements for a truck while Hart started sifting the present from the past. He didn't have to be at Punanai for his pee test until after lunch.

Hart was discouraged before he even worked up a sweat. There was too much stuff and all of it loaded with memories. He was surprised to find items he thought he'd thrown out years ago. They'd been tucked away under things and behind larger items. Why had he hung on to them? His mother's silverware stopped him cold. He only used the set once the whole time he was here, but that's not why he balked. His mother had loved this set and had never let it tarnish. Seeing it discoloured now felt to him like a betrayal of her and her memory.

As a practical matter, sending it off to Value Village where it could be discovered and loved again was the right thing to do. He imagined himself coming across it in five years' time, when he was free again, and taking it home with him under his arm. That image popped like a bubble when he imagined himself trying to polish it. That wasn't going to happen. It didn't seem right to him that all he would do with it if he found it again was stuff it unused back into some dark, cramped space. Hart wondered if there was a word to describe an object not in use, one that you didn't know how to maintain but couldn't bear to part with.

When Sean returned from his errands, he earned his keep by supervising the division of the spoils. Hart's job was to examine and decide. Sean's job was to box it up and label it. The small pile was for things that had been spoken for.

The guys — many of whom were still in treatment — would put it to good use. Sean had arranged to rent a pickup truck so they could deliver it.

The larger pile was being donated to the Salvation Army because they were willing to come by with their truck. Larry Lorne had promised to keep Hart's record collection for him until he got out. They were aficionados and they got each other. His one treasure of treasures would be safe.

———

The place was starting to look ready. They had been hard at it for three days, living on takeout food and energy drinks. As the sun was beginning to set, Sean put on a fresh pot of coffee. It looked and felt like the natural end to the workday. Sean took his coffee and sat down in front of the television to catch the sports scores.

Hart sipped the bitter, satisfying brew, looked around the apartment where he'd lived for fifteen years, and sighed. It was a sound stage now, one dimensional and ridiculous, with all the things that made it seem real sitting in the hallway, waiting for the diaspora. For a time, this space had presented a credible face to the world; it seemed real enough, what with his paintings and his photographs tastefully marshalled on the walls, the faces of all the people he'd worked with and the teams he'd played on, recalling a fanciful, storied past. Had any of it been true, even for a day? Or had it all been staged, like a wedding picture taken to fool immigration?

There were pictures of old girlfriends and glamorous vacations. His high-end electronics, his vinyl record collection, and his deeply comfortable recliner identified him as a successful man enjoying the comforts of life. But it was all an illusion grounded in souvenirs, consumer goods, and bric-a-brac.

Sean came back into the kitchen tearing up his Proline ticket. Hart was still adrift and not ready for company. He turned his back to Sean so that he could master his feelings.

He started blabbing, trying to hide whatever he was feeling under a tarpaulin of words. "This is the only place I've ever thought of as being mine."

Sean lit a cigarette and made himself comfortable at the kitchen table. "Must feel funny, seeing it all packed up."

Hart took down a photo from the wall and joined Sean at the table. He wanted a smoke but he knew that if he took one now, he'd have to go through the agonies of withdrawal all over again when he was back in custody. That intolerable outrage was within his power to avoid. He handed Sean the photo. "Can you find me in that?"

Sean saw a playground full of running kids. "You sure that you're in there?"

Hart reached across the table and pointed to himself. He was the skinny kid with the mullet doing a dance at the top of the jungle gym.

"Who took the shot?"

"My dad. He was a shutterbug for a while after he got sick. It kept him busy." Sean handed him back the photo. Hart smiled as he ran his fingers over the glass, trying to take it all in. "I knew all those kids. I only remember a few names now."

Sean ground out his cigarette in the ashtray as he blew a plume of smoke away from his host. "Thinking about the past makes me sad."

Hart spied another picture and got to his feet to retrieve it. He looked at it carefully before he handed it to Sean. Narrative was replacing nicotine. "This was the house next door to ours. My aunt and uncle lived there. They were the first couple on our street to renovate their bungalow and turn it into a three-storey monster home. That was the way you told the world what a big noise you were in the eighties. I was still in public school when this was taken.

"There was a better picture of them. He was tall and bald and she round and blond. They looked out of place on the dance floor but they got along. They only had each other and that was enough."

Hart held the framed photo in his hands with the reverence that a portal to the past deserved. "They bought an old family restaurant, tore it down, and turned it into a condo development. But they saved a few of the bright-pink booths and the jukeboxes that hung on the wall at table height. They put it all back together at home as a kind of party room. The finished product looked like the set of *Dirty Dancing*. It was fun. I had all my birthdays there."

Sean started to do a dance step. "Where is that waitress with our burger?"

Hart smiled as he tapped the glass in the frame with his knuckles. "They added pinball machines and milkshake blenders and put up a menu with sandwiches for ten cents each and coffee for a nickel. They even had a cash register with buttons that you had to push down hard to open. That's where they kept the nickels that you needed to make the jukeboxes and pinball machines work. It was the coolest place on earth."

Hart carried his coffee into the living room and took up his tale from the La-Z-Boy. "Duffy and Glad were the same age as my parents, and after my dad got frail, they started relying on me to do the heavy lifting. After I shovelled their snow or raked their leaves, they'd let me play pinball on their Hi Dolly machine. I got so good at it that I could play all evening for a nickel."

Sean lit a smoke and settled himself on the couch. Hart carried on, "When my dad died, I was away at college. Mom, Duff, and Glad had nurses in and they hired someone to cut the lawn. I lost track of the place. Then one day my mom said they'd both gone to a nursing home. A real estate sign went up on their lawn, and the next day the house was sold. A week after that there was a big orange dumpster out front. There was the party room, all in pieces again, even the pinball machine — all of it going to the dump. It made me feel so sad. I loved that stuff."

Sean shook his head. He'd packed up a few versions of himself. Putting it all together while he pulled his life apart was bittersweet. "What are you gonna miss most on the inside?"

"Chinese food and movies on the big screen."

"Not women?"

"You can't miss what you don't see."

Sean still wasn't sure if Hart knew how to handle himself inside. "Are you scared?"

"Nah. I only have to spend a couple nights in the Don this time, then it's off to a nice, quiet minimum-security prison."

Sean brightened. "You gonna break out?"

"Only if I eat the fish sticks."

Sean didn't know how to express what he was feeling. "I wish I was going with you."

"That's a funny thing to say."

"Yeah, I guess it's nuts, but — I don't know — I feel like you're important to me somehow. I've had more fun since I met you." That was too much. Best not to say things like that at all. Second best to leave it where it lay. It was Sean's turn to hide his feelings. "Read me your speech again."

"No, it's too awful to read when I don't have to."

Sean asked the million-dollar question. "Are you going to say something else tomorrow?"

A little smile crept across Hart's face and threatened to grow into a smirk. "Not if I know what's good for me."

Chapter 43

Hart was delighted to see Father Phil getting himself a cup of coffee at the meeting. He gently shouldered his way through the throng to say hello to his new friend. "What are you doing here?"

Phil looked up as he poured something that looked like cream, and that might actually turn out to be cream, into his coffee. "This is my home group."

"So this whole 'get sober' thing isn't just something you do for the rubes from nine to five?"

"No, it's weekends and evenings too." He looked Hart up and down with a practised eye. "So how are you holding up?"

Hart grabbed a coffee cup, but before he could fill it, a large lady in a floppy hat got her shoulder between him and what he wanted and then refused to budge as she caught up with her friends. He stood quietly with his empty cup in his hands as he thought about how to reply to Phil's question. The lady was oblivious to him and in no hurry to move now that she had what she wanted. Hart felt stupid standing there with an empty cup in his hand, too embarrassed to make his desire known. He put the cup back down on the tray and moved away from the happy coffee scrum — his eyes registering a deep and dangerous resignation. Phil noticed but said nothing.

Hart and Phil found a spot to talk. "I've had the most astonishing couple of weeks. I was on a high for a while when I was in treatment — the pink cloud experience is what the guys call it."

Phil's face filled with light. "What a feeling. Every walk is a parade, every sandwich is a banquet, and every fool is a wise man. It's a classic reaction to early sobriety."

Hart smiled. "I guess this is all old stuff to you."

"No, what you experienced is what we theologians call Grace. It's a gorgeous feeling."

"The guys at Punanai say it lasts ninety days and then boom, it's gone. Kind of like a new video game. Crap, I didn't even get a week."

Phil smiled and moved into Hart's personal space. "I'm going to let you in on a little secret. I've been sober for thirty years and I still feel it on a daily basis. Are you surprised by that? Now, I don't feel it at the floating-on-air level, but for me it's always there. And getting back to you for a minute, what a delightful change."

"Really?"

"Oh, yes, it's palpable. The last time we talked, you were pretty discouraged. How do you feel about what's coming up for you now?"

"I spent the last week cleaning out my apartment. I had to pack up everything I own and give it away. It was … I don't know … felt the same way it did when I had to pack up my parents' place after they died. Without them there to love it, none of their stuff meant anything. It was all so sad and worn out. It got me thinking about my own life."

There was a pause as he changed gears. He wanted to tell Phil everything, but he was still sorting out and boxing up his reality.

"I'm churning inside. I guess what I'm trying to say is that I'm feeling more than one thing. The feelings are swirling around inside me and getting mixed up with ideas and memories and fantasies. I'm afraid of going to jail and I'm angry at getting caught and frustrated that I can't go where I want to go and do what I want to do. But when I get finished feeling sorry for myself, I start to feel deeply for that lady and her kid."

A faint look of hope dawned in Hart's eyes. He was looking at Phil as if, somehow, the answer he was searching for could be plucked out of his coat pocket. Feeling had taken him to a dangerous place. Thinking had, so far, organized it and boxed it up and only faltered when it was time to put an address on the label. Only words could put this deal together. Two people sharing consciousness.

The feeling of loss and despair had snugged its way into his gut like a tick. Here, at last, victim and perpetrator found common ground. The journey home that Hart and Alice had begun in separate vehicles became a common journey.

"My kind of craziness killed her. Going to bars and drinking and talking tough and driving home drunk was fun. It made me feel alive and important. But it was all make-believe. Stuff that gets in the way — like the shit you have to pack up when you move. I did what I did because I was empty. I couldn't stand the way I felt and I didn't know how to change it. So I sat around the big table at Clancy's and talked shit and pretended I had the world by the tail. But that stopped working when that little girl stood up in court and had her say."

Hart felt a shiver move up his spine. His cheeks flushed and moisture dampened his palms. The triple hit. Head, heart, and gut. He thought about his mother's kitchen knife. The one with the bent blade.

He had to sit down. "That lady deserved better. She was the one living a real life, with other people she loved and who loved her. The thing I learned in the last three weeks is that my life doesn't mean anything, because it was only about me. What difference does it make where you live a life like mine? Here or in jail?"

Hart looked up to check out Phil's reaction. The old confessor had his game face on. He was a deep, slow-moving river: calm and peaceful on the surface but dark and private in his depths. You could not see to the bottom of him. But he was busy sounding the depths of this troubled young man. *This is the knife edge of hope and despair. Which side are you going to land on?*

Hart read the old priest's calm as encouragement. "Phil, I've had my head up my ass. My money, my work, my opinions, my way. I was right all along. I saw it first. I knew better than anyone else. If we bet on a football game and my team won, that made me better than you. Those were the big important decisions in life. I was the guy who always took a stand against the so-called experts. I called them on their shit every time … except when it mattered."

Phil, always intuitive, knew exactly what to say. "You've had a lot of people telling you what to think."

"I'm never going to know if I was driving that car — but I agreed to get in. I know that much about it. Why didn't I refuse? Why didn't I offer to pay for the cab ride home and stop Connor from driving? I coulda done that. I'll tell you why I didn't. I was drunk. And I wanted to go. That was all that mattered to me as I stood at that bus stop. I can almost hear myself saying 'turn up the radio' and the squeal of the tires."

Phil was taken aback. Had he known all along? "You said you didn't remember that night. Did it come back to you?"

"No, that's not how I worked it out. Objects hold memories for me. Packing up my apartment felt like I was reading my biography. There it was, my whole life spread out in front of me like evidence at a trial. Not knowing is bad but I made my peace with that. But that didn't mean I couldn't get to the bottom of this."

Phil sat down beside Hart and put his right hand on the back of his chair. The distance felt right to both men.

"I know what I was thinking and feeling that night. Stuff like that happened all the time. I woulda done what I always did. The thing that makes this episode different is that I was so drunk I was in a blackout. I'm holding two ideas together here with spit and bailing wire, but I think I finally have it right. If I was going to jail for something that someone else did, that would be wrong. But I'm not. I'm going to jail for getting into that car."

Phil had a quick look around to make sure they were out of earshot. This was new growth and it couldn't bear much weight yet. Still it was rooted in something worthwhile and enduring and, if given a chance, maybe it would become something more.

"The court's giving me a break. This coulda been so much worse. I could be a quad, or Alice Gibson could be dead — there's no end to what coulda happened. Still, one real life lost is enough. The thing that turned this around for me was when you talked about Perry Mason getting me off. Going back to my old life. Pretending that nothing that had happened made any difference. I never felt such despair and … and powerlessness as I did the day after our talk. I woke up in darkness and felt nothing, and I was certain I'd feel that way for the rest of my days."

Phil smiled. "So why didn't you jump in front of a train?"

"It's so stupid. I had to do the dishes. Reg caught me sleeping in, and he gave me a boot in the ass and told me to get downstairs and do my duty. I'd left Larry Lorne down there to do the work while I felt sorry for myself. Big betrayals, little betrayals, was there no bottom for me? I was in a free fall. Having to get out of bed and go downstairs to do the dishes saved me. It wasn't much of a reason to live, but it was more than I had when I was lying there alone in the dark."

The chairwoman had taken her seat at the head table and was beginning to fuss with her papers, making sure that she had everything she needed to run the meeting. This flurry of activity said, more clearly than any spoken word, that the meeting would shortly come to order. Both men picked up on the subtle cue.

Hart picked up the pace. "While I was washing up the pots and pans, I realized that I like to do things. Work is important to me, always has been. I liked my partner and I felt good knowing I'd done something, anything, for someone else. A day later, it occurred to me that prison wasn't going to be so bad. This next part is crazy. That car crash took away everything I had, everything that was in the way, everything that blocked my view. The job, the friends, the alcohol, the money — they're gone now. All I have left is me. I was too afraid to be real when I had my freedom. I had too much to lose. And I was afraid to lose it because it was all I had. Now I'm going to have to learn how to be real without any of that stuff and while I'm in jail."

The chairwoman banged her gavel.

Phil gave Hart a hug. "Channing, you're a man worth knowing."

Chapter 44

Sean Miller was back at Clancy's for the dinner hour. He was out of treatment now and running out the string at Hart's apartment, so he had no one to answer to. In the old days, he'd have had no trouble blending in with this group. Two drinks and he'd have fit in with these guys like they'd all gone to high school together. Alas, sobriety had one drawback — Sean was no longer drinking the poison, so he couldn't be on the team. No exceptions.

Sean wasn't exactly sure why he was there. Tonight was his last chance to go to a meeting with Hart, and he would have to move his feet to get there on time. But something had drawn him to Clancy's. He was full of contradictory feelings. He was still thinking about justice and revenge, but he was also curious to have a second look at this other living room where Hart had spent almost twenty years of his life. These fat guys with bad tattoos had been his family and his friends, and this beer-soaked industrial carpet had been the very earth under his feet. Hart's name was still on the Grey Cup score chart; he'd won third prize. Sean wondered if Clancy was holding on to the money for him. The Hart he knew didn't belong here any more than he belonged in jail, and that insight made Sean feel unexpectedly sad.

He leaned back in his chair and sipped his coffee. Hart was back in court for sentencing at 9:00 a.m. tomorrow and, for him anyway, the clock had run out. But here at Clancy's, nobody was even aware that tomorrow existed. Booze was funny that way; it made a person feel so connected to strangers that only the here and now mattered.

Sean had come to get to the bottom of the irksome Connor. The monster who'd so very badly messed up his friend. No good could come of this, he knew that. But Sean wanted to know, he finally just wanted to understand. Was this bastard all oil and ball bearings? Is that how he got away with it? Did he sell drugs, take bets, buy stolen goods, and kind of have the run of the place because of it? Did the punters need him so badly that they couldn't imagine their lives without him? So much for the herd but what about the cowboy? Did he get a sick satisfaction out of fucking people up, like Czombo did? Was he born with the slick tongue of the serpent?

Bill the Thrill had filled him in. He knew what to look for this time. Connor wasn't an imposing figure. There was no hint of either raw power or sophistication in his clothing or his manners, and no hint of the master criminal either. He was dressed like everybody else, needed a haircut like everybody else, and had a big belly peeking out like a pale tongue from under his badly distended T-shirt.

Sean was convinced that Connor was guilty, that he should be the one going to jail, but the incident with Bill had soured him on a vigilante approach. He couldn't simply beat the truth out of the man, although he had to admit that there was a certain savage satisfaction in thinking about that. He'd been hoping for weeks that Hart was going to remember something, but he hadn't, and even worse was the new direction his conversation was taking. Hart said Connor's role in his troubles was a distraction. What idiocy! All that mattered was who was driving the car.

The only sympathy he could muster for Connor was this: What man could honestly say that he'd go to the police station, look a sergeant in the eye, and tell him what had really happened when they already had some other mutt by the collar? The pillorying that Hart received would be nothing compared with the treatment Connor would get. Confessing, going to jail, getting sued, and coming clean — what did any of that crap really mean anyway, when you had a pot of beer in front of you?

It was a play. Like the ones the Sunday school put on at Christmas. It made a point, but it wasn't convincing in and of itself. A trial was a half-hearted way of maintaining the appearance of accountability and fairness in a world that was happily organized around the principles of privilege and corruption.

But still, in the human spirit — not in all people perhaps, but certainly in some, and maybe even in most — there was a thirst to know what was real and what wasn't. Sean was consumed by this desire to know. The knowing might not change anything, but the darkness needed to be pierced, needed to feel the fear of discovery.

Chapter 45

Hart and his lawyer were huddled together in the interview room outside the court. Levy wanted to be certain that Hart was ready to read his lines this time. The lines as written, without editing.

Levy did the talking. "Channing, I want to make sure you understand what's going to happen. The decision about what to do with you has already been made. You're getting a five-year sentence and a lifetime ban from driving. You're going to be given an opportunity to say something before Judge Sullivan hands down her ruling. Nothing you say is going to change that outcome. Say the words on the sheet as best you can, and if you lose your place, remember this — you're trying to say you're sorry, in as few words as possible."

That didn't jibe with the gospel according to Prison Bob. He could hear his diminutive friend's Scottish lilt in his ear. *Your job is to look like the fella who was in the evil place at the unlucky hour.*

The patronizing look on Levy's face sent the newsprint flying off the roll in every direction until it covered the length and breadth of the printing shop floor to a depth of several inches. Stop the presses! Stop the presses indeed. The pea had never been under the cup; it had always been hidden in the lawyer's palm. Hart remembered what Prison Bob had said. Bob was a criminal with no scruples about lying, but somehow that only enhanced the value of this insight.

They don't care about what happens to you any more than they do about that lady. This is all about appearances, nothing more.

That was what all the scorn and disgust and shaming had been about. Make your man hate himself. Do that and jail became a much more attractive proposition. It evened the score. It cleaned the slate. It stopped all the unwanted attention and pain. Why not go along with them? Who wouldn't prefer a warm comfortable lie to a truth that rubbed you raw? The truth solved nothing. The lie put everyone back to sleep. Until a little girl looked over her shoulder at the sound of an approaching footfall.

Hart looked at Levy and saw him for the first time. "This is a puppet show."

Levy didn't like his client's tone and started to look a little concerned, knowing that cornered men frequently forget where their best interests lie. "Buck up. You're getting a sweet deal here."

"Lucky me."

Hart walked into the empty courtroom and found a good spot on one of the benches. It was quiet, almost peaceful. It would remain so until they let the public in. He checked for the fiftieth time to see if he still had his toothbrush. He'd made a lot of money in his time, but an hour from now, all he'd own was a suit and a toothbrush. And an hour after that, the suit would be going into mothballs. The toothbrush was going to be his one consolation.

The court came to order. Summers got to his feet when the clerk called a case. They did a remand. It happened with the next two cases. They were getting rid of the easy ones. Hart didn't mind, he was in no hurry. It felt good to sit there in a suit, looking like an expert witness waiting his turn to put everything into perspective. That would all change when his name was called. Jurisprudence had designs on his dignity but hadn't laid hands on it yet.

With a nod from the judge, a line of shackled men shuffled out the door and another cohort took their place. Judge Sullivan instructed the bailiff to admit the public. Behind him, Hart could hear the sound of spectators taking their places, led, as always, by the Gibsons' minister and the press. He felt a tap on his shoulder. Sean, Reg, and Father Phil had arrived. When he saw them, a tear rolled down his face. They sat next to him on the bench and suddenly the world didn't seem so awful. It was odd. He'd dreaded this moment, and now that it was here, he felt calm. But then the clerk called his name and the whole world changed. His rubbery legs defied his commands while his heaving lungs ached for air.

He took his seat at the defence table and looked at Levy, who smiled at him. He felt his gut go sour. He wondered for a moment how much more awful this would be if he'd had a jury staring at him, if he'd been trying to read his fate in their faces. But he didn't have the energy to pursue that thought.

Judge Sullivan had her game face on. "Mr. Hart. You have entered a plea of guilty to the charge of vehicular manslaughter causing the death of Margaret Gibson. Have you anything to say before I pass sentence?"

Hart got to his feet and took a moment to orient himself. The last time he'd risen to address the court, he'd been ill prepared. The room had defeated him. He'd swallowed a deadly draft that day. Fear of public speaking and of being judged had made common cause with the deeply felt shame of watching an orphaned child cry. It had, predictably, bettered him. The terror he felt in that moment was back, but this time it hung awkwardly on to his lapels, as if trying to unbalance him. As yet, it had failed to press its thumb on his carotid.

What a choice. Tell the lie devised by your lawyer or risk being seen as a heartless monster. Genuine wasn't on the menu. He couldn't bring himself to say the four lines that he was supposed to utter. They checked the required boxes. Remorse, accountability, vulnerability, and the willingness to change. They were the worst kind of self-hatred. He understood that now. The words he'd spoken in their place were no better. They thrust him back into the world of betrayals — a world in which there was no hope of release. A realm where every action was taken in the sure and certain knowledge that, no matter what he said or how he said it, no one would believe him, and all his frantic thrashing around had to end with a trip back to the madhouse and the brutal judgments of the prisoners and guards. He took a breath. He wasn't going to drown a second time. He wasn't going to read the four lines. He smiled as he thought about Prison Bob in his new role as patron saint of bank robbers and drunks.

Anne Sullivan was pleased with what she was seeing. Hart had lost the baby fat and bewildered look he'd acquired in the Don Jail. His skin was clear and his shoulders squared. This wasn't the defeated and demoralized man she'd seen forty days ago.

Good on you, Doug. Maybe now we'll get the truth.

Hart's voice didn't let him down this time. "I actually have quite a lot to say, Your Honour."

Levy looked perturbed and spoke to Hart sotto voce. "Oh no, don't you dare…"

Hart looked around the courtroom and, to his great surprise, felt a little giddy. "Your Honour, I want to thank you and this court for your patience. Ever since the accident, I have been hounded by the police, psychologists, lawyers, newspaper reporters, addictions counsellors, and busybodies — all of whom are after me to tell the truth. But it's a funny kind of truth they're after. They want me to tell them that they've been right about me all along. Well, they haven't been."

Levy hated this. He cringed when Hart punched the word *accident*. He pulled urgently on Hart's sleeve and delivered his message in three staccato notes of equal length and intensity. "Don't. Do. This."

Hart smiled and looked Levy straight in the eye. "Piss off," he whispered, and then resumed his peroration: "The whole truth, Your Honour, is that I don't know what happened and I never will. I have no memory of the car crash. I could be completely innocent of this crime or as guilty as the tabloids say I am. I've had to accept that."

The room was silent and every face blank. Even the crazy prisoners chained together in the gallery knew they were hearing something quite out of the ordinary. Maybe something they could use.

"I've always been horror-stricken about what happened. But I feel bad about it in the same way that you do, from an emotional distance. It's been impossible for me to feel remorse for this crime because a part of me still believes I didn't do it. And that makes me more of a monster, doesn't it? No accountability and no remorse."

He blew out a stream of air as he went on the offensive.

"But since the whole world needs to know what I'm thinking, let me tell you what's in my heart. I've worked this out. I'm going to do some hard time. I'm not going to follow the advice of my fellow prisoners, who tell me that I need to have a come-to-Jesus moment in jail and own up to what I've done. They say that works with parole boards. They like men who've learned their lesson — or at least say they have."

There was a guffaw from the prisoner's box.

"I know from talking to other prisoners that the guards and the jail shrinks are going to label me as incorrigible because I won't admit my guilt. They're going to conclude that I'm at risk to reoffend because I won't tell them what they want to hear. But how would that not be a lie?"

Levy looked sadly into the distance. *The judge knows all this. Couldn't say what I told you to. Got to be the star. What a moron.*

"I'm going to be regarded as the lowest of the low because I haven't done a man's crime. Jail logic says I could've killed a prisoner's wife as easily as Margaret Gibson, and so when they beat me black and blue, they'll come off as heroes, guys willing to do what's needed to keep their women safe."

Summers moved uncomfortably in his seat, trying to decide whether or not to say something. His gut told him to stay out of it.

Levy was aware of what could happen next, and he dropped the whisper for an audible warning. "You're not doing yourself any good. This deal isn't set in stone."

Hart looked at him blankly, praying that Levy was going to forget himself and say, *Read the damned speech I wrote for you!*

Judge Sullivan listened to Hart's words, looking neither distressed nor outraged. The Gibsons were sitting at attention in their seats while their emotions milled and jostled like pulp logs crashing into a boom.

Hart was trying with all his might to pretend that this was no different from the Straight Up meeting. All he had to do was tell the truth without giving it that little tug that it needed to serve his best interests. He was sorely tempted. "For those of you who didn't hear that, my employee, Mr. Levy, has determined that I'm not doing myself any good here by speaking my truth. He's wrong about that. I'm preventing a soul murder. I only hope that what I need to say doesn't come across as insolence. Before I go away to prison, you're going to know how I feel about this."

Reg and Phil were beaming. Sean looked angry enough to throw something.

"We've made a bad bargain here. Yes, a terrible crime was committed. And we all want justice. You're vulnerable because you want to go home knowing you've caught and made an example of the person who did this terrible thing. You want to feel good about the fact that you've solved the problem. The mad dog has been locked up. You're even willing to give a guy quite a break on his jail time if he confesses. Why is that? I'll tell you. Your worst fear is that you have the wrong guy. It does you credit that the very thought of getting this wrong makes you squirm. Let's think about that for a second. What if you've made this worse? You see, you don't have any more certainty here than I do. I can't remember and you don't know. You want certainty but you can't have it any more than I can. And that's where we find ourselves. We have that in common."

Everyone was wondering, *Where is he going with this?*

"Am I a monster? Do I deserve to be here? None of us is ever going to know for certain." He ached to turn around and see how his friends were receiving this. He didn't care about the prisoners or the spectators or the press. He'd even given up on the judge. She wasn't his mother, after all. What mattered was the truth, even if it started a riot. "Still, I accept my fate. The one thing I know is that you're never going to see me in a courtroom again. I'm here because I'm an alcoholic and I put myself in harm's way by drinking."

Anne Sullivan looked up from her papers. Could it be that simple?

A racking smoker's cough from the prisoner's box filled the silent courtroom, taking hold of the feelings of everyone who heard it. Hart let the din die down. "I didn't know that before, but I know it now. I could've been killed or horribly injured in that car crash. I'm taking the view that I'm lucky to be alive and grateful that maybe I'll get a chance to do something good with my life before I die."

Anne Sullivan's tone was a marvel of clarity and calm. "But, Mr. Hart, one vital question remains unanswered. How do you feel about Margaret Gibson, whose life was lost? How do you feel about her child, Alice Gibson, who was injured and will be feeling the effects of this tragedy for the rest of her life?"

Hart took a full minute to consider his response. He could feel his pulse in his ears. He'd actually finished everything he planned to say. He was thinking with his mouth open now. He was certain for a second that he could hear Reg's voice.

Don't put a bandage on her corpse because you feel bad about yourself.

"That's where my thinking hits the wall. I don't know the answer to that question. Accidents happen to people every day. There's a randomness to these things. But, also, an inevitability." He paused for a very long time. It sounded as if he was stymied. Had a long, impressive strand of posturing finally petered out?

Levy and Summers exchanged an annoyed look. Why was Sullivan letting this go on?

But then Hart's voice changed the way a singer's does when it is properly warmed up. "This accident was different. It was the inevitable result of drinking. It was only a matter of time before something happened. Time and luck run out sooner or later. The car crash was entirely arbitrary — which night, which mishap, and in which manner."

Friction alone could never have produced this gem. That one process would have worn everything into a powder. This insight needed pressure to give it a final form. The sting of self-interest left him, and he saw only what had been there all along.

"If Margaret had left ten minutes earlier or ten minutes later, she'd still be alive." Alice Gibson's head went down on her aunt's shoulder. You didn't have to hear the groan. The gallery was alive with feeling. "But her good fortune might have been fatal luck for someone else. Drinkers can't stop themselves." That sounded like the start of an excuse. Shoulder muscles tensed and jaws tightened everywhere in the gallery. "Something outside our control has to happen before we can regain awareness. That's the way it is when you live in a fog and invent the rules to suit yourself as you go along. I couldn't see then that what I was doing was wrong. The booze changed the way I felt about everything. It's only now that I'm sober that I can even begin to try and sort it all out."

Judge Sullivan took up her pen and began to scrawl furiously. The prisoners were uniformly perplexed. Summers and Levy landed on adjacent squares with *She's had enough of this shit* and *Now you've done it.*

Hart saw the lawyers' reactions, heard the intake of breath from behind him, and it gave him pause. A rivulet of sweat ran down his arm. "I'm acutely aware of what it feels like to lose a part of my life. I've lost a big chunk of mine. Alice has lost even more. Neither one of us is ever going to be the same."

The silence of a free fall in a dream overtook him. Time slowed down to a frame-by-frame view. A tale told twice couldn't possibly be untrue. Ambiguity had to give way to something nobler. He thought about his mother's paring knife. The one with the crooked blade that left a distinctive mark in the fruit. Her favourite knife, ruined by her husband's carelessness opening a beer. She could have thrown it out and gotten another. Why keep it? It had to cut him to the bone before it cut him free.

"Margaret lost it all. I don't know what that feels like. I don't even know what it feels like to be real and loved and needed the way she was. The thing I'm hanging on to for dear life this morning is the possibility that I'm not out of chances. I may get another kick at the can. I get to learn from this experience. Margaret doesn't. I feel her loss intensely. I'm ashamed of the part that I played in her death. Getting into that car was inexcusable and inevitable and unfathomable."

He sat down in his chair.

———

The bailiffs took Hart away. One minute before the sentencing, he could be kissed and hugged and supported, but once the awful sentence of the law was spoken, he was untouchable. Hart was still wearing the same suit, he was still in the same room, but he was on an altogether different planet now. He looked a little stunned as they removed him.

A few moments later, he felt foolish. Here he was, dressed up in his best suit, heading back to the Don in a van filled with strangers, all of whom were wearing identical orange jumpsuits and bracelets. After the speech he'd just given, someone should have cued the happy ending. Well, at least the cops wanted him. He was going back to his old nightmare, but it held no terror for him this time.

The man sitting opposite him was muttering into his beard. "Can you believe that friggin' bitch Sullivan? Boy, what I would like to say to her. You were there, what did you think, buddy?"

Hart looked at the man and felt genuinely sorry for him. He looked devastated. "I wasn't in the court when your case came up. What happened?"

The look of sorrow on the man's face was genuine. "That bitch looks up from her precious papers and makes her little speech with my whole family sitting there. 'Mr. Gerard,' she says, like she's going to be all respectful, 'your conduct upsets me. Why do you feel it's necessary to walk into a suburban bank branch with a shotgun and discharge the weapon in the presence of a grandmother with a heart condition in a robbery that only netted you three hundred and twenty-five dollars? Many of the people present were badly traumatized. Why can't you put a bad cheque through the machine like everybody else?'"

Hart smiled and wondered what St. Bob would have to say about this. *Sullivan really is nuts. I think I love her.*

Chapter 46

Phil had his head bowed in prayer. Sean sat stone-faced, looking angry, while Reg waved and wiped a tear from his eye with his handkerchief as Hart was led away.

The three men lurched to their feet and made their way into the long, dark, umbilical corridor that attached the justice system to the rest of the world. The hallway was littered with victims and perps, with lawyers for and lawyers against, with unhappy relatives and friends, all learning to wait and hope in vain.

Phil insisted on crossing the road and getting a coffee at Fran's. Sean wanted a Tim's, but Phil wanted a booth and a piece of apple pie. The waitress seated them and left them to read the menus while she ran for the coffee pot.

"I can't believe how well that went."

Sean was stunned. "You think that went well?"

Phil looked over at Reg to check out his response. Reg smiled. He'd seen the same thing Phil had.

"Sean, that was the best outcome anyone could've hoped for."

"An innocent man in jail seems good to you?"

"He wasn't innocent."

Sean was angry. "Connor did the crime and now Hart is in jail!"

"That doesn't make this a bad thing."

Sean looked at Reg to see if he was buying this lunacy. "What about you? Do you think this was a good thing?"

Reg smiled at Sean. "I'll answer your question if you promise to let me speak for two minutes before you trample me."

"You got a deal," said Sean, leaning back in the booth and folding his arms in a gesture that said, *in two minutes I'm going to straighten the pair of you out.*

Reg looked over at Sean before he spoke, trying to gauge his mood and find a way into the conversation that wasn't going to provoke an angry response. He was agitated at the loss of his friend and didn't know how to vent that except in anger, but this wasn't the same lunatic who'd stormed through the house hurling accusations at the staff for allowing thieves to steal his coat. Nor was it the man who'd glared daggers at him in the hallway after he'd wound Hart up like an alarm clock. This was a man who was saying, *I want the truth more than even the savage satisfaction of drawing blood.*

"What Phil and I are happy and excited about is Hart. He gets it. The addiction is over. That's all that matters. The rest of this stuff is neither here nor there."

"That's crazy! He's in jail for something he didn't do!"

Reg smiled. "You know, you're right about one thing: It's crazy, but a good crazy!"

Phil waded in. "Sean, we just saw what a theologian calls a *moment of clarity* and what a behavioural scientist calls a *psychic change*. The two things describe essentially the same event, but they're coming from different disciplines. Until you have experienced one of these moments, it's hard to recognize them, let alone understand what they mean for a person. These events change lives."

When the waitress arrived with the pie and coffee, the table fell silent. For some reason, it felt wrong to talk about what had happened in front of her.

Phil took the lead. "Sean, when you were a kid, say about ten years old, did your parents ever play this game with you? On a Sunday, when all the relatives came to visit, they'd call you into the living room and ask you if you liked girls, then they would all sit there looking solemn, while you thought about how to answer the question.

"When my parents did this with me, I said, 'No, I don't like girls. They smell funny, they don't play baseball, and they're a pain in the ass.' Then, suddenly and unexpectedly, the room roared with adult laughter and I didn't know why. I had answered their question honestly, so why were they laughing at me? I remember my dad picking me up and sitting me down on his knee. He gave me a hug and said, 'Don't worry, Phil, someday it will come to you.'

"Later, when my dad tried to explain sex to me, he made a very bad job of it. He was embarrassed and awkward, and he made it sound as appealing as a trip to the dentist. But then, one magical day, I got my first sexual feelings, and on that day, the whole world started to change. Moment of insight, spiritual awakening, psychic change, call it anything you like. That is what we just saw. No one could've prepared me for that moment. For a couple weeks, I didn't connect those feelings to anything sexual, all I knew was that something was different.

"The point is that everything in my world changed. I stopped being a boy and I began the process of becoming a man. I remember watching *The Tonight Show* with Johnny Carson, and for the first time all the jokes made sense. I used to watch my older brother comb his hair for an hour before a date and think he was being pretty stupid, but now I was inside his head, I understood why he was doing that. I looked at my mom and dad, and I could see how these feelings bound them together.

"A year later, my dad called me back into the living room when the relatives were there and asked the same question. 'Do you like girls, Phil?' This time I answered. 'Yes, Dad, I like girls.'"

"You're talking in parables, Father."

"*Parables* is actually a good word to choose. A parable is a story you can tell in front of your enemies without them catching on to the fact that you're calling them out on their lies. That's what Hart did. He told them what he thought of them and their bullying and deception and posturing. They thought he was talking about a court case, when really he was talking about something quite different and quite special."

"I'll bite, what was he talking about?"

"His soul."

"No such thing, Father."

Reg and Phil exchanged a glance. "The kind of truth we're talking about, our truth, makes no sense to the vast majority of people in this world. But it's nonetheless the truth. These transformative moments look like nothing, but they change everything."

"Your two minutes are up. You guys aren't making any sense. No matter what happens, you jump to your feet and yell hallelujah."

Phil wanted to get to his pie but the conversation wouldn't give him leave. He settled for a sip of coffee. "Sean, what we're saying is that recovery is experiential. It's something that happens in your body, just like when you go through puberty and get your sexual feelings. People can try and describe the experience to you all day, but you can't understand it or even begin to appreciate it until you experience the feelings in your own body and in a way that makes sense to you. Even then, you're only at the edge of it."

Reg jumped in. "Hart was already serving a life sentence. He was going to sit at the big table at Clancy's Tavern, sucking his teeth and talking trash with Bill and the rest of that pack of assholes until the ground opened up and swallowed him whole. He was so dumbed down by the alcohol that he thought he was on the winning side. That, my friend, is a wasted life. That is soul murder. That is a life sentence with no possibility of parole." He paused and shifted uncomfortably in the hard-backed chair. "Now he's seeing reality. He's not worried about what cops, judges, or lawyers have to say anymore. He's answering to his conscience and maybe even the God of his understanding. Who knows how deep this runs? What is certain is that he has a shot at a real life again."

Sean opened his mouth to speak but nothing came out. He wasn't buying this bullshit, but he had to admit, part of him really wanted to. This whole theory was whacked as far as he was concerned, but he just couldn't reconcile the looks on their faces as they spoke. These guys were not lying. In a way, it was easier to trust Phil and Reg than it was to untangle what they were saying.

Phil put his hand on Sean's forearm. "Sean, if this hasn't happened for you yet, try and be a little bit patient. You're still healing. Try and remember what we talked about today and maybe keep an eye out for it."

"So you're saying this is going to happen for me too?"

"Yup."

"Any idea when?"

"Nope."

Sean practically emptied the sugar shaker into his coffee before giving it a vigorous stir. "This isn't very scientific."

Phil knew that already. "Try and look at it this way: The night of the crash was the lowest point of his life. When he was lying there in the wreck, he had a lot to do. He had to climb out of the vehicle, out of his addiction, and out of the false version of himself that he'd been showing the world for years. Hart's addiction was mortally wounded that night. Today you saw it give up the ghost. Did you think he had that in him? Does anything other than that matter? He's alive now and moving in the right direction, and for that I say thank you, Jesus."

Reg studied the granite jaw of his sparring partner. *Is such a thing possible for you, Mr. Sean Miller?*

———

Sean spent a miserable night on the air mattress and awoke stiff with an ache in his hip. Hart had let him have the key to the place until the end of the month. It was a little lonely here with only the TV and the fridge, but it was nice to have a place with a lock on the door again. It had been quite a while since he'd been this well off.

Sean had lived rough for long periods in jails and on construction sites out west. It wasn't the bedding that was bringing him down, it was the emptiness and the unfairness of all this. If someone like Hart couldn't get a break, what hope did he have? Reg and Phil were doing the best they could, but they were wrong. Sending an innocent man to jail was horrible. Didn't anyone care about that bastard Connor, dealing drugs and laughing it up at Clancy's? The smart part of him thought, *If no one else cares about this, why should I?* But it burned. *Those two old bullshitters are bent. A fanatic and a fool. Doesn't anyone care about justice anymore?*

Sean remembered the first time he'd gotten into real trouble when he was a kid. A bunch of guys had been playing baseball, and when the game was over one of the older guys offered them a ride home. He said it was his father's car. It wasn't. When the cops pulled them over, they all had the good sense to get out and run. Sean didn't, mostly because he hadn't done anything wrong but also because he still had some respect for the bulls in those days.

They took him into custody and his dad had to leave work to come and get him. It occasioned a terrific beating — apparently, he was supposed to know if a car was stolen simply by looking at it.

Maybe that's why this bothers me so much. The two things aren't the same, but it's hard not to compare them. Maybe some of this anger I'm feeling is really about me.

There was a knock at the door and Sean tensed up. *That'll be the super here to boot me out.*

He went to the spy hole and looked out. A young woman was standing in the hallway. He opened the door and was very surprised to see that she was holding a casserole dish. It smelled good.

She smiled at him shyly. "I'm Mary from down the hall. Is Channing here?"
Sean smiled. "He's gone."

"Will he be back?"

Sean said it as gently as he could: "He's gone to jail for five years."

A tear came to her eye. Sean invited her in. She put the casserole on the counter and helped herself to one of the milk crates that still passed as furniture.

Sean looked suitably embarrassed. "The truck took all the good stuff yesterday. I'm squatting here till the rent runs out."

Mary looked at him. "Are you a friend of Channing's? Mr. Hart, that is?"
"Yes."

"I don't know if he knows who I am. I used to speak to him sometimes in the lobby when we passed. He was always very kind to me. He'd treat me like an adult when I was just a teenager. I liked that."

Sean liked her. She was real. He felt for just an instant as if he'd never seen a woman before.

"When I read about what happened in the newspapers, I couldn't make sense of it. He wouldn't do something like that. But he never came home. The mailbox got full to bursting, and the mailman asked when he was going to be back, but no one knew. There was a follow-up story every day in the paper. One about him and another one about the little girl and then one about the funeral for the mom." She started to tear up.

"It must have been hard for you."

"We didn't know what to think. Then last month, I saw him in the lobby. He was opening his mailbox and getting his stuff. I looked over at him and, well, I-I panicked. I practically ran out the door, trying to get away from him. When I looked back over my shoulder, I saw him standing there. I think I hurt him pretty badly. I felt awful, but I was too embarrassed to go back and make it right."

Sean smelled something other than home cooking in the air. "So that's why you made the casserole."

"I wanted to do something. I wanted him to know I believed him, and I still care about what happens to him, and to say how sorry I am."

Sean nodded. He thought about what Phil said. He thought about the three questions. He wondered if he could ever have anyone in his life as wonderful as Mary Pearson.

Mary had said her piece and she felt better. She looked over at Sean with curiosity. "Now I feel kind of stupid. He's gone and all. Are you hungry?"

In a way you would have a hard time understanding. "Help me serve this and I'll tell you the whole story," he said.

Chapter 47

Peter caught up with John at Flannerman's. John was having a moment. He was hanging around the main lobby, enjoying the scent of the floral displays and the warmth of the sun on his face. His expression was so peaceful, it looked like he'd fallen asleep. An instant of pure bliss, a moment in which it occurred to Peter and possibly even to John that melting into the light and forgetting all their cares might not be such a bad thing. Could it all hang on wanting it to happen?

"John, we need to talk."

Another trampled epiphany. John looked him up and down. He could see crazy in his eyes. Oh no, *he thought,* you've had another great rush of blood to the head, another pathological insight of staggering proportion. One that scatters all the other staggering insights of pathological importance like pigeons put to flight by a barking dog in the town square. My very own lazy Lazarus.

The fat man grew impatient with the silence. "About the light, John. We need to talk about the light."

Peter was standing over him with his fists dug into his hips. There was a scowl on his face and dark flashes of rage around his eyes. He was here to intimidate. Well, John wasn't one to be bullied. He was as tired of Peter's interruptions as he was of this room, this conversation, his circle of acquaintances, and the endless stalemate that had become their entire existence. John was in no mood to hear another of Peter's theories, so he offered up a refreshing new one of his own.

"You mean the snout, don't you? I saw a snout. Like an elephant's trunk — a large disagreeable orifice."

Peter held his arms straight out in front of him with his palms facing outward. He looked like the god of wind about to lay waste to a forest. "John, you need to stop saying that. You didn't see a snout. You saw a light. God would never do such a thing. He'd never convey us to the Promised Land in anything that undignified. It's obscene. I find it very distressing to think that everyone I ever loved somehow got vacuumed up. That's not the way God would call us out of this world. It ruins my whole remembrance of my beloved Aunt Mary."

John couldn't stop. "I can see her fat little legs now, wiggling, her hanging on to a nose hair for dear life..."

"Naff."

John had him in the right frame of mind and so he relented. "My cocaine clients would not have a problem with that. They put all kinds of things up their snouts: cars, recreational vehicles, boats, motor homes. Sometimes they put their whole lives up their noses."

Peter was trembling. He wanted something very badly. *"Is that the nub of your joke?"*

John played the vexing innocent. *"Peter, it's a witticism. Besides, I did see a snout, and I also saw a pair of ratty eyes that reflected light back from the darkness. We simply saw two different things, that's all. That doesn't make either of us liars. Anyway, what's got you all hot and bothered?"*

"Well, apart from your intractable insolence, the only other annoying thing was the article in the Toronto Star *about death and dying."*

"Did they say anything new?"

Peter vented his impatience by raising his voice and emphasizing certain words. *"No, they're clueless,"* he said in reference to the authors of the article, and it was clear he thought that John shared this characteristic with them. When that subtle insult fell unanswered, Peter seemed appeased. He carried on with his new preoccupation. *"But they did raise a question that got me thinking, and now I would like to talk to you about it. They quoted the Apostle Paul, who said we would be raised from the dead in new imperishable bodies."*

John couldn't help himself. *"I remember the quote — something about getting the extended warranty."*

Peter slowed down his speech and enunciated each syllable of his answer once more. *"That is not what he said and you know it. The perishable cannot put on the imperishable because flesh and blood cannot inherit the Kingdom of God."* John could tell Peter was still angry with him. His eyes were blazing and he'd fixed him in a no-nonsense stare.

The thin ghost feigned interest, hoping to bait him again. *"And he was some kind of big expert because...?"*

Peter seemed to regain his composure. *"I doubt very much if St. Paul had even our limited insight into the problem of life after death."*

John looked at Peter and then at the room they found themselves in and he relented for the moment. He posed as one who'd been shamed and was now ready to shoulder the burdens of reason once again. *"Well, the evangelizer formerly known as Saul certainly lacked our perspective,"* John said in an even-handed way as he rose from the pew and made his way over to the stained-glass window that showed the very moment when Saul ceased to be and St. Paul began. *"I was never convinced by the road to Damascus story. It always reminded me of the best wide-eyed excesses of the book of Mormon."*

That was a calculated swipe. Peter hated it when people attacked religion, any religion. It made him nervous. Peter thought that goofing around really could deliver the wrath of the Almighty. *"John, please let's not get too abstract. We don't want to string this conversation out all morning simply because you have nothing better to do. We're onto a seam of pure gold here. Our salvation is at hand."*

"Well, your brow is furrowed, so I'm going to give you full rein. Tell me what's in your heart."

"We have hung this painting upside down. Freezing the body was the wrong thing to do."

Well, butter my toast. Second thoughts! From Peter? On the sacred science of cryogenics of all things. *John returned to his pew to consider the ramifications of this.* "What? Doubts at this stage of the master plan? Out with it, before it ruins your whole day!"

You could tell that Peter was still refining this first pressing of the oil as he spoke. "What if the Greeks had it right? What if there is a soul? Maybe that's what we are, you and I. Think about it. Here we are, two disembodied persons sharing a conversation in the same world we used to inhabit, only now we're invisible to everyone who is still alive, but we can still talk to each other. We have our memories, our interests, our intellect, and our senses, and because of this we can still learn new things — all without the encumbrance of a body."

He fixed John in his fiery stare, and all that poor man could think was, If metaphysics is a bolt, then surely this kind of bullshit is the nut. *He attempted to temper this new insight.* "But not all of the facts fit, Peter. Souls are supposed to be immortal. You know, immortal soul and perishable body. We're on a short leash here. We're on the glide path to drooling idiocy. We only have so much energy, and then it's poltergeist time."

Peter started to flap his arms. "That's the point. That is the very point. Do you remember me telling you about Walter?"

"The old perv down the street, the one with the big eyes for the young ladies?"

"That's a bit jaded, even for you, John. He was a very fine fellow when we knew each other. I want to try something out with him."

"Let it all flow. I'm completely in your thrall."

"When you mock me, you make me so very angry, and you do it all the time!"

"I'm sorry, Peter. I'm passing the time. I admire you sitting here all day, selflessly deluding yourself. You're like your late friend Barry in a lot of ways. A real firebrand."

Peter's face said murder. "You're a fine one to talk, after that failed business at the ZiggZagg club. That still bothers me. We damn near took part in a murder just to see if the light showed up when someone died in disgrace. I still feel sick about that. There are consequences to things, John. Things you never consider!" *He turned away in disgust and fixed his attention on the floor.*

John offered up a weak mea culpa. "Yes, a bad bit of business."

Peter started climbing the ladder of righteous indignation that would elevate him and diminish John. "Your crackpot theories never pan out."

John looked over at the stained-glass representation of Jacob's ladder and had to smile. What an aid that rickety structure would be to them in their current difficulties.

Peter was coming to a point. "That whole experiment may have been a good idea, but it was inconclusive. We need to try something new — a more controlled *inquiry. I'm going to go and stay with Walter. The light has to come for him soon. When it does, I'm going to throw him into it."*

John was shocked. *This was the kind of depravity he'd expect from Jack. Lighting up a ghost with a match was out of character for Peter — he was no Rosedale strangler.*

John turned to face Peter. "Why would you want to do that? I thought you liked him?"

Peter put his hands in his jacket pockets. "The plan has always been to find a new home for my brain in a much younger and more vigorous body. I want to take the world by the ear and shake it until it ponies up what it owes me."

John was taken aback. *There it was — without the use of torture or intrigue to midwife it into the world. The whole crazy sordid truth dropped in his lap like the New Year's ham brought home from the butcher's shop.* Is that what this is all about for you? How often have I wondered?

Peter had to move. His thoughts were filling him with energy. "But here's the thing, John. If we get an imperishable body in the next life, I would be a fool to hang around here and try to clone the old one. No, I may have had the right idea, but the wrong method. I may be the biggest obstacle in the path to my own salvation. What if my consciousness continues to decay, even after I put it in a new and vigorous body? What a disaster that would be — eternal dementia — a permanent poltergeist. No, I need to know what I'm up against before I make an irrevocable choice."

The sticky logic that was flowing out of Peter and binding him to a grander purpose was, so far, failing to adhere to John. "So where does Walter come into all this? How does stuffing him up Jumbo's nose help us with our inquiries?"

Peter's eyes sparked fire, but he pretended he hadn't heard. "We need to see once and for all what happens when the light gets hold of a ghost. Perhaps the light only comes for us. That would explain why it leaves the dying alone. If we throw Walter into its path, we'll know more than we do now. The light is going to get him anyway; he's too far gone to duck, and besides, it isn't right what he's doing, ogling those girls. It's indecent. He'd never have done anything like that before he became ill. No, he needs to be sent on his way! It's the best thing for everybody. His lingering is spoiling an otherwise fine reputation."

That actually made a crazy kind of sense from a cause-and-effect point of view. Though it was surprising how easily Walter of sainted memory had been repurposed as cannon fodder.

John got to his feet and sat on the stone windowsill beneath the stained-glass rendering of Jacob's ladder. He was almost transparent when backlit by the bright sunlight. He's right about one thing. All our theorizing about the light hinges on it showing up when someone dies. But it never seems to. Maybe the light is only interested in ghosts. Perhaps some other force we're immune to gathers up everyone else. There has to be a way to resolve this.

John turned to Peter, who was inhaling the vapours of a pot of fresh coffee that the staff had set down for the next service. "You've given me an idea, Peter.

The buzzards are circling this poor old prick at Punanai. A Mr. Jacob Hutton. He's a wealthy slum landlord, and he's drinking himself to death. He's yellow, fat, red-eyed, and so full of ammonia that his pee smells like a commercial cleaning product. The smell of rotting organs follows this guy around like a dog."

Peter's eyebrow betrayed his interest; he was checking John's arithmetic. "Do you think he's going to die soon?"

"The counsellors were against bringing him in. I heard them talking it over. When he was at St. Joe's, he paid cab drivers to bring him booze. The doctors there got fed up and wanted to get rid of him. His family wanted him in treatment. His wife cried all over the manager for an hour before she got her way. He sits in his room all day, muttering to himself about the big condo he's going to put up at Yonge and Bloor."

"He owns that site?"

"He used to — he drank it all away. Now his former partners own it. They gave him the boot. They've set to work digging the foundation, but this old fool thinks that it's all going to be his again someday. He has a lawsuit going, don't you know? I think we should set up a deathwatch on Mr. Hutton and put your man Walter in the same room with him."

Peter moved closer into John's space without realizing how pliable this made him look. "Why? What will that do?"

"Well, I'm beginning to think that the light only comes when we meet as a group. I don't think it can track us when we're alone."

"Well, yes, after our last meeting it's hard to refute that point."

"So if we put all our eggs in one basket..."

"I see what you're saying. If the old man does die, the light might take Walter too. But wait a second — I take your point more fully now. If the light takes Walter and leaves what's his name, or vice versa, that's a kind of answer for us."

John's theatrical training took over and he struck a heroic pose. "Exactly! The process of elimination."

Peter's brow was still embroiled in worry. "But how do we get Walter to come to Punanai?"

"Peter, the man is a poltergeist. His idea of self-expression is hitting his face on a wall and groaning. We'll outsmart him."

"He doesn't have any energy left. He can't go very far."

"Good, let's tucker him out. When he gets to Punanai, we want him to be on his last legs anyway so he can't wander off."

The scowl left Peter. "I must say, I feel ever so much better now. I feel encouraged. All our recent failures have been devastating for me. Without the council to turn to, where are we? I was so annoyed with you when we started, but now I think we may have something here. This sounds like it might work."

"Well, it's either this or daytime television, my friend. Let's go get Walter."

Chapter 48

Francis Dover was watching for Kaiser from the window of his office. Kaiser pulled into a parking spot at the far end of the lot and got out of the car. He didn't want Dover seeing his ride. The Toyota took the opportunity to continue running for almost thirty seconds after it had been switched off. A puff of black smoke announced to the world that a man of modest means had arrived.

"I need to use your bathroom," Kaiser said as soon as he walked into the lawyer's office.

"Second door on the left."

Kaiser gave Kate a wave after he'd hung up his coat. She looked up from her desk and smiled.

Oh shit. She saw the car.

"I owe the boss five dollars because of you," she said.

Kaiser stopped in his tracks and gave her a quizzical look. "How so?"

"I figured we'd never set eyes on you again. You look like the sensible type."

"Don't pay up yet, this is a long way from a done deal."

"You give a poor girl such hope," she said as she returned to her duties.

Kaiser finished his business in the washroom and regarded himself coolly in the mirror as he washed his hands. *So this is the way the story ends. I could've shut up all those guidance teachers, cops, and relatives simply by saying, Just you wait … someday I'll be a beekeeper.* He shook his head as he dried his hands. *This has to be two million dollars the hard way.*

The drive to the Spraklin farm took twenty minutes. Dover used the time to explore Kaiser's character a little further. "How long have you been working at the treatment centre?"

"Fifteen years."

"Do they take good care of you?"

Kaiser cocked his head to the right and placed the three middle fingers of his left hand at his jawline. He looked like he was searching for a pulse. "No, they claim to be as poor as church mice."

"Are they?"

Kaiser sat up and looked over at Dover. "Church mice always lie about money. They own IBM. They have bucks but not for the likes of me."

"Top-heavy?"

"The ninety-nine and the one."

"It's the same everywhere."

"Even in your profession?"

"Especially so. Lawyers are like Icarus — we don't make money if we don't soften up the wax. We don't get close enough to melt it, but we need to be a little singed to get a real payday."

Kaiser looked around the interior of Dover's Prius and wondered when the last time was that he'd helped himself to a sunburn. *Maybe never.* "Tell me more about Chester."

"There's not much to tell with him. He's been reliving the same year ever since he was fourteen. I think it's fair to say he has above-average intelligence but it's not anchored to anything."

"What about bees?"

"Well, everything he says or does is about bees in one way or another, but his thoughts — what can I say about his thought process? It's chaos. That's why he needs the bees. They anchor him in this world."

"Sounds a bit like his brother."

"Chester is the kind of guy who would quite happily try and calculate the final value of pi on a sheet of foolscap until he fell over dead from dehydration. He doesn't feel his needs the way other people do. He's oblivious to the cues that guide your life and mine. For him, there's no past or future. There's only the present, and the present is always about the bees. Where are they, what are they doing, what do they need, and what needs to be done today to ensure their wellbeing? Without the bees, he'd be lost."

"Is he certifiable?"

"If he didn't have the bees, he would be."

Kaiser had a dark thought. Dover could've scooped this whole thing and no one would ever have known. He could've shut Chester up in a nursing home and counted on him being dead or deranged in short order. If one farm is worth two million, then both farms are worth five. Kaiser felt a newfound respect for his companion. He understood the Icarus crack now. But where did that leave him? Was he really going to inherit here? Or was he a patsy in some kind of nefarious scheme? The question begged to be asked. Who had Chester left his bees to?

"Why are you taking such good care of this guy?"

Dover smiled. "It's why I became a lawyer. I realize that I'm a little old to be an idealist, but that's what I am and this is what I do — perhaps not unlike you, Mr. Kaiser, working for a very low wage at a very important job."

"But look at me, I'm old and tired and have nothing."

"I find myself wondering if Ian Spraklin knew that."

"You said he was limited."

"Ah, but he was shrewd. You know, he may only have spoken to twenty people in the last half of his life. You obviously made an impression. Perhaps he was drawn to the bee-like qualities in your character."

"But here's the question: Do I need to be taken care of or am I the caregiver?"

Dover checked his rear-view mirror and began to pump the breaks. "You have to go slow here. The farm is on the right. The driveway is full of potholes."

"He should have this graded. He's going to break an axle."

"Chester doesn't drive. He doesn't see the need."

"So how does he get to town?"

"He doesn't mostly, and if he really needs something, he either phones in an order or hitchhikes."

"He's living in the nineteenth century."

"Indeed he is, my friend."

"So how is this going to work? Are you going to introduce me?"

"There's no point in making a plan. He may greet us warmly or wave us off with a shotgun."

"Then what?"

"We could go and get a coffee and come back an hour later and get a different reception."

Kaiser cast his thoughts back to the way Ian behaved in treatment. That was the way he had been too. His focus was always on what he was looking at.

Dover honked the horn once as they came to a stop outside the farmhouse. "He knows the car."

The Spraklin farm was in its dotage. Its once pristine monoculture was giving way. Fine, rich agricultural fields had become pastures. Trees planted as windbreaks had overstepped their boundaries. Did the restless ghost of the first Spraklin — the one who tore tons of fieldstone from the very earth to clear these fields and build these fine stone walls — look down from heaven in horror to see all his labour coming undone?

The main building was box shaped and looked like an old construction boot that had been soaked and dried in the sun many times. It had taken on a rounded shape at the corners and was the kind of structure that you could go through with a try square and never once find a right angle. There had been plenty of them once upon a time. You could tell at a glance that a skilled carpenter had put this place together. But the building had an organic feel to it. Like it was a little boat afloat on the ocean. It adapted itself to whatever change was in the offing but never once attached itself to anything of permanence.

There was a front door that faced the main road and looked like it had never been opened. Anyone trying to enter or leave the building by this portal would have to negotiate a three-foot drop. The side door that opened into the kitchen from the porch was the main entry. The porch was low slung and decorated around the posts with wooden scrollwork that looked like Canada geese. The building wasn't on a foundation; you could see field stones supporting the beams and keeping the house up off the ground.

From the courtyard, Kaiser could smell a wood stove. The porch was stacked high with hardwood covered by a plastic tarp. Behind them to the left was a well-built and maintained fieldstone barn.

Two centuries of storms had damaged the barn, but it had been expertly repaired. On the upper story, a coat of red paint was fading rather badly to reveal the aging grey surface of the barnboard underneath. Kaiser glanced through the open double doors as he lit himself a cigarette. It was still a working barn. It wasn't fancy or modern, but it was orderly and clean. He could see a stack of wooden beehives piled on top of each other at the far end of the structure. Chester could do carpentry.

"Shall we go in?"

Kaiser nodded. As they approached the porch of the farmhouse, a little man with big ears and thick glasses came to the door. He was about five foot two and as thin and weathered as a cedar rail. He wore faded blue jeans that were ripped around the knees and a lumberjack shirt. Kaiser could see the family resemblance, both in his face and taste in clothing. He could've been looking at Ian.

"Lawyer, who've you brung?"

"Chester, this is Mr. Kaiser. He knew your brother."

Chester looked Kaiser up and down for a moment. "Not dressed for the field."

"Only here for a visit today."

"Have you strewn my late brother?"

"Not as yet, Chester. We need to talk about that. May we come in?"

"Bees need tendin'."

"I thought they were asleep this time of year."

"Bees always need tendin'."

Dover walked toward Chester like he'd been invited in and, after a moment's hesitation, the old man gave way and allowed them to enter. The kitchen was a window into the past. Kaiser had grown up visiting old farms like this in PEI. There was a very old oil cloth on the table and, in the corner, he could see hurricane lamps full of kerosene and ready for use. The place was heated — if one could fairly make such a claim — with a wood stove, which meant it was either always too hot or always too cold in the kitchen.

The wear marks on the floor indicated the sweet spot was close to the stove. There was a little daybed that Chester had been sleeping on since the weather got cold and a stack of original Hudson's Bay blankets piled on the table beside it. Presumably, he'd move to one of the bedrooms when the weather improved.

There was a pump in the sink, and Kaiser saw a washtub full of dirty dishes being brought slowly to a boil on the stove. The floorboards caught Kaiser's eye. They were as long as the building and had all been cut rather roughly from local hardwood. They had a sway to them. A marble released at one end of the room would roll toward the centre and halfway up the other side before it would run out of momentum and return to the centre. In the high traffic areas, the top half inch of the floor had been worn away, and moisture and uneven heating had twisted all the boards into a tight knot.

The floor was the temperature of the ground outside, so Kaiser left his shoes on and his overcoat open. The room smelled of acrid smoke mixed with the heavy, greasy odour of a thousand fry-ups. There was grease everywhere and it looked like no one had restored order in the structure since Mrs. Spraklin had gone to her reward. The furniture was handmade in the nineteenth century and worn right down to the springs. All the chairs boasted pillows and blankets as a defence against unwanted pokes and stabbings.

Dover went to the pump and filled an enormous kettle with fresh spring water. "You're going to like the local water, Mr. Kaiser. Chester has the finest well in the country."

Chester had lost interest in his visitors. He curled up in his favourite chair by the stove and wrapped himself in a blanket. Dover rested the kettle on the stove while he opened the fire door to see what was happening. There was a good bed of coals but not enough to bring a kettle to a boil, so he added some small pieces of hardwood. Kaiser was surprised by the tingle of pleasure he experienced hearing the clank of a wood stove opening and closing. He remembered the sounds from his youth. His aunt Ella would cook for a family gathering of over twenty people on her wood stove and never think twice about it. Ella's stove shone with a burnishing oil that she applied once a month. Chester's reminded him of the wood furnaces that the men kept in their hunting camps.

"Have you eaten today, Chester?"

There was no response.

"Kate asked me to bring you a plate of sandwiches. I'm going to leave them here on the table."

There was no need. The old man was out of his chair and moving toward the food. Kaiser was intrigued. Chester started wolfing down the sandwiches like he hadn't eaten in a day or two. He barely took time to chew, and the look of joy on his face said all that needed to be said. While Chester was busy, Kaiser opened the refrigerator and took a peek. It was dirty and jammed with all kinds of jars and bottles, but there was edible food inside. Chester was starving to death because he had no one to remind him that it was time to eat.

This guy needs to be in a home.

Dover found the teapot and gave it a good rinse under the pump, then went hunting for some cups. He carefully examined several before he found three he could live with. They, too, had been in service while Victoria was still on the throne. The saucers no longer matched the cups and there were dark stains in the cracks, but they still held hot liquid. Kaiser picked up one of the cups and had a look at it. This cup was never designed for someone with hands the size of his. He chuckled when he recalled how funny his uncle Ted always looked trying to drink from his aunt Ella's good bone china with his thick, weathered, calloused farmer's hands. He always looked like he was trying to use one of teacups from a doll set. Chester was fully engaged in the sandwiches and Dover had the good sense to leave him in peace while he ate.

Kaiser smelled the room. There was a dampness that pervaded the place. He knew that if he took a wrecking bar to the walls, he'd find a layer of plaster supported by wooden laths, then some heavy timbers, a run of field stones, and an enclosure of sand. These old places held the damp like a sponge but were proof against the wind. The sand in the walls would be moist to the touch this time of year.

Time had gotten a bit behind in its work here in Lakefield. The last vestige of a century past was still living and functioning in a way that called the modern world into question. Kaiser looked over at Chester and saw him for the first time. He belonged here. He was like the kitchen table: handmade from local lumber and set down for purposeful service for a hundred years or more.

This is normal for him. He must look at modern houses and appliances and wonder. My world would seem very strange and frightening. But this is where he belongs, and the only thing he has to offer to the world is his honey. Every other valuable thing that his parents had put away or saved is hopelessly out of step now.

Chester looked up from his empty plate and at Kaiser as if for the first time. "You that city fella?"

Kaiser smiled at the old man. "I grew up on a farm like this, but yeah, I'm a city fella."

"It's hard work in the country. You look soft to me."

Kaiser looked at the poor, skinny old man and wondered if he'd seen a reflection of himself in a mirror anytime in this new century. It was hard to tell what Chester had looked like as a young man. His small head and jug ears had probably condemned him to a life of taunts and retribution. There was no muscle on his frame and who knew if there ever had been. His fingers looked like the blunted stubs of cigarettes, twisted and bent.

"Did you make the beehives in the barn?"

"Like, I did."

"They look very fine."

"Look means nothing to a bee. Are they snug? That's the thing."

The conversation lurched to a full stop. Kaiser let the silence lag on for five minutes before he spoke again. "Do you know who I am, Chester, and why I'm here?"

"For the bees, young fella — you're here for the bees. I've been run ragged lookin' after Ian's hives. Worthless lot of parasites. Worse than wasps. Mostly dead by spring, I reckon and hope. Ian was stubborn. Wrong bees. They don't belong here. Thin blood. Sour honey. No good can come of 'em. Let the cold take the young and the devil take the rest, I say, and good riddance."

Dover handed Chester a cup of fresh tea — one brimming with honey and canned milk. Was it the food and the company that had brought the old boy out of his funk or the subject of bees? Either way, he was on a manic high and enjoying himself. Dover had a happy look on his face and contented himself with occupying a chair while Kaiser and Chester spoke.

"What needs to be done with Ian's bees?"

"My brother was a fool. He believed what he read and not what he saw. He was always packin' up his bees and sending 'em somewhere or another, to some orchard or farmer's field. He made some money, I'll give him that. But it's not the order of things. Bees stay put and go lookin' for their food. It's not right to send 'em someplace and then, just when they're findin' their way, yank 'em back. Ian was a monster. But he's gone now. I want no truck with his devil hives."

"What do you want me to do?"

"I don't care. Kill 'em, farm 'em out, let 'em die in the cold. That's what a businessman would do. But if you wanna learn how to do this right, I'll show you. I can't last forever and if I don't show someone, then everything I learned will die with me, and that includes my bees. I won't have that — not if I can help it.

"This is how it's gonna be. You go back to the city and get yourself a good pair of work boots, some horsehide gloves, and a sleeping bag. It's the dead of winter and there's not much to do. But you be back here, young fella, no later than March thirty-first, and we'll see if we can make a man of you. Oh, and dump my brother off at that treatment centre if you haven't already. That's where he wants to spend eternity. Damned fool that he was — early, middle, and late."

Fin

CPSIA information can be obtained
at www.ICGtesting.com
Printed in the USA
LVHW040811060922
727630LV00001B/151

9 781771 805711